Artura x Thorn

Queen of Poison & Fire

Tiffany Parker

NIMUE & CO PUBLISHING

NIMUE & CO PUBLISHING
Located Sydney, Australia

Copyright © Tiffany Parker, 2023

This is a work of fiction.
Names, characters, places and incidents either are the product
of the author's imagination or are used fictitiously.
Any resemblance to actual persons, living or dead,
events or locales is entirely coincidental.

All rights reserved.
No part of this publication may be reproduced or transmitted in any form or
by any means, electronic or mechanical, including photocopying, recording,
or any information storage or retrieval system, without prior permission in
writing from the author/publisher.

For more information, address:
enquiries@tiffanyparkerbooks.com

Book design by Tiffany Parker
Map by Tiffany Parker

ISBN 978-0-646-88785-2 (PAPERBACK)

*Dedicated to anyone kept awake by a book boyfriend.
Add another to the pile.
Long live King Thorn.*

Also by Tiffany Parker

Daughter of Ashes
Rule of Shadow & Stars

TRIGGER WARNING

This book contains themes of infant loss, sexual assault, rape, abuse both mental and physical and torture.

The Northern Kingdoms

Naiva

Lanceris

CIMRAN

NIMUE

Hafan

Isle of the Old Gods

Ocaran Sea

CHAPTER ONE

"Nerium oleander?"

Old, sea grey eyes buried beneath thick, salt and pepper brows narrowed on my face. He sucked in a deep breath, studying me with frustration.

"Do you propose healing? Or death?"

"Depending on the day of the week?"

"*Artura*," he warned.

I smiled serenely. It was the way of things between us. He taught, I listened. There would be banter and eventually, when I'd worn the old man down, he would dismiss me for the day. It had been that way for years now, ever since I'd learned to read and began to study under him. The fact that I was now twenty-four had little bearing on my disdain for forced education.

"Testing my patience is one thing," Emrys warned. "Deliberately failing to learn is another. All I want for you is to be the very best that you can be. Or at a base level, *not* take life."

"Even if it's deserved?" I asked, brows drawn together in mock confusion. Because the reality was, if ever I saw fit to use my talents for evil and not good, I would have a damned good reason to do so. And there would be no confusion about it.

Emrys sighed heavily through his nose, nostrils flaring. "*Girl.*"

I stood to my feet, putting away the collection of worn cloth bound books Emrys owned, his most valued possessions in the world. We had little but in case of a fire, I was under strict instructions to save the tomes first, him second.

"Trust me when I say that I know these dusty things inside out. I could heal anything from a wart to dysentery. You've taught me well. Have faith in that. And don't stress, Emrys - it ages you something fierce."

"*You* age me, Artura."

I steered him away from the scratched wooden table, directing him towards one of two beds at the end of the small cottage we occupied.

"It's just yet another thing I excel at."

Emrys shook his head, rubbing a gnarled hand across the side of his face and into eyes lined with deep crevasses. The day was young, the sun not yet at its apex in the sky. However, with every passing season, Emrys struggled more and more. With the chill outside now, Autumn only just kissing the land, his joints ached. I was beginning to feel alone more than anything in the cottage, watching him rest while I worked by the fire, maintaining our simple lifestyle.

"Sleep," I instructed. "I'll go into the village, fetch some lunch."

"Don't-"

"Cause a scene," I finished. "I'm well aware. Rest, Emrys. You're a grouchy old bastard when you don't."

I donned my shawl and picked up a fraying woven basket. As I closed the door, I glimpsed Emrys groaning as he sat down on the edge of his bed. The mattress dipped in the middle, looking more threadbare than I was happy with. Maybe tomorrow I would distract him somehow, get him out of the house so I could swap his mattress for mine. I could make do. He wouldn't. Not for much longer.

Our cottage sat on the outskirts of Naiva, a small town itself on the outskirts of a kingdom in ruins. The last twenty-odd years, things had steadily grown worse. Food was scarce on a good day and if you could find it, you'd pay in one way or another. Either losing a hand to steal or losing a little dignity, begging horizontally in some dingy brothel for scraps.

I'd never particularly minded living so far out of the village. It was a quiet life beneath constellations I would never learn all the names of. The sky was full of wonders by night and I'd long ago fallen in love. The stars were my company beyond Emrys, silent friends and companions that never left. Even on clouded nights, they were still there, ever loyal.

I knew Emrys' decision to live in solitude was more for my benefit. Things were dangerous, he said. Life beyond our village was corrupt. War had ravaged the kingdom for little over twenty years in something the king declared to be The Exoneration. The kingdom was polluted by sin. Witchcraft and sorcery, debauchery of every kind. Whores, murderers, thieves and gender betrayers. The king had made it his personal mission to cleanse the land of its tainted blood, no matter what.

The fact that he'd left it as little more than a charred husk was a negligible fact.

Healers were targeted among witches. To many, there was no distinction, no trust in medicine. If it couldn't be explained to a simpleton, it was evil. And the only way to fix it?

Fire.

Burn, burn, burn.

I headed through town, spotting the markets nestled in the heart of it. Makeshift tents covered baked goods and homespun thread. Clothes sewn by widows of The Exoneration. They were numerous in a way that broke my heart. They had lost the most. Loved ones who had fought another man's battle while he sat back in luxury. The dead left behind children and wives who struggled to comprehend and survive the new world they'd been dropped into.

I kept to the side of the road, out of sight of the majority who filtered about. Never to be seen. Always tucked away. It was only two years ago that Emrys permitted me to travel to the village alone. At twenty-two, I had never gone anywhere on my own, save for a rebellious moment or two where I had snuck out of the cottage. I'd thought myself invincible on my first lone outing - something I soon discovered was *not* the case. I learned the hard way that day.

And now, at twenty-four years of age, I heeded Emrys' warnings, followed his instructions and abided by his conditions. I didn't fight them. Not when rape was more common than a bar of soap. 'Saintly' was be the word I used to describe the level of patience I had for the old healer. Many others wouldn't have done so well staying within four walls their whole life.

Truth be told, I did it out of love. Not that I would ever admit that to him.

The village was bustling in that way small villages bustled - people moved about, barely talking to one another, and when they did, it was gossip and nothing more. With a population of several hundred, most everyone knew one another. I knew only a select handful and it was one specific woman I searched for now.

I glimpsed a head of jet black curls, bouncing around a petite, pale face. Her eyes were equally dark but alight with an inner fire that burned intensely, no matter how her husband treated her. No matter what her father had done.

No matter what - Soraya looked on the bright side.

She chased after a little boy with blonde hair and stained clothes. His cheeks were ruddy and he screamed in delight when she caught him around the middle, hauling him up into the air. When he saw me, he tapped her arm and pointed. Soraya put him down, breathless.

I didn't wait a moment before taking her by the hand and hauling her through the village. An old apothecary stood in ruins in an abandoned part of town - a reminder of the king's firm hate for anything even remotely resembling witchcraft. Simple herbs were enough to trigger his wrath and so now, healing was done under the table along with your ordinary, everyday dirty deals.

I thought there was a certain degree of excitement in the sleight of hand Emrys and I lived day by day.

He said it was exhausting.

Soraya didn't fight when I pulled her into the charred building. The fire had been put out quick enough, residents fearful that it would spread and destroy homes that had been painstakingly put back together twice already. I was grateful. The building had fast become a sanctuary for Soraya and I.

"Artura," she scolded, folding her arms like a petulant child. "You can't just-"

I put a hand over her mouth. "I *can*. And I *will*."

She teasingly poked her tongue out, licking my palm and giggled when I pulled my hand back.

"You're mad. They'll find out."

I shrugged. "Fuck them."

I stalked forward, Soraya stepping backward in time with my steps until she hit a blackened wall. I lifted a hand to her face, lightly stroking my fingers across her cheek. My hand trailed down her slender neck, bobbing on a hard swallow and pricked with goosebumps. Down her breasts and peaked nipples that heaved with every sharp intake of breath. When I reached her stomach, she shifted restlessly.

"Artura…"

"Yes?"

I pulled at her skirts, lifting them higher and higher until her thighs and hips were bared to me. Not for a second did her dark brown eyes, flecked with gold, leave mine. She stared, mouth falling open as my hand stroked along the soft skin of her inner thigh, heading closer and closer to her core.

"I've missed you," she whimpered.

I smirked. "I know."

Her brows furrowed. "Don't pretend you didn't miss me, too."

I pushed my lips against hers, my tongue darting out and licking across the seam of her mouth. She parted, letting me in to taste how sweet she was. Soraya always tasted of honey and cinnamon and it drove me insane. I kissed her like a woman starved, desperate, tongues and lips moving in unison, promising to devour.

"You know I missed you," I breathed against her lips. "I always miss you. I miss you even now."

Her face softened, her hand brushing a lock of hair so dark it matched her own, away from my face. "I'm here, Art. I'm all yours."

My fingers plunged into her core, hurried and eager. She was deliciously warm and wet, ready for me. Soraya cried out, fingers digging into my shoulders as she ground down against my palm. I felt her clench around my fingers, tightening with every rhythmic thrust. Biting her lip, a squeal stole past her lips before a hand flew to her mouth to stifle a moan.

"No. Let me hear it." I kissed along her collarbone, pulling the neckline of her dress aside. "I need to hear you scream."

She shook her head, onyx curls bouncing around her face. "They'll hear. We'll get in-"

I added another finger, silencing her, and the words died on her lips. Because I knew what she would say. Someone would find out that the adopted daughter of the taboo village healer and the bakers daughter/blacksmiths wife were fucking.

Gender betrayal, as the king had put it.

When reduced to the simple term of 'fucking', it was easy to pretend I could walk away, leave Soraya behind. It was purely about pleasure, scratching an itch. Nothing more.

Except it wasn't. Every part of me craved Soraya like she was the sweetest wine and I, an unrepentant alcoholic. I could get drunk on someone like her. Someone new and shy. Someone who would tremble with little more than a heated gaze.

Someone who looked at me and didn't see the mess I felt inside.

I'd had other lovers before her. Some halfway decent - marriageable, even. One was a far cry from that, though. He wasn't who I thought he was. Emrys forbade me to see him again and I'd only been too happy to agree. However, when it came to Soraya, Emrys had never once tried to stop us. We never spoke of it but I knew he knew about our affair. At heart, Emrys was a romantic. He believed in free will, in choosing those you wanted to spend your life with. His heart had shattered for innocent Soraya when she was wed three months ago to a notorious thug.

Falling to my knees on the dusty, blackened floorboards, I surged forward and tasted her. My tongue slipped across her clit, savouring the sweet muskiness that I craved too much. She was dripping for me, no longer in control of herself as she wound a hand through my hair and ground against my face. I moaned, the humming vibrations only adding to the wave of sensations crashing over her. Through every lapping of my tongue and sucking of my lips, I moved my fingers in and out, in and out.

As I crooked my two fingers forward, touching the one spot I knew would break her, I felt Soraya tighten and her whole body locked up. A moment later, panting and breathless, release flooded through her. My hand grew slick against her mound and when I pulled it away, I lifted my fingers to my lips, tasting. She was sweet there, too. My sweet, sweet Soraya.

"Let me touch you," she begged, reaching out for me on shaking legs.

"No. I just wanted you."

Her eyes narrowed. "So...you *used* me?"

She folded her arms, looking as bossy as the day I'd met her when we were eight and she'd told me I couldn't wear a green dress because it made me look like the witches they'd burned three towns over.

"I didn't *use* you. I satisfied you. I doubt that husband of yours can do as much."

"Whatever happened to equal give and take, huh?"

I combed my fingers through my hair, smoothing it out before wiping a hand across my face, still damp with her release. "If someone else is hungry and you are not, do you feed yourself as well as them?"

Soraya cocked her head to the side. "What is that supposed to mean?"

"It means you were hungry, I was not."

"You know nothing of my appetite," she replied, matter of factly.

"Actually, I have a very good idea of your...*appetite*," I crooned, eyes twinkling with mischief. "Besides, I don't need to be finger fucked today, thank you very much. I'm still sated from last night." I smiled, smug.

Soraya snorted, pushing her skirts back down and dusting them off. I helped her, soot covering the back of her pale blue dress. With any luck, the evidence of fire would be passed off as dirt from the streets. Our soil was mostly ash nowadays, anyway. I didn't like to think just how much of that ash contained human remains.

"Firstly, don't be crude. It's unbecoming of a young lady."

"Bold of you to assume I'm anything lady-like."

"Secondly," Stray continued, speaking over the top of me. "You share one bedroom with Emrys. Please don't tell me you pleasured yourself with him not even an arm's length away."

I picked up my basket, moving towards the door. The splintered wood was hanging by a single hinge and had been ever since we'd first entered the burned apothecary. How the door hadn't fallen was a miracle.

"Of course not," I replied. "I much prefer the stars to watch while I unwind."

"Incorrigible."

I shrugged, winking at Soraya as she followed me out.

CHAPTER TWO

Emrys sat outside on a moss-covered rock, one I'd sat on many nights while watching the stars appear one by one, waiting for one constellation in particular - Nemeniah, the King Slayer - to appear. He'd grumbled as I led him from the cottage, wispy grey hair ruffling in the early morning breeze. Sunrise had come and gone and in the later morning sun, he looked frailer than ever. I grimaced, noting the way his shoulders slumped forward, how his spine seemed to show even though he wore several layers. His face was beginning to hollow and his skin looked more translucent with every passing day. It was something I saw in the faces of the elderly when they were nearing death and it worried me, leaving a sickened feeling in my gut.

Not that I could ever accept that Emrys would one day die. No, he was immortal. In my mind, he would outlive us all, be the one person surviving the end of the Northern Kingdoms. He would rule Cimran and Nimue from a comfortable home with a fireplace that held more than a couple of small, half-rotted logs. Emrys would have his pick of every kind of dish - eat just as King Helmar did in his castle in Lanceris.

He had to. Because once he was gone, I had no family left. Not a soul.

I headed back inside, wiping my hands on the apron tied around my middle. It wasn't that I was precious about dirtying my clothes but rather that I'd not been able to dry my only other dress. After several days of rain, everything felt damp - even the brick walls of the cottage seemed to be slick with it. And so, after wearing my dress for three days in a row, I had now resorted to an apron to hide the stains.

Emrys' mattress was light as I pulled it off the frame. A cloud of dust settled around my shoulders when I placed it against the wall before moving my own mattress across the small space between beds. His comfort would trump my own every time, without fail. After everything he had given me, no sacrifice, small or big, seemed enough.

Because the truth was, despite a decades long war raging around us where food shortages and the stench of death were a daily occurrence, I'd had a happy childhood. Of course, there were bad memories with the good but even those were threaded with bursts of joy. Emrys would encourage me to smile through the hard times for they never lasted long. I believed him. After all, he had lived far longer than I.

I set about changing the sheets on each bed, bundling the dirty ones into a pile and placing them in a fraying wicker basket to wash later. I peered out the window to check on the old man and saw he was still where I'd left him.

Ten minutes later, our home was tidied and I went out to enjoy the sunshine beside him.

"Shall we begin?"

I suppressed a groan. "Would it hurt to have a day off from study?"

"One day missed could be the difference between life and death, Artura."

"It's nice out here." I laid back in the browning grass, closing my eyes. "Let me rest."

"Up, girl."

I cracked open one eye. "The older you get, the more stubborn you become - you know that, right?"

He chuckled to himself. "What's the point of being old if I can't throw my weight around and demand things?"

"Emrys, you've no weight on you to throw. If this breeze picks up, you'll be a kite in the wind."

Silence fell, save for the sounds of birds nearby. Naiva was surrounded by mountains and the Forest of Ember, so named because of the sheer number of times it had been set alight. Some swore now they could still see glowing remnants of fires as they passed through. The forest made me shudder at the mere thought. It was said creatures roamed within it - the likes of which you'd die at the very sight of.

"A natural emetic," Emrys said, eyes crinkling as he squinted against the bright light. "What would you choose to induce vomiting and how would you prepare it?"

Sighing, I pushed myself up, folding my legs underneath me. When Emrys insisted on a lesson, there was no point in refusing. He would get his wish one way or another.

"Blessed thistle."

Emrys turned his head towards me, giving away nothing as to whether he deemed my answer correct or not. "And?"

"Steep it in hot water for ten minutes. Serve and vomit to your heart's content. Perhaps also lose a few pounds while you're at it."

His mouth pressed into a thin line, the creases around it deepening. "Why do I get the feeling you're of a mind to weaponise the tea rather than use it to aid the sick?"

I shrugged. "If the occasion calls for it."

"Sometimes I feel I am doing the world a disservice by handing you so much knowledge."

"To be honest, I think you'd be doing the world a disservice by *not* handing me so much knowledge."

A butterfly flitted past, its wings a mixture of sunset orange and crimson. I watched as it darted among dandelions, gentle wings stirring the fluffy seedlings, sending them floating through the air. Eventually, winter would take hold, killing the last traces of the puffs that littered the hillside. I always looked towards spring and the beauty it brought.

"Other properties of blessed thistle?"

"Milk production," I replied. "But not too early in a pregnancy or else it could stimulate uterine contractions."

"Which would?" he prompted.

"Potentially end a pregnancy."

Emrys nodded, satisfied. "We must be careful when preparing remedies for common illnesses. Many can harm just as much as they are known to help."

"Dual purpose," I laughed. "Just the way I like it."

Emrys dug his walking stick into the earth at his feet, using it to hoist himself to standing. "Sometimes, I very much worry about what you'll become when I'm gone."

"You needn't worry, old man. Because you'll never be gone. I know for a fact you'll haunt my every waking moment."

He grunted and as he walked away I heard him mutter, "Someone has to watch out for you."

Laying back down once more, I watched pillowy white clouds float past. None held an ounce of rain and for that, I was grateful. I hated being cooped up in the cottage - not when I'd only so recently been granted freedom to go about as I pleased. It wasn't that I hated my home. I truly did love it. It was just that I also loved the world beyond it, the sense that there was so much out there to see and learn about. I was but one small speck amongst the heavens and while that caused others to fear, it left me with only wonder.

I shoved up the sleeves of my dress, feeling the warm rays caress my skin. After so many days like this, a light smattering of freckles covered my nose, cheeks and arms. The older women in the village tutted and shook their heads. In their opinion, it was imperative that a woman be flawless with perfect ivory skin. All they saw where I was concerned were imperfections. And I loved every single one for that reason.

My eyes drifted closed and I fell into a deep sleep.

*

When I opened my eyes, the sun was falling to the western horizon. Night would fall soon and I'd barely accomplished half of what I'd intended. I jumped to my feet and ran into the cottage, slowing when I saw Emrys sleeping soundly. I pulled on my shawl and grabbed a basket before making my way into the village where I stopped by a grocer, picking up fruits and vegetables. Everything in the cottage was gone after being confined during the rain. I made a face as I turned an apple over in my hand, noting that it had been deliberately placed rotten side down to attract customers. But then I realised that was the way they all were and settled for the best of the bunch that I could still cut the rot from.

The baker didn't care for me much. Tiram was Soraya's father and in his eyes, I would bring nothing but trouble to his only child. Trouble, he didn't realise, was the spice of life.

One I was abundant in by virtue of being a healer and well, me.

It was a silent exchange as I handed over two crowns for a loaf of freshly baked bread. The ingredients were inferior to what Lanceris had and it gave the bread a dusty texture but in Naiva, so far away from the world at large, beggars couldn't be choosers.

I glimpsed a familiar face down the street.

"Raya!"

Spying the head of dark curls, I called out to my best friend. Soraya didn't turn but I could have sworn her footsteps picked up as she rounded a corner. I sped up behind her, breathless when I finally caught up.

"Soraya, stop." I swiped a hand across my brow, wiping away beads of sweat. Despite the lateness of the day, it was still humid, autumn struggling to kick the last vestiges of a brutal summer. Nightfall would blessedly bring the crisp caress of what a soon-arriving winter promised.

Soraya froze, barely moving a muscle. I walked around her, smiling. But when she raised her head, that smile melted away only to be replaced by horror.

One side of her face was mottled purple and black with bruises lining her jaw and cheekbone. Her eye was swollen shut and puffy. Her bottom lip was also swollen, a deep split down the centre. As she looked up at me, that lip trembled. I reached out a hand, tentative fingers probing.

"What is this?" I whispered.

Stay focused, I reminded myself. *Focused and clinical. Treat her like a patient. Assess the damage. Consider treatment options. Do not run off and take matters into your own hands. That would be disastrous. And definitely don't make a scene in front of everyone - that would be equally disastrous for her.*

Soraya shook her head, wincing. "It's nothing."

I sighed heavily through my nose, nostrils flaring with loosely controlled fury as all thoughts of professionalism eddied. "Did I stutter? What the *fuck* happened, Raya?"

She glanced behind me, her unaffected eye wary. "The horse bucked while I was cleaning near the forge. It's my fault. I wasn't watching."

Not for a second did I believe her.

"Really? Does this horse happen to have a drinking problem and go by the name of Erisk?"

Soraya stayed silent, eye darting to the ground.

Erisk Matrov had married Soraya to wipe a debt incurred by her father. The 'wedding' had been rushed and while many brides welcomed the day with smiles, Soraya had heralded hers with bitter sobs. The blacksmith was known for his temper, with many landing on the wrong side of it by doing next to nothing. I was among those.

All I'd had to do was exist.

It was no secret I enjoyed being the source of his ire.

I sidestepped Soraya, headed for the village centre.

"Artura, stop."

I ignored Soraya, moving faster. My feet pounded over dirt-covered streets, teeth grinding together. When I reached the smithy, I didn't hesitate.

"You cock-sucking, son of a bitch," I spat, coming to a stop before Erisk. He was a beefy man, a full head taller than I with inflamed cheeks. To hear him put it, that was a byproduct of working near the forge though the rest of the town knew well enough it was from the ale he constantly reeked of. "Did you touch her?"

Erisk put down the wheel rim he'd been working on when I appeared. "She's my wife."

My fingernails dug painfully into my palms. "Exactly. *Wife*. Not punching bag. What happened this time?"

Erisk took a step towards me. I refused to back down. "Who says I touched her? The bitch is clumsy."

Behind me, I heard footsteps. I glanced back, spotting Soraya standing several feet away. In the presence of Erisk, she always looked impossibly small. As though through mere proximity alone, the man stifled any traces of confidence she held when I was with her. Because the woman I looked at now was nothing like the one I knew. This creature was a ghost, living with one foot in this world and the other in the After. She barely existed. And it was the drunkard before me who was the cause of that.

"Let me guess," I ground out. All I could smell was the stench of his stale breath laced with alcohol. If he were anyone else, I would fear for his safety, working near a forge while intoxicated. Instead, I sent up a silent plea to the Mother that he'd fall in head first. "She's so clumsy that she ran into your fist repeatedly and you were helpless to stop her?"

"Who's going to believe you anyway?" Folding soot-smeared arms across his chest, Erisk smirked down at me.

I stepped closer to him, enjoying the way his eyes widened imperceptibly, how he struggled not to inch backward away from the fury that fuelled the fire in my veins.

"I couldn't give *two shits* if no one believes me," I said. "Because *I* know the truth. *Soraya* knows the truth. *You* know the truth. And if you ever lay a godsdamned hand on her again, I *will* come for you. Make no mistake. The things I could do to you, you would never recover from. It would look like an accident. Erisk drinking too much yet again. So be warned. She is not yours to touch. You're not even to so much as look her way without her consent. Understand?"

I watched as thoughts ran through his head before he finally settled on one. At my eye level, his hand clamped down into a fist.

It was my turn to smirk. "Try it. I *dare* you."

Slowly, Erisk lowered his arms to his side, jaw clenching and unclenching. I didn't take my eyes off him as I moved to Soraya's side, taking her by the hand. I led her back through the village to the outskirts where a rocky road led up the side of a hill to my cottage.

"Artura," Soraya whispered.

"Hush. You shouldn't talk."

"Neither should you," she replied, voice wobbling. "Not to Erisk."

"If he makes things worse for you, I will step in." It was a promise. One I meant with all my heart. I would destroy him if he dared hurt my best friend, the woman I loved implicitly.

Soraya yanked her hand out of my grasp. "You don't get it, do you? Every time you stand up to him, I bear the brunt of his wrath. Every time you remind him that what I am to you he could never be, he hurts me. You say you will intervene but you cannot be there at every moment. When he comes for me in the dead of night, you're not there. It is I and I alone who waits before the executioner without a chance of salvation. Every single time I suffer at his hands…and you can do *nothing* to stop it."

I reached out for her hand again, stopping only when she pulled away.

"I care about you."

Soraya's uninjured eye glistened. "Then leave things be, Artura. Please. Erisk will only escalate."

"Then leave."

"It's not that simple."

I threw up my hands, already frustrated because this was a conversation we'd had many times. "How is it not? By the Mother, I swear. Pack your things and come with me. I *will* protect you."

Soraya barked out a harsh laugh. "Protect me? How? Remember Daria? What they did to her when she left her husband? They whipped her in the square, Art."

My face darkened. "I remember."

The gashes had been deep and required dozens of stitches. Emrys and I had worked on Daria all night long, applying tinctures and spoon-feeding her broth to keep up what little strength she'd retained. When the sun rose, her husband had come for her, pulling her out the door as she whimpered in agony.

"Come with me," I whispered. This time, when I reached for her hand, she didn't pull away. "Let Emrys look at you. For me. Please?"

Soraya finally nodded.

Emrys was still asleep when we walked through the weathered cottage door. I roused him and he jerked awake, eyes wide as he looked around. Despite his age, the moment Emrys saw Soraya's face he bounded out of bed, joints audibly cracking.

"Camomile," he instructed, all business. "Boiled water, cloth. The willow bark salve, too."

I retrieved the water and cloth first and Emrys set about cleaning Soraya's face. She put on a good show, suppressing winces and refusing to pull away as Emrys probed her cheekbone.

"Not broken," he concluded. "You were lucky."

Luck wasn't something I would have attributed to the situation. I hated the word. Hated the implications that sometimes, the universe decided to cut you some slack. That somehow, everything was beyond your control. I wanted to make my own luck, bottle it and keep it. Never fall into fate's hands again.

To be the arbiter of my fate.

I sat beside Soraya while Emrys worked. A cloth soaked with camomile was placed against the side of her face, soothing the tender flesh. Soraya breathed a sigh of relief.

"I would say I hope this is the last time," Emrys spoke quietly, voice gravelly in the dim of the cottage. "But I think we both know that won't be the case."

"Someone needs to do something about Erisk," I replied.

Emrys shrugged, the movement full of exhaustion despite how long he had rested. "What can be done? Until people value a woman's worth, no one will stand up to her husband."

"I will. I *do*."

"And look how far it gets her, Artura."

No one spoke as Emrys applied the salve to Soraya's face. When he was done, he excused himself, returning to his bed to rest once more. I guided Soraya's head into my lap. She closed her eyes and breathed a sigh as I stroked her hair back, gently detangling the knots that had formed. Whenever Erisk hurt her like this, her appearance suffered. Emrys had mused once that it was Soraya's way of trying to deter Erisk. That somehow, if she could repulse him, he would leave her be.

Except we both knew Erisk wasn't that kind of person. He would never leave Soraya be. She was nothing more than property to him, something he believed he had the gods-given right to use as he saw fit.

"I'm sorry," Soraya whispered. "For this." She waved a hand towards her face. "For everything."

"Don't. Don't go there." A lump formed in my throat. "Don't start apologising, Raya. None of this is your fault."

She was silent but I knew she didn't believe me.

"I love you, Art. I will never stop loving you. No matter what Erisk does. You're the one thing he can't take away from me."

The lump threatened to choke me so I settled for a nod and a gentle squeeze of her shoulder.

Because that was exactly what I feared: that one day, Erisk might actually take Soraya from me.

CHAPTER THREE

I slept fitfully.

Dreams of faces contorted by swelling and bruising plagued my mind as I squeezed my eyes shut against the harsh light of day. Except the air was still cold and the cabin around me dark. My eyes flew open.

Out past the window beside my bed, I had a full view of Naiva. On any given night, it was merely a black mass against the landscape, rooftops contorting the horizon line as you looked towards the northern sea. But tonight, it was glowing.

I jumped from the bed, closing the distance to Emrys in a single step.

"Wake up. Quickly, Emrys," I whispered, shaking his shoulder. "Something's happening."

Emrys groaned, eyes flickering open. I left him to fully rouse as I bounded out the door. The grass felt like pinpricks of ice beneath my feet as I ran, stopping at the top of the road leading from the cottage into town.

Fire ravaged the landscape, houses and shops consumed by twisting flames. On the wind, faint screams met my ears.

Errant fires weren't uncommon, not this time of year when hearths needed to be stoked throughout the night to ward off the chill. But there was something in the air, something different about these fires.

Fear. I could practically smell it, sour and foul.

"My god," Emrys breathed beside me.

"Get back inside," I ordered. "Now."

"What are you intending to do, Artura?"

I tucked my hair behind my ears, a few onyx strands almost luminescent in the moonlight. "I'm going down. I need to help."

"You mean to see to Soraya."

I was already halfway down the slope when I called back, "And what of it, old man?"

She was ever present in my mind as my bare feet tore across gravel and dirt. I felt the soles of my feet blister and scrape in my hurry to reach the town. What normally would have been a ten-minute walk took only a couple of minutes to run and when I stopped by the printers, I was panting. I rubbed a hand absentmindedly across my chest, soothing the ache.

That was when I saw it - white. Everywhere.

My heart sank.

The last time so many in white had graced Naiva, an apothecary had been burned and four lives ended.

The Cleanse. A band of King Helmar's men who enacted his laws to their fullest extent. Unlike other kingdoms, the king didn't send out soldiers en masse, hoping that so many would do the job effectively enough. Rather, Helmar sent an elite grouping of highly trained soldiers, finely honed weapons in his arsenal. The group was comprised of those he swore to fight against: murderers, rapists, thieves. I was convinced, after witnessing the horrors carried out by The Cleanse all my life, that there was no good - only one form of evil or another.

Men with hardened faces surveyed the village. Several laughed as an elderly woman fled down the street, the hem of her dress on fire. I ran after her, recognising her as a seamstress from the market.

"Marva, stop!"

The old woman halted, her face panic-stricken. For a moment, she didn't recognise me. But as I took a discarded blanket from outside the butcher and extinguished the flame, her face relaxed.

"Artura," she sobbed. "It's happening again. We didn't *do anything*."

"I know." I held her arms, fearing she would fall. Behind us, the creaking of a door sounded. "We never do."

"Here," a gruff voice commanded. "Give Marva to me."

Silas, the butcher, held his hands out for the seamstress. I led her to him, waiting only long enough for the door to close before making my way through the village, headed for the smithy and the home Soraya and Erisk shared above it.

"What have we here?"

Something roughly caught my arm and sharp pain radiated up past my elbow and into my shoulder. I spun, finding myself looking into the eyes of a man with hair as red as the fire that raged around us. My throat burned with the cloying smoke that clung to him.

"Unhand me," I said through gritted teeth.

He only laughed. "Spirit, I like that." And then leaning closer, he murmured, "Especially breaking it."

I tugged again on my arm, trying to break his hold. He was strong, they all were. Members of The Cleanse were bred and trained for war - and not a war that would be fought equally. They were prepared to eradicate, to destroy and tear apart, to play dirty if necessary. Their will was that of the king: that witchcraft and magic be wiped from the land and if that wasn't an option, to cleanse it by any means necessary. At their hands, more blood had coated the earth than rain in the last two decades.

My wrist throbbed in his hand as his eyes danced, watching me squirm. Without pausing to think, I drew up my knee and threw it between his legs. The effect was immediate as he dropped to the ground with a groan, freeing me.

I only made it a few steps before more hands latched onto me. This time, two soldiers.

"Fucking cowards," I spat as they carried me down the street. "Attacking in the dead of night. Why not come by daylight and fight as equals?"

"Funny that you think your little shit-hole is equal to Lanceris in any way," one of them replied. He smelt of smoke and his white tunic was blackened. One of the soldiers who had started the fires, then. He, I decided, I hated the most.

"You're right. We are *not* equals. We are above you and always will be." I suppressed a wince as the other soldier's hand tightened around my upper arm. "Those who do the dirty work of King Helmar are worth nothing more than the ashes at their feet."

"What a way to speak of the dead."

I looked forward, spotting a man who was clearly the captain. He wore the same white tunic but his was emblazoned with the crest of King Helmar, one that only his closest and most trusted wore. I considered it more a target than anything, a clear indicator of who ought to die first.

"Dead you put there," I replied.

He waved a hand at his men and they let me go. I rubbed my arms, letting blood rush through to my fingertips.

"What is a young woman such as yourself doing out so late in naught but her shift?"

I refused to glance down and give him any impression that I was ashamed or embarrassed. "It wasn't exactly high on my list of priorities to change into something more formal when I saw you razing my home."

He clicked his fingers to someone behind me and a moment later a weight settled over my shoulders. I glanced down and noted a sparkling white cloak woven with gold thread. Immediately, I shrugged it off, letting it fall to pillow atop the dirt.

"Cold night like this," the captain said, placing a hand on the hilt of his sword where it was bound to his side. "One might catch their death."

"You would only be so lucky."

I shuddered but not from the chill on the air. Phantom weight from the cloak, belonging to a member of The Cleanse, felt sticky as honey, though far from as sweet. I would never be rid of the feeling of it on my skin.

"It's a wonder," I said, hands balling into fists, "that your uniform is still so pristine with the blood you've shed."

The captain merely smiled. "Years of practice make for a clean killing, maiden."

I wanted to say that I was no maiden, no one for him to speak to. That I did not need of his services. I wanted to tell him to go to Hel and stay there because that was where every one of The Cleanse belonged. Only, I knew that would lead to trouble. I'd witnessed enough in years gone by to understand that The Cleanse did not take kindly to insults.

Blow smoke up their arse, I'd once heard Silas say. *That's the only way to survive the bastards.*

"I must beg leave, your grace." I bowed, hoping the captain didn't see how it was more mocking than anything, how my mouth had puckered at a title he didn't deserve. The Cleanse did nothing with grace.

"I'll have someone escort you home."

"Why? In a place that I know as well as the back of my hand? No need. I'll find it faster than I would with your... *assistance*."

I hurried away before the captain could speak again, feeling his eyes on my back as I went. I hoped that the lateness of the hour, the near starless sky would conceal how see-through my shift was. Every inch of my skin broke out with goosebumps.

Fire hadn't yet spread to the east side of the village and when I arrived, the smell of smoke was faint. I banged on the door of the smithy, not stopping until I heard footsteps on the other side.

"Quit it," Erisk growled, wrenching the door open, clearly unsurprised to see me waiting on the other side. "She's safe."

I didn't give him a chance to object as I pushed the door wider and slipped inside. "I'll be the judge of that."

The flight of stairs to the home Soraya and Erisk shared groaned under the weight of the two of us. I hurried faster, imagining every possible scenario where the entire thing collapsed, injuring and trapping me in a home I was not welcome in.

When I came to the landing, I looked around in the dim. My eyes landed on a bundled figure, sleeping beneath a patchwork quilt. I breathed a sigh of relief.

"Told you," Erisk grumbled.

"Don't let her out of your sight," I instructed. "Not tonight."

He knew as well as I did that there were nights Soraya slipped out, walking to 'clear her head.' He had deluded himself into believing that to be the truth - rather than the reality of Soraya coming to the cottage where we would lay under the stars to talk, touch. Commit one another to memory.

He had the common sense at least to nod in agreement.

With one more glance at Soraya, I headed back down the staircase and out the front door, closing it softly behind me. I wiped my hands on my shift, removing the clamminess from my palms, and took off back to the village centre where people raced about carrying pails of water. Laughter rang all around as The Cleanse watched the battle before them - the one of an all-consuming fire and a people struggling to defeat it. Already, two homes had been taken, the members of each household standing in their shadow, fighting tears welling in their eyes. No one would mourn - not fully anyway. Once The Cleanse left, the town would weep together. Not a soul dared give a single soldier the satisfaction of seeing them break.

I took a bucket from an onlooker with defeat clear in their eyes and raced down the hill to the well. Men were taking buckets, filling them, and passing them back. One took a quick look at me before deciding that questioning a woman's involvement was a matter best left to another time. He filled the bucket and passed it back. As I ran, water sloshed at the sides, dampening my shift where I held the bucket close.

I lost count of the number of trips it took before just one home was doused. By the time the fire was mere embers upon the earth, every inch of my body protested, my feet felt raw and my neck jarred from the weight of each pail of water.

A slow clapping sounded from all around as The Cleanse applauded.

The captain I'd met some hours before strolled forward.

"A noble effort," he congratulated with a smirk. "Truly impressive. The king's grace has been extended to you this night with the burning of only several homes."

"Leave," someone begged.

The captain ignored them. "A message to you all. King Helmar knows of your treason. He knows of the fugitives you harbour. Produce them now and be spared his wrath. Give them over to us and instead, be rewarded."

"Rewarded?" I spat. "What reward can Helmar offer that we would possibly want if *this* is his grace?"

The captain's eyes roamed over me, his smirk widening. "Are you sure you do not want that cloak now, maiden?"

I clenched my jaw, returning his gaze. "There are no fugitives here. Be gone and tell your king to go fu-"

A hand settled on my arm. I glanced behind me to see Emrys, a warning clear in his eyes.

"Any way we can be of service to you and yours," Emrys said, "we will be sure to do so. For now, I think the night has grown rather long and we are each in need of rest. Tomorrow, sirs. Let us wait until then."

The captain eyed Emrys, taking several steps closer. "You look familiar."

Emrys straightened. "So I've been told by many. I am a common man with a common face."

"No," the captain replied slowly, calculating. "Not at all common, I suspect."

I held my breath, eyes darting between Emrys and the captain. It wasn't until the captain turned his attention from us that I let loose that breath.

"Return to your homes," the captain ordered. "Tomorrow at noon, a meeting will be held in the town square to see the king's justice meted out."

The Cleanse moved as one, leaving the town like the smoke from the fires, carried on the wind.

"What was that about?" I whispered.

"Memories," Emrys said, "are like sand, slipping through your fingers. Remnants inevitably remain. And I'd rather they didn't."

CHAPTER FOUR

By the bleary looks on everyone's faces, it was clear sleep had been a rarity through the remainder of the night. The sun shone down overhead but did little to dispel the eerie chill in the air. The citizens of Naiva surrounded the town square where at the heart of it, a pyre had been erected.

Foreboding and ominous and not seen in eighteen months. To see another again was too soon. Though I imagined that even if it had been a decade since the last Burning, that would still be the case.

The captain of The Cleanse stood beside the pyre, surveying the crowd. His gaze was sharp and brutal in its intensity and when his eyes locked on mine, I shuddered. His only response was to raise the corner of his mouth before continuing on to the people beside me.

"Last night," he called moments later, "King Helmar demonstrated his grace and mercy. A place such as this deserves to be wiped from the earth. Twice now, in the past two years, we've been required here to remedy the infection that plagues you all."

"I'd say that's a decent track record," I muttered under my breath.

Emrys grunted.

"Give up the treasonous scum you harbour and be spared," he continued. "Let your home escape unscathed once more by the grace of King Helmar the Pure."

"Unscathed?" someone shouted. "Liar! Our home is lost to us and you talk of grace? You're the ones that ought to burn."

The captain didn't even flinch. His white uniform was still just as pristine as it had been during the night. I wondered where they'd slept, he and his men. Then I realised that I couldn't have cared less. All I wanted was for them to be gone. Far, far away from here.

"I know that look in your eye, Artura," Emrys warned quietly. "Don't be a fool."

"Better I a fool than someone dead."

I took a step forward and when the captain's eyes snapped to me, I was grateful for the thickness of my dress, no matter how much I was sweating underneath. Last he'd seen me, I'd been little more than downright indecent. But from the look in his eyes, I knew he wouldn't have minded. Rumours of The Cleanse preceded them - a band of evil that did the very things they claimed to put an end to. In the early days of The Exoneration, the Cleanse had done as they wished and little more than a year later, we as a kingdom saw the firstborn of a generation that was every part its title: The Forsaken. Children born of rape as The Cleanse moved throughout the land, a disease that infected innocents with their seed, siring children that were treated lower than the very dirt that now cultivated no life. Some were in Naiva, one of the few towns that had not shunned those who'd had no hand in their fate. An orphanage adjoining the church housed exactly twenty-three children, their ages ranging from twenty-two to just six months old. Life beyond the orphanage was difficult for The Forsaken and so, even once they reached adulthood, each soul remained within the safety of its four walls.

"There are no fugitives here." I clenched my jaw to stop myself from shaking, steeling my nerves. "They left for Reynar during the night while you burned our homes. If you leave now, you might catch up in time."

The captain's eyes narrowed. His copper hair was swept back from his face this morning, revealing a long straight nose ending in a slight hook. His jaw was solid and his mouth at a permanent slant. Perhaps that was why he always seemed to be smirking at me. Then again, it could have just been that he could see right through me, straight into the heart of the lie I was crafting.

"Convenient that it would be Reynar they left for. That would require boarding a ship to sail around the mountains, would it not?"

I shrugged, hoping the movement looked casual and not as tense as it felt. "If you think your horses cannot handle the terrain then I would presume that to be the best path, of course. But then again, it's entirely your call. The longer you stay here, the greater the distance they put between themselves and your men."

The silence surrounding us was deafening. I couldn't hear the familiar blackbird song that seemed to always ring through the village. Even the wind had died down, creeping on tenterhooks through Naiva. The captain took three steps, closing the distance between us.

"What is your name, girl?"

"Ar-"

"Orletta." I glanced back to look at Emrys who'd spoken. He cleared his throat and repeated, "Her name is Orletta."

"Is that so?" The captain reached out, gloved fingers the smelt of smoke gripped my chin and turned my face towards his. "Orletta. Not a name I've heard of before."

"We've never met before," I simply replied, falling in line with Emrys' lie easily.

"Indeed. However, I distinctly recall hearing another call you Artura."

A small squeak sounded to the right of us, a squeak I'd recognise anywhere. Soraya and I had spoken before the village came to a standstill around the pyre. Had the captain been listening? He didn't strike me as a man who let down his guard for even a second. And being in charge of The Cleanse meant that he had many pairs of ears at his disposal.

"Orletta is a pet name," I hastily replied. One lie to buy out another. "Artura is the name of my birth."

"An interesting name. Do you know its origins?" I shook my head. "Artura was the name of the eleventh queen of Cimran. She ruled for ninety years until she was murdered in her sleep by her son."

"Unfortunate for her," I breathed.

"Quite. Many consider the name to be bad luck. We do not name our children after those who die in such a grisly fashion. It bodes for an unhappy ending to such a young life."

"Perhaps some see strength in the name instead," I replied. "After all, it's a rarity for one to rule more than a decade let alone nine."

The captain's head tilted. "Except, of course, our beloved King Helmar."

"Long live King Helmar," The Cleanse said as one, the residents of Naiva numbly echoing after them.

"Of course." I gave a tight-lipped smile and spoke through gritted teeth. "Long live the *king*."

"Tell me, maiden," the captain went on, circling me. "Do you know what has befallen Reynar?"

I shook my head, an icy chill running up my spine. It wasn't uncommon for Naiva to not receive news beyond the Forest of Embers and the mountains. Many didn't make the journey, knowing it would take a considerable amount of time to circumnavigate the terrain. And at this point, paying your way onto a ship was costly. When few could afford to eat three square meals, fare for a sea crossing was simply unattainable.

"At present, Reynar has been levelled," the captain explained. Horrified gasps echoed around us. "See, they, too, harboured fugitives. While we were able to apprehend three, two escaped. They fled through the mountains."

"That hardly seems smart. I'd have much rather braved the sharks and swum." I was babbling, I knew I was. It happened when I got nervous.

And the captain knew it, too, could sense it. He smiled, a predator closing in on his prey.

"Reynar is no more. Those who fled would not return. So you see, *Artura*," - I didn't like the way he said my name, it felt greasy, like he was trying to be intimate in a way that felt violating - "I know you've told me an untruth. That pretty mouth of yours has lied to me and that's not something I tolerate lightly."

I gulped. A bead of sweat trickled down the back of my neck. But I wasn't about to beg forgiveness - even though I knew what was coming. The last thing I would do on this earth would be to beg on my knees for mercy from men who didn't know the meaning of the word. So when strong hands gripped my biceps and pushed me to the ground, I didn't fight. When a knife sliced down the back of my dress, baring my skin to the distant sun, I didn't flinch.

And when the crack of a whip sounded, followed by a stinging pain so sharp I felt it in my very bones, I didn't cry, didn't so much as whimper. I took the punishment, fingers digging into the dirt beneath me as I forced myself to remain on all fours. A dog to be whipped by The Cleanse.

I counted the lashes, imagining a death for each strike.

First, the soldier holding the whip.

Then the red-haired one who apprehended me last night.

The short stocky one who'd laughed as Marva ran in terror, skirts alight.

Another death with the soldier bearing the torch, burning Naiva.

And finally, the captain, the man responsible for it all.

I ignored the soft hands that reached for me, trying to help me to my feet as the soldiers backed away. If I took help now, they would win. The Cleanse would see yet another citizen of Cimran broken.

I refuse to break.

Clenching my jaw, I pushed myself to my feet, keenly aware that my bodice hung wide open to reveal each lash.

Good. Let them look. Let them see. I cannot be broken.

"I'll give you one more chance," the captain said, holding his hands behind his back as though our conversation weren't the knife's edge on which two lives balanced. "Where are the fugitives Naiva is harbouring?"

I let the blatant hate show in my eyes, blazing as I stared down the captain, and pulling my head back, I spat. The wad of saliva landed square in his right eye.

"Fuck you," I ground out.

Was it silent before? I was wrong. *This* was the very definition of silence.

The captain pulled a handkerchief from his pocket and wiped his face. Then, with a click of his fingers, I was pushed yet again to all fours and whipped a further five times. One wound blended into another until my entire back was on fire. Dark spots clouded my vision and I bit the side of my tongue until I tasted copper, forcing myself to remain conscious.

Do not break.

Those three words were a chant in my mind, a silent prayer and petition to any gods who deemed Naiva worthy of a second glance. We had long ago been forsaken by the gods, old and new. Now, they were little more than fairytales told to children by candlelight. I'd been one of those children. Even then, I wondered how such powerful beings could turn a blind eye to all they'd created when it was falling into the grip of chaos.

I hated them. But that didn't stop me from praying to them when I was desperate.

I swayed on the spot, fighting to remain upright after pushing myself to my feet.

"One more chance," the captain repeated. "Do not squander my generosity. It would be a crime to further mar skin as beautiful as yours."

"You'd know all about crimes," I breathed.

"I didn't catch that," the captain said.

I raised my head. "I don't know where the fugitives are. And even if I did, I wouldn't tell you."

The captain's face darkened. "Another five lashes and you'll be unconscious, maiden. Remember that."

I stayed silent. Because I knew he was right. Already it was a fight to stay awake when my body craved rest so furiously.

"Here."

It was spoken so quietly, I thought for sure I had imagined the word. But then a murmur echoed around the crowd and slow, scuffing footsteps neared. I kept my eyes on the captain, knowing that the moment I looked away would be the moment he might strike once more. I'd lived near beasts great and small long enough to know that you never let them out of your sight.

"It is I you seek."

The voice was feminine and when I looked up, I found a girl. She couldn't have been older than seventeen and as she stood several feet away from the captain, she shook. Her muted brown hair was tied back in a low bun and she wore clothes dirtied with dust and mud from many days of travel. Wide blue eyes glistened while tears streamed over pale cheeks. I didn't recognise her

However, I knew I'd not soon forget that look of fear mixed with resignation.

The captain drew his sword and pointed it at the girl.

"Witch," he snarled. "Today, you will burn."

The girl whimpered. "I'm not a witch, sir. I ran because I was afraid."

"You were seen performing a spell in the woods by one of your townsfolk."

"Cleaning a kill," she cried. "That's all. Food has been scarce and I hunted that day. I know no spells of any kind, honest. All I did was kill a rabbit to feed my family."

The captain remained unmoved by the free-flowing tears the girl shed. If anything, his face hardened more, turning to stone. Devoid of all feeling.

"The tales I could tell you," he began, "of witches at the hour of their death who plead for their lives. You will be but another nameless face burned today for treason. King Helmar has declared the land be purged of witchcraft. You and your kind are a blight."

Her face crumpled as she began to sob in earnest. My heart thudded in my chest, searching for some way to help. But I was already on borrowed graces. The fact that I'd not been arrested was a small mercy.

Mercy. Ha.

"Where is the other?"

The girl shook her head. "She was burned by the fires that took our homes before we left. I couldn't keep her alive and she didn't make it. Her body is in the mountains, buried beneath a pile of rocks."

This seemed to satisfy the captain. Perhaps he'd thought he wouldn't get even one fugitive and was cutting his losses. Still, I suspected someone would search the mountains to be sure. Helmar spared no trouble or expense when it came to his mission.

With a look, the girl was carried towards the pyre, hands and feet bound. She was screaming long before the torch lowered, before the tinder curled under the heat of the flames. When her skin blistered and her cries grew faint, The Cleanse walked away. She would be left for the good people of Naiva to clean up. Justice had been served and there was nothing more for The Cleanse to do.

*

"Sit still."

My jaw ached. For an hour straight, I'd clenched my teeth while Emrys cleaned my wounds. The walk to our cottage had been a long one and by the time we made it, tears old and new marred my face.

"I'm trying," I whispered, voice cracking.

Emrys said nothing and I was glad of it. I knew what he'd say. That I should have kept my head down. Remained silent.

Let events unfold without interruption. I'd brought this pain upon myself. He would then lament that while he hoped it would, this would likely not teach me the lesson I so sorely, desperately needed.

I always spoke up. I never learned.

"Why are they doing this?" I asked, staring at the fire burning low in our hearth. "What can they possibly hope to gain from a few deaths? The entire kingdom fears Helmar as it is. Won't this only cause a revolt?"

Emrys sighed, dabbing with a cloth, softening blood mixed with dirt that had dried too fast in the sun.

"Men like King Helmar, they fear that which they hold: control."

"How?"

"He fears losing it." Emrys wiped near my lower back where it was tenderest and I winced. "Anything gained through violence never truly belongs to you. One day, Helmar will have that control taken from him."

"Couldn't happen a moment too soon."

"I agree, Artura. Unfortunately, I fear we have quite some time yet before Helmar is overthrown. He's clever. He knows his enemy and uses that knowledge to his advantage. The people of Cimran fear him, yes, but they fear the lie he has spun even more so."

"That magic is evil?"

"Yes."

"Do you think it's evil?"

A pause. And then, "No. I do not."

"Do you fear it?

"No."

"Why?"

Emrys dropped the cloth into a bowl and picked up a salve, one we'd used on Daria after she'd been whipped in the village centre eighteen months ago. I sighed at the first smear of it against my inflamed skin, drinking in the cooling relief it brought.

"People fear what they do not know."

I lifted my head, ignoring the stinging that radiated down my spine as meh skin pulled taut with the movement. "Do *you* know magic?"

Emrys didn't answer. Didn't so much as look at me.

CHAPTER FIVE

I didn't leave the house all week.

Whether it was cowardice or self-preservation, I didn't know. All I did know for certain was that the moment I showed my face, I would be met with sympathetic looks.

Sympathy was the one thing I could tolerate the least.

I didn't want it. I didn't want people to see me and think that I had been helpless as I was whipped by The Cleanse. I wasn't helpless - never in my life had I let that be an option. Everything had been my choice and mine alone. I refused to be made a victim.

And so I hid away.

Like a victim.

Or so Emrys said.

"You know," I drawled early on the fifth day, "for someone who wants me to learn my lesson and never repeat what happened in the village, you're trying awfully hard to get me out of here. Here I was thinking you'd prefer I sit in the corner like a naughty child to think about what I've done."

The old man chuckled to himself before turning to look at me with a grave expression. "Artura, I've raised you from birth. I know perhaps best what you need. To stay up here in this cottage, that is not it."

"I'm sore."

"Boo hoo."

I poked my tongue out at him. It was the only movement that was truly pain-free.

The criss-crossing wounds on my back were healing slowly but surely under the careful ministrations of the healer. Emrys checked my back three times a day, applying salves and insisting I let fresh air get to it. So I'd taken to napping on a blanket in the sun, letting the warm rays caress my back. It was invigorating and had become the part of my day I looked forward to most.

"Are they still there?"

Emrys knew who I meant. "Yes. I suspect they will be until soldiers return from the mountains."

To confirm what the young girl had said - that the other fugitive was indeed dead. How long it would take The Cleanse to scour mountains that rose so high they were engulfed by clouds, I did not know. All I knew for certain was that so long as The Cleanse were in Naiva, none of us were safe.

*

Emrys made the slow journey into the village. A meeting was called by the captain with the senior most members of Naiva. It wasn't a meeting Emrys could refuse. Had the old man avoided detection, he could have perhaps stayed in the cottage, kept his head down until the meeting was long over. Except he'd made the critical error of speaking up whilst I crafted lie after lie to the captain.

I puttered around the cottage, tidying and sorting through the chaos that had unfolded the past week. Emrys wasn't exactly organised, so far as healers went. He claimed to know where everything was, what the unlabelled tinctures and pots of salve contained. With little more than a sniff, Emrys could discern between most remedies he'd concocted, even name specific ingredients they contained. A skill I highly doubted I would ever possess.

I put those to the side, deciding to leave them for him to sort through later.

The pain in my back had faded considerably so I cleaned. Changing sheets that were still stained with my blood and likely always would be now, sweeping the floor of debris blown in by the wind. Just as I was preparing a stew for supper, a hurried knock sounded pounded at the door.

I pulled open the door to find Soraya standing on the threshold, a panic-stricken look etched across her face. Deep purple half-moons hung under her eyes and her face looked sallow and gaunt. Before she could speak, I took her by the hand, pulling her inside.

"What is it?" My hands fussed over her, searching for an injury. Her whole body had changed since I'd last seen her in the town square. Her shoulders now hunched forward, defeated, but the energy radiating from her was one of pure, undiluted fear.

"I held out as long as I could," Soraya said, her voice hysteric. "I really did but he's so much bigger than me. And I'm not exactly what you would call strong…"

I frowned. "What do you mean? Did Erisk hurt you again?"

She hesitated.

"Raya?"

"Something like that."

It took a moment before I comprehended her meaning. My heart thudded to a painful stop and my mouth fell open.

"No."

She nodded. "I forced him to wait two months, Art. I swear. I'm so sorry."

"Stop." I held up my hands.

"Please don't hate me."

That caught my attention more than anything else. "Hate you?"

"I betrayed you. I slept with him. I-"

Before Soraya could say another word, I pulled her against me, pressing gentle kisses to her forehead, her temple, and her lips. I cradled her head in the crook of my neck, one hand smoothing the wild curls from her face while the other stroked her back in hypnotic circles. Soon, her breathing evened out.

"Betrayal is not even a thought I considered," I whispered. "We both knew this would happen eventually. I don't hate you. I still love you - so much that it hurts."

She sniffled. The material of my shift under her face was damp.

"But...you said you made Erisk wait two months. It's been four since you were married."

Soraya froze in my arms.

"Oh." My chest tightened. "How long have you known?"

"Since last week," she replied. "I suspected when my monthly was late but that's also happened before because of stress so I didn't jump to conclusions straight away. But then it never showed and...well. I've been vomiting nonstop this week. Haven't stomached more than bread or water."

I pulled back from Soraya so I could see her face. Her sea-glass green eyes, ones that normally held so much life, the brightest spark, were dull. Dead. There was nothing of the woman I knew in them.

"Does Erisk know?"

She shook her head. "No. And he won't. *Ever*."

I snorted. "That's not how pregnancy works, Raya. Eventually, he will find out."

Soraya bit her lip. She turned, walking to the hearth where the stew was bubbling in its pot. I noticed now that the dress she wore was black, one usually saved for funerals. She was in mourning. For the woman she wanted to be, the woman she spoke of when we were children. I wondered if had Soraya known what was coming, what she would have done. Because she'd once sworn death would be better than a loveless marriage.

"No," she whispered. "Erisk won't find out. Not if you help me get rid of it."

I stared, processing her words. Of course, it was far from uncommon that a woman would want to rid herself of an unwanted pregnancy, especially in times when feeding the mouths that already existed was more and more difficult. And while I knew Soraya would be the most doting mother, I also knew her well enough to know that she would rather be childless than have one with an abusive husband.

"If Erisk finds out…"

"I don't care," she snapped, whirling to face me. "I don't give a shit, Artura. This is *my* life. I'll not have myself bound to that demon in more ways than this." She threw up her hand, showing the simple wedding band she'd worn for four months now.

"What if you get hurt?" I protested. "These things are never safe."

"Don't be such a hypocrite. You've done this before. I know you have."

I clenched my jaw. That was a memory I'd rather have forgotten permanently. "You have no right to bring that up."

"Don't I?" She laughed. "Because from where I'm standing, it seems to me that you won't offer me the kindness that was offered to you."

"I was thirteen."

"And I'm twenty-three! Big difference."

"There is, Raya. A *very* big difference." I ran a hand through my greasy, unwashed hair, desperately wishing this was not my reality. "Childbirth could have killed me at that age."

"Childbirth will kill me *now*. If I bear this man's child, I am as good as dead." Her face crumpled and then she was sobbing, her chest heaving. "Please don't make me do this. I can't. Artura, I can't."

I closed the distance between us, pulling her against my chest. How long we stayed like that, I didn't know. Holding Soraya through her world crashing down, I realised that I was holding onto her by my fingernails. She was precariously close to slipping away from me forever. If I lost her, I would lose myself in kind.

"It might not work," I quietly said into her hair. She smelled of rosewater. It was always soothing but now, it made my skin prickle because it was a reminder of what I stood to lose.

"Anything. I'll try anything." She wiped her nose on her sleeve. "I have tried. Art, if you knew how much I have tried over the last week. I've not fought the blows Erisk has dealt and my skin still aches from the scalding water I sat in till it turned to ice."

I sighed, bowing my head to hers, and closed my eyes.

"Okay. I'll help you."

Her only reply was to place her palm against the side of my face, fingertips twining in my hair.

"We should wait for Emrys."

"No."

"Raya, I don't know enough."

"No." She pulled back, lifting her chin. "We do this now."

"What do you think will happen by waiting another hour?" I asked. "That Emrys will say 'no'?"

"He might. He's a healer. Who values life more than a healer?"

"He's also sympathetic to your situation."

Soraya's gaze narrowed. "We do this now, Art. I've waited long enough."

By the stubborn way she held her head, I knew there was no winning this. If I didn't help her, the possibilities of what else she might attempt were endless. Women had been known to throw themselves from the tops of staircases, to have people kick them in the stomach. Some attempted to make abortifacients by themselves only to get similar herbs confused and instead of taking one life, took two in the process.

I left Soraya by the fire and moved to the shelf where Emrys' tomes were stacked. I sifted through them until I found the one I was looking for. I'd looked at it only days ago, searching for emetics after the lesson Emrys had given. On the eighth page, I found it. A remedy for uterine contractions that would almost certainly eventuate in a miscarriage.

"Are you sure about this?" I asked, looking up at Soraya.

"Yes."

I sighed, nodding. "Hand me the mortar and pestle."

I set about pulling ingredients for the tea that would rid Soraya of the child she didn't want. Dried tansy flower, mugwort, yarrow and pennyroyal oil. I ground the ingredients together before adding them to a muslin pouch, tying it with string. Ten minutes later, the pouch had steeped in boiling water, the aroma strong in the small confines of the cottage.

"Once you drink this," I said, holding a chipped mug full of the tea, "there's no going back. Nothing can be done to stop the miscarriage. You *will* lose the child."

"Give it to me." Not a request. An order. Soraya's eyes burned. "Let's be done with this nightmare."

I hesitated, holding the steaming mug in my cold hands. A chill rolled up my spine and the distinct feeling that we stood on a precipice of something much bigger than ourselves was all-consuming. Yet, I shook myself mentally, erasing the thought as I handed Soraya the chipped mug.

I had expected her to sip slowly. The liquid was bitter, that much I remembered from when I was thirteen. It had taken me a full hour to drink, willing myself not to throw up. Sometimes I imagined I could still taste it at the back of my throat. Except Soraya didn't stop, not until the last drop was drained from the mug. She placed it on the tabletop with an audible thunk and stepped back.

"Sit, rest," I said. "We should see some changes in the next half hour."

I went back to sorting through the cottage, tidying things that had already been tidied before. Anything to distract from my present reality - that I was committing one of the gravest offences under King Helmar's laws. To take the life of the unborn, was punishable by beheading. It was, in part, the reason why the king sought out witches and healers, for the instances in which they'd supplied a woman with a concoction of some kind to induce miscarriage. Emrys had made one for me all those years ago without a moment's hesitation as I bore the results of a crime the accused would never be punished for. And now, he did so for others but after much careful thinking. Perhaps that was why Soraya had been so insistent that we not wait. If Emrys refused her, what choice would be left? There was no other healer for miles. No way for her to seek help when Erisk was always so close by. Even now, she risked much by sneaking out to see me.

There'd been next to no real thinking here this evening. Only action. Because ultimately, there was nothing I could refuse Soraya, the woman I loved more than life itself.

Just as I was pulling the stew from the fire, I heard a gasp.

"Art, I-"

I placed the pot of stew on the table and turned to find Soraya staring at her stomach. No, not her stomach. I followed her gaze to the floor beneath where she stood. Dark liquid pooled there, staining the floorboards.

"It's happening," she gasped, something like relief in her voice.

The hairs on the back of my neck rose. Something didn't feel right. It was happening too fast, the bleeding too heavy given the short time that had passed since Soraya had drunk the tea. There should have been cramping for some time first but instead, blood slipped down her legs, freely flowing like the waters of a creek in spring.

I rushed to the bed, pulled my blanket, and put it on the floor.

"Come here."

Her face changed from relief to confusion. "What?"

"I need to check you."

"Why?"

I gritted my teeth. "Don't argue."

Soraya sat down on the blanket and a moment later I'd lifted her skirts past her hips. Her white undergarments were soaked crimson and at her core, the fabric clung to her.

"It's working, isn't it?" Soraya lifted her head.

I didn't reply. This was beyond what I knew. I suddenly felt way out of my depth. I had made a mistake, one I couldn't remedy. And Emrys was far into the village with no way of contacting him. Even if I could have, what could be said? He was surrounded by members of The Cleanse and what I'd done would certainly earn me a noose or flame.

"Everything will be fine," I said, hearing the barely controlled hysteria in my voice. "Just stay still."

I knew Emrys kept vials of a tincture known to induce blood clotting. It was the one thing he was constantly asked for with the way Cimran had been in recent years. I searched through the unlabelled bottles he kept, looking for the one with amber liquid. Scrunching my eyes shut, I tried to remember what he used to make it. There were so many ingredients used in the medicines Emrys made - some interacted badly with one another. Whatever I gave Soraya could either save her or make things far, far worse.

I glanced behind me to where she lay on the blanket. Her face was pale and blood had begun to pool around her. My hands shook as I continued my search before finally landing on the smallest bottle. The liquid looked a little darker than I remembered but it was definitely amber in colour. I plucked it from among the others, uncorked it and fell at Soraya's side.

"Drink this." I tipped the bottle to her lips and she gulped it down in three mouthfuls. I'd seen Emrys give much larger amounts to those injured in battle. Soraya bled far heavier than any of the men we'd attended to.

She gasped. "That burns."

"It'll help," I promised, though with every passing second I became less and less certain. The liquid shouldn't burn, if anything it was sweet like the candy we treated ourselves to once a year on the summer solstice. I pulled her skirts back and saw that the amount of blood had tripled.

"I feel tired," Soraya murmured, sounding groggy. "I need to sleep."

"Do *not* sleep," I demanded. "Please, Raya. Just stay awake. I'm going to fix this."

Except I didn't know how. I was lost. All I could do was stare in horror as Soraya paled to the colour of parchment. Her eyes were too dark in her face and her skin was clammy.

Like ice. The ice cold of encroaching death.

"Stay awake," I breathed, tapping her cheek as her eyes closed. "Please, Raya."

All I could do was hold her. I'd made things worse. The clotting mixture hadn't worked and the knowledge that in my haste and desperation I'd given her the wrong thing made my gut twist. I could feel the woman I loved fading away. She was cool water in my palms, slipping through my fingers by the second.

When her chest fell on another exhalation, it didn't rise.

CHAPTER SIX

Frozen. That was how Emrys found me sometime later. I sat in a puddle of Soraya's cooling blood, feeling my legs grow sticky with it. Knowing that blood crusted under my nails, an indelible reminder of what I'd done, made bile burn the back of my throat. Her head was cradled in my lap. A face etched, in my mind, now a mask of death.

Emrys said nothing, just fell to my side on frail legs, knees cracking too loudly in the small confines of the cottage. He placed two fingers against Soraya's throat and a moment later, pulled back silently, hand shaking.

"What happened here?"

I couldn't speak. Formulating words was no longer something I knew how to do. The only thought crashing through my mind and body was that I wanted to join her. A world without Soraya was a world I did not want to live in. I'd always wanted to think what she and I had was something I could just walk away from, that at the deepest level, we weren't connected the way I now knew we were. Somewhere,

I heard an owl hooting through the night and a wave of pain coursed through me. How could the world continue to spin when my own had come to a crashing halt?

"Artura."

She looked so peaceful, despite the way she'd died. Her death had been swift and panicked, too fast for me to stop. Somewhere, in the back of my mind, there was a voice mocking me.

You couldn't have stopped this. Her death was inevitable. The moment you granted her your assistance, her life's thread was cut.

An angel of death. Emrys had joked years ago, when I began my studies as a healer, that I was more inclined to become just that. Perhaps his words carried a kernel of prophecy.

"Look at me, Artura," Emrys said. He took hold of my chin, tilting my face to his. "Breathe. You've gone into shock. What happened?"

Slowly, I regained my senses.

"Raya...she...she's pregnant."

"Did she lose the child naturally?"

I couldn't answer, my mouth silently opening and closing like a dying fish. Fitting. I was dying with every second that passed.

Emrys reached out for the teacup on the dining table, sniffing the dregs at the bottom with a frown. He then looked beside me to the vial that had held the amber tincture.

"What were you doing with this?" He held it up, tilting it back and forth. Nothing more than a single drop remained, glowing like liquid gold in the dim firelight.

"She was bleeding out," I whispered. "I tried to stop it."

"This isn't right," he replied. "This would have thinned her blood, not helped it to clot."

Killer, my mind taunted. *Nothing more than a killer.*

"Raya didn't want the child. I thought I was helping her." Hot tears leaked from the corners of my eyes and ran down my cheeks. I'd always been one to say that tears were cleansing but now, they were damning, evidence of my failure. "I made her the tea you made me."

"Oh, sweet girl." He brushed hair from my face where it stuck to the salty tears. "Why didn't you wait for me?"

"She didn't want to. Didn't think you would be willing to help."

At that, Emrys sighed heavily, and that was answer enough. He would've helped - would have done it right, too. Soraya wouldn't be growing cold on the floor, more and more by the minute. She'd be alive and in my arms, smiling because, with a simple tea, she would be free of Erisk's full control. At least for a little while longer.

"I want her back." No sound came out, only the formation of the words. But Emrys knew.

"It's not that simple."

At that, I looked up at him, a spark of hope flaring within. "That implies it's possible."

"If anyone found out, we would simply be exchanging one life for another."

"The conversation we had the other day," I said, thinking back to the night Emrys had tended to my wounds. "You said you didn't fear magic. I asked if that was because you knew it but you never replied. Do you, Emrys? Know magic?"

His head whipped around, wispy white hair floating around his head like a halo. Because at that moment, that was what he was - an angel, my chance at salvation, at bringing back the one person I loved more than anything. Emrys moved around the cottage, ensuring rattling windows were firmly shut, closing curtains and finally, locking the door. When he turned back to me, his face was grave.

"If this happens, Artura, there is *no* going back."

No going back. Words I'd cautioned Soraya with not more than an hour ago.

I held her tighter, bending myself around Soraya as though I could protect her still.

"Anything, Emrys. I would do anything to bring her back."

He nodded, thinking quietly to himself. The familiar crease between his thick brows formed as he crossed to his collection of tomes, pulling one out that we never read from. He said it was because the knowledge within was outdated, that there were more modern, simplified practices. I'd never questioned it - not when studying was the last thing I wanted to do. Perhaps if I *had* studied more, Soraya wouldn't be gone. We wouldn't be in this gods awful mess.

"Bring her closer to the fire," he instructed.

I had little in the way of upper body strength so settled for pulling the blanket Soraya died upon. It was my favourite blanket in the whole world, the only treasure I had left of my mother. She'd died in childbirth, spending only a moment with me before slipping into the After. And now, the woman I loved had also died upon it. I should have burned the damn thing, rid myself of the curse so clearly woven into the fibres.

"I can bring her back," Emrys said. I opened my mouth to speak but he held up a hand. "Magic demands balance and payment. I can only return her to this world with the payment of blood."

"Take my life," I begged. "I don't care. Just bring her back."

While I spoke, Emrys ripped open the front of Soraya's dress, baring her chest. A chest I'd spent many nights with my ear pressed against, listening to the steady beating of a heart that was now painfully silent.

He shook his head, rubbing a gnarled hand across his face. "Your life is not needed, simply your blood. Hold out your palm."

I did as I was told, holding my hand out to Emrys. He positioned it over Soraya's heart and in one quick movement, drew a pocketknife across the lifeline on my palm. From there, blood pooled and when Emrys turned my hand to the side, it dripped over Soraya's breast, over her heart.

"Keep your hand there. Keep the blood flowing."

Emrys took that same pocket knife and made a vertical incision along Soraya's breast, a line to match the one on my palm. He then rocked back on his heels with a groan and opened the tome. The pages were blank. Were it not for the worn exterior, I'd have thought it to be a brand-new book, ready to record valuable knowledge. I watched as Emrys flicked through pages before finally stopping at one. It was loose in the book, held in only by the thickness of the spine. He removed it and turned to the hearth.

Words appeared, brought into being by the light of the fire - a sprawling cursive running corner to corner. It was a language I didn't know. But with the way the words slanted and dipped, the light smearing leading towards the right that indicated a left-handed author...that was Emrys' writing.

Emrys narrowed his eyes, his lips moving fast around words I couldn't hear.

He turned to Soraya and placed a hand on her forehead. A metallic tang filled the air, burning my nostrils.

Magic.

It was everywhere, potent and all-consuming. Twining with the very fibres of my clothing, leaving an indelible mark upon my body. It raised the hairs along my arms and stung my eyes like the salt water of the ocean. Magic filled the room like smoke from a fire, cloying and choking but also bearing a sense of freedom with it. In magic, there were possibilities, second chances. Life.

I watched and waited with bated breath. I was so consumed by Emrys' touch upon Soraya that I almost missed the way the wound in her chest parted, how it seemed to drink in my blood as it continued to pool there. I gasped but Emrys ignored me, pushing on with the nonsensical words he uttered.

A moment later, he drew his hand away.

"Did...did it work?"

He held up a finger, brow furrowed.

And then -

"Her chest," I breathed, watching as Soraya's breasts rose and fell rhythmically once more.

Emrys replaced the paper, the words quickly disappearing as it left the light of the fire. He closed the tome and returned it to the shelf. When he returned, he held a bandage in his hands and wrapped my palm. The blood was already clotting and I barely noticed the dull ache, too busy watching Soraya's face.

"Yes," he finally replied, checking her pupils and placing a hand beneath her nose. "Soraya is alive."

A sob escaped me. "Thank you, thank you, thank you."

"*Never* speak of this," he warned. "Or else we'll both be dead by sunrise."

I had no intention of telling anyone.

Soraya's breathing grew steadier and finally, she opened her eyes, blinking against the light of the fire.

"Everything hurts," she groaned, clearing her throat.

Emrys held out a cup of water. I helped Soraya up so she could sip. As she took a tentative mouthful, her gaze flickered between Emrys and myself.

"You were-"

"Asleep," Emrys concluded, his eyes issuing a warning his lips dared not. "For quite some time."

Soraya frowned, staring into the distance. "No."

"No?"

"I wasn't asleep."

A cold chill seeped and crept over me, coating every inch of my body. "What do you mean?"

She turned to look at me, her eyes wide. "I was with the Mother. I saw the After."

"Must have been a dream," Emrys said. I looked at him and saw worry deep in his old eyes. It was rare for the old man to worry, so when he did, I knew things were far from good.

Soraya struggled to her feet, using the table as leverage. "It was no dream. I was there. And then I was being ripped away. It felt like my very flesh was being peeled from my bones."

I said nothing. The relief in Emrys' eyes that I chose that moment to stay silent caused a flicker of guilt. Too often I'd spoken when I shouldn't have and it had gotten me in trouble. Except now, it wasn't just my life on the line, but his, too.

Soraya looked at me, her expression morphing into one full of horror. "Witchcraft."

I swallowed hard.

"I was *dead*, Artura. I should have stayed dead. That much I know. The very fact I'm here now - the departed don't just rise of their own accord."

"Soraya, please-"

I reached out for her and she stumbled back, still coated in blood, her black skirts turned to something resembling midnight. For the first time, I saw the one thing on Soraya's face that threatened to break me because it was the one thing I dreaded more than anything.

Hate.

Pure, unadulterated hate.

"You've tainted my soul," she breathed, pressing a hand to the incision at her breast, now little more than a thin silver line, likely unnoticeable to many. "The Mother will not take me back now. I am damned for all eternity because you could not accept what was."

Emrys said nothing, merely bowed his head. I'd drawn him into something that would be the death of us both. I saw him slowly resign himself to his fate, the fight leaving him as his shoulders slumped.

"Do you not know by now?" I replied, eyes full of wild desperation. "I cannot live without you."

"So you would rather damn me?" Her eyes were ablaze as she looked around the room. "What you have done, Artura - it's evil. Vile. Wicked. You should be beheaded for this."

I flinched. Truth be told, I'd known Soraya would have had a problem with us using blood magic to bring her back. But I'd also been so certain of her love for me that I hoped she would forgive me in time. Forgiveness, however, was clearly the furthest thing from her mind as she backed away towards the door.

"Please don't leave," I begged. "I love you, Raya. I would have done anything to bring you back."

She shook her head. "That was your first mistake. You should have let the Mother take me."

When she tore the door open and fled into the night, I fell to my knees, feeling my heart shatter into a thousand pieces.

*

"It's not a matter of 'if' but rather 'when,' Artura."

I sat at the window, staring out at the predawn light. It was beautiful, inky shades of purple and crimson. However, all it reminded me of this morning was the blood that stained our porous cottage floor. Blood I'd spilt.

"Do not fret."

I snorted. "How can I not? I've ruined three lives this night."

"What I did, I did of my own accord, girl. Be sure of that."

"So I've ruined two lives. That's infinitely better, thank you."

"Sarcasm does not suit you."

I drummed my fingers on the windowsill, restless. "Allow me this one indulgence when I'll likely not live to see another sunrise."

A warm hand touched my shoulder and I drew in a steadying breath, attempting to hold the tears at bay. If I broke now, I would never recover. I would go to my death a blubbering mess. Far from the stoic, brave death I'd always envisioned I would have. With my tendency towards back-talk, wilfulness and sarcasm, it was only ever a matter of time before I pissed off the wrong person.

I just never imagined it would be the woman who held my heart.

"It was a morning much like this when you entered the world, Artura."

"Things might have been easier if I had died that morning, too."

Emrys squeezed my shoulder. "No. One death was enough that day. More than. Ever since then you've brought me nothing but joy. I do not regret raising you. Not for a second."

"I'm guessing you never envisioned that I would be the death of you," I muttered bitterly.

He chuckled, the sound wheezy. "No, I always knew you would be the death of me. I may be an old man now, but I also was twenty-four years ago, Artura. Raising such a...*spirited* girl was not something I had planned for myself."

"And you never had children? Before me?"

He shook his head, pulling a seat up beside me. His body creaked in unison with the old, worn-out wooden chair.

"My lifestyle was not conducive to children. Besides that, I never really planned on them."

"And then I came along," I finished.

He smiled. "And then you came along."

I was beginning to realise just how little I knew about Emrys and the sixty-odd years he'd lived before me. The realisation that I was too late to ask all the questions that now bubbled in the back of my mind, was a painful one. Instead, I settled for the one question I'd asked time and again. The one question he had never answered.

"How did you know my mother?"

He thought for a moment, wrinkled mouth pulling down at the sides. "Best let the past stay in the past, Artura. It will do us both no good to dwell on what might have been."

What might have been.

Those words struck me as odd. They alluded to something else, something much larger than the narrative I knew. I had always imagined my mother to be just an ordinary woman, one who had sought out Emrys' ministrations and then entrusted him with her child when she succumbed to a fatal childbirth. To think there was more...

No. It was too late for wishing and hoping, for wanting things that never were nor could ever be.

Best let the past stay in the past.

"They're here," he muttered, suddenly looking up.

I followed his gaze out the window to where half a dozen horses bearing riders in white approached the cottage. They were unhurried. Inevitable. I had always thought death to be swift and even just hours ago when it took Soraya, I still believed that. Only now I saw death to be patient. It came for everyone.

And now, it had come for us.

CHAPTER SEVEN

They didn't knock. There were no courtesies for those accused of witchcraft. Just strong, calloused hands that pulled us from our home with naught but a word. I looked back, committing the stone walls and simple furnishings to memory before I was tied to a horse and led away.

No one spoke. No one needed to. We were under no misconceptions about how this would play out. Emrys and I would be taken into town to be burnt on a pyre.

Or beheaded.

Or both.

Some were 'lucky' enough to die twice over.

Emrys watched his feet as we walked side by side. The soldier riding ahead of us held the ends of two ropes, each connected to Emrys and I. My wrists had been bound tightly and already I could feel pins and needles in my fingertips. But what use did I have for hands when I was due to die within the day? They could take every part of my body. Soon, it would not matter.

The thing that hurt most of all was the knowledge that after everything we had shared between us, Soraya had sold us out. She'd reported what Emrys and I had done to The Cleanse, there was no other explanation for it. All through the night I hoped against hope that she would have a change of heart. But then her horrified face would flash in my mind and I knew that it was the end.

I wondered what she might have told Erisk, the tale she would have needed to weave for him. There was no hiding the copious amount of blood staining her skin or the wound upon her breast - faint but not faint enough to someone who knew her intimately. Did she divulge every detail to her husband? How she'd been carrying his child, one she died attempting to abort?

We were led into the village, its occupants still very much asleep at the early hour. I was grateful that there wouldn't be an audience to my demise. Part of me wanted to save face somehow, hide the truth of what transpired. And that surprised me. Because not once had I truly cared what the small-minded people of Naiva thought.

Perhaps I *had* cared all along. Death simultaneously confused and enlightened.

I saw the captain of The Cleanse outside an inn, waiting for us atop his horse, a stallion the colour of stormy skies. When his eyes landed on Emrys and I, he smiled. It set my blood running cold, pure ice in my veins. The predator was back and he was about to win.

Usually, executions were carried out in the village centre and that was where I'd supposed we would wind up. Except, the horses led us through the village to the seaside where tents were erected. Looking around, I saw that there were twice the numbers of The Cleanse than I originally thought. Each man was awake and dressed in uniforms that hid the truth of what they did. No one would suspect that someone dressed in a colour so pure could be the perpetrator of such heinous crimes.

For me, white had become synonymous with evil and death thanks to The Cleanse.

A large tent stood at the centre of the camp. Outside it, Emrys and I were unbound before being ushered forward. The canvas tent resembling more of a small home, dwarfing the surrounding tents, clearly belonged to the captain. Inside, the decor was grand. The best of everything - including a plush bed that made my own look like little more than firewood. Off to one side, there stood a desk littered with maps and a decanter full of a dark liquid. The captain picked it up, pouring himself a glass.

"Care for a drink?"

Emrys shook his head. I merely stared, clenching my jaw. The captain had no real intention of giving us anything. It was a show, a front. Pretence after pretence, an attempt to prove more to himself rather than anyone else that he wasn't the scum of the earth.

Say nothing. Say nothing.

"Quite a tale reached my ears in the night." He sat down in a leather-bound chair at his desk, leaning back. Taking a deep sip from his glass, the captain then rested it on his bent knee. "Care to enlighten me on what you were doing?"

Emrys cleared his throat. "Only what was necessary. If I see someone in need, I offer my services."

The captain's lips quirked to the side. "And those... *services*...do they happen to be of a forbidden nature?"

"What is forbidden to one is permissible to another," Emrys replied with a small shrug. "So I really cannot say."

The captain nodded slowly, smiling to himself. "I see."

"Since we are to die today," I said, my throat thick. "Then the least you could do is tell us your name. I'd prefer to know my murderer at the hour of my death."

The captain drained his drink, setting the glass atop a map of the northern kingdoms, Cimran and Nimue. To the southwest of Nimue was the Isle of the Old Gods. A stretch of land thought to be the birthplace of rarely revered deities, figures who did little for us. From my vantage point near the map, the world looked small. I would never explore it. Never see the places I heard tales of. Come face to face with creatures both foul and majestic. A pang of regret ran through me at all I would be giving up.

Still, I couldn't bring myself to regret the decision that had led me here. I refused to. I wouldn't be worth my salt if I went back on the belief I held - that Soraya was someone worth risking everything for - even dying for. And even though she had betrayed my trust, she would live.

"Azazel Brone," the captain replied. "At your service."

"Interesting concept of service," I snapped back, feeling my temper flare.

So much for saying nothing.

"Maiden, wherever your kind exists, exterminating them will always be a service I will gladly partake of."

"And just what do you mean by 'your kind'?" My eyes scoured Azazel head to toe. "From where I'm standing, only one of us is guilty of unspeakable acts and it is certainly not Emrys nor myself."

At that, Azazel's eyes narrowed. "Emrys, is it? Curious name. I told you that you had a familiar face but that is an even more familiar name. You don't hear it so often in Cimran. It's not native here."

Emrys said nothing, his lips forming a thin, shaking line. I glanced at him because something felt off. This was the second time Azazel had said the old man was familiar. For someone who lived a quiet life in Naiva, it seemed strange that a captain of The Cleanse would recognise him.

"If I'm not mistaken," Azazel continued. "King Helmar once had a healer by the same name. But he disappeared some years ago before The Exoneration." The captain stalked forward, stopping a mere handspan away from Emrys. "Now, you wouldn't happen to be that very same healer, would you?"

Emrys kept his eyes on Azazel, face deadpan.

A sharp crack sounded around the tent. I heard the sound before I registered the movement. Azazel's arm was still lifted halfway when I saw the blood seeping from a cut on Emrys' cheek, made by the heavy solid gold signet ring Azazel wore. I lunged forward but only managed to brush against the captain before I was pulled back by a soldier.

"You son of a bitch," I spat. "Don't you dare touch him."

Azazel looked amused, his lips twitching up at the sides in that smirk I already hated to my very core. "Dear maiden, you are in my world now. I will do as I please." His hand reached out and his fingers found my neck. As they stroked down between my breasts, he said, "Touch whom I desire. Your will is no longer a concern. Here, I am *god*. And you will kneel before the day is through."

My fingers itched to wrap around the captain's neck, to squeeze until the bones in my fingers broke from the pressure. More than anything, I desired for this man before me to bleed. I wanted his blood to join that of the fallen whose own blood covered our streets.

And I wanted it to be slow.

Painful.

Drawn out.

I wanted him to suffer.

"Bring in the complainant," Azazel ordered to one of his men. A moment later, the tent flap lifted and in walked two new people. "I believe you're very well acquainted."

Something in me broke as I watched Soraya's face. No warmth lingered there, no familiar light in her eyes. The spark I'd seen in her all those years ago when we met was replaced by a hatred so intense, it threatened to burn everything and everyone in its wake. She was clean now, no longer coated in blood, though she once again wore black. A thin veil covered her face, a sign of mourning. Beside her, Erisk stood in matching black attire, his shirt and tunic freshly pressed. He openly sneered at Emrys before turning on me.

"Pray tell, my lady," Azazel said, his tone turning gentle. "What took place this night?"

Soraya lifted her head, and pulled her shoulders back. She looked to Erisk who nodded. Not once had I ever seen her seek direction from the man. Detest for Erisk Matrov ran deep. Now, however, she looked utterly dependent on the scum.

"I was taken, sir, by these two present. They..." She drew a deep breath. "They did things. Horrible, unspeakable things to me."

"Such as what?" Azazel prompted.

Soraya looked again to Erisk.

"Tell him," her husband ordered through clenched teeth.

"Everything happened so fast, sir," she continued. "All I know is that before they took me, I was with child. When I came to, my child had left my womb. They killed me and brought me back to life through their dark magic. Now my soul is marked." She sniffed, delicately wiping her nose with an embroidered handkerchief. I recognised it as her late grandmother's, one of the precious few valuable heirlooms Soraya kept. Only the best needed to be displayed while putting on a show. "The Mother will never again accept my soul into the After. I am *lost*."

Erisk put a protective hand on Soraya's shoulder. "I want them to pay for what they've done. For taking my firstborn before he met this world." It took everything within me not to lunge at him. Only the look on Soraya's face as her eyes met mine kept me rooted to the spot.

She loathed me. There was no possible way to fabricate the disgust on her face. For saving her life, she reviled me with everything within her being.

"If you do not make them pay," Erisk continued, "then I will. Judgement at my hands will not be swift."

"Well, your hands do have practice meting out your sick form of judgement, do they not?" I bared my teeth at Erisk.

I know the truth. Soraya knows the truth. You know the truth.

He understood. For a finite second, his puce face paled.

Azazel waved his hands. "They will be dealt with, rest assured. King Helmar is not in the habit of pardoning those who partake in magic - *especially* blood magic. It is the most forbidden kind."

"I want her dead."

My head whipped around, meeting Soraya's eyes. Surely I had imagined her speaking but again, she repeated.

"I want her dead. She killed my baby."

"No." Something in me snapped. This was it. The moment I broke and lashed out at the woman I loved despite the way my heart ached something fierce. "*You* killed your baby. *You* didn't want it. *You* came to *me* and *begged* me to put an end to your misery."

The anger in her eyes flickered, a candle caught in a breeze. For a moment, I hoped she would see reason, stop this when I had only done as she wished. But her face hardened to stone once more and I knew she was lost to me.

"Regardless," Azazel said. "The very act of performing blood magic, be it on a human or a rodent, is punishable by death. However, I'm intrigued by your accomplice, maiden." Turning to Erisk, the captain asked, "What do you know about Emrys?"

Erisk took a moment to answer, surprised that he'd been consulted. "I was a child when he came to Naiva. He's operated as a healer ever since. Brought the girl's mother with him, too. My father knew he was trouble the moment he appeared on our streets."

"Do you happen to know where Emrys came from?"

Erisk shrugged.

"Well, we shall find out," the captain continued. "I feel a journey to Lanceris might be in our best interests. After all, *Emrys*, should you be the healer I think you are, you are very much a wanted man."

I glanced at the man who had raised me, hoping to garner some sort of understanding. Instead, he stared resolutely at his feet. Now I was really kicking myself for not knowing anything about his life. To a degree, I'd always been a little self-possessed, uninterested in the majority of those around me. But I should have tried harder to learn more about the man who cared for me as his own. On some level, I felt like I had betrayed Emrys.

"So we are not to be executed today?"

Azazel smiled, the expression chilling rather than warming. "I hate to disappoint you, maiden, but no - a stay of execution. For now. When we reach Lanceris, we will determine who your companion is. From there, it will be in the hands of the king."

The king.

Any hope of a quick death just flew out the window. King Helmar was known for a particular variety of cruelty. He had chambers specifically catered towards torture. Stories reached every corner of Cimran of how he would tear the nails from fingers and toes one by one. How he had a jar full of teeth extracted from those he 'played' with. King Helmar was the cautionary tale told to children to keep them on the straight and narrow.

I felt my insides turn watery.

Do not break.

I clung to those three words as though they were a cliff I was in danger of falling over. I held on with my fingertips, desperate to adhere to them, to make those words my beginning, middle and end - my whole world. Break now, and I would never recover. I would succumb to everything they had in store for me.

But maybe, just maybe, if I could hold it together I could escape. The journey to Lanceris would take a week at minimum, weather permitting.

No. I wouldn't break *down*.

I would break *free*.

CHAPTER EIGHT

We left that morning. The tents were packed with precision within the hour. Azazel, eager to return to Lanceris and get to the bottom of just who Emrys truly was, ordered The Cleanse onward.

Emrys refused to speak. He'd looked at me twice: once as we were taken to a nearby tree and anchored to its thick trunk, and then once more when I spoke.

"Why does the captain say he knows you?" I whispered, eyes on the soldiers moving about the camp. "*Are* you wanted by Helmar?"

Emrys simply shook his head, silencing me. I went back to assessing the situation around us, counting the number of soldiers - twenty-one - and deciding the best way to escape. I held no weapons and even if I did, my lack of knowledge regarding their use would surely end in me injuring myself before I even made a dent in another. I could run, though admittedly, not far nor fast. And there was Emrys to consider. At eighty-five, he was frail and moved slower than a glacier.

Getting him away from The Cleanse would prove to be the trickiest aspect of any escape plan.

Soraya hadn't so much as looked at me as Erisk ushered her from Azazel's tent. My heart ached and with her leaving, she ripped away the parts of her that had moulded within me. Emrys once said that we never truly move past the ones we lose. Perhaps he was right. It certainly felt as though I would never let go of Soraya.

The red-haired soldier I'd met some nights ago while Naiva burned approached with a roughly corded rope. His eyes gleamed but his mouth formed a hard line as he wound one length of rope around my waist and wrists, leaving enough to tie to the back of his horse. He repeated the process with Emrys.

"Be careful," I spat when Emrys winced. His withered skin was bright red and already blistering beneath the harsh fibres of the rope.

"*Be careful,*" the soldier scoffed. "No mercies for the wicked."

And there were none. Travelling that first day was brutal and arduous. I had never been particularly athletic. Most of my time was consumed by lessons with Emrys. I'd not paid nearly enough attention in light of what happened with Soraya. I was a mediocre healer who could patch a scuffed knee or offer tea to soothe an upset stomach. Emrys' hopes for me were all for naught. We were in this position because I'd squandered my time at his side. I should have focused more, consumed knowledge the way the old man intended. Instead, I had been too wilful, and done nothing.

And by doing nothing, *everything* had happened.

My ankles ached and my feet throbbed with blisters from my worn boots by the time we stopped to make camp. The Cleanse went about erecting tents at the base of the mountains.

Tomorrow, we would wind our way around, leaving the Forest of Embers firmly behind with every single one of its haunting ghosts. The crossing was too precarious to take horses through the mountains and the thought of another week of walking made me miserable.

"This is yours," the red-haired soldier said. He tossed a musty-smelling blanket at my feet.

I eyed it suspiciously. "What is it for?"

He smirked. "To sleep. If witches sleep, that is."

"Could we have a tent?"

Laughter racked through him and he shook. "A tent? Little witch wants a tent? I thought your kind was all about nature. Well, now you get to be *real* close to it. No tent. Complain again and there will be no blanket either."

I bit my tongue, tasting blood. It was cold by the mountains, their topmost peaks capped with snow throughout the year. The icy winds barrelling down the jagged rock face hit our backs with enough force that the mountain itself might have been collapsing upon us. Emrys sat beside me, eyes hollow. I picked up the blanket and swung it around, covering our shoulders.

"What are you doing?" he asked, startled from whatever reverie he was trapped within.

"Keeping you alive."

"What for?" Emrys yawned. I'd barely kept up with the day of walking. It was nothing short of a miracle that he had managed so well. I worried for tomorrow, for how he would fare on the journey around the mountains. The road ahead looked to be a treacherous one. Already I could see it would provide an uneven footing at best. I'd rolled my ankles on smoother paths and now as I stretched, found myself gritting my teeth through the pain.

No mercies for the wicked.

"I'm going to get us out of this," I replied, pulling the blanket higher to cover the backs of our heads. "I don't know how just yet, but I promise I will."

He patted my knee. "Nothing is getting us out of this except divine intervention from the Mother herself."

"Fuck the Mother."

"Artura."

"What? What has the Mother done for us?" I threw my hands up in the air. "All we did was help Soraya and now we're on a death march across Cimran. Helmar will personally torture us and we will *beg* for a death that will not come. The king is a sadistic child who treats prisoners as nothing more than toys to be broken apart."

Emrys sighed, his shoulders hunching. "We do not speak ill of the Mother."

"I will speak of her however I wish. What has that bitch done for us lately? We've starved and fought for years and for what? To die aiding someone who was in trouble? No. The Mother has had plenty of opportunities to help us and she's not done a thing."

Wrapping my arms around Emrys to share what little warmth I could provide, we leaned back against a boulder, our meagre windbreak, enviously watching as The Cleanse went about preparing dinner. They slow-roasted meat, deer and wild pig hunted along the way. The smell of spices wafted back to us on a cool breeze, making my mouth water. It had been too long since I had last eaten. The stew I'd made for dinner had gone untouched and still hung above a now extinguished hearth. Neither of us had much of an appetite once Soraya left. Would anyone go to the cottage? Or would the stew be left to grow mould; the furniture, tinctures, books and beds to collect a thick layer of dust in the coming months and years?

The cottage. My heart squeezed at the thought of my home, now lost. How long would it be before someone laid claim to it? Ultimately, all abandoned buildings were eventually claimed under the law of 'finders, keepers' - the one consistent thing, aside from death, since The Exoneration. Would anyone do such a thing, though? Or would what happened that fateful night damn the stone walls as much as Emrys and I were now damned? The cottage would fall to ruin, infested with rats, overrun by the bushes and grass surrounding it. It would become a symbol of the evil Naiva had once borne witness to.

I would rather they burn it to the ground.

Movement to the right caught my attention and I turned just in time to see Azazel approaching. In his hands, he held two bowls of food.

"Eat. We've a long way to walk and not enough horses for you to ride upon. I'll not have you pass out before we reach Lanceris."

I took the food warily.

"It's not poisoned," he said, guessing my thoughts. "I'll leave that to King Helmar."

When he left, I tasted the meat first just to be certain. Minutes passed and all that happened was the clenching of my gut, growling for more. I handed Emrys a bowl of blackened meat and tore into my own. When we were finally sated some minutes later, I yawned. The blanket around us smelled strongly of horse as I huddled further under it with Emrys.

I closed my eyes and prayed for a dreamless sleep.

*

My best chance of escape would be by night.

Stumbling along behind a horse that defecated every half hour and left its droppings to cake my boots in a thick layer, I studied the procession. There were soldiers in front and behind. Being on foot, I had no hope of outrunning one of them. Their horses were trained nearly as well as their riders. All I would achieve by fleeing during the day was another flogging. The thought of a torn-up back in addition to blistered feet made me want to vomit.

Emrys and I had been separated for the walk, anyway, thus making an escape by daylight that much more difficult.

Nighttime, then.

All I had to do was keep my eyes open long enough.

I needed a weapon. Something was better than nothing, I supposed. There was a snowflake's chance in Hel that a member of The Cleanse would willingly offer me anything. They would likely laugh and beat me for the audacity to dare hope. So I kept my eyes on my feet, watching, waiting. When a particularly sharp-looking rock appeared, I feigned a fall and stashed it away in the bodice of my dress.

"Up," barked a soldier. "Clumsy bitch."

The insult rolled off my back. I'd heard worse in the past day and a half of travel.

Darkness fell what felt like an eternity later. Once again, we were fed dinner. No lunch, no breakfast but at least dinner was sizeable. My stomach ached as I inhaled the bowl of watery stew.

"Tonight," I whispered to Emrys.

He didn't acknowledge me.

"We're leaving tonight," I repeated, shaking him by the shoulder. "I'm getting us out of here."

"How do you suppose to do that? I am an old man, Artura. I cannot run."

It was a truth very much at the forefront of my mind. A truth I refused to let disrupt my plans.

"I will carry you if that is what it takes. If you don't come with me, I won't leave at all."

"Do not be foolish. My life has been long and I am content. Artura, you should go. I can distract them."

I raised an eyebrow.

"Hopefully," he added, his smile hollow and not reaching his greying eyes.

The crescent moon was high in the sky before the last soldier fell asleep. One kept lookout over the camp, not bothering with Emrys and I. We were tied to the same tree as the horses, making it clear that we were nothing more than animals to the soldiers.

I pulled the sharp rock from earlier out of my bodice. It had cut into my breast for the better part of the day and its sudden absence made me sigh in relief. I set about sawing into the rope, a slow process with my hands still bound. It took longer than I thought it would and by the time the last fibre snapped my hands ached. Turning, I took hold of Emrys' hands.

"No," he mouthed. "Run."

My eyes pricked with hot tears and I shook my head.

"Run," he repeated, jaw clenched in the way it did when he, himself, was attempting not to cry.

There was no use arguing with him, I realised. And staying would do neither of us any good. He was right. My good intentions to free us both were just that - good intentions. Not a realistic plan, not a feasible one even in the slightest. It was either one of us or neither escape and as Emrys made no move to stand, I accepted his decision with a cracking of my heart. I leaned over him, planting a soft kiss on his weathered forehead.

"I love you," I mouthed.

Words said far too little to someone who meant far too much. I regretted every moment of stubborn silence up to this point. I should have told Emrys more what he meant to me. Should have thanked him every day.

He nodded. It was enough to convey how he felt.

I waited for the soldier on watch to turn his gaze in the opposite direction before I took off at a run. Every inch of my being screamed out in agony as I pushed myself harder and harder, heading for a copse of trees. My boots were still damp inside from the snow surrounding the mountains, and it had hardened the horse faeces to a rock-like coating. Blisters popped and grated on my heels.

I did not stop.

The tree line came closer and closer and then the world was tilting. Trees disappeared from view before all that was left was the clear night sky above. I panted, my ribs aching from the impact, as a face came into view.

"I'm surprised it took you this long," Azazel drawled, looking towards the copse of trees. "For future reference, those trees would offer you no protection."

I pushed myself to sit upright. "They look like decent enough protection to me."

Better than being amongst The Cleanse, I silently added.

Azazel cocked his head to the side. "You truly are a small-town, small-minded girl, aren't you? Have you any idea the creatures that dwell within those trees?"

I gulped. Had I nearly thrown myself from one evil to another? Most likely a worthwhile trade-off, but still.

Azazel reached down, hoisting me up by the elbow. "Shall I show you?"

The captain's eyes danced with mischief as he looked down on me, noting the fear rounding my eyes. "Hmm. I think I will show you, actually."

Before I could object, Azazel was pushing me towards the tree line. It was then that I heard it. Growling. Low, carried on the wind. The closer we came the more I became aware of how the air around us vibrated. We stopped mere feet away from the copse and that was when I saw it.

A face so hollow it looked more like parchment pulled tight across a skull supported by an elongated neck. Beady eyes locked on me and a black tongue wound out, licking at lips that were no longer there. The creature's arms and legs were long and spindly but its rounded belly protruded, almost pregnant-looking. It watched me, assessing me in a way that made the hairs on the back of my neck stand on end.

"Preta," Azazel said, completely at ease. "Should you ever find yourself near one, be rest assured that any death I could offer would be a mercy comparatively speaking. Now, do you still wish to flee? Or shall I take you back to camp?"

I sized up the creature, the preta, wondering which one would be the lesser evil. Soldiers who desired my death for justice or a creature that thirsted for my flesh out of need?

I knew which one might be easier to reason with.

"Take me back," I whispered, the words like ash in my mouth.

Do not break.

CHAPTER NINE

"I am willing to bet good money-"

"Of which you currently have none."

"-that if I were to try and crack my fingers right at this very minute, I would completely sever eight out of ten. They're frozen stiff."

Emrys peered over his bowl. This late into the journey with supplies dwindling, dinner resembled something closer to the mud at our feet.

"The same amount of pressure it takes to bite through a carrot is all you would need to bite through a finger. Best you do not play with them. They're more fragile than you think."

I sighed. "At the end of the day, all I want from my fingers is the ability to do this."

I threw up a vulgar gesture towards the circle of tents. One of the soldiers, a man I'd learned was called Malik, frowned. For seven days we had all journeyed together and now, Lanceris was within sight. Another half day of walking would put us within the city limits.

"Do not bite the hand that feeds you, Artura."

"I won't." I smiled sweetly. "When they feed us something better."

Emrys drained his bowl. His face looked sallower now than it had when we left Naiva. Worse, even, than the two-year famine we'd survived a decade ago. Half the night I spent in fitful sleep, dreaming that he wouldn't make it. The other half I stayed awake to ensure he was still breathing. A constant wheeze, audible on every exhale, had formed in his chest from walking sixteen hours a day. The Cleanse looked no worse for wear. Granted, they were on horseback. The one time I'd removed my shoes so far, it had been to discover my stockings caked in blood, my feet raw and tender.

"This is likely as good as it will get before the end," he reminded me. "From here, everything is downhill."

"Physically and metaphorically."

"Thankfully for the former. These old bones wouldn't manage another incline. Never thought I would wish for a dungeon where the only options are to sit or sleep."

Or be beaten, tortured, maimed and 'played' with, my mind helpfully added.

I was under no illusions that we weren't simply jumping from the frying pan into the fire. Travelling to Lanceris with The Cleanse was never going to be high on my list of ideal situations but the men had been kind enough. In the sense that they ignored Emrys and I, gave us a blanket to sleep with and made sure we received dinner each night when our joints were too frozen to properly sit upon the marsh-like ground. Not one soldier had tried to have his way with me, either, which was nearly unheard of for a woman taken by The Cleanse.

Lanceris would be a different story.

A horror story, to be sure.

"Promise me," Emrys began before pausing. He reached out and took my hand.

"Anything."

With a look, his sea-grey eyes chastised me. "Never agree to uncertain terms."

"It's you, Emrys. I would agree to bite through my carrot-esque fingers right here and now if you so desired."

He placed a kiss with chapped lips on my temple. "You are a fool, Artura. But a loveable one at that. No. Promise me that no matter what happens, you will deny me."

"Deny you?" My brow furrowed. "I don't understand."

He looked uneasily towards the camp before deciding it was safe to continue our conversation. Every night, The Cleanse had listened in. Hoping to garner information on fellow 'witches', no doubt. I had been tempted to speak nonsense, to craft and weave fantastical stories purely to mess with them. Yet, as Emrys had so bluntly put it once, my tongue would get me killed.

It wasn't the first time someone had said as much.

"There are certain...individuals in Lanceris who would happily see me dead. My chances of salvation are long gone by now, Artura. For you, though? You *might* stand a chance. Regardless of what happens, you must say that you were held against your will by me."

"Against my will?" I almost smiled. Nothing he was saying made sense. "When have you ever known me to do anything I didn't want to do?"

Emrys waved a hand. "Say that I stole you away, kidnapped you. Whatever strikes your fancy - you've always had a knack for twisting the truth." At that, he smiled before his face turned grave once more. "The king must not know of the life I gave you. Deny it, deny me, and be saved."

"I don't understand, Emrys."

His eyes softened as he placed an icy, frost-bitten hand against my cheek. Around us, snow began to drift in mesmerising patterns and a thin layer of ice had formed on the Arraila River we camped beside. For three days now we had followed its winding, muddied banks. Occasionally we stopped so The Cleanse could fish for whatever still lived in the frigid waters.

Were it not for the bone-aching chill, the scene before us would have been beautiful. A river, frozen in time, and powder-light snow that blanketed a slumbering landscape.

I couldn't bring myself to truly appreciate it.

"One day, if you somehow survive this, you will understand. Just know that I love you. You were the daughter I never had and for that, I cannot thank you enough. You've brought joy unlike any I've ever known and with you, my life is complete."

"Please." I pulled his hand away from my face, willing myself not to cry. "Do not say goodbye. There is still a way out of this. There has to be."

"I raised you to believe that anything was possible, Artura. But in Lanceris? Nothing is certain except death."

*

If I followed the Arraila River, I would eventually make it south to the Ocaran Sea. From there, a ship to the Southern Kingdoms. I could be free. Could have a life.

Instead, I found myself following a branch of the river around slate grey mountains, looming towards darkened skies. Noon had barely arrived and already it appeared to be dusk on the outskirts of Lanceris. It only compounded the foreboding, ominous feeling covering me thicker than the sleeting snow.

Even Autumn dared not venture near the capitol, leaving it firmly in the grips of an eternal winter.

The city was nestled in a unique position that made invasion something of an impossibility. Surrounding all but one side of the great city was the Dearmond Mountain Range. The western horizon was completely obscured from view by rocky slopes that rose at a sharp incline, making climbing near impossible. And should you somehow find yourself at the summit by one miracle or another, you would surely die on the descent. An added measure that ensured safety for Lanceris was the forking of the Arraila River. It ran around the mountains and city in a neat, incomplete circle. There were tales of nixie that once lived in the river. That they had been loyal to the kings of old, helping to defend the city from those dimwitted enough to gamble with their lives.

But now, as we approached, there were no real signs of life within the river, not even the fish we'd eaten for dinner the past few nights. It was eerily still and quiet. Spanning from one mountain to another were heavy wrought iron gates. Spikes rose out from the top, sharpened to a point so fine it would slice a man clean in two. As The Cleanse, Emrys and I came to a standstill before the gates, a heavy clicking sounded from the other side before they swung slowly inward.

The streets were quiet as we moved through. Every inch of my body was covered in a layer of grime that would not soon be forgotten, no matter how long I scrubbed. Curious faces peeked out from the corners of windows and doors cracked open no more than a wary inch.

"They all know why we're here," I whispered to Emrys.

"Not many outsiders come to Lanceris and those that do are usually guilty of one crime or another," he replied.

I squared my shoulders, glaring at a auburn-haired woman my age, peeking hesitantly through a curtain. "Except us."

"That depends on where you're standing, witch," Malik growled as he sauntered past atop a chestnut stallion. "You look mighty guilty from where I sit."

"Tell me," I replied, sounding bored, "is your mount supposed to have one arse? Or two? I can't make out the difference between your stallion's rear and yourself. All I see is double."

Malik's lip twisted in disgust as he turned and rode ahead, leaving Emrys and I behind.

"Your *tongue*," Emrys began.

"Will get me killed," I finished with a wave of my bound hands. "I'm very aware. But if I am to die anyway, why not do so being true to myself? You've always said I'm too brazen for my own good. I'd hate to leave that behind when I've so few vices left."

"King Helmar runs a tight ship within his walls. Anyone who even so much as questions him is either thrown out or executed," Emrys continued. "He'll not tolerate lip from an accused witch, Artura."

I scowled at him and said nothing more.

Lanceris was utterly lifeless. Not a plant to be seen, streets clean but devoid of any real life. In Naiva, it was distinctly the opposite: a ball here, baskets there. But in Lanceris there was nothing beyond smooth stone walls and an eerie silence that weighed heavily. It felt too clean, too clinical. Cold, uncaring - a reflection of its master.

My face ached. For the past eight days I'd clenched my jaw so hard, I felt my teeth beginning to shift. Pain radiated up past my temples and formed a headache that had me wanting to shut my eyes and sleep.

The journey through the streets of Lanceris took longer than the journey from last night's camp. We were a slow procession without an audience, standing on customs alone. I began to fidget with the rope around my wrists. The skin beneath them was raw and blood had dried around the fibres of the rope. Emrys was no better. With another step, he stumbled. Instinctively, I reached out to catch him before he could fall. The rope went taut and I fell short of the man who had raised me. His frail body sprawled across the brick road.

"Help him." I looked at the soldiers nearby. "Please. Someone help him up."

The Cleanse looked between one another, silently questioning who would lower themselves to help those accused of magic. In the end, it was Azazel who dismounted. He walked down the procession line to where Emrys was sprawled, unmoving on the stones and with a surprising tenderness, lifted him to his feet.

"Not much further. Do not die on me now, not when we're so close to discovering who you are."

Emrys kept his eyes down, his new standard response.

The palace came into view minutes later. It was just as the rest of the city and gave a clear unwelcome. I shuddered in the shadow of it, looking upwards to where high-arched windows were carved to keep watch over the citizens of Lanceris below. I got the feeling that there was little that happened in the shadow of Dearmond Mountains that King Helmar did not know about.

The doors to the palace were already open, our arrival expected. With no one in sight on our journey from the main gates, I wondered who would have alerted the king to our arrival. No doubt he had his spies everywhere, though, those who were one with the shadows. It was the way of Helmar. He had eyes and ears in various nooks and crannies throughout his kingdom.

The Cleanse dismounted from their horses as the first new faces I'd laid eyes on all week appeared. Stablehands took hold of the reins and lead the stallions away. All buildings looked the same here, one lifeless mottled grey to the next. A faint stench of manure floated from the direction the stablehands and horses headed. I wrinkled my nose but at the same time, it reminded me of Naiva and my heart ached all over again.

My home was lost to me.

We climbed the stairs, Malik holding both ropes that led to Emrys and I.

The outside of the palace was deceptive, I soon found out.

When we entered, all I could see from wall to wall was finery. Plush rugs woven with ornate designs covered polished stone floors. The walls were decorated with paintings twice the height of a man. Each painting bore the precise, highly detailed faces of men with hard expressions and a ruthless glare. The kings of old. There was no humility about them and if the stories were true, then that wasn't at all surprising. They were rulers who cared little for those living beneath them. They took spoils and wealth during war and rather than use it to benefit their people, they used it to live in a disgusting excess of luxury.

Solid gold sconces held candles on the walls. They illuminated the windows I had looked through only moments earlier - windows I now saw were stained glass, depicting images of the old gods. I looked to one, a female I knew to be Ceres, and sneered. So many put their faith in one deity or another and believed them to be the grand architects of our fates.

If they were, their designs were lacking. Severely so.

Soldiers peeled away until eventually, only Azazel, Malik and one other remained. He was big and burly and had scarcely spoken on the journey. I decided I perhaps liked him the most. He clearly didn't want anything to do with me and the feeling was mutual. Azazel glanced back as we came to a stop before wooden doors that reached towards the cathedral ceiling. He looked between Emrys and I, contemplating before shaking his head and pushing against the door with the palms of his hands.

Beyond the doorway was elegance at its finest. Everything was covered in gold and inlaid with jewels every colour of the rainbow. Even the woven runner leading from the doorway seemed to be spun with gold thread. My eyes followed it, mouth slightly ajar, until I reached the end of it and realised where I was standing.

The throne room.

And at the end of that golden runner, perched atop a throne with a back that rose clear towards the ceiling, was a man that made my blood run cold.

King Helmar.

CHAPTER TEN

"Witchcraft. Blood magic. Gender treachery. These are the crimes of the accused, your highness." Azazel straightened from his stooped bow with a flourish that made me want to snort.

But I didn't dare. Not when I stood before *him*.

King Helmar was a middle-aged man with keen eyes. Those eyes saw right through me, made me feel impossibly bare as I stood before him on aching feet. His shoulder-length hair was flecked with grey but had once been black as midnight. Sideburns met with a thick, closely cropped beard that surrounded a thin-lipped sneer. His skin was golden but in places took on a leathery quality from days spent in the sun. He was dressed in finery befitting the conqueror of Cimran - deep crimson and jewel tones. I counted seven out of ten fingers sporting obscene gold rings with various jewels nestled between claws.

I stared at him with unbridled curiosity. Gazing at King Helmar was like looking at the reaper - I saw my end, my executioner. I saw unceasing pain and suffering before I was finally granted entrance into the After. I saw hate and loathing as he returned my stare.

But there was something else in the way he looked at me. A morbid sort of curiosity, much the same way the boys in Naiva toyed with a dying animal. I was marked for death and he was already devising ways to bring me closer to the brink of it.

"Azazel," he drawled, gaze leaving my face. I breathed a sigh of relief. "These are crimes I've no real need to mete out justice for. Why not burn them where you found them?" His gaze raked over me from head to toe. "Why bring filthy witches into my home?"

"Your majesty, I believe this one" - Azazel grabbed Emrys by the shoulder, shoving him forward onto his knees before the king - "might be the healer that escaped."

Helmar waved a hand, silencing the captain of The Cleanse.

"I see the similarities," he replied. "Except I was told he was dead."

Beside me, Malik shifted restlessly on his feet. King Helmar's piercing stare turned on the soldier.

"Was that not what I was told, Malik?"

I could have sworn I saw the soldier twitch, his hands shaking before balling into fists. His upper lip developed a light sheen of sweat and he licked at chapped lips.

"I- Your majesty, I swear on my life that I killed a man of that name."

I jumped when a dark, booming laugh split the silence of the throne room.

"Did it not occur to you to be absolutely certain?" Helmar stood from his throne and descended the steps before him. He closed the distance between Malik and himself. He now stood so close that I caught a whiff of the sickeningly sweet scent rolling off him. My stomach flipped.

"Well, I…"

"You didn't think that perhaps a task given to you by your *king* warranted precision and excellence?"

Malik bowed his head. "I swear on my life, I did not know."

Azazel cleared his throat. "My king, we still need to ascertain if this man is who I believe him to be. On the suspicion that he might be the healer, I deemed it necessary to bring him to you."

Helmar stood resolute in front of Malik. Despite being a foot shorter than the soldier, his presence was overwhelming. I understood now why he was feared, how his armies had managed to sweep through Cimran uncontested. I fought and trembled with the need to shrink back.

Do not break.

I forced myself to lift my chin, only to catch the king's attention.

"*You*, however," Helmar said, sidestepping to stand before me. "You do look familiar. The ghost of someone I once knew."

For once in my life, I found it incredibly easy to remain silent. Helmar smiled and it sent a chill rolling straight down my spine. For all the lavishness surrounding us, the room felt icy, the master of it unwelcoming and vicious.

"Keep your secrets then, witch," he continued. "You will break. Once I'm through with you, that is."

Of that, I was almost certainly positive I would. The wicked gleam in the king's eyes told me he had many things in store for me, plans formulated within mere minutes of my arrival. I couldn't fathom how a mind could work in such a way, to be so attuned to evil that it took little more than a cocking of the head before every wicked thought was laid out into a neat plan.

"Take them below," he said as he turned back to the dais upon which his throne stood. "I shall see to them later."

Azazel and Malik ushered us out of the throne room. All along, Emrys had kept his eyes down on the floor beneath his feet. For the first time, I knew beyond a shadow of a doubt that the old man was hiding something from me.

Something that would either save us.

Or kill us.

*

'Below,' as it turned out, was directly beneath the Dearmond Mountain Range.

A series of winding staircases were carefully carved from the mountain itself. Each step, steep and slick with a dampness that permeated every inch of the surrounding space, led us directly beneath the southern side of the mountains. I lost track of how many twists and turns, likely all devised as a countermeasure against escape. With each and every step down, hope ebbed away.

I was beginning to understand that despite a decades-long war that had ravaged so much of Cimran, I'd lived a rather sheltered life. My involvement with the darker side of the kingdom extended only to helping Emrys treat the wounded and witnessing the odd Burning. There was much I was still blind to. The seedy underbelly of a senseless war that I couldn't begin to comprehend.

Yet as I came to a standstill upon the very last step, I was greeted with a sight that made my gut clench.

Crude cells were carved into the mountain, each one sealed with metal bars and a door bearing a heavy padlock. These cells were used to hold the kingdom's most infamous traitors, or so Azazel said on the journey down. No matter what image I had conjured up in my mind, it paled in comparison to what I now saw. Blood stained the floor of each cell we passed. One cell had been abandoned some years ago, leaving a nearly fully decomposed body behind. The skeleton bore strips of decaying cloth and sat huddled in the corner, showing that whoever it was had died in the foetal position. I could feel the phantom touch of fear emanating from the cell and was glad when it was put behind us.

I started to get a sense of just how truly awful things had become in Cimran. It was as though the war was an oily slick, covering every blade of grass and drop of rain. It was an atmosphere, hanging heavy upon the frigid chill. There was no escaping the brutality that had torn apart so many lives.

Not even down here, beneath the mountains that guarded the very heart of evil.

Azazel unlocked a cell door and waved a hand aside with all the respect owing to a lady of the court being ushered into a formal sitting room. As I moved towards the doorway, Malik pulled me back. He drew a dagger from his belt and swiftly cut the ropes around my wrists. I nursed my hands close to my chest as I entered the cell.

Emrys was placed in a cell opposite. It was slightly off-centre to my own and I could glimpse only a partial view. As his door was locked with a heavy click, he held onto the bars.

"Be strong," I whispered.

"Strength will do you no good down here," Malik said. He threw a smile my way, one that made me taste bile in the back of my throat. There was something about him that had my flight instincts ramping up. He then cleared his throat and held up a splayed hand. "Five house rules for the duration of your stay in our fine lodgings: one - no screaming. I am the warden here and if I get a headache, you get a whipping. Two - mealtime is at five each evening. Notice how I said meal*time*. Singular. That is because you will get one square meal a day. Which leads me to the third point - no complaining. I hate it. Complaining will get you a whipping. Fourth rule is simple - you bleed, you clean it. Notice the cells that were stained with blood? The only way you escape cleaning is when you die. And make no mistake, you *will* die. Not a soul leaves here in anything other than a wooden box - if there is anything left of you to go into a box, that is. With that, the final rule is simple - no escaping. Do not even try. It's futile. This place is a maze and you'll get lost before you can scratch your arse. Any questions?"

Malik looked between Emrys and I. Emrys shook his head.

"You, witchling?"

I narrowed my eyes at the use of the word. "One question: where did you find it?"

"Find what?" he replied, winking.

"Find the fucking audacity to lock up innocent people."

His face hardened and he stalked towards my cell. I refused to back away. Before I realised what was happening, one hand whipped out, taking hold of my throat. I gasped as his hand grew steadily tighter, cutting off air and blood flow.

"Little bitches who cannot keep their mouths shut don't do so well down here. Remember that."

He threw me back, deeper into the cell. I fell to my knees, gulping down painful lungfuls of stale air. I rubbed my throat, already aware that before the day was out, there would be a handprint bruise collaring me. Gods, I wasn't going to last one miserable fucking night here. Not if this was how things were beginning. Helmar hadn't even arrived yet.

When I looked up, Malik was smiling.

I glared, letting the pent-up rage from our journey shine through. "I'll be sure to."

Once again, Malik smiled and I fought to suppress the shiver it induced. His footsteps echoed as he retreated down the hallway.

"What now?" I asked Emrys. His eyes were sad as he looked up at me.

"We wait."

"For what?"

Emrys laid down, mirroring the foetal position of the skeleton, and turned away from me. So low that I almost missed it, he murmured, "Death."

*

Emrys taught me mythology as a child, a brief intermission from herbs and tinctures and poultices. It was perhaps my favourite subject, discovering stories older than time, passed down from one to another in various ways. In our lessons were tales of gods and monsters, mental images conjured that stayed with me even now. Occasionally, Emrys would manage to obtain a book with carefully painted pictures depicting the old gods. The first deity I remembered seeing was the God of Death and he didn't at all line up with what I'd imagined him to be. Because the God of Death seemed to be nothing more than a man.

And I never for one second anticipated that he would look like King Helmar. Because surely that was who Death was - a sick, sadistic king who took twisted pleasure from torturing those he held beneath the mountains.

My stomach growled in the dim light of the cell and I pushed my hands against the fabric of my dress, attempting to silence the noise. Dinner was a measly bowl of flavourless oats, a cup of milk and bread. Sustenance enough to keep a prisoner alive for however long Helmar intended on using them. I'd had to pick out two cockroaches and gagged on every mouthful but I ate semi-gratefully. After all, they could have refused me food. Why waste precious commodities on those about to die?

A shrill scream echoed down the hall, following a sickening cracking sound. I glanced across to Emrys' cell and found him leaning against the wall, legs bent and arms wrapped around them. From where I sat, I could see him shiver and shake. I wondered at the likelihood of the conditions under the mountain killing us before the king did.

The scream came and went for what felt like hours. But that was the funny thing about time down here - a minute felt like an hour and an hour felt like a year. Sleep was difficult to come by through what I assumed was the night, though it was impossible to tell. No light filtered into the cells, save that of torches in iron sconces on the walls.

I smiled at Emrys, even though I had little left within me to smile about. In some perverted way, I was glad to have a friendly face nearby. Even if that did mean that friendly face was also doomed. Emrys' mouth twitched up at the side, the closest he'd been to showing any emotion since leaving Naiva. I tucked the image away in my mind, saving it for when I needed it most.

My eyes drifted closed and I let my mind turn blank, trying to drown out the screams growing fainter by the minute. I dozed off at some point because the creaking of hinges woke me with a jolt. Heavy boots stood in the doorway, shiny and gleaming in places with a thick, dark liquid. I recognised the rusty smell of blood and as my eyes moved higher, I saw that the intruder was covered in it. Silvery grey tunic and deep blue pants splattered with droplets of crimson, some of it already browning as it dried.

King Helmar looked down his nose at me, eyes narrowing. Everything in my body froze.

"Stand, witch," he ordered.

I wasn't idiotic enough to refuse the king, not if I had any remaining scrap of hope to escape. I pushed up the wall, willing myself not to fall as my legs shook.

His head cocked to the side as he assessed, his eyes roaming over every inch of me. I wanted to slide back down the wall, hide my face in my filthy hands. I didn't want this man looking at me, seeing me not just as the enemy, but as something vile.

"Remove your clothes."

I balked mid-thought. "Wh-what?"

The words were barely a whisper.

Helmar's jaw clenched and unclenched. "Remove...your...clothes."

Even though everything within me screamed to fall into line, to blindly obey, there was also that part of me that shied away, wanting to protect the last thing I had - *me*. My body was my own and save for one dark time at the age of thirteen, had been shown to the precious few I desired. Yet here was the king of Cimran, demanding I shed the last ounce of control I maintained. Demanding that I hand over my entire being to be toyed with without a fight.

Slowly, I shook my head. A split second later, Helmar was in my cell, hand around my throat. I felt him lift me, my toes barely touching the stone floor. His other hand produced a knife which he brought to my collarbone.

"Do not take me for a fool, witch," he hissed through clenched teeth. "Your kind are whores and you will be treated as such."

The blunt side of the knife slid painfully across my skin until it reached the neckline of my stained dress. As the king forced the sharp side downward through the fabric, the tip of the blade cut between my breasts. I whimpered, breathless as he held my throat in his calloused hand.

Cold air bit at my chest as the king released me. I staggered, clutching at the wall. My dress was half cut, half torn open by a blade I now saw was covered in blood - both my own and foreign. Perhaps the other prisoner whom I'd heard earlier, their screams still ringing in my ears.

Helmar took a step backwards, crossing his arms. "I heard my captain whipped you in Naiva. For your insolence and lies."

I brought my arms up, banding them across my chest. "Yes."

"Strip. I want to see the scars."

This time, I didn't fight, didn't refuse his request. I had barely caught my breath and should the king decide to take me in a chokehold again, I might pass out. If that happened, the king could move on to Emrys.

That cannot happen, I told myself, steeling my nerves as I pulled the sleeves of my dress down my arms, goosebumps rising along my skin.

"Turn."

I faced the wall, lip quivering. I hated the word that came to mind: *vulnerable*.

Only once in my life had I been so and even now, over a decade later, it still left a sour taste in my mouth.

Once again, I felt his touch though this time, it was gentle. A caress that made me shiver. He stroked down my back, his rough fingers searching for phantom wounds. My back had healed too well with Emrys constantly attentive, caring for me day and night. The remedies applied had taken care of the wounds and my skin healed without a trace of the punishment I'd endured. The king's fingers searched from my neck to my lower back, silently questioning.

"Well," he finally said and I could hear the smile in his voice. "I have my work cut out for me. I wonder just what it will take to permanently mark this pretty little back. Tell me, witch, are you ready to test your limits? Are you ready to play?"

CHAPTER ELEVEN

King Helmar walked ahead, leaving me alone once more in my cell. Slowly, I poked my head out, searching up and down the hallway. There was no sign of Malik. No other prisoners with their cell doors swung wide.

"Come," Helmar commanded, not bothering to look back. He was a man used to getting his way.

Emrys stood clutching the wrought iron bars of his cell with a bony, white-knuckled grip. His eyes were wide, full of unbridled panic. It terrified me. All my life, Emrys had been the rock from which I drew strength. He had held me up, been the solid foundation in a world where there was none. But now - now he seemed weak, lost. There was nothing he could do to save me.

Clutching the bodice of my dress to my chest, I followed after King Helmar. His footsteps echoed off the mountain walls, louder than the booming of a cannon. Each step felt like a fist pounding against my chest in a silent promise. *Thump, thump, thump. Death, death, death.* A taunting rhythm, whispering of terrors yet to come. I was careful not to get too close to the king though I knew that wouldn't last long. Before the day was out, we would be much, much closer and I, all the worse for wear - if not dead. A lump formed in my throat at the unspoken possibilities. The screams I'd heard before still echoed in the quiet, telling me that in the end, there would be only pain.

We passed a set of steps that I recognised would lead back to the castle and instead turned down a grittier, rougher hallway. The rock walls before had been smoother, polished, but here, the walls were sharp. I reached out to touch the rock, all jagged angles that looked as slick as the edge of a blade. I wondered if they would slice just as well. I had heard from others in the past that sometimes the best escapes are the ones we carve open in ourselves, in our wrists, arms, veins - on any part of our body, really. Perhaps if I needed such an escape, the mountain might suffice. I could end my suffering at my own hands, and be rid of the nightmare I was trapped in.

"Do not," Helmar snapped. "If anything is going to make you bleed this day, it will not be Dearmond."

I shuddered at the threat inherent in his words, withdrawing my hand.

The hallway ended in a barred door, much the same as the one in my cell. Helmar unlocked it and as the door swung wide with a screech, I felt the blood drain from my face.

This cell was bigger by far, nearly as large as the cottage had been. But that was where the similarities ended.

Against one wall there stood a dark wooden table bearing various tools. A hammer, a crowbar, a dozen or so knives, something shaped like a corkscrew and others I didn't have the names for. What I did notice was the dried blood clinging to each one. Above the table were hooks holding weapons.

Swords, daggers, axes and maces. Whips and floggers, their leather cords ending in sharpened shards of metal.

I felt fingers stroke down my back.

"Do not worry, witch," Helmar whispered, his mouth too close to my ear. "Those are for later."

Nothing witty came to mind as a new wave of horror swept through me.

I turned away from the table only for my eyes to land on a bed. There was something off about it, though, and in the dim lighting, it took a moment before I could work out what it was. Atop the bed was a blanket of spikes an inch long and roughly half an inch apart. There were so many that at first, it looked to be seamless, solid. I knew without going further that each spike would be razor sharp and should a body be placed atop the bed, it would be pierced from head to toe. Not deep enough to fatally wound, but rather enough to cause insurmountable pain. Dried blood covered the base of the bed between the spikes, drained from gods knew how many bodies in the past.

To the right of the bed was a tub big enough to bathe in. Not that anyone would want to, not when it was full of a murky sludge that had perhaps once been water. I couldn't be certain. Something floated on the surface and I recognised the fuzzy green for what it was. Mould.

"Water torture," Helmar said as he crossed the room.

"Should it not be water, then, if that is what you intend?" I whispered. The stench that wafted from The Tub made my gut clench. It was everything I could do not to be sick in front of the king. If I showed weakness now, he would have won without a fight.

"It is the act, not the means."

King Helmar came to a stop before the table, hand floating over it as he examined the tools before him.

"Witch, do you know what it is to break one's soul?"

He was silent for so long that I eventually whispered a very quiet, "No."

When he turned back to me, his eyes lit in wicked delight. "It is to have *power*. I intend to have power over you before I allow you to enter the After. Death will be a sweet release but one you must first *earn*."

My knees shook.

"Every day, I will bring you here," he promised. "Every day, I will extract the truth from you by any means necessary. I will find out the whereabouts of your companions."

"I have none," I replied. A cold sweat enveloped me. "I'm not who you think I am."

He simply smiled in return, showing a row of perfectly white teeth. "That is another thing I will take from you, along with your control. I will take your lies, and turn them into a weapon against you. For every lie you tell me, another punishment. Make no mistake, each one will exceed the other until eventually, you will beg for the end. And, my dear, *everyone* begs eventually."

In the face of this new horror, something deep in me was prepared to beg now. Then I thought of Emrys alone in his cell. How if I left, he would be at this monster's mercy.

Do not break.

"I have a proposition for you." The words sounded braver than I felt.

Helmar arched an eyebrow. "You are hardly in a position to bargain."

I swallowed hard. "For as long as I do not break, you will not touch Emrys. Take me instead."

"And why would you do this for someone who has committed treason against me?"

Because he's my only family. The words were on the tip of my tongue but instead, I bit them back. That knowledge would be just another weapon for the king to use.

Promise me that no matter what happens, you will deny me.

With Emrys' plea echoing in my mind, I kept my mouth shut.

"Fine. But I will do you one better," the king continued. "If you can escape the mountains, I will offer you a pardon."

My eyes narrowed. "Malik said there was no escape."

"Should anyone try hard enough, escape is always possible." King Helmar smiled as he moved to the cell door. "There are a series of tunnels beneath Dearmond. Dozens upon dozens, though most conclude with dead ends. Three, however, lead to the other side of the mountains. Should you manage to find your way out of even *one* of them, I will grant you a full pardon for your crimes."

I eyed the king warily. It seemed almost too good to be true. "What about Emrys?"

"Transferred to the city prison where he can live out his days…in relative peace."

"You mean without torture at your hands."

The king shrugged. "As I said, peace."

The city prison was known for its lax security. Many had escaped in the past. It wasn't so much an actual prison as it was a holding centre for those society had cast off. Should anyone manage to escape, a blind eye was turned as almost always, the escapee fled the city and was no longer a burden upon Lanceris. If I had any chance of getting Emrys away from King Helmar, perhaps this was it.

Hope bloomed in my chest. "The catch?"

Helmar's eyes narrowed. "Ah, a clever witch, it would seem. The catch is that you will not have more than an hour each time and *I* will be tracking you. Every step of the way. Outrun me, outsmart me, and freedom could be yours."

"How do I know you're telling the truth?"

"You do not," he simply said.

I heard what was unsaid behind those three little words - *you do not but you will try anyway if you are desperate enough.*

"My torture is to be trying to escape?"

Helmar shook his head, pushing the sleeves of his tunic up. "No. We will partake of the delights this room offers first."

I glanced around. "If you hurt me, how will I run?"

Already I was thinking of the bed, of the thousands of spikes pressing into my delicate flesh. I could almost feel the sinking needles driving into my back. All it would take was one wrong move, one errant nail piercing the wrong part of my spine, and paralysis could erase that faint glimmer of hope.

"That," he said, "is not my problem. Now, let us begin."

*

"Something easy to break you in, shall we?"

Helmar walked around the room, touching various instruments of torture, things that had brought many before me to their knees. I steeled myself, bracing for the worst even though I knew in my heart I couldn't even begin to comprehend the dark places this man's mind could go.

Finally, he came to a stop beside the tub of mystery sludge.

"I think it might be best that I go easy on you today. I'll save the bloodletting for another time." He grinned before adding, "No matter how eager I am to see your pretty flesh drip for me."

He crooked his finger, gesturing for me to approach.

Emrys, I reminded myself. *This is to save Emrys.*

I moved to stand near the king. The smell in this corner of the room was overpowering. My jaw ached with how tightly I clenched it, as though I could will away the nausea if I tried hard enough. The sludge was a mixture of brown tones and floating chunks. What I had thought to be mould was indeed that but alongside it, much to my horror, I saw what was undeniably human waste.

Gods, fucking Hel. What in the almighty, arse-kissing Mother is this?

"What's in it?" I asked faintly, face paling. Even though I knew, I silently begged I was wrong.

"Failure," the king replied. "The result of many who could not master their visceral reactions."

Before I had a moment to comprehend the king's meaning, he placed a hand around the back of my neck and plunged my head into The Tub. I barely had enough time to suck in a breath before I was enveloped in a slimy texture that assaulted all of my senses. I fought against his hold, willing myself not to gasp for air. My lungs ached with every passing second until the pain was so acute, I thought I might pass out. Just as I was about to open my mouth in desperation, I was yanked backwards.

I landed on the unforgiving stone floor, gasping. Every breath felt like a blessing and a curse. I was alive yet I could smell nothing but the filth that now coated me like a second skin. My stomach heaved and I bent over, upending what little food was still in my stomach.

When I finally looked up at the king, he was smiling. "Good. Now put it back in."

My lower lip trembled along with the rest of my body. "Wh-what?"

He nodded to the mess on the floor. "That. Add it to the failures of those gone before you.

I stared at the king, waiting for him to say it was some sick sort of joke, a test to see how obedient I could be. But he stood resolute and unwavering.

"You want me to...*this*...and put it in...*there*?" A new wave of nausea washed over me.

Failure, he had said. *The result of many who could not master their visceral reactions.*

I understood now.

Helmar cocked an eyebrow. "I could always retrieve your friend. Perhaps he'll fare better than you did."

A voice inside my head screamed '*NO*.' Emrys could not ever step foot in this room. He was too old, too frail. He wouldn't survive what the king had in store.

Then again, I wasn't certain *I* could even survive if this was what Helmar deemed 'easy.'

I shifted forward, kneeling before the vomit on the floor.

"Keep going." Amusement coated his tone.

I didn't look up at the king. All he would see was the raw hate in my eyes. In that moment, I hated him more than I had ever hated anyone. We heard stories in the village of vile things done during the war, tactics used by The Cleanse to keep the citizens of Cimran in line. This surpassed every story.

'Hate' was beginning to feel too benign for the way I felt. No, this was pure, unadulterated loathing taking hold.

I scooped my vomit into The Tub with cupped, shaking hands, the mixture making a sickening noise as it joined the sludge. Was this what others before me had gone through? I decided I didn't want to know. If there was any hope of me surviving, it would be by solely focusing on getting through each session in the torture room so I could then seek out an escape through the tunnels.

"On your feet," the king commanded. I obeyed and felt my dignity slowly draining away. "Now, we are going to do this again, witch. We will continue to do this until you can stop yourself from being sick. Until you can take your punishment."

A shuddering breath whooshed out of my lungs. "I've done nothing wrong."

Helmar came to stand so close to me, that I could only just smell his breath, stale and tinged with alcohol, over the stench of The Tub. "By virtue of birth, you are guilty. As such, you will suffer the deserved punishment."

Once again he took me by the back of the neck, only this time, I was ready. I turned and lifted my knee, connecting it with his groin. The king grunted, his other hand whipping out to strike the side of my face. I tasted blood in my mouth.

"Try it again," he wheezed, face red and full of rage. "I dare you."

I spat in his face a mouthful of blood-tinged with vomit.

"This is how it's going to be, is it?" His gaze was deathly calm, the quiet before a hurricane.

Preemptively, I drew in a deep breath before he shoved my head back under the sludge. I focused on slowing my mind, exhaling as little air as I could manage. I counted slowly in my head.

Twenty-eight, twenty-nine, thirty.

Ice cold air hit my face as I was pulled back from The Tub. Helmar shoved me onto the floor, my wrist connecting with the stone first. A sharp pain ran up my arm and I cried out. I pulled my hand to my chest, tenderly probing. I'd seen enough broken bones growing up to know that my wrist was most definitely snapped clean.

With a mixture of both pain and nausea, I fell forward, heaving once more. There wasn't much left in my stomach and what did come up was all bile. My throat burned something fierce and tears sprang to my eyes. I could feel my hair, dark and limp, plastered against the side of my face. The tendrils that fell over my breasts were clumped with a foul mix of vomit and feces.

"You know what I'm going to tell you."

With one hand, I scooped up the bile and put it back in The Tub.

"Good. You're learning. Obedience can be rewarded. Insubordination will lead only to punishment."

Helmar knelt to my level, his head cocked to the side. He reached out and took my broken wrist, ignoring my silent sobs as he turned my hand back and forth, and bent it up and down. My vision grew black around the edges.

"Please…"

I hated that I was begging, especially so early on. The lone word was ash upon my tongue, a betrayal of the hope that I would survive this. How was I going to save Emrys if I couldn't handle a single day? I would fail and he would be next. The man who had given me everything would be subject to torture because I couldn't muster the courage to withstand whatever Helmar would throw my way.

"I think we've done enough for the moment," he finally said. "I hadn't anticipated broken appendages today but perhaps the gods are smiling down upon me this morning."

I was very certain, that if any gods were turning an eye upon this forsaken place, they would most definitely *not* be smiling.

No matter how little the gods, old and new, cared.

King Helmar crossed the room, returning the corkscrew I hadn't realised he'd been holding. I tried not to think about what he intended to use it for. He picked up a rag and wiped his hand and forearms. Why wasn't the concoction in The Tub affecting him the way it did me? Had he truly been in this room so long that he was that desensitised to it?

"The tunnels," he said, his back still to me. "I will give you a five-minute head start, a show of good faith that you will be better behaved tomorrow. After that, I will come for you."

He said nothing else, just bent over his table of tools, now using the rag to clean each one. Not that it did much good. Most of them were so covered in dried blood that I doubted anything would make them look clean.

A minute passed before I realised my time had started. Four minutes. I scrambled to my feet, head spinning, and ran for the cell door. It was now open and I ran straight through it, down the hallway and past the staircase. King Helmar said I needed to escape out of the mountain through the tunnels. Escaping up the stairway would likely lead to The Cleanse. One evil to another. Frying pan to the fire - not that I knew which was which at this point. One was as bad as the other. I took a turn, headed back towards the cells and continued straight past.

The walls were jagged, just as they were near the torture cell. As I continued down tunnels, one after the other, the walls came closer and closer.

Narrowing, perhaps to a dead end.

I turned around, moving back to another tunnel I'd spotted just moments earlier. I had no way of keeping track of the time as it passed but a pang of dread told me my head start was up. Helmar would be after me any moment.

The tunnel I moved into was so dark I could barely see my hand in front of my face, leaving me with no choice but to slow down. My lungs ached anew and I held my limp wrist to my breasts. The torn bodice of my dress was hanging on by a thread, stuck in parts with the concoction from The Tub.

"Little witch, little witch," called Helmar, his sing-song voice echoing off the walls. "Come out, little witch."

I stumbled in the dark, my bare feet damp with water run-off from somewhere in the tunnel. I stuck my hand out, half crawling, feeling my way. My fingers found rubble on the floor as it sloped upwards. Just as I was debating turning around to find another path, I recognised what I was touching.

Bones. Dozens of them, fragmented and discarded in the abandoned tunnel. There was no denying it as my fingers skated across a mandible lined with chipped teeth.

I yelped, letting it go only for the mandible to clatter along the floor, the sound impossibly loud. I froze, listening, waiting. The hammering of my heart rang in my ears, drowning out all other sounds.

A burst of warm air tickled my neck.

"Found you, little witch."

CHAPTER TWELVE

Emrys waited until the king's footsteps had receded into little more than distant whispers before turning to me.

"What happened?"

I sat in my cell, cradling my wrist - the now *very* broken wrist Helmar had dragged me back to the cells by. Silent tears streamed down my face. Tears of pain and agony, shame and embarrassment, hatred and anger. I imagined dying, not surviving long enough to save Emrys and myself. Then I imagined surviving, to one day exact vengeance upon Helmar. I would raze the city by hand - broken or whole, if necessary - and drag him down to his torture cell. Shove his head in The Tub until his lungs burned for oxygen. Peel the skin from his flesh with the rusted tools he kept. Crack his bones one by one as he lay upon the bed of nails and make him beg, weep.

Just as I had begged and wept.

"Artura." Emrys smacked a hand against his bars. "Tell me what happened."

Slowly, I looked up. And lied.

"Nothing. Nothing happened."

I knew he didn't believe me. Not that I cared much at that moment. This was all about protecting him, ensuring that he wouldn't die as an innocent man in some forsaken cell.

Although, he wasn't innocent and nor was I. We each bore the damning weight of guilt. Because we *had* used blood magic. Emrys had been so confident bringing Soraya back from the dead that it stood to reason he'd done it before. However, we were good people. There were others who deserved imprisonment below Dearmond Mountains more than he and I.

"Do not lie to me, girl. What happened? Did he hurt you?"

At that, a laugh erupted from my aching chest. It rolled into a manic fit where eventually the whole hallway echoed with the sounds of uncontrollable laughter.

"Shut up," a voice growled. Malik appeared, brow furrowed with irritation. "If you're in such good spirits, perhaps the king should come back down and finish the job."

That only made me laugh more. After one day, I was losing it. How would I last long enough to find a way out?

The answer was simple: I wouldn't. We would both die here.

The thought was a sobering one and my laughter abated. I settled and suddenly felt more tired than I had ever felt before. The kind of tiredness that you felt deep in your bones, right to the marrow. I laid down on the cold stones, not caring that I'd not yet eaten dinner, and closed my eyes.

*

I slept like the dead. However, in the depths of such all-consuming sleep were paralysing nightmares. Images of the torture room with King Helmar's instruments. Then the image of me running through the tunnels, wildly searching for freedom. I saw a light only to be pulled away just as my fingertips brushed the edge of the outside world.

When I awoke, it was like emerging from a heavy fog. I rubbed at my eyes, crusted with dirt and remnants of The Tub. A blurred figure stood before me and as it slowly came into focus, my heart thrummed a panicked rhythm.

"Get up, witch," King Helmar said. He stood with his arms folded across his chest, a less than amused expression on his face. Somehow, I got the feeling he expected me to be waiting for him at a moment's notice, forever poised and ready to follow him to Purgatory, the name I decided seemed apt for a room such as it.

Forever caught in the middle.

Not dying. Not living. Simply existing.

Every inch of me ached as I forced myself upright.

"Ready?"

No. I followed him anyway.

Emrys reached out, taking the hem of my dress as I walked past. There was a silent plea in his eyes. For what, I didn't know. In the past day, I had pleaded *for* anything *with* anything and *to* anything, only to come to a painful realisation. No one except for ourselves would put an end to this horror. I shook my head at him, not even having strength enough to speak, and moved past his cell.

Purgatory stunk as bad as I remembered, perhaps more so. I wrinkled my nose as I entered, eyes averting The Tub. At least, should Helmar force me back into it today, I hadn't eaten the night before. There would be nothing for me to bring up. Passing his sick and twisted test would be easy.

Yet it wasn't to The Tub he walked, but rather a new table, brought down sometime after I'd last been in the cell. It stood in the centre of the room and had I not looked closely enough, might have assumed it to be ordinary, perhaps taken from one of his dining halls. But then I noticed that bolted to each corner were iron cuffs. They dangled off the edge of the table, glinting in the low lighting of Purgatory.

"You did well yesterday."

"I didn't have a choice."

Helmar shrugged. "Everyone has a choice. You chose to fight, to survive. A satisfactory performance. Most people do not fare so well on their first excursion into my realm."

I almost couldn't bear to know but a morbid sense of curiosity made me ask. "How many people have been in here?"

He didn't hesitate as he answered, "One hundred and thirty-eight. Thirty-nine with you. Forty if you do not survive and I bring in your friend."

I closed my eyes. So many souls had been brought into a place devoid of humanity. "How many survived?"

"Two."

"Did they find their way out?"

"One did. The other I was paid a handsome sum to release."

One. One person had escaped through the mountain tunnels. It was all I could do not to fall to the floor and weep bitter tears. One in one hundred and thirty-eight had escaped. That didn't exactly bode well for my chances of survival. A shiver ran through me, overriding the constant shivers induced by the frigid conditions below Dearmond.

"Table," he instructed, not looking at me. So certain that I would obey like the well-behaved dog he thought me to be.

I sat on the edge of the table.

Woof, woof.

"On your stomach."

I shifted to my side and rolled over, keeping my skirts down as I went. I might as well have not bothered for in the next moment, Helmar shoved them up to the tops of my thighs. I felt his calloused fingertips run down the back of my legs. He fastened the iron cuffs to each of my ankles before doing the same with my wrists. The table was longer than I was tall and he pulled my arms taut to properly fit the cuffs. One ache rolled into another, reaching a crescendo when he fastened a cuff to my broken wrist.

"Scream," he said, "and I will start the count over again. Be silent, and I will reward you."

"With what?"

"Five extra minutes in the tunnels."

Trembling, I nodded before setting my cheek against the cool wood and closing my eyes.

The first hit was such a shock that I flinched, nothing more. I don't know what I expected. Pain, certainly, but something more acute perhaps. Glancing out the corner of my eye, I noted a thin cane held in the king's hands as he brought it down with a swift flick against my thigh. One hit after another, again and again and again. By the dozenth, I was whimpering. Helmar hadn't said how long this would go on for, only that if I didn't make a sound, I would be rewarded with extra time in the tunnels. But as one hit was quickly succeeded by another, I felt my resolve turn paper thin and begin to wane.

On the sixteenth, I cried, tears leaking from the corner of my eyes.

Helmar chuckled. "Took you long enough."

The next hit was harder, faster. From there, he picked up the pace. The backs of my legs were on fire. I scented blood, felt trickles of it running down my legs. I began to cry in earnest, sharp, racking sobs that shook my entire body, silenced only by the sheer force with which I bit the insides of my cheeks. My pain only seemed to spur the king on, sending him into a frenzy.

The first hit against the soles of my feet sent a new wave of pain coursing through me. Once, as a child, I'd stepped on broken glass. The ball of my foot was sliced open, the cut so deep I couldn't walk on it for a week. Then, it had been the worst kind of pain imaginable.

I was wrong.

Straining against the cuffs, trying in vain to get away. I bit my lips to muffle my cries.

"That won't do," the king chided. "Only silence will save you from this."

My heels, my toes, the balls of my feet. Over and over. Even if I stayed silent, and somehow was...*rewarded* with extra time in the tunnels, running wouldn't be a possibility. Hel, crawling might not either with the state of my wrist. I would be utterly incapacitated and entirely at the king's mercy.

Eventually, my tears ran dry. My body went limp against the table as the king administered the final hit. He stepped back, cocking his head to the side, quietly appreciating.

"Beautiful," he whispered. "Nothing more stunning than to see skin pinked with a cane."

I doubted my skin was simply 'pink.'

Unfastening the cuffs, the king hummed to himself. I inwardly cringed at his touch when he pulled me up to sit on the edge of the table, only for that cringe to be the furthest thing from my mind when new agony swept through me.

"Notice how you cannot sit?" He smirked. "Just try to run now, see how far you get."

Bracing my hands on the edge of the table, I stepped off.

And promptly fell to my knees.

My feet were raw and bloodied. The moment I tried to stand again, they gave out. I ignored the sounds of Helmar's unbridled laughter as I planted my one good palm against the stone floor and crawled to the cell door.

*

Every movement was agony and that was putting it mildly.

I knew for sure now why the walls of the staircase were smooth stone while the walls of the tunnels were not. The rocks of the Dearmond Mountains were indeed like the edge of a blade, perhaps sharper. The one time I made the mistake of putting my hand out to steady myself on my aching feet, my palm had promptly been sliced open. Blood trickled down to dampen my sleeve, yet another bodily liquid to stain my skin. I'd been familiar with the smell of blood from a very young age but never my own. Not until I matured and nature took its course. Blood from an open wound of my own, however, turned my stomach.

King Helmar didn't give me a head start. I hadn't been silent enough for his liking and he pursued me within a minute. I felt a tug on my hair, dry and crusted, followed by a strong jolt backwards before I landed on my back, staring up at King Helmar.

"I'm disappointed. You got much farther yesterday."

I had full use of my feet then, you fucking prick.

Sharp pain radiated through my side. Instinctively, I curled in on myself, discovering the source of the pain as the king withdrew his boot from near my ribs. Each new bolt of pain melted into the next until I was lost to the raging sea of it.

"Back to your cell." He spat, a wad landing on the side of my face. "Tomorrow, we'll try again."

As Helmar walked away, he called back, "I heard witches were something to be feared but all I fear is how little time you may last."

A moment later, Malik appeared beside me. I flinched when he extended a hand.

"I won't bite," he grunted.

Hesitantly, I took hold of him, using his muscled forearm to pull me to my feet. My foot, slippery with the blood still oozing from dozens of cuts, slid across the stone floor. Malik swung me up into his arms.

I didn't miss the subtle wrinkling of his nose on a deep inhale. I knew well enough how badly I reeked.

"Let me."

I was exhausted. From walking, running, fighting. Even keeping my eyes open was excruciating. I longed to sleep like the dead once more but if I kept this up, I would join them in no time. Some comfort, at least, to know this might be over soon.

"He's a hard man," Malik said as we walked through one tunnel after the next. "But a good enough master."

"I wouldn't ever put the king and the word 'good' in the same sentence," I wheezed. "The man is a brute. And a sick one at that."

Malik grinned. "True enough. But he's also a man who knows his mind and stays true to himself. It's a rarity nowadays when the common folk sell their morals and beliefs for a scrap of bread."

"That doesn't make it any better," I shot back, my breathing slowly evening out with every passing second. "Saying Helmar is a man who knows his own mind implies he is somehow better because of it. Quite the opposite. Perhaps he knows who he is. That only makes him more dangerous because he knows his baseline. No one truly discovers their limits until they run into them headfirst, usually at the expense of someone else."

"No." We turned down another tunnel but it was hard to separate one from the next. "The king knows his limits. If you think he doesn't then he hasn't reached them with you. Yet."

"I don't want to consider how far he can go." My words were barely above a whisper but Malik heard them over his deep breathing. As much as I wanted to be far, far away from him, his warmth was welcome after feeling so incredibly cold the past week.

"Suppose you'll find out eventually."

We left the tunnel and emerged into a well-lit space with smooth walls. I was coming to realise that smooth walls meant luxury beneath the mountain - or at least, Dearmond's version of it. Smooth walls were for those you did not wish a long and painful death upon. Rough walls were for those you loathed with every fibre of your being.

"What place is this?"

"Wardens quarters."

Malik sat me on the edge of his bed. It was the softest thing I'd touched since leaving the cottage and a sigh escaped me before I could stop it. While it did reek of ale, it also held a comfort I had acutely craved the moment my home was left behind.

Malik returned a moment later with a bucket of water. Steam rose off the top of it as he dipped a stained cloth below the surface. His calloused hand reached towards my face, beads of water dripping from it. I shrank back.

"Figure you could use a clean," he explained with a wink.

Unease bloomed in my gut, a voice in my head screaming for me to run.

But how? How could I run on feet so badly damaged as mine? It was nothing short of a miracle that I had managed what I did in the tunnels. The only way out of the warden's quarters was by crawling on my belly like a snake, using my one good arm to pull my beaten body along.

I wasn't going to give anyone the satisfaction of seeing that.

Malik's other hand gripped my arm and he wiped it roughly. The cloth felt closer to sandpaper. Was this some new form of torture? Offering a deceptive kindness? It felt more akin to psychological torture. I wouldn't have put it past King Helmar but he was nowhere in sight.

"Please," I said, trying to swallow. My throat felt as torn up as my feet did after screaming for so long. "I just want to go back to my cell."

Malik ignored me, moving onto my other arm. There wasn't much cleaning, more a general smearing of caked-on dirt that tainted the clean water. It ran off my arms in rivulets, staining my already ruined dress.

When he took hold of my broken wrist, I quickly pulled my arm away.

Malik froze.

His hand moved fast as it whipped across my face. Tears I didn't know I still had sprang to my eyes.

"Bitch," he spat "Are you too good for my charity? My pity? Too high and lofty when you're nothing more than a traitorous witch. You're nothing."

I didn't move. Shiver after shiver ran over my already over-sensitised skin.

Malik turned and moved to the door - a solid wooden door. No bars to peer through. The warden was afforded privacy where the prisoners were not. He peered outside. Was he going to leave? I changed my mind. I would gladly crawl back to my cell if Malik left me even for a minute.

Instead, he pushed the door closed and turned towards me. A sneer marred a face that might have once been beautiful, long before war and senseless fighting plagued Cimran for over two decades.

"You don't want my charity? That's fine." Deftly, his fingers undid the belt securing his tunic. "I'll give you nothing. I will take and you won't say a fucking word. Will you, witchling?"

CHAPTER THIRTEEN

I lost count of the days. The only true way to tell time would have been by tracking the bruises, stacked upon one another like the rotting autumn leaves. Watching them fade from fresh red marks to dark purple splotches, and eventually onto brown and yellow. Tones I had all seen in a sunrise or sunset.

Not that I'd seen either one lately.

We fell into a familiar routine. I would wake to the sounds of heavy footsteps that the stone walls sang of long after he was gone. King Helmar would unlock my cell door. Depending on his mood, I would either be invited out or barked at like a dog. The latter was becoming more common. Purgatory never seemed to be clean beyond King Helmar's prized tools. I'd become well acquainted with The Tub - something which now contained far too much of my blood, waste and sick. The mere thought of it was enough to turn my stomach. My hair hadn't been washed since arriving and now it was stiff, moulded into an everlasting bird nest atop my head. Helmar would 'play' with me until he deemed me ready for the tunnels. I was only ever ready when I'd sustained an injury that would make an escape, at minimum, difficult and at most, impossible.

It didn't stop me from trying. And I did. Every time I got a chance at the tunnels I pushed myself harder than I ever thought possible. I learned to keep torn strips of fabric from the underskirt of my dress tucked somewhere on my person, no mean feat when my one dress was disintegrating before my very eyes. The king had decided he liked it best when he drew out the chase and routinely gave me a five-minute head start. I took the time to bind my hands so I could better feel my way through the tunnels without fear of slicing open my palms.

Once, I got close. First, I'd smelt fresh air. It was more intoxicating than any wine I had ever tasted. I followed it forward, chasing the scent. Next, I heard a roaring. It filled my ears. A sound I hadn't heard in forever. Rain. My heart thrummed faster and faster with every step. I glimpsed a ray of muted light that no torch could ever produce.

And then I was being pulled away, away, away - the only sounds that of my screaming echoing through the tunnel.

After that, I tried to retrace my steps each time. But it was hopeless. Too many twists and turns through identical tunnels. To have freedom so close only to be ripped away had done more to my lack of confidence than any beating administered at the hand of the king.

Emrys learned to no longer ask questions. My answer was always the same: *nothing*. Nothing happened. Not. A. Thing. I was fine.

Am I bleeding? Yes.

Am I torn? Yes.

Can you see bones trying to poke out of my wrist as they slowly heal at a crooked angle? Also yes.

Would I ever divulge the truth of what went on in Purgatory? Definitely not.

And then there was Malik who had dropped all pretences after that first visit to the warden's quarters. No more did he feign gentility and care, instead shoving me roughly through the doorway at any opportunity to take me in ways I would not soon forget. The damage he had done, though he used no weapon, was equal to that of the king. What Malik did left its mark on me in different ways than what Helmar achieved. Mentally, emotionally - the things that were hardest to heal. Nightmares of sword and dagger had melted into rough hands and my face being shoved into a musty-smelling mattress. To an ache deep in my core that never quite healed and near constant bleeding despite being starved so thoroughly that my cycle had come to a crashing halt. I took it all, though. Dealt with each day the only way I knew how: losing myself in the dark recesses of my mind.

If I fought, Malik would be just as cruel and merciless as the king.

If I gave up control of my body to his use, I was sometimes rewarded with food and food was integral to my plan of staying alive long enough to escape and free Emrys

Not once had I cracked, begging for my life. Although I begged for leniency, mercy, I'd not yet pleaded for death to take me swiftly. The stakes were far too great and the prize far too sweet. To see Emrys out of harm's way, that was all I wanted now. So I stayed silent, with the occasional snide comment. Part of me still lingered somewhere deep below. Very, very deep. But lingered nevertheless, a constant reminder that no matter how hard Helmar and Malik tried, they couldn't destroy me completely. There was always going to be that ember of fire burning within.

It wasn't for lack of trying on their part. It felt like they daily redoubled their efforts. My chant and prayer 'do not break' had become so all-consuming that I thought of nothing else beyond surviving. I clung to those words with my fingernails, refusing to give up.

Do not break.
Do not break.
Do not break.

*

Something scraped across the floor of my cell. I looked up towards the sound to discover Malik pushing a bowl of food towards me with the toe of his boot. I was exhausted after another long day. This time, the king had slowly torn my fingernails back one by one until I passed out. It was strange because, in the grand scheme of things, it wasn't the worst the king could have done. I'd come to learn his tastes were darkly sadistic. The things he conjured up in that twisted mind of his made me question if he was even human. But the pain of fingernails being pulled was unlike any other.

"Eat. The king wants to see you."

I stopped mid-reach. "He already did today."

Malik grinned. I hated the way it lit up a nauseating mischief in his eyes. "You can be sure to point that out when you see him. Hurry."

I was starving and did as I was told, drinking the watery soup straight from the crudely carved wooden bowl. I'd learned not to move my lips too much while I ate, lest I wind up with splinters in them. The soup was bland and tasteless but at least contained chunks of meat. Most likely rat but I was long since past the point of caring.

At some point in the last week, my dress had finally disintegrated to the point of being unwearable and I now wore a threadbare tunic from a deceased member of The Cleanse. If I paid too close attention to the feel of the linen on my skin, it burned like acid. Dressing in clothes that had once belonged to a murderer made me feel dirtier than The Tub ever could. Beneath the fabric, my ribs were a little too pronounced, hip bones a little too sharp. One meal a day for what was most likely several months now had reduced my already petite body to next to nothing. I felt hollow inside. There were no mirrors or glass to see my reflection beneath the mountain but I knew it wasn't good by the way Emrys looked at me with raw pain in his eyes.

I put the bowl on the floor and pushed myself to my feet. "I'm ready."

A lie. I was never truly ready.

Following Malik past the cells, I mentally steeled myself for a second venture into Purgatory. Only once before had I been to Purgatory twice in one day. It was after I'd fought back, stabbing the king with a discarded, rusty nail through the back of his hand. He'd shown no hint of anger and set me loose in the tunnels. After dinner and once Malik delivered me back to the king, he'd served his own cruel form of justice: that very same nail was driven through my hand, nailing it to the table. Helmar left me there all night as punishment.

Never again did I fight back. Outwardly at least.

When we bypassed the hallway leading to the torture cell, I grew suspicious.

"Where are we going?"

Malik didn't look back as we began to climb the stairs that would eventually lead us back to the castle.

"Do you know what I am, witchling?"

"No." *I don't care.*

"A soldier."

"And you take orders."

"Yes. Without explanation."

We ascended in silence but just as the final staircase to the castle loomed ahead, Malik shoved me through a side passage. Another set of stairs delivered us into a room full of paintings, each one taller than a man and painstakingly painted over hours and weeks. When Emrys and I arrived at the castle, I had seen paintings like these but only a few. This room held dozens upon dozens, lining the walls barely a handspan apart.

"Wait here."

Malik left me standing in the middle of the room. I was suddenly aware how out of place I was. I stunk. Gods, the scent that wafted off me could made my eyes water. And the layer of filth on my skin was so thick I would likely have to scrape it off. I didn't belong in a room so grand.

King Helmar's expression when he approached only confirmed that.

"What am I doing here?" I asked, voice quiet. What the king had done to me below the mountain worked. I feared him. The only other emotion left that could stand a chance to rival that fear was the unquenchable loathing I felt.

Helmar tucked his hands behind his back, eyes narrowing on me. "What do you know of your heritage?"

I blinked to clear my eyes of the ever-present layer of dust from the cells. "My heritage?"

"Where you come from."

"I know what heritage means," I replied. "I just know nothing of it."

The king nodded to himself, my answer confirming whatever he thought. He cocked his head, a silent order to follow. I walked behind Helmar to the opposite end of the room where a door was concealed beneath the wallpaper and wainscoting. He pushed against it and it clicked open.

Inside were two paintings.

One was of a woman sitting on a throne. A commemorative piece from a wedding, judging by the layers of ivory lace and satin that swathed her thin frame like a cloud. The other held the same woman coupled with a man, both dressed in exquisitely crafted navy attire. I squinted and recognised a much younger version of King Helmar. Why were wedding portraits in a hidden room? During the reign of a king, portraits were front and centre of the castle, a memory of the might formed through a binding of two kingdoms. Except these two paintings were tucked away. Almost as though they bore a silent shame.

"My first wife," Helmar said, his voice near my ear. I jumped.

"First wife?"

He sighed. "And your mother."

Everything came to a standstill. I waited for a laugh, a snide comment about how a 'witch' such as myself could even for a second consider herself to be of noble birth. Nothing came - only Helmar with a solemn look in his eye.

"I don't understand."

"Figured you might not. I can't imagine she would have wanted you to ever find out."

I looked at the single portrait of what had been King Helmar's first queen. I noted some similarities between us. We both had the same inky hair, darker than a midnight sky. The same silvery blue eyes framed by thick, dark lashes. Her nose was sharp and pointed, however, whereas mine was more rounded at the end. I glanced over my shoulder to where the king stood. His nose was rounded.

Inwardly, I shook myself. *It's just a nose, Artura.*

"I never knew my mother," I murmured, looking up at the portrait. "There was nothing for her to conceal. She died in childbirth."

"Oh, I suspect she did. It's the way of these things."

I frowned at his last two words. *These things*, as though dying in childbirth were no more than a simple, everyday tragedy. However, thanks to the decades-long war and the effect it had on everyone, dying in childbirth was, in fact, just that: an everyday tragedy.

"Princess Iseult of Galdua, who then became Queen Iseult of Cimran. She and I were married when I was twenty-three. She was only eighteen and the daughter of a king on his deathbed. His only wish was to have his daughter wed and cared for before he passed the crown onto his only son. I had ascended to the throne the previous year upon my own father's death and also wished for a wife to rule at my side."

"I pity her," I replied. "She did not know who she was marrying."

Helmar nodded. "True. Though neither did I." The king took a seat on a red velvet armchair, tenting his fingers in front of his face. "Iseult came to be with child not long after our wedding. I was overjoyed, as one might expect in a new king. My bloodline was secured with little difficulty. Except there were trials. Iseult lost the child before her third month. Nevertheless, we tried again and this time, succeeded."

His face darkened as he looked at the portrait of the queen on her wedding day. There was a pure youthfulness about her, one unmarred by the evil ways of the king. I wondered if this story would end up similar to mine. If she had ever found herself beneath the mountain.

As though sensing my train of thought, the king chuckled.

"No. I didn't touch her. I didn't even lay with her during her confinement, so fearful was I that I would jeopardise the well-being of my unborn heir. Seven months we abstained and then late one night, when one of her ladies-in-waiting came to fetch me, it was with news that my wife had gone into premature labour. The child was early and survival would rest solely in the hands of the gods. Iseult gave birth to a son. He was…sickly. Pale. Small. The midwife told us to prepare for the inevitable. Perhaps it was for the best. No kingdom can thrive upon the shoulders of the weak."

"I'm sorry," I whispered. Because even though the king was a monster, no one should have to endure the death of their child. Emrys had held the hands of many mothers in Naiva, bearing the loss of a child far too soon. I sat by his side every time. And every time I mourned right along with those childless mothers.

"I do not want your sympathy," he spat, enunciating the last word sharply before rubbing a hand over his face. For a moment he looked older than his near fifties. "That was the night I learned who my bride truly was. A witch. To save our ailing son, Iseult drew upon ancient blood magic. She fought to retrieve his soul from the After before it took hold of him completely. The child was in limbo, you see. But she could not. She failed. And my son died in my arms. I was furious but also determined to have an heir. So we tried again. And again. And again. Each pregnancy lasted less than the previous, as though the gods themselves sought retribution for the evil Iseult called upon. After many attempts, however, Iseult came to be with child again. The fourth and fifth months passed. We began to breathe a little lighter, easier. Perhaps this child would be born at term, healthy."

I tried to imagine how it must have been for the queen - a woman whose sole purpose was to produce an heir to her husband, the king. She had tried and failed for so long. Queens had been executed for less.

"I caught Iseult practising magic once more late one night," he continued. "She was out in the gardens, chanting before a fire. The fire seemed to move before her, bend to her will. It was...*unnatural*. I realised then that she'd ensured the continuation of this pregnancy through magic alone. But it was also through magic that my son had died. I...I struck her."

Hardly surprising, I thought bitterly, feeling the phantom sting of his hand across my cheek. But there was a subtle sorrow in the king's eyes, as though he truly regretted his actions. Yet, I knew him to be a master manipulator, twisting and weaving words and emotions, like thread on a loom, to whichever way suited him best.

"By the next morning, she was gone along with several members of my court. The Cleanse took great pains tracking down each one of them, executing them for treason. To abandon their king, it was inexcusable. Iseult, however, proved difficult to track. Along with one other - my healer."

"Emrys," I breathed.

The king nodded, his eyes locked on mine. "Yes. *Emrys*. Though back then he was known as Alhemrys. He had been my healer since I was a child and then became responsible for the care of the queen. I thought I could trust him but soon realised my folly. I always wondered what happened to the two. Where they went. Now I know."

I was silent. There was nothing for me to say. His words swirled around my head, confusing and clearing all at once. Questions were answered while many more were raised.

"You think I'm that child? Iseult's child?"

The king smirked. "Think? No, I do not *think*. I *know*."

I couldn't believe what I was hearing, and yet...

"How long have you known?"

His lips pursed as he watched my face. Finally, he said, "A while."

Something in me cracked. Though he'd not said exactly how long, the implication was there - he had known while torturing me, while slicing into my body, beating me, shoving my head into a vat of filth and human waste. It made sense now why he was adamant I was a witch. After all, many were through birthright alone, magic passed along as easily as any other familial trait.

Betrayal flooded all of my senses. Emrys had lied to me. He'd let me be tortured for months while promising me that I'd done no wrong. Only I had, hadn't I? Through virtue of my birth alone, I was genuinely guilty of being a witch - regardless of whether I possessed any real magic myself.

The thought that I deserved every single thing that happened made me want to be sick. I fought the urge and only very narrowly won.

"Why?" It was all I could think to ask.

"I see you in her."

A simple reply and a full explanation. He wanted to punish Iseult and since she was dead, the only way to do that was through me.

Punish a memory.

"I am of your blood."

"Perhaps. But magic has tainted yours," he replied, wiping dust off his sleeve. "Therefore, you are no child of mine. Though you do possess...certain qualities of my own. Truthfully, I admire your ardour. I would admire it even more post-mortem. Personally, you do me a great disservice by still breathing. Fortunately for you, my advisors believe you can be of far more use alive."

Bile rose in my throat. "And how, pray tell, could I possibly help *you*?"

King Helmar stood, motioning for me to follow him back into the main room. I squinted in the bright light, scrunching my eyes shut for a moment. Too long had I lived in darkness. Sunlight was an all-out assault on my vision.

"Not I, but rather your kingdom."

"You just said I was no child of yours. And besides, long ago I decided this to be no kingdom of mine. Now that I know who fathered me, I will gladly leave this place to the crows if given half the chance."

Helmar snapped his fingers and a servant appeared with a tray laden with richly smelling food and wine. The king took a seat at a table that had been set up since we were sequestered. The servant handed him a silver goblet full of red wine and he drank deeply.

"This kingdom is yours by birthright."

I tried not to look at the meats and cheeses, the freshly baked bread and fruits that smelt sweeter than I remembered. My mouth watered.

"So I am to be your daughter and princess when you see the need for it?"

"When will you learn, Artura?" I flinched. He'd never used my name before. The sound of it on his tongue was all wrong. "Everything is up to my choosing. Ultimately, I am the arbiter of all that happens in Cimran."

"Except for my death, it would seem. That was promised to me."

His eyes glinted like the diamond raindrops of the chandelier overhead. "Oh, make no mistake. Death is promised. Just not this day."

"A heartwarming thought."

"When you burn upon the pyre? Heartwarming indeed."

Silence fell over the gallery as the king ate, the only sounds his chewing and the odd moan of appreciation. It was no secret that despite the famine throughout Cimran, Lanceris had the best of the food trade. The king was top priority.

Emrys said it would amount to nothing if all that was left to rule over was a kingdom of bones. A king with no one to control was no king at all.

"So you intend to use me for your benefit? What am I to do? Scrub the floors? Darn your socks?"

Helmar threw an orange peel on the platter before him, wiping his mouth on an embroidered napkin. "If your husband sees fit. Personally, I would have you performing much more menial tasks."

I frowned, wondering just how much exactly the king knew about me. "My husband? I am not married."

Tearing apart a chunk of what looked to be sourdough, something Emrys had bought for me as a treat on my fifteenth birthday after scrounging coins for weeks, the king spoke around a mouthful.

"Ah, but you will be. See, your arrival posits an interesting idea, one brought to my attention just this morning. My daughter, Cerana, is due to wed King Juriel of Nimue by the week's end. Now, why would I send my beloved child when I could simply send you instead? Juriel is a fool. All he expects is somewhere warm to stick his cock each night. My daughter does not deserve a loveless marriage such as that. An accused witch, however? That would do nicely as punishment. For now, anyway."

My eyes narrowed. For all I knew, I was simply being given from one evil to the next.

"I am to be married off? To what end?"

"To my own," King Helmar replied. "Your union with Juriel will benefit Cimran greatly. For a worthless whore, King Juriel will provide me with additional soldiers, weaponry. Everything I need to end this tireless, though worthy, crusade against evil."

My hands began to shake and I clenched them, ignoring the pain in my fingertips where my nails had once been.

"In a word, my marriage will be a marriage spawned of hate," I shot back. "All to murder a handful of people who do you no harm - who have *never* done you harm. Innocents. For fuck's sake, you claim that I am one of them but you did not know about me until recently. How could I have possibly hurt you in any way? You did not know me!"

Helmar stood, his chair clattering backwards against the mosaic-tiled floor. He closed the distance between us in only a few short strides. When he came close to my face, I smelt the rich aroma of wine lacing his hot breath.

"Witches," he spat, "are a blight upon this land and magic their great weapon in a war *we,* the righteous, endure. Every single one is guilty of treason and shall be executed in a manner so befitting. Be grateful you are not yet among them, though I promise you, witch, I will come for you. All I need is your marriage to form my alliance and then you are of no further use to me."

By the time he was finished speaking, we were nearly nose to nose, his finger dug into my chest in silent accusation. I willed myself not to take a step back.

Do not break.

I tilted my chin up. "I can hardly see King Juriel playing by your rules if you slaughter his wife."

Helmar snickered. "Who says I'll slaughter you? No, it will be as though you simply passed away in your sleep. The fool will be none the wiser and by contract of marriage, forever bound to our treaty. I will have my vengeance upon not only you but your kind as well."

"Upon a people who *do you no wrong*." My words came out as a strangled cry. I had never paid witches any mind. They went about their lives in peace as I did with mine. But senseless murder would never sit right with me. More so after all I'd endured in Purgatory.

"Upon your filthy whore of a mother," he spat back. "You are seed of the rotten apple. Born of her flesh and blood. Just as evil as she was."

"I am also of your flesh and blood so if I truly am evil as you say, then perhaps I got it from *you*."

Helmar raised his hand, a fist forming before he gritted his teeth and pulled it away. The king sat down in his chair once more, downing the remnants of wine in his goblet.

"If your mother knew that I now have the one thing she treasured most... Well, that thought is worth all this bloodshed."

"This war was always about her." Not a question, but rather a truth that finally settled within. The realisation that Helmar had brought a kingdom to its knees, all because of one woman, was a sobering one. How could anyone hate so much? Cause so much destruction all to enact revenge upon someone who died so long ago? It made no sense but then, nothing did in Cimran. It was a kingdom without reason. If the king wished it, then it was so - no matter what.

But I knew, also, that it really was possible to hate one person so ardently that you would do anything to ruin them. After all, if I had the chance, would I not also tear apart a kingdom to destroy one man?

In a heartbeat.

He half shrugged. "In part. She was certainly one catalyst, yes."

Thousands upon thousands dead, all because of the hate Helmar carried for one woman. I wanted to walk over to his table, pick up the steak knife and plunge it into his ice-cold heart. I wanted to twist and dig with the blade, slicing into ribbons the one part of him that should have contained even a shred of decency. Instead, I drew in a steadying breath and spoke clearly.

"You forget one vital part of your plan."

Helmar chewed on another slice of orange. That particular fruit was worth almost its weight in gold. Oranges only grew in the Southern Kingdoms and would have cost a pretty coin to bring into Lanceris. And here he ate it, leaving too much flesh attached to the peel as he discarded each piece. A waste of food from a waste of a man.

"I forget nothing," he muttered.

I smirked, feeling brave for the first time in weeks. "I could tell Juriel of your plan to have me killed."

"True," Helmar replied, nonchalantly. "You could do that. But then I would have to kill Alhemrys - sorry, *Emrys* - and I very much doubt you would appreciate such a thing."

I started forward as rage flickered in my gut like a fire, stopping only when the king held his hand up, his gaze not once meeting mine.

"Don't you dare touch him," I hissed. "You promised him freedom."

"Yes, *if* you escaped the mountain which you clearly did not. So he will remain below at my pleasure."

I felt that tentative bravado wavering. I was no longer beneath Dearmond yet I'd failed worse than I could have possibly imagined. Emrys was there alone now, at the mercy of the king.

A mercy I knew first-hand did not exist.

"Remember what I said, witch," Helmar said, waving his hand in dismissal. "I am the arbiter of all things. My will shall be done."

CHAPTER FOURTEEN

I didn't return to the cells. All that was needed for me to be ushered out of the gallery was for Helmar to wave his hand nonchalantly. A short woman wearing a pristine white apron with her hair pulled back into a severe twist scuttled forward. Hand outstretched, she stopped abruptly with a stifled yelp when she realised just how filthy I was. I followed her in silence through the castle, passing countless closed doors, each one deathly silent beyond it, until we stopped outside an open one.

The room within was as grand as the rest of the castle. Gilded ceilings and polished floors, richly coloured tapestries and a four-poster bed with a sheer, tied to each post with a white satin bow. The dozen pillows and thick knitted blankets covering the bed looked softer than anything I'd ever seen.

"Keep your hands to yourself," the woman instructed as she flitted about. "Gods know I've enough to do without scrubbing your grubby fingerprints off the walls."

"I was raised better than that," I replied, lost in thought.

"If you pardon my saying so, girl, you were raised by a traitorous old fool. I doubt very much you were raised correctly at all."

"Why? Because I couldn't tell you which number of forks are needed per individual for a feast? Or because I don't wear corsets and cross my ankles when I sit?"

"Of course not," she huffed.

"Or is it perhaps because I dance about naked beneath a full moon chanting sweet nothings to the almighty Mother?" I would have been lying if I said that the change of events hadn't reinvigorated me somewhat. I felt the old me stirring beneath the surface, that first flicker lighting up the ever-persisting dark that clouded my mind. "Sometimes I even bathe in a cauldron while drinking blood."

"That mouth of yours will get you killed, you know," she muttered as she pulled clothes from an ornate wooden wardrobe.

"So I've been told."

She moved across the room - a room ludicrously large for just one person - and placed the bundle of clothes atop a stool beside a porcelain, claw-footed bathtub.

"In."

I didn't move, my momentary change in mood fading away instantly. The only tub I'd been near recently was the one I still wore a reminder of - mentally and physically. The thought of fully submerging myself in any sort of liquid, clear or opaque, made my skin crawl. My breathing quickened, chest rising and falling rapidly. My head grew light. The room spun.

No. Not The Tub. I can't. Not again. Please, don't make me.

No longer in Purgatory but still tormented. And now I would enter a loveless marriage, carrying that weight for gods knew how long.

Helmar was the gift that kept on giving.

The woman's face softened ever so slightly. She knew. "It's clean, child. Just suds and lavender oil. Come and see."

She was right. As I approached, the scent of lavender and something headier enveloped me. Every nerve was instantly calmed as I peered over the edge to glimpse steamy water ringed with pearlescent bubbles.

"Well, it's clean now," she went on. "That's not to say it won't be once you're in it."

I pulled the tattered tunic from my body. It didn't seem right to put the filthy fabric on floors that likely had never been sullied by more than the odd muddy boot. The woman wordlessly held out a basket and I placed the tunic in, not a bit sad to see it go.

"Soak. I'll be back momentarily."

Every inch of my skin burned as I slipped into the piping hot water but I welcomed it. It had been too long since I'd felt halfway normal. As ribbons of murky water curled away from my skin, I felt something in me crack, something I had been holding back for too long. Tears fell in earnest as my body shook with heaving sobs.

I mourned the life I'd known, the life I would have had if I had stayed in Naiva. I mourned the torture experienced over the past months, and the fact that there would be evidence of it on my body for the rest of my life. I mourned seemingly small things like a scar on my knee from when I'd fallen because my feet were too torn for me to stand. Subtle reminders were the worst kind. They snuck up on you in moments you thought you were doing well.

And most of all, I mourned Emrys. For the fact that he was still below Dearmond. Would they tell him where I'd gone? Or would he have expected that eventually, I would just not return? That I might have succumbed to injuries at the hands of the king and no one bothered to tell him that I was dead.

A darker thought emerged. Would Helmar use my absence as a weapon? Would he terrorise Emrys with some tale of how I'd been pushed beyond the brink, my body abused in ways only the truly twisted could imagine? Emrys cared. That was perhaps his greatest weakness and strength. It would crush him to hear some of the things Helmar had done to me. Then there was what had occurred between Malik and I - that would break him the most, I thought, especially in light of a decade ago. After the events in the weeks following my thirteenth birthday, what Malik had done would destroy Emrys more than anything else. Emrys had apologised for too long after that dark time for failing to protect me. He would think this was his fault, too, as though he somehow could have prevented what Malik had done.

I didn't notice when the woman returned. Or that she brought a servant girl with her. The two set about cleaning me, pouring water over my head, detangling locks that were so filthy they'd become ratty, matted dreadlocks. I resigned myself to a shaved head as the second woman tutted about the futility of it all and lamented over a second broken comb, the teeth stuck in random knots. Shame overwhelmed me even though there was nothing I could have done to prevent the damage and lack of care. I sniffled quietly but slowly, ever so slowly, my hair detangled and dripped down my back as it once had.

The water was black before I knew it. The second woman helped me to my feet while the first directed new servants to empty the bath. I waited as they took away water that reminded me too much of The Tub in Purgatory. Once it was refilled with clean water, I stepped back in and the women continued their careful ministrations. I closed my eyes and focused only on the healing that came with being clean.

The second woman left. The first dressed me in a thick nightgown and stockings. She added a shawl before steering me to a stool where she once more combed and finally braided my hair.

"Sleep now." She patted me twice on the shoulder. "Tomorrow I will return to you."

I must have looked lost because she gently touched my cheek - the first genuine human contact I'd had in a very long time. A tear leaked out of the corner of my eye as a shiver ran through me.

"Blessings come to us in strange ways. It might not seem like it right now, but this marriage is a blessing."

She turned and left, closing the door behind her. I was asleep before my head hit the pillow.

*

I woke with a jolt, coated in a fine sheen of sweat, sometime around midnight. The fire had gone out, now reduced to nothing but embers, a faint, eerie glow on the other side of the bedroom. I heard no murmurs beyond the bedroom door, no footsteps creeping by.

I slipped from the bed, built so high off the ground that I'd needed a step stool to climb in. Everything in the castle seemed a little too big, a little too grand. A sickening display of wealth while the rest of the kingdom scrounged together basic meals daily; while children wore clothes riddled with holes, so thin that they did little to keep out the winter chill.

Pulling a blanket from the bed, I wrapped it around myself, turned the door handle silently and peered out into the hallway. No one was around. Darkness filled the space, save for the faint glow of a torchlight down the end of the hall. It cast eerie, haunting shadows up the walls. I shivered.

My footsteps were silent as I crept down the hall, halting every so often to listen. I wasn't sure exactly where I was going. And if I got to somewhere useful, what could I hope to do? Escape with nothing but the clothes on my back? I was woefully underprepared to make a run for it. To escape both an evil monarch and a marriage I didn't want.

The thought of being married off to a complete stranger turned my stomach. I braced my hand against a cool wall bearing a tapestry detailing the first Burnings. I would be married by the end of the week to a king I knew nothing of. Although, if Helmar were to be believed, then I knew one thing about my intended - that King Juriel wasn't exactly bright.

Perhaps escape would be easier under his watch.

Blessings come to us in strange ways.

Strange indeed.

I continued on and eventually found myself outside the throne room. I shivered and hurried past, wanting to put as much distance between the symbol of power and myself as possible. So preoccupied with getting away, I didn't register the sound of a second pair of footsteps until the person belonging to them took hold of me. Another hand cupped my mouth, stifling my shriek.

"Witchling," breathed a voice I knew too well. Malik's breath smelt strongly of ale. "What are you doing down here?"

He didn't release me. I wondered if he spoke only for his benefit. King Helmar certainly did. I had come to realise in the past months that some people spoke only for their amusement, not particularly caring for answers or clarity. I'd rather they shut up altogether.

Malik's hand on my arm tightened. "I'm going to take you back to your room and you're not going to make a sound, do you hear me? Or else you'll wake the king and I know you wouldn't want that, would you, witchling? Wouldn't want Helmar to take you back to the cells for a little fun."

I shook my head, sweat beading at my temples. Slowly, Malik pulled his hand from my mouth. I barely had time to catch my breath before he swung me up by the waist, winding me as his shoulder dug into my stomach. My fists beat against his back in silent protest, trying in vain to have the soldier release me. When he opened the bedroom door and swept in, every hair on the back of my neck stood on end.

Malik threw me down onto my bed, my head snapping back against the carved headboard.

"Leave," I demanded through gritted teeth.

He was already undoing his belt, a smug smile on his face. "Or what? You'll make me regret it? Remember, you *owe* me. For every scrap I gave you, every moment of kindness-"

"That was *not* kindness," I snapped, prodding my scalp. A lump was already forming. "Do not delude yourself into thinking you are capable of kindness."

"You owe me for keeping you alive."

Malik waited for me to speak, to say something. Nothing came.

Because the fact was that in the warden's quarters, I'd never really tried to fight. When Malik was done with me, I was usually fed something more substantial than the slop given to prisoners. But now? Now, I wanted to fight. I wasn't below anymore. I was one step closer to freedom.

And I wasn't giving that up for anything.

Do not break.

I rolled myself off the opposite side of the bed just as Malik dropped his belt to the floor.

"Good. I like the chase." His smirk was pure predator.

I ran across the room, unsure where to go. During the bath, the servant women had trimmed my hair, some parts far too matted to detangle. While most things from the evening were cleaned up, the scissors along with a brush and comb had been left behind. I made a beeline for the dresser. Three feet away, an arm encircled my waist, hefting me into the air. I kicked out my feet, thrashing every which way in an attempt to free myself. Malik walked back towards the bed and this time, when he threw me down, he covered my body with his own. The heavy weight of him on top of me pushed the air from my lungs. Every instinct cried out for me to run, escape him. Somehow.

But I was small and weak from my time in Purgatory. Malik, honed and built for war, was used to throwing around full-grown men. One tired female would do little to stop his intentions.

He wriggled, shoving his pants further down while one of his hands pinned my wrists above my head. I clenched my teeth so hard they might have cracked under the pressure. Every inch of me ached with exhaustion but I continued to fight, to try and roll him off me. Malik's free hand whipped sharply across my face. Stars and lights danced before me as the room spun. Another slap and shadows edged around my eyes, threatening to pull me under.

Malik's hard length pushed against my thigh. My legs clamped together and with a grunt he dug his knee between my legs, trying to force them open. With a quick twist and pull, I managed to free one of my hands. Before I could second-guess myself, I reached for his face, found his eye and pushed my thumb in as hard as I could. He roared and released me to cup his face in his meaty hands. Blood coated my thumb but I paid it no mind as I fell off the side of the bed and half crawled, half stumbled towards the dresser and the scissors.

With shaking fingers, I clamped down on the cold metal just as my ankle was painfully tugged on. My stomach hit the hard floor, sending a sharp pain lancing through my hips and ribs. Malik didn't let go of that ankle and when he tugged it again, I rolled onto my back. He stood over me, dressed in only his tunic. My gaze landed on his erect cock, looming over me, and when Malik saw me looking, he smiled.

"I told you I like the chase." His words were raspy, voice thick. "I like a fight. And I always win."

Using what little strength I had left, I pushed myself up and threw the scissors upwards, straight into his groin.

Malik screamed and toppled sideways. Blood pooled around him as the same hands that had only moments ago covered his injured eye now held onto his damaged manhood.

"You *bitch*," he swore. "You motherfucking *bitch*."

I scrambled back on all fours until my back hit the wall and held the scissors close to my chest like a talisman, something to protect against the evil before me. Malik's eyes were wild as he looked from his groin to me and back again, as though he couldn't quite believe I'd had it in me.

Truthfully, I almost couldn't believe it.

"I will kill you," he seethed, voice breathy.

"Enough."

We both turned our heads at the same time towards the speaker. My chest constricted yet again when my eyes found the cold, unfeeling ones of King Helmar. He stood just inside the doorway, clothed in a black robe. The servant woman who had helped me bathe hid behind him. As Helmar looked around the room, noting the evidence of struggle, his stony expression changed to one of amusement.

"Malik, you know the time for play has come to an end."

The soldier spoke through clenched teeth. "The bitch stabbed me."

"Consider it a minor payment for the enjoyment she's given you these past months. A bargain, I'd say."

I stared at the king, my panic and terror turning to red-hot hate.

"He tried to rape me," I spat. "Again."

Helmar raised an eyebrow. "A pity he did not succeed. *Again.*"

I opened my mouth to speak, stopping only when I noted the woman shaking her head, her eyes wide. Instead, I pressed myself harder against the wall, praying it might swallow me whole, and save me from the dark reality I now found myself trapped in. A reality where torture and rape were the bread and butter of those who held all the power.

"Malik, clean up," Helmar instructed. "Then return to your post. Find some other cunt to warm your cock. If you still have a cock by morning, that is."

The soldier threw a final loathsome look my way before hobbling from the bedroom. Without so much as a backward glance, Helmar followed suit, leaving me alone with the servant woman. She hurriedly closed the door and ran to my side.

"Silly girl," she muttered, pulling me to my feet. She clucked her tongue at my bloodied nightgown and tugged it off, ignoring my bruised and scarred body. Had she seen others like me? I'd expected her to gawk unashamedly. After all, I would have in her place. Something about the cool indifference oozing from her told me this wasn't the first time she'd borne witness to Helmar's cruelty. "Defending yourself here will get you nowhere."

A clean nightgown was pulled over my head and I shoved my fatigued arms and bloodied hands into the sleeves.

"Should I have just let him attack me?"

The woman cursed under her breath before replying. "No one is expecting you to accept your fate. Just to let what will be, *be*."

"That sounds an awful lot like accepting fate." I struggled to suppress a yawn and failed.

The woman tucked me back into bed, below sheets Malik had rumpled only mere minutes ago. I could still smell him. Sleep would be hard to come by, and possibly altogether impossible this night.

"What is your name?"

She looked up at me, grey eyes softening, and dropped the edge of the quilt. "Verity."

"Verity," I echoed. "Thank you."

If it wasn't for Verity, the night might have ended very differently. I decided I liked her. She was the closest thing I had to a friend in the castle now.

"You've three days here," she replied, a small crease forming between her brows. "Do try to keep your head down. There are far worse places to be, child."

CHAPTER FIFTEEN

"Fuss again and I will cut it all off."

I clamped my lips together and stared at the vanity mirror. Verity tugged on a braid that pulled at my scalp enough to make my eyes water. It wasn't the first time she'd threatened to make me bald and I was certain it wouldn't be the last with the sheer level of preparations yet to come. King Juriel and his delegation would arrive the following day.

My wedding day.

I shuddered at the thought, nausea roiling in my gut.

Tonight, a feast to celebrate. Celebrate what, exactly? Verity couldn't be certain. All she said was that King Helmar eagerly awaited the wedding.

In other words, he looked forward to securing more soldiers in his war to wipe out witchcraft, magic and healers across Cimran - all because of his hate for one woman who dared defy him. The thought that my wedding would facilitate countless murders was enough to make me sick. Yet I was powerless to stop the wheels put in motion. This was a sea I was lost to, bound to be tossed by wave after wave with nothing other than survival on my mind.

Verity tugged again and I winced.

Her eyes narrowed. "By all means, show up at dinner looking like a street urchin and see what happens. Princess Cerana will be dressed properly. The king will expect you to be also."

"The king doesn't care about me," I muttered.

Verity tied off the braid. "On the contrary, you are very valuable to him."

"What a joy it is to be considered little more than livestock to be traded."

She pursed her lips and started on another braid. My hair was once again returned to silky, endless black. The end of several braids hung curled down my back, one over my shoulder. I toyed with the end of it restlessly, smoothing the hair through and around my fingers to soothe my nerves, just as I had done as a girl.

"Livestock live a good life in these times. They're more valuable than gold."

I snorted.

"Laugh all you want but is this not preferable to the mountain?"

At that, I sobered. Verity was right. As awful as it was to be closer to King Helmar, to have my body sold off in marriage, I did prefer not to be beaten and tortured daily. Not that I didn't still bear the evidence of it. Fine scars covered my collarbones and chest, made by the pointed tip of a double-edged dagger. Each cut had been shallow, though deep enough to leave a lasting reminder. Sometimes I wondered if the king enjoyed seeing the scars more than the blood. On more than one occasion, I'd caught him eyeing their pale lines, a glint in his eye.

My back was thatched and puckered. I'd looked in the mirror a day ago and that was more than enough. 'Deformed' was the word that came to mind. Verity had said I was being too hard on myself, that it really wasn't so bad. In the short time I'd known her, I'd come to realise she sugar-coated the harshest truths.

My face was no better. One half was covered in a blotchy bruise from where Malik hit me. The other side bore a long scar, one of the oldest on my body. It trailed from my temple to my jaw. Growing up, I had always considered myself to be beautiful. I had the flawless, creamy skin women paid Emrys a good deal of money for. He made them tonics and tinctures to produce a glow that could never be properly manufactured. Yet now, the creature staring back at me was far from beautiful. She was hollow, a badly damaged shell. Worn and cracked and leaving little of her former beauty behind. I hated looking at myself - and it had only been a few days near a mirror since leaving Naiva.

As though sensing my thoughts, Verity placed a gentle hand on my shoulder. "I have a plan for that, child. Do not worry. Makeup can cover a multitude of sins."

'Sins.' Perhaps that's what it was - evidence of my guilt. Because whether I liked it or not, I was guilty in some way. Association with magic was as damning as committing the crime yourself. Never mind the inherited guilt of being born of Queen Iseult.

Ultimately, I didn't have it in me to tell Verity that what I most needed covered was the emptiness I felt inside. There was no easy fix for that.

When Verity was done with my hair, braids were criss-crossed behind my head, forming a lattice pattern. There would be no one other than the king, Cerana and his advisors at dinner so makeup was kept minimal - just enough to diffuse the discomfort everyone would surely feel should they deign to look my way. I was dressed in a blue, long-sleeved, low-cut dress. Somehow I got the impression that this was for the king's benefit more than anything. A peace offering of a kind from Verity for waking him the other night. Inwardly, I recoiled at the thought but couldn't damn her for the gesture. She had no idea who Helmar was to me. As far as she was aware, I was simply another whore degraded by his hand.

The dining hall was as equally grand as the rest of the castle. A gilded chandelier laden with dozens of dripping candles hung over the centre of a long dining table. Droplets of wax hit the wooden tabletop and I stared at them, watching each one dry in the cool air. Because despite the fires roaring in their hearths around us, the atmosphere at the table was practically arctic.

No one spoke as King Helmar ate and drank first. It was customary to allow the king to sample everything - after the servants sampled each plate to ensure nothing was poisoned - before anyone else had so much as a sip of water. I held a hand against my stomach in an attempt to muffle the growling sounds of hunger. I was still kept to a similar meal schedule as under the mountain, the only real difference being the quality of food given.

Finally, someone picked up their fork and the rest of the table began to eat. I forced myself to slow down, to chew rather than inhale whole morsels of lamb. I ate through one plate and eagerly took more when offered. Halfway through a third plate of roast vegetables and roasted lamb, I felt queasy and pushed the leftovers away.

Princess Cerana watched me out of the corner of her eye, just as she had done from the moment I arrived in the dining hall. She was stunning, clearly taking after her mother rather than Helmar. Her hair hung in vibrant crimson waves down her back and her skin was almost as white as snow. Luminous green eyes framed by thick, dark lashes took in everything around her with careful scrutiny. Cerana carried herself like the woman of noble birth she was - the woman I would have been had things been *very* different. Every movement was effortless, graceful and poised. Watching her was mesmerising and for a brief moment, I understood why Helmar didn't want to marry her off to King Juriel. She was a person to be protected, kept safe at all costs. Cerana was not the kind of princess you sold for personal gain. From the way the king looked at her, he held nothing but love for his daughter.

And then there was I, his firstborn, loathed and abused because of who my mother was.

The remainder of the table was full of men talking amongst themselves. Some voices rang out over the others, boasting of victory in the war and conquests. Tales of Burnings and raids were recounted at length to the ringing sounds of laughter. Each story made my mood darken more and more. I forced myself to think about something else.

This time tomorrow I would be a wife. Married, wearing a ring that might as well be a pair of heavy iron shackles, binding me to a man I'd never met. Would King Juriel be kind to me? I was no fool to believe he would expect nothing of me as his wife. My duty would be to produce a suitable heir. Beyond my womb and cunt, however, I would be of no use to him. Perhaps I could eventually lead a quiet life in Nimue, rarely seen and barely heard. That, I could settle for. And who knew, maybe in time I could garner enough favour with Juriel to secure an exchange for Emrys. Surely Nimue had something other than soldiers and weapons to offer King Helmar. Everything has a price. Even the life of a healer guilty of treason.

Emrys just needed to survive long enough for that to happen.

I didn't notice the scraping of a chair beside me until someone cleared their throat.

"I don't believe we've met."

Princess Cerana smiled at me in that manufactured, polite way all royals did. To appear normal, even warm - to seem kind on some level. I returned her smile though there was nothing but emptiness behind my own. I longed to return to the bedroom, crawl under the quilt and sleep - even if it did put me one step closer to a marriage I didn't want.

"Pleasure, princess."

She inclined her head, fiery curls falling over her shoulder. "I believe thanks and well wishes are in order."

"You have nothing to thank me for," I replied. I picked up my goblet and drank deeply, instantly feeling the alcohol rush to my head. Blissful release. For the moment, anyway.

Her smile faltered. "Actually, I do. While I do not wish it upon anyone to be wed to a man such as Juriel, I am thankful that you offered to take my place."

I nearly choked on my mouthful and swallowed painfully. "I offered?"

"It was very kind of you."

I felt a pair of eyes on me and when I glanced around the room I found those of King Helmar. There was a warning inherent in the way he looked at me. A warning I dared not ignore.

With a manufactured smile plastered across my face, I turned back to Princess Cerana. "Of course, your grace. To be of service to Cimran is an honour."

"My blessings and hopes for a happy future to you, cousin."

With that, the princess left the dining hall, planting a kiss on her father's cheek on the way. I returned Helmar's gaze with an equally hateful one of my own, wondering what the hell he'd told Cerana about me. Cousin? A twisted truth if ever there was one. No doubt the princess had no real idea of who I was. Did she not at all wonder where this supposed 'cousin' had been all her life? But then, royals, as Emrys had once said, bred like rabbits. Throw a rock in a city such as Lanceris and you'd likely strike noble blood. To suddenly have a long-lost cousin surface would have been far from surprising.

Helmar's gaze was unflinching and in a rare moment of boldness, I sneered at him.

I would go through with this wedding if for no other reason than to escape him.

*

The window of my bedroom looked out across Lanceris and by night, the city was a patchwork of stars. Darkened, sleepy windows mirrored the sky above, showing a snippet of life beyond the castle walls. I sat on a stool beside the window, head resting against the cool glass. For hours I'd sat here, watching a life I had never been particularly jealous of until now. I would happily trade places with anyone below if it meant escaping this arranged marriage.

The streets were quiet save for the odd patrolling soldier. Even by moonlight, Helmar ran a tight ship. Fear of the king coated the air so thick it was a greasy film suffocating all traces of life.

My wedding dress hung across the room, brought in by Verity during dinner. I glanced at it, admiring the fine lace detailing, and the fullness of the skirts. Whoever had made it was talented, gifted even. But it had clearly not been designed for me. There were additions sewn onto it, little scraps of fabric to hide the evidence of Helmar's predilections. What had once been a low-cut, sleeveless gown now bore a high collar and sleeves down to the wrist, made of a lace thicker than that of the rest of the gown. Just looking at it made me sweat. Despite the chill of winter, I would boil under the fabric.

Perhaps from stress more than anything, but boil nevertheless. Fitting, since I was in hell.

A veil accompanied the dress, hanging beside it. When tried on, I could scarcely see my hand inches from my face.

"How am I supposed to walk with this on?"

Verity half shrugged. "The king will give you away. You'll not need to see, girl. Simply follow. Silently."

I would marry King Juriel blind in more ways than one, it seemed.

Offered, my arse. I would sooner offer myself to the jaws of a lion than to a loveless, faceless marriage - especially one that would result in senseless genocide.

I returned to looking out the window, ignoring the abundance of lace and misery.

Below on the street, something was stirring. I couldn't hear anything so far above the city but I felt it, a humming in the air. A moment later, a procession came into view. Dozens of horses and carriages, carts and wagons. Soldiers clad in armour and carrying banners bearing the winged sigil of House Sorega.

King Juriel had arrived. Early.

I watched as the procession drew ever closer to the castle, winding through silent streets. Just as when Emrys and I arrived, there was no one to greet the king of Nimue. Members of The Cleanse stood aside to permit the delegation passage through the streets but were watchful, careful and wary of the outsiders. The Nimue delegation reached the castle and beyond my bedroom door, I heard a commotion.

A moment later, Verity entered.

"Get dressed," she snapped, eyes frantic. Her hands fussed about the wardrobe as she searched.

I moved to her side. "What's happening? It's well after midnight."

The wedding wasn't due to happen until late the following afternoon. I still had time, didn't I? I wasn't so ready to give up what little ounce of freedom I still possessed. Because even if I was a prisoner, I was not tied to a man for life in the eyes of the gods. I was still my own person and every remaining minute of that was precious.

"I don't know, girl," she huffed, tugging my nightgown over my head. "All I've been told is to get you dressed and to the throne room."

Verity made quick work of dressing me in swathes of fabric. Being of a similar cut to my wedding gown was where the similarities ended - this gown was of such a deep black it swallowed any nearby traces of light. Appropriate, considering I was in mourning. She drew my hair back into a low bun and hastily applied makeup, muttering about how the darkness would conceal most of the blemishes anyway. I knew enough about the woman to not fuss and to simply take everything she did without complaint. When Verity was done, I barely glimpsed myself in the mirror - wide-eyed and struggling to conceal the terror on my face - before she ushered us from the bedroom.

The walk to the throne room felt like an eternity. Along the way, I spotted officials and soldiers scuttling about like bees in a hive. Some appeared busy, I suspected, so as not to draw unwanted attention. Idleness was as much a crime as magic.

"What on earth happened?" I whispered. Something felt wrong. Very wrong.

Verity said nothing, just hurried me along faster.

King Helmar stood before his throne, pacing back and forth with a look on his face that made me want to shrink back. I had seen him look angry in Purgatory, but this was downright murderous. I dug my heels into the stone floor as Verity pushed me closer. When the king finally exploded, I didn't want to be anywhere near him, lest I be caught in the fallout.

Helmar grunted at my appearance before turning to one of his officials, a thin, bony man with grey hair I recognised from dinner.

"Where are they?"

"Coming, my lord."

I lowered my eyes, staring at my booted feet. Slowly, I counted to one hundred and then backwards. Just as I reached twenty-nine, the throne room doors scraped open. Everyone hushed, all heads turning.

A small man entered on his own. He reminded me of the squirrels that lived behind my cottage in Naiva. Brave when they needed to be but for the most part, skittish. The way he held himself told me that he hadn't come of his own will. But as he halted before King Helmar and bowed low, he mustered enough courage to look the king in the eye.

"Well?" Helmar demanded. "Where is he? Pulls me from my bed in the middle of the night. There ought to be a damned good reason."

The little man's lips pressed into a thin line. "My apologies, your highness. King Juriel passed away."

That caught my attention. A small sound fell from my lips. Verity pinched the underside of my arm in warning.

"Passed away?" Helmar's eyes narrowed. "How?"

"His heart was ailing in his old age. His death was not unexpected."

"We have a treaty," Helmar growled, temper flaring in an instant. His eyes darkened to a hellish black.

To his credit, the messenger didn't balk.

"We have every intention of honouring that treaty, Your Majesty."

Helmar descended the steps leading to his throne, approaching the messenger. "And how, pray tell, do you intend to do that with no king to wed?"

The messenger opened his mouth to speak but the words that came out were not his own.

"There is a new king."

Everyone's attention turned to the main doors where a man stood.

My heart thundered in my chest because he truly was the most breathtaking person I had ever laid eyes on. Clad in black leather, armour and a white fur cloak, he stood a head above the rest. His hair was nearly as inky as my own and swept back in a leather thong, revealing a long nose and thick brows. His eyes were pure sea glass green, a colour so vibrant that no painter would ever be able to replicate it. His mouth was full, one corner lifted in a smirk, and despite the neatly clipped beard he wore, I suspected there might have been a dimple hiding underneath. Tan skin boasting of days in the sun covered his forearms. I caught myself wondering if he was that golden beneath the armour, if he was as muscular as he appeared to be.

Whether he felt like sin and lust to the touch.

"Who are *you*?" Helmar demanded.

The man walked forward, completely at ease. I admired the way he looked at the king without a shred of fear or trepidation. His footsteps did not falter when Helmar puffed out his chest and lifted his chin, trying to close the gap between their heights - a considerable gap given that Helmar stood atop the dais bearing his throne. On an even footing, the stranger would tower over the king. When he came to a stop several feet from Helmar, he inclined his head in a simple acknowledgement.

"Prince Thorn of House Sorega," he said, voice smoother than velvet and deep enough to send a pleasant shiver scuttling along my spine. A voice like that could have told me to throw myself from a bridge and I'd have complied with haste. "Though I suppose you may refer to me as *King* Thorn now."

Helmar stalked forward, standing almost toe to toe with King Thorn of House Sorega who didn't budge and if anything, seemed amused. His eyes flickered up and down Helmar, weighing up the man before him. I could tell from the look on his face that King Thorn was far from impressed.

"And who are you to claim the seat of the king?"

"I am the king's firstborn."

Helmar's eyes narrowed. "I didn't know Juriel had a son."

Thorn's smirk widened. "I suppose there is a lot you did not know about Juriel. Like for instance how he was on his deathbed when he signed your godsforsaken treaty."

King Helmar's face reddened as his jaw clenched and unclenched in time with his fists. "That treaty is binding. To break it will cost you dearly."

"Oh, I'm fully aware," King Thorn continued. "And as my messenger said, Nimue has every intention of honouring it. A marriage with a king was promised and a marriage with a king you so shall have."

"What? You?"

King Thorn glanced behind himself before sweeping his arms about the room. "Yes. *Me*. Unless you see any other kings wandering about?"

Helmar snorted, throwing his hands in the air. "Have it your way then. Something is better than nothing, I suppose."

King Thorn inclined his head once more before turning his back on Helmar. I didn't miss the way Verity's mouth popped open in surprise. No one turned their back on King Helmar, the so-called 'Great Defender of Cimran.' The level of disrespect that came with it would cost you your freedom.

And your head.

"Till tomorrow then."

I watched as Thorn left the throne room, barely keeping a lid on the rising panic in my chest. The last two days I had mentally prepared myself for marriage to King Juriel and although I'd not once laid eyes on the old man, it was what I was braced for. But this, a marriage to his *son*...

Definitely not something I was prepared for, though there was a part of me deep within that was excited by the prospect. I would have been lying to myself had I said I wasn't attracted to the young king. It had been instantaneous, my body awakening after a long slumber, one I had been deep within since leaving Soraya behind. His presence made my very core vibrate with need. After Soraya, I assumed that part of me was dead, murdered by her betrayal. I didn't think I could ever desire another.

Until now.

Until *him*.

"A young king," Helmar said, a sly smile on his face as he turned to me, "will do just nicely. After all, it is the young ones that have the most to prove. He may yet be the kind of husband to break your spirit."

CHAPTER SIXTEEN

Preparations for the wedding were well underway by the time Verity arrived at my bedroom just after dawn. For the first time in months, I had been fed breakfast, morning tea and lunch - not out of kindness. I strongly suspected that having a bride pass out from malnutrition on her wedding day would not bode well for any treaty brokered between the two kingdoms. My stomach ached from the sheer volume of food consumed and for a brief moment, I wondered if my wedding dress would even fit. But then I remembered who it had been made for. A princess who had never in her life been starved, who had all the right curves befitting a woman who would one day be farmed out for her true purpose - to bear children to another king, ensuring the continuation of his house. I looked down at myself and saw only bones poking out where they had no business to. Including my wrist, healed at an angle too awkward to be ignored.

It was a sober affair, preparing for the wedding. Verity kept quiet save for the odd instruction to turn this way and that. My hair was woven into an intricate braid and then tied back at the nape of my neck. The low knot of braids and curls was so large I could see it rounding outwards when I looked at my reflection head-on. A sweeping of hair was carefully draped across the side of my face to conceal the thin scar, still a little pink in the faint afternoon light.

Makeup was applied in layer after layer, so heavy that my skin could no longer breathe. When I looked in the mirror, I didn't recognise the woman staring back. This one was entirely different. Her face was painted to look alive and rosy, to give the appearance of free youth and beauty. But deep in her eyes there laid the truth - there was nothing but an immense emptiness and sad resignation to her fate.

"You look lovely," Verity finally said as she took a step back. "No one will know."

I sighed. "I will."

"That's why we have the veil, child. So in case your face gives away the truth, it will at least be hidden."

I fell silent, my fingers picking at the skin around my nails. It was a nervous habit, one developed beneath the mountain as my nails slowly regrew. After King Helmar had forcibly removed them for the first time, they had itched something fierce while healing. What started as absentminded scratching turned into a nervous tick, something to soothe in a place where there was nothing to quiet my mind. Sometimes I didn't even realise I was doing it, like now. Verity placed her hands over my own, kneeling beside my chair.

"Take heart," she whispered. "King Thorn may yet prove to be a good man."

"That won't be seen until it's too late," I replied.

"It's already too late, child."

The sun drifted downwards on the horizon, sliding behind thick grey clouds that threatened more snow. A light smattering covered rooftops already but the worst was yet to come. A storm had been warned. Fitting for the day.

The wedding gown weighed heavily on my shoulders. Yards upon yards of tulle and lace surrounded me, hiding the bleak reality of my small size after months of torture and abuse.

"I'm being swallowed whole," I muttered.

Verity merely clucked as she pinned the dress to fit better at my lower back. She continued to fuss, cinching in here and there. Despite Princess Cerana and I being the same height, our bodies were vastly different, no thanks to her father.

"This will have to do," Verity finally said as she stepped away, eyes roaming over me from head to toe. "If I pull it in any more, King Thorn might throw you back like an undersized fish."

"Now there's an image I needed."

"Perhaps he can fatten you up when you return to Nimue."

That was yet another thought I'd refused to entertain. As much as I wanted to put distance between Helmar and myself, leaving my home was a terrifying idea. I'd not once stepped beyond Cimran's borders and as much as I dreamed of adventure, the cold reality was that someone of my standing would never have the chance to venture far. It was a mere dream, never to come true.

Yet, in just a few day's I would depart Lanceris, cross the border of Cimran and Nimue where strategically placed outposts full of grunt soldiers stood watch, and find a new home.

With King Thorn.

I gulped, feeling sweat trickle down my back. The neckline was two firm hands squeezing my throat, slowly suffocating me. I shook out my arms, trying to down as much air as I could before fear pulled me under.

Do not break. Do not break. Do not break.

The words looped through my mind, bringing me back from the downward spiral I was in danger of riding.

"Shoes."

Verity held out a white slipper made of the softest satin. I put my foot into it and then followed with the other. The thought that I wouldn't run very far in them crossed my mind. Had Helmar thought of that, too? Would someone be watching me at all times to ensure I followed through with the wedding?

As if I had any say in the matter. Regardless, I would do this for Emrys, a thousand times over and then some more. For the man who had raised me as his own, I would sell my soul to the devil to ensure the protection of his. Get through the wedding, get to Nimue, make good with the king and then plead like hell to trade for Emrys' life. He would like Nimue, a kingdom fraught with nothing worse than the very best. It would be a safe haven for Emrys to grow old...er.

Three sharp knocks sounded at the bedroom door.

"It's time."

*

The throne room was decorated lavishly. No expense had been spared on the wedding originally intended for King Helmar's beloved daughter. I knew that had I been the intended bride all along, the affair would be less than decent. Most likely in one of the stables behind the castle. Wreaths of baby's breath and lemon myrtle hung throughout the room, lining the aisle, and draped across the backs of rows of chairs. A plush indigo carpet ran up the centre of the room, cutting through masses of bodies with nameless faces.

Suddenly, I felt incredibly alone.

An arm looped through mine.

"Make one wrong move," Helmar muttered under his breath, his mouth close to my ear, "and I will be with Emrys tonight. He will get to experience the fun you and I have had. Perhaps I'll begin with The Tub just as I did for you."

I said nothing, only shrank beneath the veil to hide the tears welling in my eyes. I breathed slowly through my nose, willing myself to stay strong.

Music played on violins, a light tune I didn't know. Any other time, I would have thought the melody pretty but now, it was the morbid droning of a funeral march. I focused on putting one step in front of the other, ignoring the tight, almost painful hold Helmar kept on my arm. I thought of Emrys, why I was doing this, and knew that failure was not an option. So I straightened my spine and steeled my nerves.

It barely worked.

"Keep going," King Helmar commanded behind a broad smile that was more barred teeth than anything.

I climbed the three steps to the dais where the throne stood and let myself be turned in a half circle by the king. I heard murmurs all around, and sensed bodies nearby but beneath the veil, my world was lonely. Then light drifted over my face as the veil was pulled away to reveal King Thorn.

This close, he was heart-achingly beautiful. His eyes were more stunning than I'd originally thought them to be. As I looked into them, I saw some dark emotion I couldn't put my finger on. He was dressed in finery, a forest green tunic and copper fur cloak that one could likely survive on the sale of for some years to come. Atop his head he wore a crown crafted of intertwining branches - driftwood, if I wasn't mistaken. But overall, there was a natural, rustic quality surrounding the young king. He reminded me of home, of everything I loved and missed with pain so acute, it sliced like a dagger through my chest. That simple thought of home was comfort enough to stem the rising panic.

The next moment, however, that panic grew when King Thorn raised his hand to my face slowly. I fought not to duck my head, hide, not when he would see me soon enough - *really* see me. Thorn's thumb swiped across my cheek, smearing the thick layer of makeup. I knew what he would see beneath it - a bruise layered upon another, both slowly healing, still purple in parts while yellow and brown in others. I shook and dug my fingernails into my palms, trying to conceal each tremor. Thorn looked down at the slight movement and drew my hands into his own. He gingerly held my poorly healed wrist and examined it closely, fingers barely touching the misshapen lump of bones.

I felt like an item in a marketplace, being examined before the haggling began.

Was this the point King Thorn would decide I wasn't worth the treaty? The thought only made me shake more because I knew what the result would be - I would return beneath Dearmond and to Purgatory. Tortured until eventually my body - or mind - gave out.

His luminescent green eyes were locked on mine when he spoke, his words sharp and cutting across the throne room.

"Who did this to my wife?"

Silence fell thick and heavy. I didn't dare breathe or pull my hands away from Thorn as he waited for an answer. His gaze fell to my cheek once more before he repeated himself.

"I'll not ask a second time," he growled with carefully concealed fury. "Who did this to my *wife and queen*?"

The way he said that one final word made me shift uneasily. A possession with a nice title. That's all I was.

Behind me, a throat cleared before a deep voice answered.

"She was punished for treason against the crown," said King Helmar. "The punishment was befitting the crime, I can assure you."

Thorn's eyes darkened to a deep jade green, the only sign of his displeasure.

"What crimes?" he asked, still not looking anywhere but me. "And why punish her when being of your blood is punishment enough?"

I tried to swallow past the lump in my throat but I couldn't. I didn't understand what was happening. Why was Thorn asking these things? Why did he even care? Helmar had said all King Juriel wanted was somewhere warm to stick his cock. I had expected about as much from his son. The only purpose I would serve was the forming of an alliance and perhaps, one day, children. If I wasn't damaged, that was. Gods knew the lasting damage I might have incurred over the past months. All I was worth was my reproductive organs and I'd not menstruated for so long now.

I felt King Helmar approach, his footsteps heavy, and my shoulders hunched. A movement that didn't escape Thorn's notice.

"Remember our deal, *prince*. Choose your words wisely."

At the mention of the word 'prince', Thorn looked past me to where Helmar stood. I could practically feel the king's hot breath against my back. I wanted to vomit.

"One you need far more than Nimue does," Thorn replied, his voice cool and even. "No contract, however, is worth tolerating the mistreatment of my wife. If you ever lay a hand on her again, I will raze your kingdom to ruin and see that you are entirely incapable of *life*. Am I understood?"

Helmar was silent, the only sound that of his retreating footsteps.

The ceremony was over quickly. In my mind, it was to be a drawn-out affair, something to be suffered through one hour at a time. Yet it became clear that King Helmar had intended the wedding to be short enough that neither party had time to back out of it, thus securing his army and arsenal.

"Under the eyes of the gods," the priest spoke, "I declare you man and wife."

I braced myself for the inevitable, the sealing of the marriage, but Thorn made no move to kiss me. A flicker of disappointment ran through me too fast to stop. I was revolting. Revolting and scarred and damaged. Not fit for a king - not even fit for a slave. Perhaps he wouldn't consummate the marriage and I might be queen and wife in title only, a fixture in his court. It wasn't uncommon for kings to take lovers. Perhaps a legitimised bastard would be heir to the throne, rather than a child born of my womb.

A small voice in the back of my mind debated whether that would be a disappointment or not, either.

I went through the motions of the evening, not talking, merely nodding instead when well wishes and congratulations were offered with little emotion behind the words. During the toast, I drank deeply, trying to drown out the misery that welled inside. There was an endless source of merriment all around and it tasted bitter on my tongue. I could not forget that along with my marriage was also the signing of hundreds of death warrants for innocents throughout Cimran. King Helmar would have his reinforced army any day now and with it, enough bloodshed to turn all the rivers of Cimran crimson.

Verity came to collect me when the evening grew late. I followed silently, gut twisting as she led me down hallways I had not stepped foot in before.

"Where are we going?"

"To the marital suite."

Marital suite. I was a wife now. Something I'd always believed would be my decision, be it to a man or woman, had been forcibly taken from me. A tear slipped from the corner of my eye and I swiped it away, makeup smearing on my fingertips in the process.

The suite was twice the size of my room. Obnoxiously large when you considered it was only for one couple. In the centre of it stood a four-poster bed set with intricately woven quilts and pillows. A fire roared in the hearth and I began to sweat under my gown all over again. It itched against my skin and in that moment I wanted nothing more than to tear it from my body and heap it upon the twisting flames.

"Here," Verity said. "I'll help you undress."

I found myself shaking my head.

"How will you get out of it on your own, child?"

"I won't," I simply replied.

Verity eyed me for a second before slipping from the bedroom. I stood before the fire, mind blank, until I heard the lock in the door click once more. I turned my head to see King Thorn standing just inside the doorway.

"You've nothing to fear from me," he said in a soothing voice as he closed the door behind himself.

While I was inclined to believe Thorn given the way he'd stood up for me during the ceremony, I replied, "Many great men have uttered those words. Many of them lied."

Curiosity flickered in his eyes and he cocked his head to the side, contemplating quietly for a moment.

"Do you think me a liar?" he finally asked.

"I think you are an untested king who will struggle to establish his rule without force." I loosed a shuddering breath. "So yes, in part, I do think you a liar."

Thorn nodded to himself as he pulled off his fur cloak and set it on an armchair.

"It is true," he replied. "I *am* an untested king. Gods, I'm not even technically *king* yet. But I've no inclination to establish my rule at the cost of my wife. I have every intention of you ruling at my side - not suffering under my foot."

"Intentions are as common as pebbles in a stream. Fulfilment of those intentions, not so much."

"Time will tell then." He crossed the room to a table holding decanters of various shapes and sizes. "A drink?"

"Please."

I'd not touched my dinner and drunk only wine. Tomorrow, my head would hurt something fierce. For now, I needed the courage hard liquor would provide. Thorn moved to my side and handed me a glass which I took, carefully avoiding his fingers. The memory of his hands holding mine had not yet left my skin, the phantom touch still ever-present. It was a heady feeling, to be touched kindly - or at least, with the absence of anger - after so long.

I downed the amber liquid in one gulp, my throat searing in the wake of it's heat. Thorn took my now empty glass and placed it on the table. When he turned back, he caught me fanning my face. This close to the fire, I was roasting alive.

"Did no one offer to help you undress?" His eyes narrowed as he took in the miles of tulle and lace.

"They did. I just needed to be alone."

He nodded, moving around behind me. I jumped, swallowing a yelp, when I felt his fingers brush against my neck as he unfastened each button with deft fingers.

"I apologise if I seem too forward," he murmured. "But I'd rather my wife not die of heat exhaustion before the day is through."

His fingers descended lower and lower until he met the final button at my lower back. Fresh air hit my damp skin and felt so good that a low moan escaped my mouth.

"I'll give you a moment to undress," he said as he headed for the bathroom. "There's a robe in the closet."

The moment the door shut, I shoved the sleeves of the dress down and let it fall into a pillowy heap on the floor. I stepped out of it, treating the bundle as something poisonous and retreated to the wardrobe. The robe that hung in amongst the other clothes was thin and designed for Thorn's eyes before my comfort. I groaned at it, feeling panic rising once more before I gritted my teeth and shoved it on.

Thorn reentered, some of his own layers removed until he was in just his pants and a light linen shirt. I tried to ignore the way the linen hugged broad, muscular shoulders. Or the glimpse of golden skin down the centre of his chest, the topmost buttons lazily undone to reveal the beginnings of a tattoo. I caught myself, eyes wandering lower, examining the man I was now bound to with sharp curiosity. He froze, eyes raking over me in kind. I banded my arms across my chest.

"Come here," he said, holding out his hand. "Please."

I moved across the room on shaking feet, coming to a stop before Thorn. Sooner or later he would see. Now was as good a time as any.

His eyes moved over my face, still covered in makeup before dropping to my neck, chest, arms and legs. Seeing scars beneath the thin fabric, he sucked in a quick breath, the sound almost pained. Some scars were puckered and still purple, no sooner to healing than the day they were made. Bruises covered my ribs from the start of the week when Helmar had used his fists. The robe stopped mid-thigh and revealed a multitude of scratches and scrapes along my legs. His eyes couldn't see the worst of it, though - the damage that was slowly rotting away within, poisoning the few untouched parts of me.

Thorn hissed through his teeth, face hard.

"I'm sorry, your grace." My voice was barely audible above the roaring in my ears.

Thorn cleared his throat but when he spoke, his voice was hoarse. "Whatever for?"

"I imagine that when you considered having a wife, you would not have wanted one in a somewhat...used condition." Embarrassment coloured my face. I wanted to run to the bed and curl up under the quilt so he couldn't see me, see the shame that clung to my frame like a second, equally bruised, skin.

Instead, Thorn reached out, his fingers gently lifting my chin so my eyes met his.

"Were you touched?"

There was something about the way he said the words that told me he wasn't asking about the physical wounds visible to the naked eye, but rather the wounds left by Malik, by the way he took me for his pleasure and reduced me to an empty husk in a way Helmar never achieved. I shook, releasing a gust of breath in one quick blow.

"Yes."

His jaw clenched as he pulled his fingers away.

"I'll see myself out." I fumbled out a curtsy like I'd watched Verity do before King Helmar and turned to leave. To go where? Where could I possibly go? I was bound to this marriage. But distance, perhaps that would help Thorn accept the manacles that were I and the trauma I wore like a glove.

I felt a hand softly take my own.

"Do not leave," Thorn whispered. "What happened to you is vile but not your fault, Artura."

It was the first time he'd referred to me by name. Until now, I'd only been his 'wife' - never *me*. Never Artura, a name that died in Naiva the moment The Cleanse tore me from my home. To hear my name gently spoken - and with kindness, no less - threatened to undo me entirely. I gazed up at Thorn.

"I see you as no less of a person for what has happened to you. In all actuality, the very fact you stand here before me with your head held high makes me think you are much, much more than I could have ever anticipated or dreamed of in a wife."

"Your dreams must be woefully underwhelming," I mumbled.

He smirked. "Not when they're about someone so strong as you, someone with a hidden fire. I see it in you, you know. I felt it the moment I arrived last night."

"Fire can burn out."

He cocked his head to the side, eyeing me speculatively. "For some." He was silent for a moment before changing the subject. "Let me care for you."

I pulled my hand from his and moved away. "I do not need your pity."

"It is not pity." I heard the smile behind his words. "But rather, adoration. My father made sure my mother had everything she needed, right up until she breathed her last. But he did not treasure her for the gift that she was. Let me treasure you, Artura, the way you deserve."

"You do not know what I deserve."

He nodded slowly. "True. But I know what you *don't* deserve and that is every single thing that has happened to you here."

I sat down in a chair by the fire while Thorn collected a bowl of steaming water from the bathroom. He brought with him a vial of clear liquid that he tipped in.

"It's not poison," he said, busying himself with dampening a cloth. "Just in case you were wondering."

I stiffened. "If I thought you would poison me, king, I did not think it would be this night. Most men take what they need before ridding themselves of burdensome wives."

He looked up at me and winked. "I am not most men."

Thorn squeezed out the cloth and brought it to my cheek, wiping away the thick layer of makeup while his free hand cupped the other side of my face. I felt myself relaxing under his careful ministrations and the water turned murky in a matter of minutes. Verity had applied at least a year's worth of makeup to my face to hide the truth - a truth now plainly seen by my husband.

He emptied the bowl and refilled it several times over, cleaning my face, my hair, and my body. It should have felt far too intimate but instead, it simply felt right. There was no awkwardness, much to my surprise, and when he lifted the cloth yet again to clean across my back, I welcomed his touch.

It went beyond cleaning a layer of makeup off my skin. In many ways, with each stroke, Thorn removed a memory from below the mountain, a harsh word spoken or a hand used too roughly. He soothed broken parts in me and for the first time in months, made me feel safe. By the time he was done, I felt relaxed - something I'd thought would never happen again. The memories were far from truly gone but for the moment were at least muted somewhat.

Thorn looked at me, his eyes filled with a heat that curled in my core.

Instantly, I felt my blood turn ice cold.

Had this all been for selfish reasons? Was he merely preparing me for him, to fulfil my duties on our wedding night as intended? Were there ulterior motives where I'd thought there to be only kindness? I was a fool, thirsty for even the smallest ounce of kindness - real or otherwise.

Thorn stood to his feet and carried the bowl back to the bathroom. When he returned, he was drying his hands on a towel.

"Will you leave now?" I asked.

He paused, cocking his head to the side as he studied me. "Not unless you wish me to. However, I will say that you are the only thing stopping me from walking down the hall to slaughter in cold blood the filth that touched you. No one has the right to raise a hand to a woman."

I snorted. "Didn't take you for the sexist type."

Thorn smiled, the expression reaching his eyes. "Let me rephrase: no one has the right to lay a hand against someone incapable of defending themselves."

I bristled at that. "I am no victim."

Thorn dropped the towel on the table beside the decanters. "I would never think of you as one. To be a victim is to be robbed of all power. There is a power in you, Artura. I see it."

I pondered his words as I moved to the bed, suddenly exhausted. Coupled with little to no sleep the night before, this day had been never-ending. I was weary down to my bones. No, to my marrow. It was an exhaustion unlike any other.

"So you'll stay then?"

"As I said, you are the only thing stopping me from committing regicide."

I pulled back the quilt and climbed in. While washing me, I'd removed the robe and still wore nothing. I had never been particularly shy of my naked body and had, for the most part, considered myself beautiful. The thought that I ought to be shy now came to mind but I simply couldn't bring myself to feel shame at being naked before Thorn. Of being damaged? Yes, there was shame, immensely so. But not of being bared before the man that was now my husband. Sooner or later I would have been exposed anyway. Might as well be now.

"Happy to be of service, in that case."

I sank below the quilt, instantly warming. Thorn removed his shirt and came around the other side of the bed. He stopped when my brows drew together, sensing my unease.

"No, Artura, I'll not take advantage of you. I know this marriage was not what you intended so I will wait. Besides, when I do fuck you, I need you to want it. Not to succumb to me out of obligation. I'll not take what is not freely given."

I didn't trust myself to speak so instead I nodded. The mattress dipped under his weight as he climbed in beside me and I fell asleep to the comforting feel of a warm body nearby.

CHAPTER SEVENTEEN

Eternal gratitude was a gross understatement for how I felt when Verity knocked on the bedroom door early the next morning, carrying a tray laden with pastries and fruits. I didn't pause before snatching up a croissant, tearing off a piece and shoving it in my mouth. Thorn sat in an armchair near the fire, emerald eyes watching me closely.

"I didn't disturb you, did I?"

I looked up at him mid-chew, raising an eyebrow.

He gestured down at himself and I saw he was dressed for the day already. "I usually wake early - something leftover from my time training in the south."

I didn't enquire further as to what training he did exactly. I wasn't sure I even wanted to know. The South was not known for its soft-hearted nature but rather ruthlessness and ferocity.

"No, you didn't wake me."

"We'll leave tomorrow morning. I've some preparations to attend to for my father's body."

Suddenly, I remembered the reason why I'd married Thorn instead of Juriel. My face flushed. What was a wife supposed to do when her father-in-law and king passed away? Was I even bound to any duties considering he'd died before I was officially wed? Did Thorn expect me to stay by his side or to leave him be, to allow him to grieve in peace? If he would grieve - I detected no hint of sadness in his eyes, only warmth as he watched me closely.

"What can I do?" I asked, dusting my fingers off.

Thorn looked thoughtful for a moment before he spoke. "Be by my side. You are my queen, after all."

"Queen," I echoed, suddenly going numb with the realisation. "Yes. I must be now."

That brought a smile to his face. "Understandably, it'll be overwhelming for a time. Just know I'll not pressure you into anything. When you're ready, we'll face this head-on."

"Why are you being so kind to me?" I blurted out. It was a burning question in my mind, one that had formed during the ceremony when Thorn defended me to King Helmar. I had never seen anyone stand up to him the way the young king did.

Thorn approached where I sat at the table. He stopped a short distance away, close enough that I could reach out and touch him if I so desired. And if I looked far enough into myself, I was certain I *would* find that desire. Something drew me to him, an inescapable magnetism.

"Tell me Artura, would you prefer I raise my hand against you? Because if you're waiting for the other shoe to drop, it won't. I'll not touch you. Not like that."

A flicker of relief rushed through me, despite the scepticism that still lingered. Had I been waiting for the catch? Arranged marriages were at best cordial and at worst lethal to one party - usually the female. Part of me had assumed the same would be true of my marriage. Thorn was tall and built like a soldier. He could force himself on me, hurt me in all the ways I'd become used to in recent months. Yet, as he looked down at me with almost a sad look in his eyes, I got the feeling it would hurt him more than myself to lash out against me.

"You said last night that you'll expect me to rule by your side," I began, thinking back to our conversation. "Do you really mean that?"

Thorn pulled out the chair beside me and perched on the end of it, resting his elbows on his knees. When he looked up, there was nothing but sincerity on his face.

"If you demanded my kingdom, I would give it to you."

I couldn't stop the jolt of surprise that shot through me. "That's ridiculous."

"Is it?" he countered. "Nimue is a kingdom that means little to me, though one I'll care for as duty dictates. I was born and bred for war, to lead my father's armies should the unrest in Cimran spread south. I don't know my people, nor do I know what it is to be a leader."

"I know nothing of leadership, either." The thought was absurd.

"Artura, you are one of the people."

"A pretty way of saying I am a commoner."

He shook his head. "It is not a bad thing. Just because someone is of royal blood does not make them honourable or just. I've known many men who came from nothing with more common sense than your king."

I pushed away from the table, walking to the fire. In the damp chill of early morning, my wrist ached. When the bones healed wrong, something in me had changed. Parts of me felt more fragile than before. And with the weight I'd lost through barely eating, the slightest breeze slipped right through me.

Thinking about what Thorn had said, I saw the truth in his words. King Helmar was a perfect example. Royal but abhorrent with not a shred of common decency for his fellow man. Not that he would ever see the men of his kingdom as a 'fellow man.' That would imply equality - something Helmar didn't believe in. He was at the top of the food chain in Cimran. I imagined he even considered Cerana to be inferior, despite his proclamation of love for his daughter.

"I can't be your queen."

I felt a hand on my lower back. Warmth seeped through me along with an all-consuming peace.

"Then simply be my wife."

"I'm not so certain I can be that either."

"And why not?"

I gestured to myself, looking down. "Have you seen me? Nothing about me cries Ruler. I'm a skinny, accused witch who's spent months in…"

My words faltered. Helmar had made it clear I was to say nothing about the cells or Purgatory, lest Emrys suffer for it. While I got the sneaking suspicion I could trust Thorn with anything, even after such a short time, I wasn't willing to risk Emrys' life on it. He mattered too much to me.

Thorn circled, eyes burning into my skin. "I see strength. I see grace. I see a courage unlike any other. All qualities that are essential in a just and honest ruler." He stopped in front of me, taking my face in his hands. Just as he had done yesterday, his thumb swiped over my cheek where the bruise from Malik's hand still lingered. His other thumb traced the scar along the side of my face. "All qualities that I see in *you*. I'll not force you to be something you don't want to be. Just know that you could be good for our people, Artura. They need someone like you. Simply stand by my side. Be with me. I have a feeling the rest will come naturally to you."

There was no denying the earnestness on his face and in his words but I still somehow managed to ignore it. Some days, *I* didn't even want me. While I'd kept to my mantra and not broken despite everything Helmar had done, I still felt lost, worn down like the coastal cliffs near Naiva. Every wave of abuse at Helmar's hands had stripped away a piece of me - pieces I wasn't so certain I could get back. And if I did, would I even be the same again?

Would you want to? A voice in my mind asked.

I couldn't answer it. I simply didn't know. Some days it certainly felt like there was no going back.

Thorn took hold of my broken wrist, his fingers lightly brushing over the odd angle of the bones. His touch was gentle and soothing, something I could come to crave more than my next breath if given half the chance. It had been so long since I'd been touched with care that I'd forgotten how much I missed it.

"I suspect you'll tell me in time how this happened," he said. "All I want to know is if the man responsible bears a crown?"

My breathing hitched on a sharp inhale.

"I have my answer, then." Thorn bowed his head and planted a soft kiss atop the bone. When he pulled away, the emerald in his eyes turned to stone. "Never again."

I let his promise sink in, hoping for the first time that perhaps the nightmare was over.

*

"Come with me."

I'd dressed in a simple pale blue dress that hung off my frame like a sack, hidden from view by the fur cloak placed around my shoulders. The fur was white and softer than anything I had ever touched. A large hood was pulled over my head, hiding part of my face from view.

Only, Thorn never took his eyes off me. Not for very long, anyway. Since the ceremony, I'd more or less remained within his line of sight through no doing of my own. He seemed to always be there, a guardian angel I didn't expect to have.

He peered into the hood now, the corner of his lips quirked up in a smile. "Please?"

I took his outstretched hand and let him lead me down the stairs. We made our way through carefully manicured gardens slowly suffocating under a thick blanket of newly fallen snow. The stables were to the side of the castle, hidden in the shade of the mountains. Each stall within the stable was occupied by a stallion much taller than I. A few I recognised from the journey from Naiva. One I knew belonged to the captain of The Cleanse. I'd glimpsed Azazel Brone only a handful of times in the last three days - and each time I had offered up one of my most scathing looks only for him to return a mildly amused one of his own.

Thorn didn't let go of my hand, his fingers entwined with mine. "This will be your horse. Her name is Kahina."

I looked up at the mare. Her coat was as white as my cloak and just as soft. Kahina had been brushed and cleaned to the point where she practically glowed in the dim lighting. She snorted softly, tossing her silvery mane as she grazed on a bag of oats.

"The moment I saw you, I knew. Artura and Kahina. Made for each other."

Stroking her flank, I smiled. The first genuine smile in months. Already, Thorn and the new life he promised felt like a cool balm to my aching soul. Healing, comforting. "She's incredible...and I fear too much. This is such a spectacular gift and I've nothing to offer in return."

Thorn chuckled quietly to himself. "I've nothing I want in return except your company. Besides, don't be a martyr. The walk back to Hafan would be far too long on foot."

"Ha ha." My voice was monotone and my face deadpan. I stroked a hand over the silky mane. "Thank you. Kahina is marvellous. And what about a horse for yourself? Or are we to share mine?"

Instantly, my mind filled with thoughts of Thorn riding behind me atop Kahina, his legs pressed either side of mine, chest flush against my back. Heat simmered low in my belly, wondering if he would be as affected by the nearness as I would surely be.

But then I shook all thoughts of his body near mine. It was too soon to think like that. Too much had happened. My soul still felt raw and wounded. These things would hopefully come back in time. Until then, I needed to heal.

Even as the concept ran through my mind, I hated it.

Thorn moved to the stall beside Kahina's where a chocolate-coated stallion stood. The moment Thorn entered, it recognised him and let out a huff, pushing its long head into Thorn's chest.

"Caderyn. He's been by my side for many years now. No finer horse in Nimue."

We spent an hour with the horses, making idle chit-chat about Nimue and what to expect. By the end of the conversation, on our walk back to the castle, I was breathing a little easier. Thorn hadn't been home in some years, returning only when he heard his father was to remarry. Instead, he'd found himself with a new wife, dealing with funeral preparations that would last for a month at least...

And with the weight of a kingdom upon his shoulders - his to now bear till death.

"Where is your father now?"

Thorn glanced up at me. "Being prepared for the return trip. We're fortunate that it's winter. He'll last the journey if we take the right precautions."

"I'm sorry for your loss. I don't know if I've said it yet but I truly am. Losing a loved one is hard. It's a pain unlike any other. I don't know what I can do but know that I am here."

Thorn surprised me by half-shrugging. "While I respected my father, I did so out of fear more than anything. There was no love lost between us. Gods, there wasn't even any means to foster it - no connection was made in the time I was with him. I was sent abroad when I was still quite young to train in the southern kingdoms and truthfully, I didn't really know him. Not beyond what I saw when I was a child. The man I knew then, he wasn't flawed and not fit to parent."

I thought of Emrys, of what I might remember of him now had I not seen him since I was a child. A twinge of pain and guilt ran through me. If I didn't save Emrys, free him from below Dearmond and deliver him out of Lanceris, he would one day be a distant memory to me just as Juriel was to Thorn. I couldn't fathom it, not when Emrys had been a constant in my life for twenty-four years.

"What about you?" he asked. "Family? Beyond what's up in there." He jerked his chin to the upper levels of the castle where the king resided.

I debated staying silent, not speaking about the healer who'd raised me. Helmar had said only that I couldn't speak about the cells and what had happened there, not about the man still kept under lock and key. And sooner or later I would have to tell my new husband of the man who raised me…and beg his help in rescuing him.

"I've only ever had one person I considered family. His name is Emrys." My voice cracked on his name and I cleared my throat. "He raised me as his own, gave me a happy life."

"Until recently." Thorn paused, emerald eyes searching. It felt as though he could see right through to my soul. With Soraya, I had thought the same but now that familiarity we shared was beginning to feel counterfeit with Thorn here. Standing before Thorn, I felt vulnerable, completely bared.

What terrified me more was that I didn't mind.

Pressing my lips firmly together, I turned and headed up the steps leading into the castle. He couldn't know the whole truth. Not now, not ever. The stakes were too high.

*

On our final night in the castle, a feast was held. Before anyone ate, they drank - and in copious amounts, too. Raucous laughter echoed off the stone walls. I jumped at every booming laugh, my nerves fried within no time at all. I was grateful to have Thorn by my side. Even when King Helmar demanded Thorn drink with him, he politely declined, instead placing his arm around my waist and holding me close.

In the past, I'd never been one to openly rely on another. Emrys had raised me to be independent.

"I won't live forever, Artura," he'd said. *"Some day, you will be on your own. You must learn to stand on your own two feet."*

Except now, my feet shook along with the rest of my body. Mere proximity to King Helmar was enough to rattle me down to my core. Thorn could sense it. It was in the way he held himself, like an asp prepared to strike. I was under no illusions as to whose side Thorn would choose at a moment's notice. After all, he'd said himself during the ceremony that Cimran needed the treaty far more than Nimue did. If given the chance, would Thorn dissolve the union between the two kingdoms? And if he did, what would that mean for me? For Emrys? Would I be safe in Nimue? Helmar had threatened - no, *promised* - to come for me, and that was with the treaty very much still in place.

Without it, I was as good as dead.

Thorn's lips brushed my ear, sending a hum of awareness through me.

"Breathe. I'm here."

I forced a smile to my face, one he instantly made a show of disbelieving with an arched brow.

"I'm fine."

"If I wanted a tale, Artura, I'd pick up a book." Calloused fingers tilted my face towards his. "Tell me, what can I do?"

I said nothing. Because ultimately, there was nothing to be done.

CHAPTER EIGHTEEN

A bath was waiting when I finally broke away from the dinner. I sighed as I dipped my fingers in, testing the warmth. Tingles shot up my arm as I swirled my hand through the bubbles, relishing the feel of the water. After The Tub and the horrors it held, I'd been afraid I would never step foot in another bath again, too terrified and caught up in unrelenting nightmares.

I began to undress. There were far too many buttons, the dress much fussier than anything I'd ever worn before. While I did have to admit it was stunning, with gold leaves embroidered across the bodice and voluminous skirts made up of pale pink tulle that fell in waves around my legs, I felt like a fraud. Thorn said I was now Queen of Nimue.

Queen.

I was the Queen of Nothing and No One. The only title I deserved. How could I rule as I was? I had nothing to offer a kingdom beyond being a womb to continue the royal bloodline.

And I doubted I could offer that much after all that happened in Purgatory.

I wriggled my hips, sliding the dress down. Behind me, I heard the faint click of the bedroom door closing. I turned, expecting to see Thorn and froze in my tracks.

"Witchling."

Malik didn't smile, there was only unmatched hate etched across a face reddened with drunkenness. He didn't wear the uniform of The Cleanse, instead wearing formal dress, the colour a dark navy embroidered with gold and sporting the crest of King Helmar upon his breast. All night I could feel Malik's presence at dinner, though I refused to look around, to confirm that he was truly there. He walked with a limp now, legs spread a fraction too wide. Still wounded from where I'd plunged the scissors. Good. The memory sparked a flare of hope in my chest. Would he try anything, knowing that I had defended myself? Knowing that I now had the added protection of marriage and a highly valued alliance - even if Thorn was nowhere in sight.

"Leave." I'd hoped the word would be a command but it was more of a quiet plea.

And I'm supposed to be a queen. Mother give me strength.

Malik ignored me, sauntering forward. "We've a score to settle."

My arms wrapped around my bare chest. At my feet, the gown lay in a heap. I was naked, vulnerable in more ways than one. I'd only narrowly escaped last time. Could I be lucky enough again?

The determined look in his eyes told me that no, I couldn't be.

"King Thorn will be back soon."

Not entirely a lie. There were things he'd needed to see to ahead of our departure. Thorn and I parted ways at the bedroom door, him giving the promise that he would return as soon as he could. Had Malik been lying in wait for me to be alone? The thought of him watching me, waiting for the perfect moment to strike, made my skin crawl.

Malik snorted. "Let the prick see."

"See what?" I trembled, hating that I did, while shuffling backwards.

"His witchling bride being fucked like the whore she is," he spat. "And this time, if anyone draws blood, it'll be me."

At that, Malik withdrew a dagger from his belt. My eyes darted to it, a lump forming in my throat. I wasn't familiar with this room, didn't know what might be used as a weapon in a pinch. My eyes remained focused on Malik while I tried to think of a way out of this. Somehow, I would have to save myself. I couldn't count on Thorn to return in time.

But I also couldn't fight. The past few days had been almost as exhausting as a day in Purgatory. My body felt weary. Even standing felt like a chore.

"You hurt me a great deal, witchling," he continued, an ugly sneer across his face, contorting what would have once been beautiful features. He flipped the dagger in his hand as though weighing it up. "With this, I thought I'd repay the 'favour.' Just because I'm physically unable does not mean you'll escape."

Making a split decision, I turned and bolted for the bathroom. Pain radiated through me as something hard pushed me to the floor. Screaming, I writhed beneath Malik. I rolled over, trying to use my legs to push him off. His hands were rough as he placed a hand around my throat, forcing my head back into the stone floor. Stars lit up before my eyes as I gasped for air. I was vaguely aware of his hand moving down my stomach, to the top of the curls between my thighs. My hands flailed about in an attempt to stop him but without air, I was fading. Lungs aching, head throbbing, I felt myself being dragged further and further under the surface of crashing waves that would surely drown me.

All at once, a roar sounded from nearby. The crushing weight of Malik's body disappeared. I choked down mouthfuls of cool air, throat burning, eyes watering. Standing beside me was Thorn, fury radiating off him in powerful waves. In his hand, he held Malik up by a fistful of his hair.

In his other hand, he held the dagger.

"Artura," he said, his voice cool and even despite the pulsing anger in his eyes. "Say the word and I will spare him."

I looked up at Thorn, the choice made long ago with the first touch from Malik.

I shook my head, eyes wide and full of fear.

One swift movement was all it took. Splatters of hot blood coated my naked body and face. I was too deep in shock to fully comprehend what was happening. All I could do in that moment was look up at Thorn as he ground his teeth together, his hand fisted so tightly around the dagger that his knuckles were white. Malik bled out, dark crimson soaking the light pink tulle of my gown where it lay.

I felt a twinge of guilt over such fine craftsmanship being ruined. And for a moment, a bubble of hysteria threatened to burst. I was more upset over a destroyed gown than I was about the murder of a man right before my very eyes.

Without a word, Thorn stooped and pulled me up, cradling me against his chest. In his arms, I felt small and weak.

In his arms, I felt safe.

"Denard," Thorn called. A moment later, a man dressed in a clean-cut soldier's uniform entered the room. He glanced from Thorn's face to mine and then to the cooling body on the floor. Without a word, he crossed the room and threw Malik over his shoulder. Malik's head lolled at a sickening angle.

How deep had Thorn drawn the dagger? No head should fall so far back, show so much bloodied flesh at the neck.

With a curt nod, Denard carried the limp form of Malik away, softly closing the door behind him.

"What will your man do with...*him*?"

"I don't particularly care," Thorn grunted. He pressed his lips against the top of my head, breathing deeply. "Most likely something far kinder than he deserves."

"He's dead." I wasn't sure if I said the words as a question or to reassure myself. "Kindness is irrelevant."

"It was him, too, wasn't it?"

Looking up at Thorn, I saw heavy pain deep in his eyes. It surprised me. Why would someone who had known me for mere days share my pain? Why would he even really care? I was no one to him other than what I had become through marriage. We were still very much strangers. Except, judging by the way he stared at me, there was a knowing there, a familiarity that only time could build.

I came undone and it was answer enough. Tears fell over my cheeks, streaking through droplets of blood. My shoulders shook with every shuddering sob tearing through me. I was vaguely aware of Thorn stopping to kick off his boots before hot water touched my skin as he lowered us both into the bath. I clung to his shirt, no end in sight to the tears I cried. All the while, he held me, one hand scooping water up and over my body to keep me warm. He moved onto my face, whether to wash away the blood or tears or both, I didn't know. His touch soothed me and the gap between sobs grew until eventually, I was silent against his chest.

"I'm sorry," he whispered, chin resting atop my head.

I burrowed further into him. "What for?"

His grip on me tightened. "You are my wife. I should have been here to protect you."

I sniffled and wiped my nose on the back of my hand. "I'm not a duty to fulfil."

"No," he replied. "You're a promise to keep."

I pulled back to look at him, noting smears of drying blood on his face. I took a cloth from the stool beside the bath and soaked it with water.

"May I?" I asked, my words barely audible.

Thorn's throat bobbed, his voice thick. "Please."

Washing Thorn, despite him still being fully clothed, was the most intimate thing I'd ever done. There was a force between us, thick and tangible, binding us in ways that couldn't be spoken. With every swipe of the cloth against his face, awareness rippled through me. The feeling was one of tendrils of fire licking at my skin, warmth pooling in my core. My chest felt tight all over again and I grew restless sitting in his lap. My thighs squeezed together, the movement slight, though it didn't go unnoticed.

Thorn's eyes became deep, dark pools as his lips parted in a silent sigh. "Artura…"

Against my hip, he grew hard and thick. I shifted at the sensation, eliciting a sharp groan from deep in the back of his throat. I let the cloth fall, my fingers sliding to the back of his head where they tangled in his dark hair, clinging to the back of his neck from the humidity of the bath. Breathing heavily, I licked at my lips.

"Just a taste," I murmured, the words falling from my mouth without warning. "That's all I want."

For what felt like an eternity, we hovered, only an inch apart and barely touching until I finally cracked. I surged forward, pulling his lips down to meet mine. We met in a frenzy, worlds colliding as I kissed the man I'd been forced to marry, a man who had awoken something in me I'd thought to be long dead. I breathed Thorn in, the smell of him intoxicating. Spice and salt and heat. His tongue slicked over mine, teasing and taunting, driving me mad. Heat pooled between my legs and I shifted in his lap to feel his hard length, my legs bracketing his own.

Pressing myself against him so hard it was almost painful, I used the edge of the bathtub to hold onto while I slid along his clothed length. The lust coursing through my veins was more potent than any drug. Never had I ever wanted anyone so much as I wanted Thorn.

No, *want* wasn't the right word.

Need. I needed him. I needed this, this release and escape.

His mouth hunted down my neck, licking, kissing, sucking. Teeth nipped at my collarbone, the slight sting only heightening my arousal. But as he lowered his head to my breast, cool air hit my face and I sobered instantly.

Thorn sensed the shift in me almost immediately and pulled back.

"Time," I gasped, still trying to catch my breath. "Give me time."

It was too much. I would combust, lose myself entirely in the bliss of him. And while I didn't exactly have much left to lose, I couldn't afford to relinquish the scraps of myself I still clung to desperately.

Thorn placed a hand against the side of my face, thumb stroking across my kiss-swollen bottom lip.

"We've only got time."

I didn't contradict him. But I should have.

*

I could tell Thorn was as sleepless as I was.

Blood stained the rug at the foot of the bed, the scent of rust and salt potent in the room. As though a phantom haunted the space where Malik had breathed his last, I averted my gaze, wary of what I might see. I burrowed beneath the blankets, night-gown tangling around my legs.

Something terrifying had shifted between Thorn and I. If I gave it too much attention, it began to overwhelm me. Here was a man I had been forced to wed - a man that, in reality, I should have never been bound to. The marriage was intended for his father and Princess Cerana. Yet as it always did, fate intervened and while I usually didn't put much stock in fate, even I had to admit there was something different about this whole situation. Something...*more*.

You only have feelings for him because he's the first friendly face you've seen other than Emrys in months, I chided myself. *It's not real. Once you depart for Nimue, the spell will be broken and you will see that this is all a farce.*

Why did that make me even more terrified?

Marriage wasn't something I'd ever truly considered. Not while I was in love with Soraya. It was an impossibility, one beyond our control. In Naiva, we'd heard rumours of gender traitors fleeing the continent for safer shores to live their lives together in peace. But King Helmar's reach was long and his influence strong. Extradition was common and always ended in the execution of those who fled.

And yet, now I found myself betrothed to a stranger - one who very quickly felt less of a stranger as the seconds ticked by. Of course, I'd one day imagined to be at least 'familiar' with Thorn but that was it. That was the extent of the relationship I had envisioned over the past three days. I was beginning to wonder just how wrong I was.

Rolling over in bed, I stared at the canopy above. Wispy cotton that seemed to move on an unfelt breeze even while the room was silent, every door and window firmly locked. It felt as though I were sleeping beneath the clouds, watching the sky drift past just as I had done so often in Naiva. Beside me, the bed shifted.

"Darling."

For a moment, I thought I'd misheard. But then I felt fingers brush hair off my shoulder. I shivered at his touch and his fingers disappeared.

"Don't," I whispered. "It's fine."

Warm fingertips toyed with the sleeve of my nightgown, stirring goosebumps along my skin as they went. I turned my head to look at Thorn, propped up on one elbow.

"What is it?" I asked, brows furrowing.

He said nothing, his fingers continuing to stir up tingles of awareness through me.

"My father was promised the daughter of King Helmar," he finally said. "Though I get the feeling it was not you. Who are you really, Artura?"

I stopped breathing.

"Artura?"

A deafening buzzing filled my head.

Strong arms encircled me as Thorn pulled me against his chest. One firm hand cupped my head, tucking me under his chin. I pressed my body to him, trying to quell the uncontrollable shaking that rattled through my core. His simple question had caused a visceral reaction within me. I fought to keep a grip on myself, to stop myself from careening over the edge I'd been precariously balanced on for the last few days. Was this how my life would be? The mere mention of King Helmar and I would fall to pieces like a poorly stacked house of cards. I wanted to believe I could be stronger than that but from all those months ago, the promise Helmar made swam through my mind:

I will break you down to nothing.

"Fall," Thorn whispered. "I'll catch you."

I shook my head, speaking between sharp, gasping breaths. "The fall is what will kill me. Not the landing."

"Then let me fall with you. I'll keep you safe."

For the second time that night, I felt myself breaking apart, clean in two. It was both cleansing and damning, evidence of my weakness and the truth I buried deep. There was no saving me from this nightmare, the one in which I tried and tried again to save Emrys, only to fail constantly. Just because I was no longer beneath the mountain did not mean I had suddenly succeeded. If anything, I was failing harder now because I wasn't there. Emrys was alone and I, in turn, was alone with the burden of his imprisonment.

Thorn's fingers combed through my tangled hair while he hummed low in my ear. The song was unfamiliar to me. The longer I listened, however, the more I detected the definite cadence of the Nimue lullabies an old grandmother in Naiva sometimes sang to children. I let the notes carry me away, painting a picture of a place that knew peace, freedom. A place where torture was unheard of and the only prisoners were those kept inside homes by warm summer rains.

At some point in the night, I drifted off. When I awoke to blinding light, I was still in Thorn's arms, my face salty with dried tears.

CHAPTER NINETEEN

Kahina was saddled and waiting when Thorn and I emerged from the castle doors. She stood beside Caderyn, the pair regal-looking as they awaited their riders. I approached my horse and stroked down her head, smoothing the silky coat. In the early morning light, she was as luminescent as the snow beneath our feet.

"I trust you enjoyed your stay."

At the sound of the deep voice, Thorn and I both turned. King Helmar stood at the top of the stairs, hands behind his back. He looked down towards us but it was on me his gaze fixed. I struggled to return it, lowering my eyes to the ground with the sound of blood rushing in my ears.

"It was…eventful," Thorn replied. He reached out and took my hand. "My bride and I shall depart for Nimue now. We've much yet to do with my father's burial and funeral rites."

"My condolences, once again."

For Thorn's father? Or for my betrothal to the new king? Helmar didn't elaborate. Either way, I doubted he was truly capable of feeling sorry for anything or anyone. The disdain Helmar held for Juriel was clear as day. The only thing I thought he might regret, perhaps, was that I'd not been married to the deceased royal. There was no denying that between Juriel and Thorn, the latter was preferable.

"My thanks." Thorn nodded, tight-lipped. His expression softened when he turned his back on Helmar and took my chin between his thumb and forefinger. "Are you ready, darling?"

No, I wanted to say. *No, I'm not ready. Not without Emrys.*

Instead, I found myself nodding.

I climbed atop Kahina with some difficulty, maroon skirts tangling with my legs. I could feel Helmar's eyes on me, criticising my every move. Cerana could ride a horse, most likely. Royal children were given such advantages, taught to ride properly. Side saddle for the ladies, prim and proper. None of this masculine riding with a leg on either side, not for a princess.

But I was no royal, save by blood, and it took every ounce of restraint within me not the throw a vulgar gesture over my shoulder at the king as I tugged on Kahina's reins and headed down the cobblestone street.

"We'll be on the western coast by tomorrow night," Thorn said from his place beside me. Caderyn kept in perfect step with Kahina. I didn't have to do anything other than gingerly hold the reins. It was like Kahina knew exactly what to do, knew to follow Thorn's lead.

"Western coast? Are we not to head south to Hafan?"

"In good time we will be with our people."

Our people. I let the thought run through my mind, struggling to come to terms with it. Because they were our people now. Not Thorn's alone. They were mine and I was theirs. Queen Artura of Nimue.

"What's on the west coast?"

"A ship."

"Yes, I figured as much," I replied dryly. "*Why* is there a ship? We've horses. Could we not just ride to Hafan?"

Thorn glanced at me out of the corner of his eye. "We're not going to Hafan."

Just as when I had arrived and then later Thorn and his delegation, the streets were empty. I began to wonder if Helmar hadn't perhaps ordered that those in Lanceris indefinitely remain within their homes. Onlookers peered through slivers of open curtains at the foreign king and his new, commoner bride. I caught confused and infuriated looks.

I was equally confused. I never anticipated that I would leave Lanceris at the side of a king and much less a husband. When dreaming of departing the city all those months below Dearmond, it was most often a coffin that provided my escape.

I didn't ask Thorn to elaborate. Until we were clear of Lanceris, the weight in my chest would remain. Guilt wore me down, too, threatening to drag me through to the centre of the earth. I was leaving, free - of a kind - while Emrys remained. How long before Helmar would tire of our bargain and take Emrys to Purgatory? Without being nearby, there would be no way to be certain of Emrys' safety. For all I knew, he could be dead by the time we reached the city gates.

As we neared the looming behemoths, a dozen more horses and riders came into view, all waiting in the shadow of the gates. Among them, I noticed Denard, stationed at the front of the group. He dipped his head.

"My lord, my lady. King Juriel is on his way directly to Hafan. The *Scylla* is awaiting our arrival."

"Very good," Thorn smiled. "Perhaps a formal introduction is in order. Artura, this is Denard Fray, captain of the guard."

"Old guard, now, perhaps," Denard replied with a small smile of his own. He inclined his head to me, his expression turning grave. "I do wish, my lady, that we had met under kinder circumstances."

I didn't trust myself to speak so instead merely nodded my head in silent thanks. Later, when I felt ready, I would ask what happened with Malik's body. King Helmar had given no indication he knew of what took place. Would a foreign king even get away with cold-blooded murder under another king's roof?

Most likely not - especially given the roof in question.

"A camp has been set up on the other side of Dearmond."

"Excellent, Denard. You have my thanks."

Kahina fell in step with Caderyn within a heartbeat as we moved on out. At this pace, it would take a full week to reach the coast, rather than a few days. However, I could count on one hand - nay, one finger - how many times I had mounted a horse before today. 'Mounted' being the operative word. As a child, I'd been bucked off before the horse took a single step. What followed was a lecture from Emrys and a concussion to rule any hangover I'd had since.

The party slowed to match my pace. By lunch, I felt more confident and Kahina was able to stretch her legs a little more. I felt the joy moving through her and it was infectious. Cold wind whipped through my braided hair, biting at my cheeks and lips. My eyes stung and I was grateful for the white fur cloak Verity had put aside for me this morning with the small trunk of clothing given for my journey.

All through the day, Thorn rode by my side and kept a watchful eye over me. We stopped several times for food, water and nature, making idle conversation. Thorn spoke at length with Denard who informed him of things that had happened unseen in Lanceris. I kept an ear out, hoping to glean what I could but the captain was careful with what he said and the volume at which he spoke. I wasn't as stealthy in my spying as I hoped and soon, contentious discussions ceased, replaced instead with inane topics.

We rode steadfastly towards the sunset. Every inch of my body ached, my joints screaming. How did riding look so natural, effortless for some when it was excruciating for me? True, our party had ridden through much of daylight, but I'd not for a second anticipated it being so difficult. When we finally came to a stop beside a clustering of black tents, I found I couldn't move. My legs were frozen on either side of Kahina and my rear felt chafed beyond anything I'd felt before.

"Darling."

Thorn held his hands towards me and when I nodded, placed them around my hip. I winced as he pulled me down and when I instantly swayed on my feet, Thorn easily lifted me into his arms. My face heated as he carried me through the makeshift camp, my arms securely wrapped around his neck. What would the guard think of their queen? I was certain that the only thing I looked to be now was weak and small. Far from the leader Thorn needed in a wife.

As though he could feel the unease within me, Thorn's grip tightened.

"Ignore them," he muttered, low enough for only me to hear. "You are my wife. If I want to hold you, I damn well will."

"They might believe that if this were not a marriage born of a treaty between our two lands."

Thorn was thoughtful for a moment as we dipped, entering a large tent. "Happy marriages have been created through worse."

A bucket of warm water was brought for me and I washed, changing into another dress, one not marred by dirt or smelling of horse. Slinging my cloak over my shoulders once more, I exited the tent, heading for the fire at the centre of the camp.

I found meat slowly roasting when I approached and the smell was utterly mouth-watering. My stomach hurt constantly after months of barely eating. The past several days had taught me the need to eat slowly until I readjusted and so I picked at my bowl, eating small mouthfuls of succulent wild pig.

The mood around the fire was light and easy among the men. I was the only woman and not for a second did they treat me differently. Whether that was because of Thorn's presence or not, I didn't know. In many places throughout Cimran, women were treated as less, something so common that most were no longer phased. It was readily accepted that women were for producing children, maintaining homes and being traded by fathers as little more than chattel.

The only real way around that was to be an accused witch or whore. The former and latter were both something I had under my belt with little to no effort.

Stars winked across the sky one by one and the chatter around me faded into a low murmur as I focused on the obsidian sky. Too long without the night had made me cherish it that much more. I settled down on a blanket and fell asleep, truly content beneath the heavens.

*

I was being cradled in a way that brought an all-encompassing peace. Blinking away the last dregs of sleep, I realised that the thing cradling me was a person. The smell of smoke and something more earthy washed over me. Beyond the seam of the tent opening, a sliver of light told me it was early morning. Dawn was only just breaking. Soon, the camp would awake and once again I would mount Kahina.

The thought had me quietly testing out the muscles and joints in my body. I moved slowly so as not to wake Thorn but it was all in vain when a loud crack made him stir.

"Are you well?" He rubbed a hand over his face. It wasn't fair that he would look so good so early in the morning. I knew for a fact I was sporting a bird's nest atop my head and my face felt dry from riding through blistering cold winds.

I looked up at Thorn sheepishly. "Aside from coming across as the inexperienced urchin I am? Yes."

"Urchin you most certainly are not," he murmured, fingers tracing the line of my jaw. I shuddered at the touch, leaning into it unconsciously. His eyes heated and dipped to my lips as they parted on a slow exhale. It felt good to be touched. No amount of tender caresses would ever satiate me after the past months in Purgatory but I was willing to try.

I wouldn't let Helmar take yet another thing from me. Not when he had already taken so much.

"Did you sleep alright?"

He was thoughtful for a moment. "Better than I have in some time. You're very warm to sleep beside."

"Is that why you held me through the night?"

Thorn's eyes twinkled and for a moment I thought he was going to say something more. Instead, he pushed off the bed, muttering something about breakfast, dressed quickly and exited the tent. I stared after him. What had I said? Did I do something wrong? In all my time with Soraya, we'd never spent the night together. Her father and then husband were equally controlling and the danger was too great. Already we had pushed the limits by sneaking off for a few hours at a time. Was there some sort of etiquette I'd not observed when sleeping beside someone else? Did I snore? Bad morning breath? Gods knew. Emrys didn't care to mention most things of that nature.

Once I was dressed and outside, I found Thorn and Denard whispering furtively amongst themselves. The captain's face was creased with worry.

Perhaps Thorn was just a grouchy man in the morning. That was fine. That, I had experience with. Emrys was a cantankerous old bastard until midday. The remedy for it was to ignore him until he got over himself and settled. So I moved to the rekindled fire and sat close, rubbing together my frosty hands in an effort to warm them. A light layer of snow had fallen overnight, not nearly as much as the past week and I was prepared to thank any gods willing to listen a thousand times over. The only thing worse than riding sore would be riding sore through knee-deep snow.

One of Denard's men offered me a bowl of porridge. It smelt of rich spices and I inhaled deeply, savouring the scent. Spices were a rare commodity in Cimran thanks to the food shortages and Helmar's stubbornness when it came to trading with neighbouring kingdoms. The deal between Cimran and Nimue was odd given how closed off Helmar kept his lands.

I ate slowly, eyes on the fire.

"I'm sorry."

Thorn sat down beside me on a rock, resting his elbows on his knees.

I swallowed. "Whatever for?"

For a moment, he looked uneasy, as though whatever he had to say was difficult. "I shouldn't have done that last night. Hold you."

I blinked up at him slowly, trying to decipher some hidden meaning behind his words. When I came up short, I raised my eyebrows.

Thorn glanced around. His men were busy dismantling tents and packing for the journey. When he spoke, his voice was low.

"After everything that's happened to you..." His voice trailed off, words silenced as he rubbed a calloused hand across his beard.

I put the bowl down on the snow. "You...what? You don't want me? I'm spoiled goods?"

His eyes narrowed at the tone of my voice, sharp, biting, even though I didn't intend it to be. The thought that he would find me repulsive due to a situation far beyond my control, it made me want to tear something apart, hit and scream till my throat grew hoarse.

The reaction was so potent that it took me by surprise.

And yet, I wouldn't have blamed him. Not for a single second. After all, was I not just that - spoiled? A king deserved a virginal, wholesome bride who knew nothing of the seedy underbelly of a world gone mad. Instead, Thorn had been given me - the complete antithesis of everything tradition demanded.

"That's not what I meant."

"Isn't it?"

"Not even a little." He huffed, looking up to a sky streaked with purple, gold and crimson. "I don't want to push you. That much I've already said."

"You haven't," I replied, almost too quickly. "I've not once felt pressured by you in any way."

That seemed to relax him a little and he visibly began to breathe easier.

"Artura, I know this isn't what either of us planned. That doesn't mean I do not wish to get it right. You are my wife and even though that may be in title only at the moment, it still means something to me."

"I don't know *how* to be a wife." I picked up my bowl, shoving another spoonful into my mouth. My appetite had waned with the conversation, as had the temperature of the porridge. I ate purely so I didn't have to look at the earnestness in his eyes. It was too much.

"Nor do I know how to be a husband," he finally countered.

I snorted. "Well, you've already killed to defend my honour so I beg to differ."

"It was deserved." His voice grew deepened dangerously, the air around us changing as the memory flitted back.

"What did happen with the body?"

Thorn took hold of my spoon, taking a bite of my breakfast. He chewed appreciatively for a minute before answering.

"Denard handled the disposal. Currently, pieces of Malik are headed several ways, all of which we do not to know about. There's no way to determine who the pieces belong to anyway. Denard knows what he's doing and I trust him implicitly. If he says it is taken care of, I do not question it. For now, though, it's best we let sleeping dogs lie and move on."

"Is this how it will always be?" I asked. When Thorn frowned, I elaborated. "You killing to defend me? I was told as a child that you should always start how you wish to finish and I think you can agree that the way we started doesn't bode well for a satisfactory ending."

Thorn smiled. "If I die protecting a wife given to me by the gods, then it will be a life well lived."

"I'm hardly a gift from the gods," I replied.

Thorn stood to his feet, light glinting in his eyes. "No, darling, you are. You are heaven-sent."

CHAPTER TWENTY

For four days we travelled, riding solidly through daylight, sleeping by moonlight. By the time we reached the coast, bruises had formed over my backside and standing had become equally painful to sitting. Hell, even just *being* hurt.

The *Scylla* was anchored a short distance off-shore, a small tender boat moored to a rock protruding from the breaking waves lapping at my boots. Even from the sandy beach, I could tell the *Scylla* was grand with an exquisite attention to detail. Pure white sails billowed, caught on a chill wind that promised a swift journey.

Wherever we were headed. As of yet, Thorn had said nothing of our destination. I was going on blind faith that whatever we were journeying towards, it was not my death. There was no reason for him to be so kind if just to kill me later on and he'd given no indication that I would be anything other than safe with him. In fact, Thorn had been nothing but attentive, making me his top priority before anything and anyone else. It was a strange, heady feeling. For so long it was

I who'd been the carer. To have the roles reversed was almost unsettling.

The ride to the *Scylla* took longer than expected. Winds grew harsher and waves higher the further we moved from shore, trying to push the little boat off course. Sailors dug their oars into the choppy waves, forcing the little boat against water cresting over the sides of the boat. My stomach rolled. I was grateful I'd been too full from breakfast to eat anything at lunch. But I shivered non-stop, my clothes drenched by the time we read the *Scylla*.

Climbing in a dress proved to be more embarrassing than anticipated. Icy winds gusted up my skirts, ballooning them around me and making it impossible to see my next foothold on the rope ladder hanging over the side of the ship. Twice I slipped, acutely aware that everyone's eyes were on me, their new queen, a total klutz. When strong arms helped me over the side of the boat, I breathed a sigh of relief. Thorn followed and then Denard. The two spoke with the ship's captain and I waited off to the side, eyes on snow-covered land.

It was the first time I'd ever been so far from Cimran. Everything was much smaller than I imagined, making the world that had seemed so big look rather insignificant. Trees were toothpicks and people mere spots against the sand. I found myself questioning why my problems had felt impassable when from my vantage point, the home I knew looked to be little more than a handful of soil dropped in the middle of the ocean.

But then again, King Helmar had a way of making even the simplest of matters feel overwhelming.

"Darling," Thorn said, his lips close to my ear. I shivered as our fingers entwined and he led me below deck. "Come with me. Living quarters down here aren't exactly spacious. We'll practically be on top of one another for a while."

I pressed my lips together in an effort to keep my thoughts to myself because I was fairly certain that given time, being on top of Thorn would prove to be a favourite pastime of mine. I then mentally swatted at myself, feeling much like the hormone-fuelled teenager I had once been, much to Emrys' ire.

We entered through a narrow door. The room behind it wasn't what I had in mind. From the way Thorn spoke of our living quarters, I'd envisioned something akin to a broom closet or my cell beneath Dearmond.

"This is as large as my cottage." I laughed. "Husband, I believe your royal birth is showing if you think this is *small*."

Thorn grinned back. "Now that I know you think this is big, it'll be much harder to please you."

I shook my head at him, moving to the far side of the room. Windows lined one wall, looking out onto the stern of the ship. Above, rumblings could be heard as sailors and soldiers moved about, preparing to set sail.

"Will you tell me now where we're headed?" I turned, leaning back against the windowsill.

"That depends," Thorn smirked, the expression stirring something in my core. The way he could awaken things in me with the simplest gestures was mind-boggling. I wasn't even certain I wanted those things awakening again, not after Malik, but I'd always been a thoroughly sexual woman. Perhaps that part of me wasn't as dead as it should have become.

"Depends on what exactly?"

He braced his hands on either side of me, gripping the windowsill. This close, I could smell his enticing scent of sea and smoke and something sweeter, almost like cinnamon. I licked at my lips and his eyes fell there, his lips parting on a sharp intake of breath. The look in his eyes turned ravenous.

It was my undoing.

I surged forward, wrapping my arms around his neck as I brought my mouth to his. The kiss was raw, fuelled by desperation and acute need to be touched in a way I'd not been touched for so long. Lips and tongue and teeth collided as I sought to taste every part of him. Thorn pulled me against him, one hand gripping my rear, the other the back of my head. His fingers tangled in my hair, destroying the plait woven this morning.

Something low in my core twisted and I felt heat coat my body. My breathing came in short bursts. When I bit down on Thorn's lip, the growl that rose from the back of his throat was animalistic and I grew slick between my legs at the sound. Sturdy hands lifted and carried me across our quarters before dropping me on the bed. After a week of riding, it felt like heaven but I didn't have time to fully appreciate it, not while Thorn stood over me, panting. I ran my eyes over him, noting the way his shirt hung open to reveal tattoos faded from years in the sun, how his hands clenched and unclenched as if he was forcing himself not to reach out to me. He shifted on his feet and I dropped my eyes to his pants, to the hard length I'd felt pressed against me. It bulged, leaving very little to the imagination. I swallowed hard.

"Artura…"

I knew what he was going to say. I could see the wariness in his eyes, the unspoken question of whether I truly wanted this.

I didn't *want* this.

"I need this," I replied with a sharp exhale. "I need you."

Needed it more than anything in my life. I needed Thorn to touch me, to erase the memory of Malik's hands, a memory that still coated my skin no matter how many times I scraped at my body, trying to remove greasy fingerprints that felt indelible. I needed to replace what had been taken from me with something - *someone* - I decided should be there.

I reached a hand out to Thorn, his own immediately going to mine, and tugged lightly. Thorn fell to the bed beside me, rolling over and taking me with him. I straddled his thighs, slowly rubbing myself against him, teasing and taunting. His answering groan was all the encouragement I needed. He was still clothed and the friction from his pants was almost too much against my thinly covered sex. I braced my palms against his chest and Thorn gripped my hips with firm hands, his fingertips digging in. He pulled me along his length once, twice. I shuddered, my core clenching on an emptiness that demanded to be remedied

And soon.

I took his mouth once more, my tongue exploring, twining with his. There was nothing slow or unhurried about the way I needed him. It was a force, all-consuming and desperate. I kissed down his cheek to his ear, biting his earlobe between my teeth. Thorn's only response was to grip harder and flip me over. I landed against plush, velvet pillows.

"Let me taste you," he whispered between pants. "Let me take away the memory of everything he did to you. Let my touch be all you know and crave."

I nodded, one hand going to my forehead as I focused on my breathing. I was close, so incredibly close to falling off the edge. When his lips kissed the inside of my thigh, I moaned.

"Again."

He kissed closer to the apex of my thighs, over and over until I felt his nose nuzzle against my curls. His hot breath ignited every nerve in my body. I parted for him, a silent invitation and when his tongue circled my clit, I cried out, the pleasure too intense. He continued the teasing dance, round and round as I squirmed beneath him.

"Will I have to teach you how to stay still?" There was a smile behind his words, a quiet mischief.

I reached out, my fingers wrapping around his hair, pulling him down in an unspoken command to continue. He obliged, licking up and down from my entrance to my clit. Fingers entered me, curling against that one spot within that threatened to tear me apart in the most delicious way possible. Everything wound tighter and tighter and tighter until in a rush, I came undone with a cry, my body shaking and shuddering, twisting and writhing beneath Thorn's still-lapping tongue.

In the aftermath, Thorn's head rested atop my thigh as I gradually drifted back to sanity. I stared up at the ceiling, wondering if the decision we had just made had been for the better or the worse.

*

The tension that evening proved my suspicions correct.

A choice for the worst.

Thorn and I sat on opposite sides of the dining hall. It was the most distance put between us since the wedding. I couldn't pinpoint why, but it hurt. Like my body had already become accustomed to his presence and without it, felt lost in a void. I'd never been the type to pine away. Either I was loved or I was not, I could not change another's heart.

But *this*. This was different.

There was no way to tell if he felt the same. The new king of Nimue sat beside his captain, talking quietly. Once, Thorn looked my way with no more than a cursory glance but for the most part, he spoke with Denard as though I wasn't really there. 'Discarded' was the word that came to mind.

After what had happened between us this afternoon, I'd expected to be treated differently.

But how? Why? After all, was I not as new to him as he was to me? Having a husband suddenly thrust upon me was more overwhelming than anything I'd been dealt yet - more so, even, than Purgatory. With that, I knew what to expect: pain. With Thorn, there was another possibility.

Happiness.

In the past months, I'd come to accept that being happy again was not a reality. Confined to the cells beneath Dearmond Mountains, there was little room for emotion. Yet now I was free. Admittedly, in a different kind of shackles, but free nevertheless. Could I believe I could be truly happy once again?

No. Not until Emrys was freed.

And if I did attain that happiness, what would I become if it was suddenly ripped away? It struck me then that Thorn wasn't the kind of person one could easily survive the loss of. If I gave myself over to him and the possible joy a life with him could bring, I ran the risk of being hurt in a way I'd not been hurt before. How things ended with Soraya had been a snippet of what was promised with the loss of Thorn.

I pushed remnants of grilled fish I didn't particularly care for around my plate while my mind wandered. Letting my fork suddenly fall to the plate with a clatter that echoed in the room, I stood from my seat. Other soldiers and sailors sat to one end, giving me a wide berth.

The night was still young and after sleeping through much of the afternoon, I was far from tired. I made my way to the deck. The seas were smoother than glass, giving the appearance of a mirror world beneath my own. Each star was reflected in an endless blanket of twinkling lights that wrapped around the *Scylla*. No longer could I see the coast, now cloaked in darkness on the distant horizon. I still didn't know where we were headed though I had worked out we were sailing south. Beyond that, my knowledge of the world at large was abysmally low. We could have been sailing for an island made of cotton candy for all I knew.

I heard footsteps behind me but didn't need to turn to know who it was approaching. I could sense him, a tingling awareness that set every nerve in my body on fire.

"Sparrow." Thorn didn't touch me as he leaned against the railing beside me. "You left dinner."

"Sparrow?" I lifted a single eyebrow at the name.

"You remind me of one. Small and resilient." He shrugged. "Besides, I've a mind to give you a name other than 'darling' - with how often I've already used the word, you might get sick of it."

"Doubtful. Though I *was* called gumdrop as a child. Perhaps you could use that."

Thorn snorted. "Gumdrop. Hardly the term of endearment from a husband to wife."

"What would you call me then? Sparrow, as you said? Or after a wild beast? A *fish*?"

He was contemplative for a moment, the only sound that of the wind whispering all around.

"Sea bass," Thorn finally said. "Wouldn't that sound pleasant to cry out as I fill your delicious cunt?"

I swatted at his arm bracing against the ship with a laugh. "I'll throw you overboard."

"No, no. Think about it," he continued before pitching his voice an octave higher and whining, "*Oh, sea bass, dear sea bass, come to me so I might squeeze that arse. With scales so bright and tail so fine, to bed you swiftly would be divine.*"

"Disgusting." I made a gagging sound, leaning over the side of the ship. "A surefire way to never get laid again."

"If this afternoon proved anything, it's that I'm irresistible."

I gently threw an elbow behind me, hitting Thorn square in the gut. "This afternoon proved that we ought to be wiser, that is all. And for your information, I left dinner because I wasn't hungry."

"No? Not even after my ministrations?" he crooned, voice like velvet.

I refused to appear affected. "Not even."

"Funny, because I certainly worked up an appetite," he continued, pulling away.

I turned towards Thorn for the first time since he arrived on deck. He wore a heavy jacket against the chill and just looking at it reminded me how cold I was. I tried to stifle the shiver that rolled up my spine but the subtle shake of my shoulders didn't go unnoticed. Thorn opened his jacket and pulled me against his chest before wrapping the material around me.

"What are we doing?"

He chuckled, the movement rumbling through me. "Preventing you from dying of hypothermia, I believe."

Shaking my head, I twisted around in his arms to gaze back at the ocean. Wrong decision. I could feel him too keenly now, was all too aware of him. My body remembered the way he'd been pressed to me just hours before and yearned for it all over again. I drew in a steadying breath.

"I've suffered through many cold winters and I'm yet to die," I pointed out in a tone that said he should know better. How could he? We didn't know one another from a bar of soap. "I mean with us, Thorn. What is happening? In the past few weeks, we've gone from stranger to spouse to lover, despite each of us saying we should take things slow. It's jarring."

"If I recall correctly, *you* seduced *me* this afternoon."

"I had an itch to scratch."

Thorn made a disapproving sound low in his throat. "An itch?"

"An itch. Nothing more."

"So what you're saying is," he began, choosing his words carefully, "that you used me for your benefit."

I scowled up at him. "When you put it that way, it sounds incredibly heartless."

"Is it not?" He cocked his head to the side to look down at me and his hair, as dark as the night, fell around his face. Phantom feelings in my fingers reminded me of how soft each strand had been. Like finely spun silk.

"Definitely not. To say I would use you implies little to no care."

"So you're saying you care for me?"

I hesitated, not knowing what to say. It was too hard to think with him this close. His scent made me drunk, my head clouded with thoughts of taking him back to bed, finishing what we'd started today. He hadn't pushed me further once I'd found release. Had I used him? Or had he merely obliged me because turning me down would have made things between us awkward?

I couldn't imagine it being more uncomfortable than things were right now.

Taking Thorn's hands, banded at my stomach, I pushed him away. He let me go, jacket falling open to expose my back to a cold, ruthless wind rolling off the ocean. Goosebumps raced across my skin and when I shivered violently, he smirked as if to say 'I told you so.'

"We've each found ourselves in a peculiar situation," I began.

"An arranged marriage is hardly peculiar," Thorn countered.

"It is when you're me."

"Enlighten me, Artura."

I walked away from him, thinking about what I could say without giving away much of the truth - a truth that was as good as a death warrant for Emrys if ever Helmar found out. From what I'd seen of Thorn's character already, I had no doubts that he would do something heroic or honourable - such as confronting King Helmar...who was so, so *very* far from honourable. But I also wasn't willing to take that chance. I wouldn't risk Emrys like that.

"Until recently," I said, my face turned away, "I was unaware of my parentage. I was raised in a small town to the north. For reasons...*somewhat*...beyond my control, I was accused of being a witch and taken to Lanceris. It was there that I learned of my connection to King Helmar."

Thorn moved to stand before me. He ducked his head to look in my eyes. The emerald of his own was almost luminescent, drawing me in. I didn't realise I'd been holding my breath until he trailed a single finger across my cheek.

"That, sparrow, is a watered-down truth if ever I heard one."

I returned his gaze unflinchingly. "It's the only truth you're going to hear."

Thorn's thumb brushed the corner of my lips. "In time, you will tell me. And when you're ready, I'll listen."

I said nothing. Listening wasn't what I was worried about.

CHAPTER TWENTY-ONE

Human refuse. My nostrils burned with the stench of it, making my stomach roil. I couldn't catch my breath, not when it meant drawing air into my lungs that carried a stench so heavy I could taste it. Scratched, bloodied palm braced against the stone floor, my fingers curling to drag my ripped nails through the grit.

Get up, I silently commanded. *Do not break.*

Yet I was dangerously close - so, so close. Of all days, today might just be the day I would break. Helmar was relentless in his efforts to punish me for crimes I did not commit. No matter to him, in his eyes, I was and always would be guilty.

A witch. Repulsive. Evil.

Get up. If not you, then Emrys. He won't survive this.

My arms shook with the exertion, sweat beading on my forehead. My teeth clenched together so tight I could have sworn cracks marred them like cobwebs, on the verge of shattering completely. Helmar didn't move, I could see his boots several feet away. Practically hear him contemplating at what point he would intervene to remind me once more that he was the arbiter of all things.

That I did not matter. I never had.

I made it to my knees before I felt another sharp blow.

Bowing over, hot liquid trickled down my temple, cheek, jaw and then neck. The only competing scent with the feces filling a bucket in the corner was now the scent of blood. I looked at King Helmar's hand where he held a crudely made club. Primitive but effective. The ringing in my ears was louder than my breathing.

I heard his footsteps before I registered the movement. A second later, a fistful of my hair was taken by one of his meaty, dirtied hands.

"Perhaps," he said, voice low, too close to my ear. I couldn't shy away, not when he held my dirt-encrusted hair so tight it threatened to tear my scalp. My eyes watered. "Perhaps, before you came to Lanceris, you thought yourself something of worth, someone above the lowly station to which you were born and raised."

The club dropped, the sound echoing throughout Purgatory. Helmar's free hand took me by the throat, pulling me up. He was strong, my toes barely skimming the floor as I gasped for air and scratched at his firm grip with torn nails.

"However, all I see is a feculent little *bitch* who is back where she belongs - amongst the filth of this world. You deserve this. Every moment."

Helmar heaved me across the room to the corner where the stench was strongest. When he released my throat, I instinctively gulped down mouthfuls of putrid air.

"There is no difference between you and this," Helmar continued, forcing my head over The Tub as one would a disobedient dog that had defecated on a rug. The sneer on his face contorted what had once been a handsome face, some time long ago. He was twisted now by hate and an evil so ingrained, it had become all he was. "From shit you came. To shit you will return."

Helmar pushed me closer towards The Tub.

"Artura!"

Something shook me. My entire body vibrated. Stench, filth. It was all around me. Inescapable.

"Artura," the voice commanded, far off. "Open your eyes. Look at me."

I wanted to obey, more than anything. But the smell, Helmar's hold on me, it was too much.

Trapped. Trapped and hopeless and lost to pain.

Cold suddenly covered me like a sheet resting over my body. I spluttered, jolting forward.

No cell. No Helmar. Just a gentle rocking back and forth and the smell of salt. My hands searched in the darkness as panic racked through me. My fingers found warmth and then I was being wrapped up in arms far stronger than my own.

"Darling sparrow."

I settled instantly at the sound of Thorn's voice. His hands smoothed my sleep-mussed hair, damp with sweat. A nightmare. Not real. I repeated the words to myself like a prayer, over and over. But I could still smell blood, the scent making my stomach clench. Pulling back from Thorn, I looked around, eyes slowly adjusting to the darkness. His own shone in the dark, moonlight on the ocean reflected in them. They were wide as he searched my face for answers I couldn't give.

That was when I noticed his cheek.

"Did I do that?" I mouthed silently, fingers hovering above three deep scratches across his cheek. As I looked over them in horror, beads of blood bloomed, one running down to his jaw.

Thorn's only reply was to take my hand in his, pressing a tender kiss against the palm.

At that, I broke, tears streaming down my face as I violently sobbed. Months of pain and heartache welled within, driving a long overdue cleansing. My howls filled the cabin. Tomorrow, I would no doubt be embarrassed. Surely the others could hear me. Sleeping quarters were close on board the *Scylla*, the walls paper thin despite the luxury all around. Voices carried all too easily.

If Thorn cared for the noise, he made no indication of it as he held me, the only grip on reality I possessed.

The dream had felt too real. A memory I was locked inside of. As trapped as I had been beneath the mountain. No matter how hard I tried, though, I couldn't fully shake the feeling of dread that filled me that day. The day Helmar had incinerated my last shred of dignity. The day I came so dangerously close to begging for mercy that the wicked king did not possess.

Was Emrys enduring that same fate now? How long would he hold out if he was? I was under no illusions. Helmar was not a man of his word - he merely gave the impression he was. The only word he adhered to was the one that promised bloodshed and pain.

"You're safe," Thorn whispered, his whiskey-scented breath ruffling through my hair. "Nothing will hurt you again."

I shook my head where it rested in the crook of his neck. "Do not promise what you can not deliver."

"Have I not shown you my loyalty, sparrow?" Thorn tilted my face up to his. Deadly serious, expression turning molten. "I would raze entire kingdoms for you."

"Why?" I asked, the word tumbling out. "You don't even know me."

For a long minute, Thorn looked down at me, eyes burning. "Because, sparrow, you are *mine*."

I pulled my face down. The intensity of his gaze was too much on top of everything. One more thing I simply couldn't deal with right now. It was then that I realised more than my cheeks were damp. My nightgown clung to my skin and tendrils of hair twisted around my neck like rope.

"Did you...did you pour water on me?"

His chest rumbled with silent laughter. "After you attacked me, it seemed the safest option."

"I'm sorry," I whispered. Shame flooded through me.

"No. You never have to apologise to me, Artura. Never."

Thorn held me for a little longer, the only indication of time passing was the moon slipping further in the sky. When I shivered violently, I pushed away from Thorn.

"I need to change."

Despite what had already happened between us the previous afternoon, he turned, offering up what little privacy he could give. I changed quickly from one nightgown to the next. Whoever had provided clothing for me aboard the *Scylla* had been generous. The style wasn't that of Cimran so it couldn't have been Verity. A small pang shot through me. She'd been the only kind face I'd known in the castle. The fact that we were together only mere days mattered little. I almost missed her. Almost.

Once I was changed, I cleared my throat to let Thorn know he could turn. Stepping off the bed, he crossed the room to me.

"What can I get for you?"

I chewed my lip absentmindedly. "Maybe some bread?"

"Hungry, darling?"

"Nauseous." Remnants of the dream clung to me, scents I would never be rid of no matter how long I tried. My stomach churned uneasily at the thought.

"I can go one better than bread," Thorn said, a sly smile making him look younger. I glimpsed the mischievous child he might have once been, long before fate bound us together. "Come with me."

We moved soundlessly through the ship, hands twisted together, until we reached a place I'd not yet been. The kitchens were still warm from ovens that had produced dinner for several dozen men. Surfaces were spotless, leaving behind a faint smell of lemon. It reminded me of home, of when I was a child and Emrys would make a concoction of lemon and vinegar to clean with. Once, I'd accidentally drunk it. Needless to say, that mistake had not been made twice.

Thorn lifted me onto the bench, hands lingering on my waist a little longer than necessary. I watched as he moved about to kitchens, pulling ingredients. Peppermint leaves and ginger were set on the bench beside me.

"Playing with your food?"

I toyed with the nub of ginger. "If you make me eat this raw, I'll revolt."

One hand lifted a pot. "Have you so little faith in me? I may be high born but I am far from the incompetent fool others of my kind are prone to being."

"Who said you were an incompetent fool?" I arched a brow. "Those are your words, not mine."

"Sparrow, even if I'm mistaken and I truly am an incompetent fool of a king, I am still a blessed one. That is all that matters."

My cheeks burned at the look he threw my way and I let the subject drop. He'd said not long ago that he was blessed to be my husband. I wasn't going to touch that topic with a ten-foot pole. If he truly knew, his opinion would change drastically in a heartbeat.

Thorn kept busy chopping ingredients, mincing ginger and shredding herbs. He pulled a pouch from off a shelf and sprinkled a fine powder into the pot before stirring it in. The liquid resembled something like dirty water but the smell it gave off was sweet and familiar.

I gasped as I peered into the pot. "Who taught you to make this?"

Thorn paused mid-stir. "Why?"

"It's a tea."

"Well spotted," he replied sarcastically.

"A tea that only few healers know how to make."

Healers like Emrys, I mentally added.

"Do I need to worry that my bride will hand me over to The Cleanse for crimes against Helmar the *Great Defender*?"

My eyes widened but the look on Thorn's face remained amused. The question had been in jest but the thought that I would turn on Thorn when he'd been so kind to me…

"No. I'm just curious is all."

Thorn pulled the pot from the stove, pouring its contents through a sieve and into a mug. He handed it to me, my chilled fingers instantly warming against the ceramic.

"My aunt is a healer…of sorts. You'll meet her in a week, weather permitting."

I took a tentative sip. The tea tasted sweeter than Emrys' brew but just having something familiar in my hands was soothing all on its own.

"Will you tell me now where we're headed?"

"That depends," he replied. "Do you intend to pounce on me again? Because I absolutely tried to tell you earlier, only to be wooed by your feminine wiles."

I pretended to gag into my tea. "My behaviour has been called many things but never that. Tell me. I'll behave."

Thorn leaned back against the opposite bench, folding his arms. His shirt was rumpled from sleep - that was if he had managed to sleep before I woke him. Perhaps he'd just lain beside me, wide awake, wondering as I often did during the day how we wound up here.

"The Isle of the Old Gods."

I almost choked on my tea. "Why the fuck are we going there?"

The corner of his lips lifted at my question. "I always wanted a wife that could swear like a sailor. And we're going there because the kings of Nimue have a longstanding tradition that I'll not relent on - regardless of how we came to be here."

"Is this the part where you offer me up as a sacrifice to some archaic god who cares not what we humble mortals do?"

Thorn's face turned serious and he closed the distance between us. His finger tucked a lock of onyx hair behind my ear.

"Darling, the only thing I'll offer is a desire to please you."

"You are incorrigible."

"The best people are."

I downed the rest of my tea in a gulp, nausea easing instantly, and handed the mug to the king of Nimue. In this setting, he looked unassuming, humble. Not at all how I would have pictured the sovereign leader of a mighty kingdom. This wasn't the image presented to us as children of a man larger than life, clad in battle-worthy armour and wielding a sword coated in a thick layer of dripping crimson blood.

No. This man was almost...domestic. I struggled to find any other word for it. He was an ordinary man. I decided I liked it far more than what I thought I'd be wed to.

*

Along with magic, one of the first things to be forbidden in Cimran two and a half decades prior was travel to the Isle of the Old Gods. Legends said that deep in the heart of the island, magic was born along with the first sunrise. It stood to reason that King Helmar would prefer to cut off at the source the very thing he sought to put an end to. I'd been told very little about the isle and what I had learned scared me. Stories of monsters that lurked in the shadows, that swam beneath the crystal clear waters. They were said to kill a man before he could muster a scream in his throat - a throat that would be sliced cleanly from ear to ear. Memories of Malik's milk-clouded eyes as his head lolled at a sickening angle played in my mind. The thought of that happening to me... My fingernails dug painfully into my palms, leaving crescent moons behind.

It was no surprise that I found myself apprehensive about travelling to the Isle of the Old Gods. Whilst my life as of late had been somewhat unbearable, I didn't exactly wish to die.

I had to wonder exactly what would draw Thorn to such a forsaken place. He was tight-lipped on the tradition he was so hell-bent on honouring. Saying only that it was important to him.

Each day passed in a blur. The further south we sailed, the warmer the weather grew until eventually, I didn't need furs when I sat on the deck, watching waves crash against the bow of the ship. We passed through something the sailors called the Eternal Strait. Here, the waters were crystal clear, giving a perfect view of that which we sailed over. Littering the seabed were ships. Some recent, only minor erosion to the body. Others were so old, I struggled to place what wood belonged to what part of the ship. In amongst the wreckage were clumps of coral, fish darting about.

"It covers the remains," Denard explained, pointing to bulbous coral the colour of sunset. "Most have faded away by now but their armour remains as an anchor of sorts for the sea life."

"Who were they?" My eyes locked on the remains of one ship I knew to be Cimranean, the sails bearing Helmar's emblem. Judging by the condition of the ship, it had gone down some time in the last few months whilst I'd been under Dearmond.

"Soldiers, sailors, slavers," Denard replied, no inflection in his voice. "Those who angered the gods."

"Do you believe in the wrath of the gods, captain?"

Denard threw me a sideways glance, lifting one shoulder in a half shrug. "Here, I believe in the wrath of the sea and nothing more. On land, it is the wrath of man. A cruel wrath. Worse than the gods, for the gods do not know what it is to be one of us, to suffer and scrape by day to day. Our fellow man does. Anyone who would wilfully inflict that pain on another is nothing short of cruel."

I turned away from the captain, not willing to show just how much I agreed with his assessment. For someone so young, he was jaded. It was there in his grey eyes, clear as the waters that carried us. I wondered what had happened to Denard to make him this way, what horrors he'd witnessed as captain of the guard for King Juriel. Would he feel the same pain serving under King Thorn? I had to believe we learned from the mistakes of those before us. Perhaps things would be better with Thorn in charge.

Though, starting his reign with an alliance between Nimue and Cimran was perhaps not the best way to go. It was something I'd thought of a lot over the past days while there was little to do on board the *Scylla*. How the alliance between the man who had tortured me for months and the man I now called my husband would affect me. I had to remind myself I was technically now queen. Duty to protect my people, despite them being a people I did not know, was imperative. Still, after months of living with it, self preservation coloured every choice I made.

My thoughts wandered as I stood at the bow of the ship, elbows resting on the polished wooden edge. It was freshly oiled and lacquered, no trace of the sun bleaching and salt staining that surely would have once been there. My dark hair kinked in the humidity, holding heat and making me sweat beneath my dress. I sighed in delight. For too long I'd felt cold, bone achingly so. I let the sun wash over me, soaking it up like one dying of thirst.

Three months ago, I was with Soraya, stealing moments in an abandoned, burned out apothecary. At the mere thought of the woman I once loved, my heart squeezed. Whilst under Dearmond, I'd not allowed myself to think on her betrayal, how everything I had done had been for Soraya. To have it thrown back in my face was a pain I wouldn't soon shake. Part of me still missed her. Her touch, her smiles, the way her fingers would absentmindedly twirl my hair as we talked quietly in stolen moments. I missed the way she kissed me, how she watched me from across the village square when she stood dutifully beside Erisk. Somehow, it felt like a small triumph over the oaf she'd married. Every time I wanted to laugh at him and say, *See? She wants me. Not you. You will never be enough.*

Except in the end, it was *I* who'd not been enough.

My eyes slid in and out of focus as I swatted away an errant tear. Something caught my attention, though, and I had to blink several times, certain I was seeing things on the horizon. A slip of jagged grey. It took me a moment but then I gasped, realising what it was.

Land.

We were here.

CHAPTER TWENTY-TWO

The tender boat was lowered over the side of the *Scylla*. Here, the water was clearer than glass and a blue so seamless that the sky and sea blended into one. Thorn stood at my side, hand firmly pressed to my lower back. Not for the first time did it surprise me how much his touch soothed and comforted. Even in the face of a place often told to children as a cautionary tale, I felt safe.

Denard called to several men, barking instructions as satchels and sacks of goods were thrown down to the two men waiting in the tender boat. I winced when a sack nearly landed in the water. Who knew how deep it was here? The water being so clear, it might have been several feet or several hundred to the sea floor.

"The kings of Nimue have traditions - ceremonies, if you will - that have been observed for over a thousand years," Thorn began. He spoke low, his voice reverberating through his touch. "While not every union has been one born out of love, it is still taken seriously. We do not marry for gain or honour. Duty is naturally a part of everything we do but we still hope that a marriage might be something more… binding."

"You're as clear as mud."

Thorn's mouth twisted to the side. "I'll never force anything on you. And perhaps I should have spoken with you before. No matter how you came to me and I to you, I still want this to mean something, you and I. You're not some tool in an alliance, some pawn to be shuffled about by men in power. You are my wife, my greatest - though unexpected - treasure. Under the eyes of the gods old and new, I want to tie myself to you, be yours in mind, body…and soul."

I was silent for a moment as I thought over his words. My experience with the practices of Nimue was well below negligible. All I knew of the kingdom was from stories told to me as a child by Emrys. Once I reached adolescence, the stories had ceased but I still remembered a few.

"You want to form a soul tie?"

Thorn nodded. "I said it last night. You are mine. Just as much as I am yours."

"I've known you less than a fortnight."

He shrugged, pulling me closer to his side. "Call it an act of blind faith."

"That's one hell of an act, Thorn."

Thorn slid his hand around my hip, turning me to face him. When my eyes found his, I saw only earnestness, the kind that implied wholehearted trust and…affection. But no, that wasn't possible. More than a fortnight was needed for such a thing.

"I don't understand why you would want to form a soul-tie with me," I said, tucking a strand of hair behind my ear. "But something is telling me I can trust you."

"You can," he interrupted.

"The only thing I can't trust you to do is let me finish a sentence," I continued. "Somehow, this feels right. I don't know why. I've known you for a hair's breadth of time but you and I…"

I didn't have the words but the look in his eyes told me he knew. It wasn't just fate. There was something more connecting us.

We climbed down the rope ladder into the waiting tender boat, Thorn going first in case I slipped - which I did - and needed to be caught…which I did. There was nothing dignified about the new Queen of Nimue falling with a squeal into the waiting arms of a king. Yet as Thorn held me with a broad smile, I couldn't bring myself to be truly embarrassed. Not when Thorn looked at me with what almost seemed to be reverence, as though he couldn't believe I was here, that he was holding me in his arms.

I flushed crimson deeper than the shade of my dress as he lowered me to the bench seat, taking a spot beside me.

The Isle of the Old Gods was accessible only through a cavernous entrance. The still waters carried us forward, an invisible tether drawing us ever closer. Nary a ripple disrupted the surface as we glided onwards. It felt as though the entire isle were coated in a peace brought by the gods themselves.

The boat slipped into the shade of the isle, the rocky ceiling replacing the too-bright sun. I looked up and my breath caught.

Littering the rocks above were lights, thousands of them. They shone like the faceted faces of a rare diamond, reflecting the water below. Some were no bigger than a pinprick but shone as brightly as the sun. Others were as large as a fist with jagged corners leading to smooth sides. As we drifted closer to the heart of the isle, my eyes adjusted and I registered that each light was a pale amethyst.

"A geode," Thorn whispered. "The isle is the largest geode in the six kingdoms."

I was breathless, lost in awe as I took in the beauty surrounding me. The roof slanted lower the further we went and at one point, I could almost reach up and touch but didn't for fear of breaking the spell. It was all so surreal, something from a dream.

"I never knew."

"Very few do," Thorn said. "It's known to the kings of Nimue and perhaps to those of Cimran. This place is so shrouded in dark tales that it's rare for anyone to journey here lest they be struck down by the gods."

"Fools," I whispered. "Every one of them. I could die happy now, having witnessed this."

It was the most stunning thing I'd ever seen and likely would ever again.

"Let's not go dying yet," Thorn murmured, pressing his lips to the top of my head. "I'd hate to be known for becoming a widower within a month of marriage."

I jumped when the tender boat bumped to a stop, one of the sailors jumping over the sides into what was now waist-deep water. Reefs lined the wall of the cavern, fish every colour of the rainbow darting about. Their scales were iridescent, almost as captivating as the amethyst ceiling above. Almost. Thorn followed the sailor, slipping into the water before turning to me.

"Come, I'll carry you."

After falling down the ladder into the boat, I didn't dare argue. Clumsiness seemed to be my core trait after Purgatory, my muscles still struggling to catch up after months of neglect. Thorn swung me into his arms, careful to not let even a single hair on my head brush the smooth waters, and carried me to a rocky outcropping. Stairs were crudely carved into the side and we climbed out of the water.

What lay directly ahead was a tunnel, winding deep into the isle. Evenly spaced along the smooth walls were torches, burning brightly, another source of light that set off the ceiling twinkling like dusk. It was from one of the wrought iron sconces that Thorn pulled a torch to light our way, took my hand and began to walk.

"Shouldn't we wait?" I asked, unable to hide the trembling in my voice. Awe and wonder from a moment before faded only to be replaced by trepidation.

"There is nothing here that can truly hurt us." Thorn squeezed my hand gently. "Nothing that would dare, anyway."

"A comforting thought," I murmured, rolling my eyes.

One turn melted into another until eventually, I realised we were heading down, down, down. How far had we come? We'd walked for ten minutes at least, the voices of the sailors now completely faded. All that could be heard were the patter of our footsteps and breathing. Another ten minutes passed and now I was certain we were well below the sea. I threw furtive looks over my shoulder. One strong wave and-

"I know what you're thinking," Thorn said, not looking back at me as he navigated the twisting tunnel. "And yes, we are safe. The old gods created this place to be a sanctuary, not a trap."

I didn't speak. The concept of the gods was one I didn't buy into. Despite swearing at and upon them, I didn't truly believe. At least not like others did. Zealots with their subservience and robes and iconography covering altars in a thick layer. Worshippers that claimed the famine in Cimran to be retribution for the disease that was Helmar and The Cleanse infecting the kingdom. On that point, we at least agreed. For me, though, the gods had done nothing and that was all that mattered. If we were pawns in their game, it was a game they'd not long since played, neglected to grow dust in some corner of the heavens.

Something floated in the air, the lilting sounds of harp strings. Surely I was imagining it, that beautiful music swelling and tugging at a long-forgotten memory. It rose and fell in a hypnotising pattern, stirring in me hope and peace and joy. I found myself breathing it in, as though I could draw its very essence deep into my soul, bottle it there and live off it for the rest of my life.

"We're almost there."

"Almost where?"

Thorn didn't elaborate as we turned around one final bend.

*

She was a ghost, surely.

A woman with eyes the colour of the geode above us and hair paler than the snow that covered Cimran sat upon a carved driftwood stool. Between her knees there stood a harp, gold and gilded and very much out of place in the cavern. Her fingers drifted from one string to the next and back again, barely touching as the music changed into something slower, quieting as we drew nearer. Her eyes studied us from under thick lashes. Well, studied me more than Thorn. To the king, she gave little more than a cursory glance before she locked onto me, looking from my face to hands, feet and everything in between.

Slowly, she let her hands fall into her lap, resting atop skirts the colour of impending dawn. The material was light and moved around her as she stood to her feet, side-stepped the harp, and approached. I fought not to shrink back. Stories of sirens and spirits filled my head.

The woman smirked, almost as if in reply to the thoughts within.

"Viane," Thorn said, smiling. "I've missed you."

I glanced from my husband to the woman and back again, shocked by the welling of jealousy that hit me. I tamped it down, telling it that I had no right to feel such a way. Thorn was several years older than I, no doubt he'd lived a life, met people.

Perhaps fallen in love.

"Nephew," she said, placing a hand on the side of his face. A flicker of her gaze told me she didn't miss the way I exhaled, nerves easing. "I've been waiting."

"Patiently, I hope."

"Never," Viane replied with an answering smile of her own. "I've waited far too long to meet your wife."

I blinked up at Viane, wondering how she knew. Had someone travelled ahead of us to give this woman the news? But no one else was here, I noted, eyes searching what I now realised was a home, though a humble one at that. A bed sat in an opening in the wall, one that looked to be created for it. A kitchen of sorts was to the left side of the space and on the opposite side of the cavern was a table littered with what looked to be…

"You're a healer?" I asked, surprised.

"Of a kind," Viane replied. "Though perhaps not the kind you expected to find this day."

I frowned, looking again around the cavern. Letting go of Thorn's hand, I moved to the table. Careful not to touch a thing. I knew how particular Emrys had been about some of his concoctions. When I reached a darker end of the table, my breathing hitched, coming faster until I was struggling to take in air that carried a metallic tang. Books with runes and symbols were stacked haphazardly in a pile. A jar of black salt and a vial of what looked to be blood stood beside a basket of bones.

And they were most certainly *not* animal.

"You're a witch." Not a question. I knew.

Viane merely smiled saccharinely. "There's nothing wrong with that."

I shook my head, leaving the table behind in my desperation to get away. It would take me quite some time to get back to the tender boat, to put even the smallest distance between Viane and myself but I had to do it. Every second I was here was putting Emrys in more danger. I was under no illusions that Helmar would find out somehow, punish the only family I had for my transgressions. This would be all the confirmation Helmar needed. That would be the death of the man who raised me, the only father I had known.

Panic threatened to choke me as I rushed past Thorn. His arms whipped out, catching me around the waist. He pulled my shaking form back against his strong, muscular chest, his breathing steady. His arms held fast, shackling me to him. I should have panicked more, fought to be freed but instead, his promises from the past fortnight rang in my ears.

You're safe. Nothing will hurt you again.

If you ever lay a hand on her again, I will raze your kingdom to ruin

If I die protecting a wife given to me by the gods, then it will be a life well lived.

My breathing slowed, falling in time with Thorn's.

"Hush, sparrow," he whispered. "Always. I will always protect you."

And I believed him.

CHAPTER TWENTY-THREE

Viane sat beside the fire, adding another piece of driftwood. On a tripod over the fire hung a cauldron full of soup. It bubbled, rich spices filling the air. My mouth watered, hunger stirring now that I'd calmed. Thorn sat behind me, a leg on either side of mine. His arms wrapped around me.

"You've come for the Oath-Taking, nephew?" Viane asked, not looking up as she dropped carrots and potatoes into the cauldron. I frowned, wondering where they'd come from. It was then that Viane glanced up, a small smile on her lips. "I serve as guardian of the isle. Provisions are delivered every so often. It would be poor form to desert the one person keeping this place afloat."

I'd pushed my sleeves up in the warmth of the fire. Thorn's fingers trailed across my bare skin, reminding me of yesterday, how he had drawn lazy circles along my spine as we wasted away the day in bed.

"We came straight here from Lanceris."

"For the best," Viane replied, spitting on the ground. "Lanceris is a boil upon the continent. I'd not spend a moment longer than necessary there."

"I still don't quite understand what any of this is," I said. Thorn's fingers didn't cease and tension lingered under his touch. "The Oath-Taking? What does it mean? What does it entail?"

Am I about to be carved up on an altar? Will I be served up to the gods of old as a vestibule for their use? Or as something to satiate their hunger?

Viane smiled, winking. "Nothing like that."

I jumped, heart pounding. "That's three times now you've done that."

"Done what, child?" She cocked her head to the side, feigning confusion. She was waiting for me, for some piece of the puzzle to slot together mentally.

"Been in my head," I replied, feeling as crazy as I sounded. "Said things in answer to that which I've not spoken."

"And why do you think that is?" she asked.

I was silent for so long that I assumed Viane and Thorn would resume their conversation. Instead, they waited patiently as I mulled things over. At last, I gasped. "You're a diviner."

Viane's smile widened. "Very good. We'll make a witch out of you yet."

"I'd rather not," I breathed. "That's what-"

I froze, keenly aware that I'd been close to saying something I couldn't so easily take back. Hiding the truth was the only thing keeping Emrys alive. I drew in a steadying breath, locking away the words that would damn him.

Instead, I said, "Witch is something I am not, I can assure you."

The woman's eyes lit up. "We shall see."

I shuddered at the thought, remembering Purgatory and the horrors it held, catered perfectly for Helmar's desires. No power on earth or in the heavens could persuade me to touch the concept of witches or magic. Not when the king no doubt still watched from afar, hoping for even the smallest reason to break our tenuous deal.

Viane handed a bowl of steaming soup to me, a wooden spoon leaning against the side. It was something more akin to a stew, chunks of what looked to be lamb perfectly cooked and falling apart before my very eyes. There were vegetables the likes of which I'd not seen for some time in Naiva, too expensive to import regularly. I brought the spoon to my lips, blowing on it for a moment before sliding it into my mouth. Flavour burst across my tongue and I was helpless to stop the moan escaping me.

"This is incredible." I swallowed another mouthful.

"I've one request and one request alone," Viane said, passing a bowl to Thorn. "And that is that my food be rich and plentiful. I'm here on my own for the most part, this is my one vice. I've plenty of time to fine-tune recipes and be my own guinea pig. There have been some…failures…along the way. I'll be sure to give you only that which I've perfected. Only the best for family."

I paused at that. Family. Till recently, all I'd ever known was Emrys, the only family I had. Soraya had come close but even then, she could never be what I needed her to be. Then Thorn had appeared, jarring and unexpected though welcome nevertheless.

But *family*. It was more than I'd hoped for, more than I dreamed of having after leaving Emrys behind below Dearmond. Despite Viane being the very thing that Helmar warred against, knowing that there was someone else on my side eased the tension constricting my chest. Thorn sensed my shift in mood, his face nuzzling against the side of my head as though to say, *I know*.

Thorn and Viane talked while I ate, filling each other in on events new and old. I gathered it had been some time since Thorn had last seen his aunt, perhaps years. There was much for the two to speak of. Despite being sequestered on an isle in the middle of nowhere, Viane spoke of events as though she'd been there herself, describing things down to the tiniest detail. As a diviner she would know more than the average person, have a front-row seat to things no one else had. Very little would have escaped her notice. She didn't seem surprised as Thorn recounted his time in the southern kingdoms, training alongside Queen Yelena's armies. He spoke of the years past, I realised, not so much for his or Viane's benefit, but rather for mine. As I sat and let the stew settle in my stomach, I learned and committed to memory what I could of Thorn.

He was a commander in King Juriel's army, something expected of him from birth. It was a stepping stone to ruling a kingdom, one form of leadership to another. Thorn missed it, the simplicity of army barracks, men who knew their place in the world. Of routine and regimen, orders given and received with no fuss. He feared ruling Nimue, for what it would mean to the finely cultivated balance that was developed in the last five years under the careful rule of his father. But, Thorn said, it would all be worth it in the end. And having me by his side was justification enough for all that was to come.

I didn't know if I agreed so much. After all, my being with him was only because of one man's need for vengeance, for total domination. Without that, we would have never met. I would have remained under Dearmond, spending my days fleeing through unending tunnels and fighting to survive Purgatory.

Viane had little to report personally. Most of what she spoke was of the world at large. Of the storms that ravaged the east, the assassination of a royal family to the west. She detailed the plight in Cimran, one I knew only snippets of due to the lack of clear information floating between towns - especially into Naiva, already relatively closed off from the rest of the kingdom. I listened attentively, equally horrified by what was taking place and amazed by the gift she bore.

I wondered if such a gift was a curse more than a blessing. And then, out of the corner of my eye, saw the corner of Viane's mouth dip down, her head bob in a curt nod.

A curse then.

*

Thorn and Viane talked for hours. At some point, I drifted off atop a blanket, head resting on Thorn's thigh. The low murmurs lulled me into a deep sleep, my first dreamless one in months. Even unconscious, I was acutely aware that something else was at play.

When I awoke, I discovered the source of my peaceful sleep.

"I wanted to help in any way I could," Viane whispered. She tapped the side of her head. "Telepatia."

The ability to speak mind to mind, to influence one's thoughts. Viane had intervened, taking away the guaranteed nightmares that plagued me nightly. I couldn't bring myself to be angry at the intrusiveness of it all, not when I felt truly rested for the first time in months.

Behind me, Thorn melted along my body. Legs bracketed mine, chin resting atop my head. His arm was slung around my waist, fingers lightly splayed across my stomach, still dipping in the tell-tale signs of starvation. Soon, hopefully, I would round out a little, not look so gaunt and near death. No queen should appear so miserable. It didn't bode well for a strong rule.

"Are diviners often practised in telepatia?"

Viane stoked the fire. "Some. It's not a common practice nowadays. Those of us who became telepatias were used by rulers for personal gain. Some of my kind grew to thirst for the power of their position, one even taking over a kingdom by dissecting the mind of their king. After that, telepatias were hunted down. Those of us who remain are tight-lipped about it."

"Understandable."

Viane glanced over my shoulder to where Thorn snored softly. "He doesn't know, does he?"

My chest tightened. "How much did you see?"

My nightmares ranged from fears of what might have happened to clear recounts of what had already taken place. What had I dreamed while Viane took away the thoughts before they could scratch the surface of my consciousness?

"Enough," she simply replied. "You've been through a great deal."

"Did you know before I came?"

Viane considered me for a moment before finally saying, "I've kept an eye on you for some time."

"Why?" I didn't dare sit up or move and kept my voice low. Thorn needed the rest. I knew for a fact that he'd lost sleep in the past fortnight with me.

"Because the gods willed it. Willed you."

"'*Willed*' me?" I rolled my eyes. "The gods forgot me long ago."

"You're wrong," Viane said. "The gods forget nothing."

Thorn shifted in his sleep, pressing me closer to him. One of us was having pleasant dreams, if the bulge pressing into my rear was any indication. I felt my face flush and shifted, trying to move away only for Thorn to follow, moulding himself to me perfectly once more.

"The Oath-Taking," I said, sliding a hand under my head. "What is it?"

Viane brushed a curtain of snow-white hair over her shoulder before tucking it behind her ear. "The ultimate commitment to another. It's a promise and vow to protect and love."

"Love?" My voice caught. *It's too soon for that.*

"I know. But love comes in many forms, is expressed in many ways." Viane sighed, something like sadness in her eyes. "It shapes the foundations we build our lives upon."

"There's no foundation for us yet," I whispered. "We've not known each other nearly long enough. Today was the first time I learned anything beyond the title Thorn carries. There can't be a foundation built upon nothing."

"I think you know enough to get started," she replied. Viane stood to her feet and moved to the side of the cavern. A chest of drawers leaned against the wall and from it, she pulled another dress. Without a backward glance, she slipped her own dress off her shoulders, not caring that she bared all and was utterly naked before a stranger. Well, somewhat of a stranger since she had admitted to 'watching' me for some time. The dress she put on was a slip of fabric that clung to a subtly curvy frame, hips that you could sink your fingertips into, breasts that rounded out in perfect form. The dress was just sheer enough that I could see the shape of her legs as they led towards the curls of her sex.

"Get started how?" I pulled my eyes away, remembering that Viane could hear everything, that nothing was hidden from her. "Until a little over a week ago, I didn't even want this." I waved a hand over my shoulder to Thorn. "None of this was of my choosing."

"No," Viane replied, coming closer to add another log to the fire. "None of this was. But what happens *now* is. Helmar is a hideous man but he does not get to decide how your life unfurls from here. You can hold fast to the trauma or choose to let go of the things he has done to you. Will that release you from the scars, physical, emotional and mental? No. But you can have a *life*. Something more than intended."

"I want that," I admitted. "But I can't move on. Not yet."

Emrys. So long as he was imprisoned, I would be frozen, unable to let go of Lanceris. The moment I let go of the stone, mountain-ringed city would be the moment my hold on Emrys slipped, sending him plummeting into a fate worse than death. So I would hold on, for as long as it took I would grip to the pain and heartbreak, the nightmares and scars that would mar my skin for the rest of my life.

For Emrys, I would make this sacrifice.

*

If the winding tunnel Thorn and I journeyed down to meet Viane had been considered long, then the one we were currently trudging through could be considered a godsdamned age. The air was damp and slick against my skin, the little black hairs that usually hung in kinked ringlets at the back of my neck were now plastered firmly against me. Even the linen shift I wore felt hotter than the thickest fur cloak I owned back in Naiva, now left to slowly rot in a chest at home in the cottage.

Thorn didn't seem at all phased by the heat as he walked quietly beside me. And I supposed that wasn't entirely surprising - not when many regions of Nimue were more on the tropical side, ranging from warm, balmy nights to monsoonal seasons. The blissful south, far more temperate and progressive than the frigid - in more ways than one - north. I felt traitorous for the surge of joy that filled me at the mere thought of Hafan. The idea of living somewhere so very different to Naiva and Cimran at large was an idea that soothed the most anxious parts of my soul. But then there was that little voice in the back of my mind, reminding me that Emrys was still below Dearmond, still suffering. Even if Helmar hadn't laid a hand on him yet, the conditions alone were enough to kill a man half his age. With a deep breath, I tucked away the spark of joy, determined to keep it bottled until Emrys could be by my side, enjoy that freedom and heavenly warmth right along with me.

My stomach growled in the quiet and Viane chuckled. I ignored her, focusing on my feet and not tripping over myself in the muted lighting. She held a torch ahead of us but as the light filtered back towards us it instead threw shadows across our path, making it almost harder to see than if there had been no light at all.

The Oath-Taking. There was a sacred place for it, Thorn had explained. Beyond that, he'd said precious little, something almost like nervousness setting him on edge as he'd turned away from me. The silence left me with a thousand questions. What would be required? Would I be made to swear promises to the old and new gods to honour and obey a man I still barely knew? Such promises had already been vowed - and quietly disregarded because I was far from obedient to anyone - during our wedding. What more was there to say? To give away? With the placing of the simple gold band on my fourth finger, Thorn had agreed to take all of me. I had nothing left to give up to him.

Except my body. Wholly and completely.

It had been some time since I last laid with a man. It had been Soraya for the longest time, and only her. Despite her engagement and then marriage, I had remained true to her. Before Soraya there were two others, both sons of a priest. The youngest brother had come first and initially, his inexperience had been cute, charming even. But I'd grown bored with him in no time at all and when his brother, Eohan, seven years his senior, returned home from Mera, it had taken all of a day before he and I wound up in bed together. From there, the relationship had been brief, barely lasting until the turning of the moon. However, it had been a passionate, tumultuous one. In the end, it was his father who brought things to an end after walking in on the two of us: me, legs spread upon the altar with Eohan's face firmly set between my thighs, tongue driving me into a state more hypnotic than any drug could muster. It wasn't until the priest cleared his throat, outrage clear in the way he bared his teeth and clenched his fists, that either of us realised we had an audience.

That had been eight years ago now, precious moments stolen when Emrys was distracted in the market. I smiled at the memory, a simpler time and place. One I would never find again.

It wasn't that I was nervous to give myself fully over to Thorn.

No. It was more that I felt stuck, frozen.

No matter how my body craved intimacy, especially after going so long without a kind touch, there was no escaping the fact that for so many months I'd been mistreated. And even that was putting it mildly. My body didn't feel entirely like my own, more like I was simply living in a shell or wearing clothes three times too big. Despite how hard he tried the other day, Thorn's hands and tongue couldn't remove a single trace of Malik's touch. It hadn't been enough and I suspected I would still feel remnants of the abuse for some time, an oily, indelible slick. I didn't know what to do with the new me and more than anything, I hated that. Malik had taken so much and now, even in death, he continued to thieve.

You can hold fast to the trauma or choose to let go of the things he has done to you.

You can have a life.

Viane's words drifted through my mind as I sidestepped a fist-sized rock. I couldn't let go - not so long as Emrys was trapped. But was it possible to let go at least in part? To release one trauma while binding myself to another? I had always been a sexual creature, free with my body, comfortable with the things I liked and wanted. It seemed strange that in the grand scheme of things, that would be the one thing I missed the most but I found myself yearning for it the way I did an old friend.

Thorn lightly squeezed my hand and I glanced up at him, at eyes the colour of crushed emeralds and sea glass. I smiled in reply to his own, the corner of his mouth quirking upwards in a half-smirk. In our brief time together, I had already decided that it was the expression I liked the most. There was a playful mischievousness to it, one that promised fun and laughter and all the good things I once had. My eyes fell to our hands, noting the way his sleeves were roughly half-rolled, half-bunched up to his elbows. How his white linen shirt clung to him perfectly, highlighting every finely crafted muscle and smooth plane. He wore loose pants, hanging lazily off hips that only an hour ago had been pressed up against my rear, and his…

I flushed at the memory, waking up to find his arousal hard against me. I could almost feel him there still, feel the quickening in my core when his splayed fingers drifted idly across my lower belly as he slept on.

"What are you thinking about?" Thorn whispered.

Viane snorted, choked and attempted to turn it into a cough. I threw an irritated glance at her back and she ducked her head a fraction, almost as if in shame.

Good, I mentally chided, hoping she could hear me. *That's what you get for eavesdropping.*

She waved a hand over her shoulder, mumbling, "I know, I know."

Thorn squeezed my hand, pulling my attention once again. I chewed on my bottom lip, debating whether I ought to answer before finally settling on, "Marital…*things*."

"Things?" Thorn's eyes danced with laughter. "Descriptive of you."

"I've not done any of *this*," I gestured between him and myself, "before. Marriage, that is."

"Nor have I."

"It's always been something monumental in my mind, something not to be taken lightly. And despite how we came to be, I want to get it right."

"As do I."

"There are things I assumed I would have in a marriage. Things like-"

"Sex?" Thorn offered up, voice dropping an octave. "I know."

I started. "What?"

"Did you think I didn't notice?" he replied. "How you pushed back against me this morning? I'm not that unobservant - even while half asleep."

"For your information," I began before pausing. Gods, this was embarrassing. "For your information, no, I didn't think you noticed. And it wasn't exactly a conscious action on my part. If you push a cock near me, I'm likely to react."

"Hopefully for the better." He winked.

I shrugged, kicking a pebble out of the way. "Depends on how you treat me."

"Is that why you hold back?" Thorn asked. "Because you worry I'll not stay true to my word? Because I swore it then and I will swear it now - I will *always* protect you. If I thought I would do wrong by you, I would in turn protect you from me, also. I've no intention of hurting you, Artura. Not when I've waited for you for so long."

"That was long for you?" I rolled my eyes, exaggerating the movement. "You only knew of me for a day, if that, before I was handed over."

"Firstly, I never saw you as property to be 'handed over.' You were, and always will be, your own person."

When Thorn glimpsed the look on my face, he came to a stop, pulling on my hand until I faced him. Up ahead, Viane also stopped.

"I mean it, sparrow," he continued, using the nickname that was beginning to stick. "You've never been an object to me. Now, an object of desire? Perhaps."

"I see your cock is still firmly in control of your brain," I dryly replied.

Thorn playfully flicked me on the nose. "Cheeky. But secondly, Artura, I've waited for you for all my life."

"You barely know me." A fact I'd already pointed out several times. I was beginning to feel like the peach-swallows that visited Naiva in early spring. They sang three notes. Again. And again. And again. Forever and always. If I had to remind Thorn one more time that he barely knew me, I would insist on having him change my nickname from sparrow to swallow.

But then, judging by what I already knew of him, that new nickname would brook nothing but innuendo and heated thoughts.

"I'm a quick judge of character."

Viane cleared her throat. "Nothing about you is quick, nephew. May we continue? I'd rather not be *here* when night falls."

In an instant, all playfulness melted away on Thorn's face. "No, you're right. Let's continue."

Twenty minutes more, bend after bend, a downward slope and an uphill climb. We finally came to the end of the tunnel and I stumbled to a stop, shock hitting me like a wave. The tunnel opened on an underground lake, directly fed into by the ocean surrounding the isle. High, high above us, the rock roof bent towards an opening where glorious midday light streamed in. I would never tire of seeing the sun, not after so long spent in darkness.

Greenery clung to the rock walls, with no traces of the amethyst geode here. Vines dripped from the sunlit opening, forming a curtain for one side of the cave.

The water was blue here, bluer than the sky I caught slivers of. But unlike the ocean surrounding the isle, this water was opaque and clouded. I could see nothing of the bottom, there were no hints of any traces of life darting beneath the surface. Slowly, I reached out a hand to touch.

Thorn pulled me back with a gentle tug, shaking his head.

Cleaving the lake's surface neatly in two was a driftwood boardwalk. Halfway down, it was sun-bleached in a neat circle directly beneath the cave skylight. Even in the stillness of the room, the boardwalk looked rickety.

"Will we have to go on there?" I whispered.

Thorn nodded. "Only for a moment."

Even a moment would be enough for the structure to collapse if it truly was as old as I feared. The Isle of the Old Gods was rumoured to be the first land, the birthplace of the world as we knew it. I highly doubted general maintenance was regular practice in such a secluded place.

Viane handed the torch to Thorn. From her shoulder she pulled a sling, bundled before Thorn and I woke this morning. When she neared the edge of the lake, she knelt, undoing the fabric to reveal two items.

A jar.

A knife.

A cord.

With a quick wave of her hand, Thorn stepped forward, pulling me along with him. He followed his aunt onto the boardwalk. It creaked sickeningly underfoot, swaying and sending ripples dancing upon the lake's smooth face. But Viane continued to be perfectly at ease and a moment later, Thorn relaxed. I sucked in a sharp breath, willing myself to calm down.

We stopped at the end, several feet shy of the vine curtain hanging just beyond the last wooden pillar. Viane unscrewed the jar, and holding it firmly in her hands, tipped out the black salt I'd noticed on arrival. She moved slowly, making a perfect circle on the wooden boards. The diviner spent a moment touching it up, double checking the circle was neat and unbroken before gesturing for the two of us to approach. Thorn stepped into the circle, pulling me along with him until we faced one another. Viane stood just beyond the salt circle. The way she held herself reminded me of the priest who had officiated our rushed ceremony a fortnight ago. That was where the similarities ended, though, as she drew the knife up to eye level, carefully balancing it lengthways atop one finger.

"The Oath-Taking," she began, "is not to be taken lightly. Once complete, soul will be bound to soul, heart to heart and mind to mind. You will be one, inescapably joined for the rest of your days."

I started, flinching at the weight of what she said. I hadn't gotten an answer before, as to what the Oath-Taking was. Only that it was a tradition Thorn wished to honour, one that his forebears had partaken of. I shifted nervously.

Viane reached for Thorn's hand, placing the tip of the blade against his wrist. Before I could speak and much to my horror, she flicked the tip of the knife across the pale blue vein. Blood began to pool and drip down his arm, the familiar stench of rust filling my nostrils. When Viane held out her hand towards me, I took a step back, feeling my heel rock on the edge of the salt circle.

"Blood magic?" My breathing came too fast, it was too difficult to focus, to concentrate. "No. I can't. I won't. That's what got me into-" I slammed my mouth shut, cutting off the words before they could fall out and damn me.

"It's alright, child," Viane soothed.

"No," I replied, voice hitching with a note of hysteria. "It's not alright. I will be hunted down. You don't understand. Helmar already thinks me to be a witch. Blood magic is a death sentence."

"You are no longer a citizen of Cimran," she replied. "You've nothing to fear, I assure you."

"It doesn't matter." Emrys was still in danger. King Helmar would exact vengeance upon him for my wrong-doings, of that I was under no illusion.

"Sparrow."

I shook my head.

"Sparrow, look at me."

Despite my better senses, I did. My eyes met Thorn's and found his to be full of tenderness.

"I promised I would protect you. With my life if need be. This is the best way I can do that."

I opened my mouth. Closed it. Opened it again and when I spoke, the words came out hushed, barely a whisper in the enormity of the room. "I'm scared. You don't understand, there are things I cannot do. There's someone-" I forced myself to breathe. "There's someone I need to protect."

It was all I could say. And even that was putting Emrys in more danger than I was willing.

"I know," Thorn replied. He switched the torch to his bloodied hand and placed his empty palm against my face, thumb brushing over the corner of my mouth. "Just as there is someone *I* need to protect."

My eyes darted about the cave, as though I might at any moment see Helmar emerge from the shadows, ready to condemn me to death. But I saw no one beyond the three of us, no threat or imminent danger.

"Promise," I said. A command, not a request.

I was putting my life in Thorn's hands - hands I'd known for not nearly long enough. Hands that had already defended me, nurtured me, killed for me. A warm rush of peace and trust ran through my chest, stilling the roiling panic. But my mind was slower to agree and fall in line, still far too logical.

Thorn swiped away a tear before it could fall down my cheek. "With my life."

Loosing a breath, I nodded and held out my left hand to Viane. The slicking of the knife across my wrist was nearly painless. How many times had she performed the Oath-Taking? On how many others? She moved deftly as she sheathed the blade in a belt at her waist.

"Blood to blood," Viane instructed.

Thorn gripped my left forearm with his own, perfectly lining up the identical incisions. I felt his blood mix with my own, warmth fluttering across my skin. I watched as two trickles of crimson merged into one, drops falling to the boardwalk. It was then that I noticed brown splotches soaked into the driftwood, from blood long since dried. Many others, then. Many before us who'd stood in this exact spot.

Viane unspooled a length of crimson cord, winding it around our hands and arms, back and forth until nearly its entire length, save for several feet, bound us together tightly. My fingers turned numb.

"Fate," she said. "Binding you together from the beginning until the end. Every decision and action has brought you here to this moment, to one another. But make no mistake, it is by fate's design that you have arrived here. This cord symbolises everything you have had and ever will have. It is your beginning and end, bound to one another from this day forward."

I watched as Viane - witch, diviner, telepatia - took the torch from Thorn and lowered it to the length of cord remaining. The frayed end caught fire and began to race. Faster and faster and faster until it neared our bound hands. I jerked back but the cord was too tight, I couldn't move.

"Sparrow," Thorn said smoothly, "look at me. Don't look anywhere else except my face."

I shook, feeling heat closing in.

"Through blood, you become one body, one mind," Viane recited, the words rolling easily off her tongue. "From fate's string, your souls become unified. And through fire, you ignite that fate, set it alight. Fire is both the strongest and weakest element. It will consume everything in its path but a mere stream can stop it in its wake. So, too, will your fate be. By sharing its burden, the two of you give it balance, bringing peace to a heady flame and safeguarding a swift end."

The fire seared across my skin - *our* skin - and I whimpered, biting down on the inside of my cheek. I tasted copper and dug deeper, willing myself not to cry, not to scream as the scent of burning flesh wafted around us. It was too much. I looked from Viane to Thorn and finally to our bound hands. The cord was slowly turning to ashes, drifting to our feet. I noticed that not a single ash flitted past the salt circle, though some came dangerously close. No, it was as though it couldn't escape as one feather-light fragment swept through the air one way, only to rebound off an invisible barrier. Silent tears poured down my cheeks as the last of the rope burned out.

"Let no one pull asunder what has been bound this day." Viane placed her hands around Thorn's and mine, each of us still firmly holding on. I didn't dare let go, not when everything ached, my skin flaming beneath the surface. Viane's touch was cool but I flinched as her skin shifted over mine, hand rubbing back and forth. Her lips continued to move, though only a whisper of sound came out now. I stared, transfixed by the rhythm of them, forming around words I didn't understand. She chanted quietly to herself, speaking words so much like the ones Emrys had spoken over Soraya's limp corpse.

Abruptly, Viane stopped chanting and pulled her hands back. There was no pain. I stared down at my arm where only moments ago there had been blisters forming from the burn. Now, there was nothing. I turned my hand over and could have sworn I still felt the rub of the heated rope.

Just as I opened my mouth to speak, eyes still on my wrist, I felt a shift and then I was falling.

CHAPTER TWENTY-FOUR

Time was a distant concept, one I couldn't have said was truly real or not.

For an age, I sank below the milky waters of the lake, further and further down. Lungs aching, head pounding, extremities tingling as unconsciousness danced closer and closer. It was a taunting rhythm, one that I dreaded but grew to hope for. I couldn't fight against the deceptive current. What had been a smooth, glassy surface was in reality hiding an undertow so strong, it felt like a vice around my body. Weighed down with nowhere to go, I sank.

There was no sign of Thorn, no indication that he had followed me over the boardwalk. I couldn't feel him nearby, sense his presence the way I'd come to so quickly. Viane was further away, still, but I didn't mind.

She'd pushed me in, dainty hands firm against my shoulder as she shoved me sideways into the lake. I hadn't been prepared, there was no more than a second to take in what air I could before I hit the surface.

Air that was running out far too fast.

Move, I begged myself. And then, more desperately, repeated, *Move*.

I couldn't. My arms might as well have been disconnected from my body - legs, too.

Further down, further down.

I'd survived Purgatory. Lived through the horrors King Helmar created, all designed to do exactly what this lake would now achieve - kill me.

Something sparked in my chest. Panic. It was a simple ember at first, every shattering heartbeat a breath stoking that fire. Slowly, panic kindled the fire into something bigger. It spread from somewhere beneath my sternum, racing through my chest, my neck, belly and into my arms and legs - the latter two still very much there and now in utter agony.

Without a second thought, I opened my mouth to scream. Water filled my mouth and nose, chasing away the last remnants of breath. I gagged against the onslaught. The water was cool as it slid past my lips but the moment it reached my throat, burned like acid.

I'm dying, I thought. *I'm dying and there's nothing I can do about it.*

Panic turned into fear.

Fear turned into terror.

Terror turned into power.

Terror turned into power?

I felt it slowly at first, a gentle thrumming pulsating from the centre of my chest. It was that of a drum beat, growing progressively faster until my entire body shook in time with its rhythm. I convulsed, bending backwards, feeling as though I were being sliced from my throat to my pubic bone. Perhaps I was still in Purgatory and the past weeks were nothing more than a fever dream. My mind was broken - that had to be it.

Helmar had done it, shattered the last shred of sanity I clung to.

Around me, I felt a flurry of water whipping past. A whirlpool spinning so fast it wrapped my sodden onyx hair around my face, blinding me. Not that it mattered - I could hardly see my hand in front of my face. The water was far too clouded, as impenetrable as the fog on an icy morning in Naiva.

Around and around, faster and faster. I felt dizzy, sick, as the water grew to speeds I'd only ever witnessed in storms. The northern lands of Cimran were prone to harsh weather, tornados tearing up homes carefully rebuilt after being destroyed by The Cleanse. For the most part, Naiva was protected by the mountains and the Forest of Embers but once, once a tornado had swept through and devastated the town. I was five but could still remember clear as day the screams and shouts, the sounds of roofs tearing off homes with little more effort than that of a piece of paper being shredded.

The water slipped past my face for a final time before it was replaced with something stronger.

Wind.

All around me there grew a cocoon of wind so strong, it scraped against my skin like sandpaper. I felt my cheeks grow raw, and closed my eyes, praying to gods I didn't believe in or trust that this would all be over. Debris whipped up around me, dirt and rocks from the lake floor. I was suspended in the middle of the wind cocoon, nausea rippling through me.

Excruciating heat continued to ripple through my body, hottest where it had grown from my sternum. I fought against the wind, gradually pulling a hand up to touch between my breasts. The shock that flooded through me was overwhelming. I'd put my hand in a fire and could feel it blistering. What I felt on the boardwalk only moments ago was icy in comparison. I would lose my hand. The pain threatened to tear me apart.

But then I felt it, a peace growing amongst the flames. Disconcerting and puzzling and abrupt. The wind around me slowed, stilled. Water lapped at my feet but stopped there. I wasn't drowning anymore. I felt cool air kiss my cheeks and warily cracked an eye.

Before me stretched the boardwalk and on it, Viane and Thorn, the latter staring at me with wide-eyed awe. The former simply looked smug, perhaps even proud. I wanted to choke the ever-loving life from her.

"What did you do?" I bit out. My throat was hoarse, the words coming out rough and low.

"Set you free," Viane replied.

I shook with rage. "You nearly killed me."

"You are stronger for it."

I stared at her, shaking now. My fists clenched and unclenched at my side. I opened my mouth to speak but no words came out. Because there were none, nothing I could say. To feign kindness only to then attempt to kill someone was vile. At least Helmar had shown his true face all along. But Viane? She was a wolf in sheep's clothing.

My head whipped to Thorn, my anger instantly flipping a switch to betrayal. "You said you would protect me. I'd have assumed that included from her."

He shook himself, resuming the calm face I'd seen just before falling into the lake. "Sparrow."

"Don't you 'sparrow' me, you lying, scum of the ear-"

"Artura," he said, voice harder. "Look."

I followed his gaze to where it fell at my feet. And shrieked.

I stood level with the boardwalk but I was far from it, so, so very far. The only ground beneath me wasn't ground at all but rather the lake itself, now once again smooth as glass. Hesitantly, I moved my foot to the side. Fragile ripples of water ran from my boot, growing wider until they melted back into the lake.

"Walk," Viane commanded.

"Fuck you," I threw back.

Either this was some sick and twisted dream or I really was standing upon the lake. How long before I fell in? I couldn't go through that again, succumb to the currents. I'd nearly died and even now, my lungs ached fiercely.

"If you want to get off the lake," Viane continued. "Then walk. The only way out is through."

"What the hell is this?" I couldn't quell the rising hysteria. "How did I get here?"

"If you want answers I suggest you move." Viane flicked a moonlight lock of hair over her shoulder. "I'm not in the business of shouting a conversation. And if you want a warm bed tonight, you'd best come with us. Personally, I'll not stay here longer than I have to. Not when the isle holds...certain obstacles."

I wanted to swear at her again but she was right. I didn't want to stay here. The Isle of the Old Gods had received its reputation through stories of monsters and bloodlust - I didn't want to find out if those stories were true.

Drawing a deep breath, one that hurt more than helped, I took a step forward. And didn't sink. The lake's surface might as well have been rock and aside from the colour and tell-tale ripples, I would have been none the wiser. I counted every step. On the twenty-third, I reached the boardwalk, almost jumping onto the relative safety of it. Relative because so long as Viane stood nearby, I couldn't be certain she wouldn't shove me in again.

And if she did, would I be met with the forgiving surface of the lake - or would it be like meeting impenetrable stone? Either way, I didn't want to find out.

"Get me out of here," I begged, letting the panic seep from my skin in a fine layer of ice cold sweat. The reality of what just happened was beginning to wear on me - and fast.

Thorn studied my face for a second, noted the way my knees threatened to buckle before he swung me up into his arms and stalked off the boardwalk and back through the tunnel.

*

"I don't understand why."

The three of us sat around the fire, a blanket wrapped firmly around my shoulders. More to hold at bay the shivers that rolled through me, though they weren't brought on by the chill. If anything, I felt warm and had so since emerging from the lake. My body felt different and if I was being honest with myself, stronger.

It didn't make sense.

But still I shook, unnerved by the events of the day. I couldn't release the anxiety that gripped me by the throat.

"You were close." Viane didn't look up from the ingredients she chopped. Stew again.

"To death," I retorted.

She shook her head, scooping an onion into the cauldron. "I tried to help you. Truthfully, I had hoped it would be done already. That your time beneath Dearmond had set things in motion and that I wouldn't be required to help."

Thorn stroked calloused fingers up my arm, a silent acknowledgement that he understood, that he was fine with the fact that I wouldn't tell him about Purgatory and Emrys.

Not yet anyway. Sooner or later the truth would need to come out if I had any hope of bringing Emrys out of the nightmare he was trapped in.

"What things?" I pushed. "You can't just nearly kill me without explanation. I deserve to know why."

I deserve not to be put in harm's way but what can you do?

After the past months, harm and I had become old friends.

"What do you know about your mother?" Viane asked, seemingly rather disinterested in her question.

I blinked slowly. "I know very little. Only that her name was Iseult, she was the queen of Cimran for a short time and Helmar's first wife. She died giving birth to me after running from Lanceris with Emrys."

"So you know nothing then about her ancestors in Galdua."

I stayed silent.

Viane nodded slowly, slicing a chunk of fat off a lump of beef. "Your mother was descended from a line of elemental witches, all born to House Igneous - House of the Flame. Fire casters and summoners. They originated from the east, a place called Alharin. Eventually, they settled in Galdua, some five thousand years before your mother was born. By then, any power was very much dormant. For some, however, that power could be awoken through something we now call Awakening. A situation so extreme that you're forced to fight, to change or adapt. Some survive, some do not. You were put through hell beneath the mountain. I assumed it would initiate your Awakening, that you would come out on the other side... *awake*. However, it wasn't enough."

My eyes narrowed and I tensed.

"Wasn't enough?" I repeated. "Wasn't *enough*? How can you possibly find the audacity to say something so foolish? Wasn't *enough*? The things he did... You have no idea what happened down there."

Viane cocked her head to the side and when she replied, it was with blistering sarcasm. "Of course. Clearly, I know nothing with my gods-given talents."

"I couldn't give two shits if you were at my side through all of it," I spat, standing to my feet to pace restlessly across the room. I needed to channel the sudden, overwhelming rage before I turned on the diviner. "Unless you were physically in my shoes, you cannot know what was enough."

"That's where you're wrong," she countered, also standing to her feet. I was grateful she made no attempt to approach and got the feeling she'd only stood to have the conversation at eye level, as equals. Just one person talking to another like nothing was wrong, like one hadn't tried to kill the other two hours ago. "The very fact that you remained the same meant that what happened in Dearmond wasn't enough to push you over the edge."

"The edge of what? Gods, you've not told me a damn thing. All you've done is try to kill me."

"I tried to *help* you," she repeated. "And it worked, did it not?"

I threw my hands up, a harsh laugh coming out. "What worked? Nothing about this *works*. I've been sold into marriage" - Thorn flinched and I tried to ignore the swift guilt that settled over me - "and carted halfway across the world to this godsforsaken scrap of land. My life is no longer my own and I have no indication that the future will be any better. Not so long as Helmar is out there. And now you speak of my mother and those who came before her. Witches? I am of no witch bloodline. I am a healer and nothing more. My..."

My words dried up at the thought of Emrys.

"The man who raised me," I continued. "He taught me everything he knew and in the end, it wasn't enough. *I* am not enough. Now you want to tell me I'm a witch because of some bloodline I knew nothing of until this month? You're deluded. I am no one of consequence."

Viane took a step forward. And then another. She moved between the fire and I, stopping only when I shook my head once in warning.

"When you were under the water," she said. I glanced at Thorn, his face a mask of concentration. "You felt something shift, didn't you?"

A breeze rustled through the cave, dancing around the amethyst geode overhead. I looked up, silent as I thought through the afternoon.

"Yes. Something..." I rubbed a hand over the side of my face, feeling grit still clinging to my skin. "There was heat and air and water." I snorted. "Hell, of course there was water. You threw me into a fucking lake."

"Pushed," she amended.

"Big difference."

"Regardless of how you came to be there, something happened, Artura." Viane closed the remaining distance and this time, I let her, my anger banking with every passing second. I was too tired to hold a grudge and the scent of dinner wafting towards me was distracting. "Awakening is a series of events that shape that which lies dormant within you. Magic. Yours has awoken this day. The undertow of the lake releases no one - no one but you, Artura. It sensed the magic in your veins and set you free."

"I would have known if I had any magic."

Surely. There was truth in my mother perhaps being a witch. All I had to go by was the word of a mad king. His tale from months ago echoed in my mind.

That was the night I learned who my bride truly was. A witch. To save our ailing son, Iseult drew upon ancient blood magic. She fought to retrieve his soul from the After before it took hold of him completely. The child was in limbo, you see. But she could not. She failed. And my son died in my arms.

I caught Iseult practising magic once more late one night. She was out in the gardens, chanting before a fire. The fire seemed to move before her, bend to her will. It was... unnatural. I realised then that she'd kept this pregnancy going through magic alone.

King Helmar's words echoed in my ears. But he'd lied about so much, he was a vindictive man. I had no way of knowing that what he claimed was true. But if Viane was to be believed...perhaps Helmar hadn't tried to deceive me. Just that once, anyway.

Viane half smiled. "We see what we want to see and are blind to that which we do not want to. You were born with magic in your blood, Artura, magic given to you by your mother and those who went before her. Now that it has awoken, you must learn to control it."

I fiddled with the hem of my shirt - Thorn's shirt. My dress was still soaked well after my time in the lake. I didn't fight Thorn when he stripped me bare and dressed me in his clothing. It felt like one giant, comforting hug and I relished the feel of the linen on my skin. Linen that carried his lightly spiced, warm scent. Pressing a sleeve against my mouth and nose, I inhaled quietly, steeling myself with the sense of safety it brought. Thorn smirked knowingly and despite the expression not quite reaching his eyes, it was still comforting.

"Did anyone think to ask me before 'awaking' my magic?"

It would be hard to consider any magic 'mine' - not when it had been drilled into all of Cimran for years that magic was evil, a curse to carry. Even now I feared an executioner would round the corner, sword covered in the dried blood of slain witches already in hand.

"I only prompted the last step," Viane said. "You forget, Artura, but I've had my eye on you for quite a while. I saw the Awakening fall into motion months ago. The day you left Naiva was the day your magic stirred. From there, it was only a matter of time."

I returned to Thorn's side, wearily falling to the ground. Immediately, he pulled me to him and I rested my head against his shoulder, breathing in his delicious scent. I knew it so well already and found myself craving it when he wasn't near. I felt like the beggars in Naiva, sniffing finely ground powders to lose themselves for one blissful moment. If those powders were anything like this, then I understood the addiction.

"You said some do not survive." I frowned up at Viane as she returned to her seat. Lilac skirts billowed out around her, the hem narrowly missing an errant flame. "Why did I?"

She stirred the cauldron once before tapping the wooden spoon against its side. "You said it yourself, Artura, many times. I heard your prayer, felt it as keenly as if I, myself, had uttered the words. *Do not break.* I do not think you to be truly capable of that. You are strong."

How many times had I uttered those words - both mentally and aloud? Far too many to count. There were days when they were all that got me through, the only thing that pushed me to endure what happened in Purgatory. Despite coming dangerously close on more than one occasion, I hadn't broken. I had remained…not quite strong, but determined. To the finish line I had crawled, weaker and far more beaten down than I'd ever been, but definitely unbroken.

We ate in silence, the only sounds that of wind whistling through the tunnels on either side of the cavern and the tapping of spoons against bowls. I devoured three helpings, ravenous from the day. It was the most food I'd stomached in one sitting in months - years, even, with the food shortages in

Naiva. By the time I was done, my stomach felt stretched to the point of bursting and my eyelids grew heavy.

Thorn had been unusually quiet through the evening, offering up only the comfort of his presence. No promises uttered or soft, soothing phrases whispered. Just his body beside mine. I didn't have the energy to push him to speak and instead just held his hand in my lap, my thumb gently rubbing across his knuckles. Viane pottered about the cavern, sorting through this and that, baskets and trunks. At one point, she stood over the long table littered with books and jars. She lifted each jar to her nose only to sniff, replace it on the table and scrawl a note in a leather-bound volume with a tattered quill.

I crawled onto the makeshift bed Thorn and I kept beside the fire. I was slowly roasting, almost uncomfortably hot despite only wearing Thorn's shirt. It hung off me, halfway down my thighs but after so many months of unearthly chill, I didn't dare remove it. I could happily be warm for the rest of my life and not once miss winter and snow and sleet.

Perhaps not as 'warm' as I'd been while fighting for my life in that damned lake, though.

"Are you well, sparrow?" Thorn's calloused fingers caressed the side of my face. He stretched out beside me, head propped up on a fist. One of his legs tangled with mine, pinning me to him. His emerald eyes were dark and flecked with hints of gold in the light of the fire.

"I don't know," I replied, giving the only answer I could.

Thorn's fingers stroked along my cheekbone, my jaw and the side of my neck. I shivered under his touch, feeling warmth pool in my core. How a simple touch from him could elicit such a visceral reaction, I didn't know. My nipples hardened into painful points as my breathing came out ragged, one harsh breath after another. His hand drifted to the neckline of his shirt, shifted as I rested on my side. It fell to show the peak of a breast. Thorn's eyes darted down, his mouth parting on a sharp inhale.

"Sparrow," he breathed.

"Yes?" I was equally breathless, my mind stuttering to a halt as his index finger slipped inside the shirt's neckline. It brushed against the sensitive tip of my nipple. There was no stopping the moan that slipped from my mouth. I was acutely aware of Viane on the other side of the cavern, still huddled over her books, and pressed a hand against my mouth.

"I would burn this world for one touch, one taste," Thorn whispered as his finger swirled around my nipple. "To have you, I would dry the seas, bring the mountains to nothing but rubble. You are a song I cannot drown out, constantly filling my head with the sweetest melody."

"Flattery will get you anywhere," I panted, arching my back into his touch.

"It's not flattery if it's true," he replied. "It's all true. I would do anything for you."

"Some might say you're whipped already, my king." I half smiled, lost to the dizzying sensation just one finger of his brought on. If he touched me more, slid his whole hand along my body…gods, I would implode. My cries would cause the isle to cave in on itself, entombing us forever.

There were worse fates.

"Let them say what they want." He ducked his head to my neck and I felt the heat of his tongue dart across my pulse. Again, I arched into him, pressing my breasts to his chest. My hips moved forward to meet his and I felt his arousal, hard against the apex of my thighs. He jerked, a strangled sound coming from his throat. "Sparrow, darling, they can say what they want. I will fall to my knees and give you my kingdom. I will do anything for you."

Lips trailed gentle kisses down to my collarbone.

"You..." I breathed. "You don't know me."

Don't know what I've done, who I am. Every horrible act I've committed, I wanted to say. But I couldn't, not when such heady pleasure was building inside me. Not when he was driving me deliriously into oblivion, his mouth and fingers promising sweet release and bliss and every good thing I had so sorely missed.

His hand left the inside of my shirt and I whimpered, feeling the absence too keenly. A second later, that whimper rolled into a moan as his hand slid down to cup my sex, already soaking wet and throbbing with need. He hissed through his teeth, the sound turning into a groan as he slicked his fingers along my seam. One finger slid between my folds to my swollen clit, gradually applying pressure until I bucked against him.

"I know you," he whispered against my skin. "You and I, we are the same, sparrow. One flesh, one blood. One heart and soul. I am bound to you and you to me. I've known you for an age. Wanted you even longer. I waited for someone like you and now that you're here, I am *never* letting you go. You are mine, Artura. *Mine*. I protect what is mine. I keep close what is mine. I am utterly devoted to *what is mine*."

On those last three words, Thorn swirled his finger around my clit, punctuating each syllable, driving home the message.

Mine. Mine. Mine.

And as I fell over the edge at the steady stroking of his finger, I realised something.

I wasn't going to mind being Thorn's one little bit.

CHAPTER TWENTY-FIVE

Muted light filtered into the cavern. It came in from cracks splintering through the geode overhead, refracting off the faceted amethyst face to dapple light all around. The illusion was that of a forest floor, specks and splotches of sun scattered about without rhyme or reason.

I woke to one such spot shining on my face, bringing me from the depths of a deep sleep - a sleep where I was dragged under by nightmares that scarily reflected my recent reality. I could have sworn I smelled The Tub and the blood that seeped into every nook and cranny of Dearmond. Could have sworn I heard Helmar's hollow laugh, the one that promised pain.

Thorn had let go of me some time during the night and so when I slipped from our bed, more a collection of blankets than anything, he didn't stir. Viane slept on, too, blissfully unaware of the daggers I threw her way. Good intentions or not, I wasn't going to soon forget the danger she put me in.

Only two days hidden away on the Isle of the Old Gods and already I was getting stir crazy. After months in captivity,

I couldn't take it anymore. I shucked on a coat and stepped into my unlaced boots before leaving the cavern behind.

The tunnel and cavern formed a T intersection. To the left, I would find the lake. I shuddered. Too soon. Even if there was a window to the outside world, so to say, I would have rather chewed off my thumbs than go near the cloudy water again. Liquids of all sorts and I were fast becoming enemies. Any other person might have stopped bathing entirely. But the thought of being dirty after months of being caked with gods knew what was enough to make me swallow the unease I felt.

I started for the right end of the tunnel, the one that would deliver me to where the tender boat was moored. I had no plans of leaving the isle - not when I knew what and who awaited me on the mainland. I just…I needed to see the sun. Even if from a distance. There was no way to tell if it was night or day within the isle. Just unending darkness broken only by intermittent torchlight.

It wasn't so different from Dearmond and Purgatory. I felt my hands turn clammy at the thought of how similar a situation I was in now. The only saving grace was that I wasn't truly trapped here. I had options, though few and limited.

Eventually, I would need to go back to Dearmond. I knew that. The very idea of it was terrifying. Why would I ever want to deliver myself back into such horror?

The answer was simple - while I didn't want to, I needed to. Emrys was counting on me. Perhaps once, he might have stood a chance at survival in the inhospitable cells. That time was long since gone now that he was firmly in the grip of old age. I thought of his fragile bones, the joints that ached not just in the cold anymore, but year-round. Would he survive long enough for me to reach him? Or would he succumb to the conditions alone, freeze to death in the endless night Dearmond provided?

Thorn knew nothing of the man who raised me. I wasn't certain of much but of that? Yes. Viane could have told him but if she did, he was the most flawless actor in the world, giving no hint that he knew the truth. Judging by the white-hot rage that filled every inch of him when Malik attacked me in our wedding suite, I doubted he would be able to conceal his feelings for long. Especially when he found out just what went on for all those months.

As I rounded a corner and stepped out of total darkness, a wrought iron sconce bearing a flaming torch blinded me. Viane had said my mother came from elemental witches. House Igneous. House of the Flame. Said that my magic had been awoken and that I must now learn to control it. There was no denying that in what seemed to be a curse, there also lurked an opportunity. Could whatever I carried be used against Helmar? He'd killed far more witches than I could count. I would be just another one in his path. But I was also sorely lacking in options, in anything useful to free Emrys. True, Thorn had an army. But what was to stop Helmar from killing Emrys the moment he saw soldiers approaching Lanceris' gates?

Nothing. Nothing would stop him. Any chance at salvation would need to be swift and silent. Completely undetected, if possible. No armies to break down city gates. No battle cries and needless bloodshed.

The only blood I hoped to spill would be that of the king.

Ten more minutes of walking and the light ahead grew, the stench of salt becoming more potent. Sea breeze wafted around me, tangling in my hair as if to welcome me back. Whispers travelled down the tunnel and as I rounded the last corner, they became clearer.

"You couldn't win a wager if your cock depended on it," someone said, their voice deep.

Another replied, almost whining. "Why does it have to be my dick at stake?"

"Because it's the only thing you value," said the first man with a booming laugh.

"Fine," the second grumbled. "I'll fold. I like my dick where it is - attached and in plain view."

A clapping sound echoed through the tunnel.

"My friend, we would never know where your cock is. Such is the case with something so small. I would need a spyglass to find it."

As the men came into view, I caught sight of one rolling his eyes. His body was lanky and his face young with an irritable expression. A much larger man sat across from him, hand clasped on the younger's shoulder. When I appeared, the two looked up, mouth dropping open slightly.

It was the younger who made it to his feet first. "My…my queen. I didn't see you there." He sketched a clumsy bow, something like panic on his very pimpled face. How young was he? I knew some kingdoms conscripted boys long before they were men. If Nimue was one of those kingdoms, I hadn't heard about it. Perhaps they were. He couldn't have been older than nineteen. So a man but still a new one, at that. There was an innocence that flashed in his eyes that told me everything all at once. He was still fresh, still new to the horrors of this world. Was this his first assignment for Thorn?

My worries were put at ease in no time at all. One look to the older man at his side and I saw what I saw in Thorn - a protector, defender. The way he stood beside the younger man, slightly in front of him with folded arms - there was a bond between the two. I looked closer at their faces, noting similarities. Same hooked nose, same slate grey eyes and copper hair flecked with gold from days in the sun.

"Brothers?"

The older one spoke first. "Yes, my queen."

"And serving together under the king."

Folded arms relaxed slightly but not enough to tell me the older brother was fully at ease. Did I carry a brand upon my forehead that said 'danger'? They both looked at me warily, like I was perhaps an asp about to strike.

"Leofred." The younger brother sidestepped the older. "Leo, if you wish. This is Edric. Pay him no mind. He's got no manners anymore."

"And Leofred," said a new voice, "has a winning hand, or so I suspect." I turned to find Denard stalking towards us, hands clasped behind his back. He moved past me towards Leo and Edric, tutting along the way. "Now, Edric, you wouldn't be trying to swindle young Leofred out of his earnings, would you? Because I am willing to bet you twice what he has that the boy is about to destroy you."

Denard bent to a rock behind the two men and when he stood up, in his hand he held four cards. He flicked through them, one eyebrow cocking in time with the tilting of his mouth.

"I'll be…"

"Damned?" Edric finished. "There's no way he could've won. I had a full house."

I'd never played poker. All I could do was pretend I knew what was happening. Emrys had tried to teach me once but for all the interest I'd paid, he might as well have tried to teach me how to shovel dirt.

Denard stepped towards Edric, fanning the cards under the man's nose. "Straight flush. Tough luck, Edric. I'm sure you would've spent those marks well at Madam Eleera's. I hear her girls can be quite…acrobatic."

"What do you mean?" Edric lifted his chin, brow furrowing. At a head taller than Denard, he could physically beat the captain in an instant. But there, deep in his eyes, it lingered: fear. A healthy dose of it, too. Denard was a captain not to be crossed.

"The bet was twice the gold Leo has," Denard said cooly.

"So? You said *you* were willing to bet. Not me." Edric jammed a thumb at his chest to indicate himself. Just in case Denard somehow forgot who the man referred to...in our grand group of four people.

Denard shrugged, pocketing the cards. He looked the picture of ease as he stood before the burly man. Edric's face was darkening to an unhealthy shade of puce.

"I never said I was betting *my* money," the captain replied. "Just that I was betting. I suggest you pay your brother. Call it restitution for all the other times you've likely swindled him out of a win."

Edric sputtered, looking between Denard and Leo and then to me. I shrugged. Queen or not, I wasn't about to put my nose where it had no business being. And a game of poker was the very definition of a place I didn't belong. I watched, hiding my enjoyment, as Edric dug through his pocket before withdrawing a handful of coins. Leo was already waiting with an open palm and a grin on his face that could only be described as 'shit-eating.' He clasped his fingers around the half dozen gold coins before promptly pocketing them.

"Pleasure doing business with you, my kin."

Edric grumbled as he walked away to sulk.

"What can I do for you, my queen?" Denard asked, his face turning serious once more.

I cleared my throat. "Um. Nothing, thank you. I just needed to get out."

He nodded, instantly understanding. "I've never done well sequestered below the earth be it mine, tunnel, mountain or dungeon. It's why I travel with King Thorn for the most part.

Days in the open, fresh air and sunlight. Barring the odd exception such as this, naturally. But the voyage here more than makes up for it."

His voice drifted off, eyes wistful. I saw in him something so similar to myself. The understanding that life was precious, that every moment beneath the sun, moon and stars was a gift, one that should never be wasted. I wondered not for the first time what had happened to Denard in his lifetime. What awful past he'd survived.

If it was one thing I was able to recognise nowadays, it was a fellow survivor.

I took a seat on the edge of an outcropping. A meter below, waves lapped against a slowly eroding rock wall. Multicoloured fish darted about between tendrils of seaweed.

"If you don't mind me saying so, your highness." Denard took a seat beside me. "You're looking better every day."

I didn't know what to say to that and settled instead for a curt nod. Chewing on my lip, I looked straight ahead to the mouth of the cave we'd ridden the tender boat through. The sky beyond the entrance was crystal clear blue. I glimpsed the *Scylla* moored far offshore, little dots moving about on the deck. Sailors and soldiers, all Thorn's men.

My men now, too, I supposed.

The enormity of my situation threatened to undo me. So much had happened lately. Deliberately not thinking about suddenly becoming queen of an entire, unfamiliar kingdom was a move made out of pure self-preservation. I couldn't afford to think about the life ahead of me. Not when the possibility of me not surviving my return to Dearmond was all too likely.

"Do you all follow Thorn wherever he goes?" I asked. "I assume now that he's king he'll have a party with him at all times but was that the case when he was a boy, also? Forgive me, I know so very little about this."

Denard bobbed his head from side to side. "Some of us have been with him since he was a boy. We travelled with Thorn to the southern kingdoms and trained together for a time. I and two dozen other men were recalled prematurely to aid King Juriel after sickness wiped out part of his guard three years ago. Thorn stayed behind. It wasn't until this past month that we reunited. I am one of eight men from the original delegation that have returned to him. The rest are still in Hafan."

"And the others on board?" I prompted after a moment of silence.

Denard looked up, something clearly on his mind. "Oh, the others were with him all along. They have a bond that will not so easily be broken. It's been for the best. Thorn's transition to king will be a rocky one. Nimue hasn't seen him since he was a boy. There was no time to prepare the kingdom for Juriel's passing, given how much he kept his ailing health to himself, so likely there will be many none too keen on what is essentially an unknown ruler."

I fiddled with my fingers, picking at the skin around my nails again. The stinging of each piece of skin torn away kept me grounded, gave me something to focus on.

"I daresay having me as a queen will not be great for Nimue either."

Denard twisted to look at me. I felt his eyes on the side of my face and flushed, deliberately not returning his gaze.

"Why do you say that?"

I shrugged, swiping away a drop of blood that bloomed alongside my thumbnail. "Change of rule is always tricky. An unknown king is one thing but bringing with him a foreign, commoner queen? One who has no idea of how to comport herself as royalty nor how to lead a kingdom? That's a surefire way to create unrest, even perhaps to ignite a civil war."

Behind us, I heard Leo trying to convince Edric to play another round of poker. One backward glance from Denard and Leo fell silent. I half smiled at the look on Leo's face, one of a child being caught painting the cat or throwing flour about the house to make 'snow.' Of course, neither of those things was something I had personal experience with. And you definitely couldn't still see flour in the grooves of the brick walls of the cottage, forever clinging to the porous surface. Of course not.

"I would like to think my home is stronger than that," Denard said. A crease formed between his eyebrows as he stared into the gentle swishing of seawater at our feet. His own nearly touched the surface and as he pointed his toe, he scooped along the crest of a small wave, breaking its trajectory. "But then again, I've seen my home grow and flourish in the past three years. Anything is possible."

I knew that to be true more than anything - that anything was indeed possible. Too much had happened lately for me to believe otherwise.

"You know," the captain said, "there is nothing I wouldn't do for my king. And to you, my queen, I extend that same courtesy. Say the word and it shall be done. I am here to serve the crown in whatever capacity possible."

I opened my mouth to thank the captain, to say there was nothing I needed. But an idea hit me hard and fast and my breathing escalated. Perhaps being queen would not be all that terrible.

An army to free Emrys? A terrible idea.

But a few men that could be trusted implicitly to scout for a direct way into Dearmond? A way that only a few had ever escaped from?

My excitement grew at the prospect.

"There is something I need to find," I began, keeping my voice steady. "An entrance at the base of Dearmond mountains. I need to find a way in for a personal matter."

Instantly, Denard's face shuttered, his eyes hardening. He stood to his feet, dusting off his pants and when he spoke, it was with an indisputable finality. "My queen, I said that you need but say the word and it would be done. But some things cannot be - no matter how hard you try."

*

"What," I breathed, hand flying to my throat, "in the sweet, ever-loving fuck is that?"

Thorn and Viane stood meters apart, staring one another down in a silent battle of wills. The latter seemed to be winning as the king fought to conceal a wince. Nothing but scathing fury and anger lit Viane's gaze, a light burning from within that threatened to tear the king apart one piece at a time…slowly…and very, *very* painfully.

Without taking her eyes off her nephew, Viane ground out. "Your lesson."

I pulled back, eyeing the mass at their feet. It was smoking. "My…lesson?"

"*Was* your lesson," she continued, "until this damned fool killed it."

Thorn said nothing but for a moment I could have sworn a flicker of pride ran across his perfect features. Even in the dim lighting, his skin was golden, eyes bright and mesmerising. But I couldn't look for long, not when the thing, whatever it was, shifted.

Thorn's boot flew out, landing a sickening smack against what must have been…gods, it had *two* faces and the smaller, far more grotesque one bore the brunt of Thorn's impact. The creature recoiled with a soft scream, almost weary sounding, and went still once more.

"One of you need to explain. Now." I folded my arms but made no move to approach. Not until I knew that the lump of scales, bones and paper-thin skin was well and truly dead. I'd never seen anything like it before, no such creatures existed so far as I was aware. Or rather, at least not in Naiva. I supposed all stories had to begin somewhere, though. Tales exaggerated from the simplest of things, drawn out and twisted to become the root of nightmares.

This was definitely the root of a horrifying one.

Viane sighed as she removed a shawl from her shoulders to drape over the mass. "This is a fire hellion, a particular type of demon that resides deep below the isle. One of the lesser, easier demons to kill."

"I beg to differ," Thorn finally said, "that demons are 'easy' in any sense of the word."

I drew in a slow breath, noting that the air was tinged with the faint stench of rot and sulphur. "That doesn't explain why there's a hellion in your home."

Viane stood straight, folding thin, though subtly toned, arms. "This was never my home. I merely reside in theirs."

I waved a hand. "I don't care for technicalities. I need to know why a fire hellion is in a bloody heap not even two feet from where I've been sleeping."

"Your husband saw fit to destroy it."

"I saw fit to protect my wife."

"If you would let me teach *your wife* then she could protect herself. She needs the sword of no man when she is weapon enough."

I cleared my throat, more so to shake the nerves twisting inside like eels. "Cut it, the pair of you. I'm gone for an hour and a demon shows up. What lesson were you hoping to instil? That nowhere in this world is safe? Congratulations, mission accomplished."

Thorn left the creature's side and moved to my own. He slid a reassuring hand up my back to my neck where his thumb and index finger massaged at a knot I didn't know was there. I fought not to melt into that simple touch but was unable to stop the curl of pleasure within as his hand went from soothing the tense muscles to gripping my neck possessively.

"Viane, I could have told you this would happen," he said, his tone very matter-of-fact.

His aunt rolled her eyes but said nothing, still seething.

"That what would happen?" I asked, suddenly wishing I'd stayed with Edric and Leo. They had offered to teach me poker, to play as many rounds as it took until I was competent. But I hadn't wanted to be away from Thorn for too long.

That was a mistake. I eyed the hellion warily. No more movement at least.

"Your husband presumed you would not want to unlock your full potential," Viane explained. "He was utterly convinced that you would be content to live your life as his little wife with no real power of your own as is granted by your blood."

Thorn growled. "Do not twist my words. I merely suggested Artura would prefer a more peaceful existence. I do not expect her to be some woman who follows me around and dutifully bears my children. I just assumed - and reasonably, mind you - that she'd rather not fight a demon if she didn't have to."

My eyes narrowed on Thorn. "What happened to not deciding things for me?"

His gaze whipped down to mine, shock radiating from him, stronger than the sulphur rolling off the demon. "You...you want...*what*?"

Viane chuckled to herself, triumphant. "As I said to you, nephew, your wife is a woman who can make up her own mind. I would suggest she develop the magic passed down to her but ultimately, it is *her* decision."

Thorn recovered, his face growing serious as he pulled me against his side. "Hardly seemed like you were allowing her to decide when you summoned that *thing*."

Viane shrugged. "I was merely preparing to teach. You took away my tool."

I looked down at the hellion, half covered by Viane's knitted shawl. It continued to smoke, dark grey tendrils snaking out from the maroon, tasselled edges. They wafted upwards, reminding me of incense in the way each tendril curled delicately through the air. The smell, however, was far from as pleasant as the sandalwood Emrys liked to burn. I swallowed hard in an effort not to gag.

"What would this lesson entail?" I asked. The idea of bearing a weapon when facing Helmar once more, even if that weapon was myself, was immediately soothing. I could be entirely unassuming. Catch the king off guard.

I could best him in a way I never thought possible.

Viane strode to the table, collecting a dusty velvet-covered tome. She flicked through a dozen pages. "The magic possessed by House Igneous is fire magic. Once, in the days when magic was far more potent, it was taught from birth, ingrained long before a child could walk. Now, that's rarely the case, as the magic does not appear in every individual and is usually discovered far too late. Your mother possessed only a trace of it but never developed her skills beyond the rudimentary basics. Perhaps why she failed to save her child."

I wasn't surprised for a second that Viane knew of Iseult and the blood magic that failed to retrieve her child from the brink of the After. In the past days, I'd learned to deal with her snooping into every aspect of my life. Not that I could blame her. After all, had I also possessed her abilities, I know I would have done a little snooping of my own. Anything to curb the guaranteed boredom that came with a solitary existence.

I moved forward and tried to peer over the edge of the book. Subtly, Viane raised it so my view was obstructed.

"To develop fire magic at your age," she continued, "there is a certain risk involved. For those taught from birth, their education contains a modicum of danger each day to create a healthy fear that grows over time to form reverence and understanding. You've not had the opportunity to develop that and being that you are now twenty-four, the only choice left to us is to essentially cram near on two and a half decades of fear in one go. Once that is done, then we can begin to control your magic."

I froze, waiting for Viane to say she was joking, that this was all a laugh at my expense. But her brow furrowed instead as she concentrated on the tome in her hands.

"I've studied this for some time now, helped others discover their magic," she mumbled as she tried to read and speak at the same time. "Admittedly, never fire magic. I've helped those of House Aquatus, House Terras and House Aeris. Igneous magic has become recessive over time, more so than the other houses. But in theory, it should be the same method."

"I'm not letting you test a theory on Artura," Thorn bit out. "Not on my wife."

"A theory is only a theory until proven, nephew. And I vote we prove that theory today."

"What would I have to do then?" I looked up at Thorn, a warning glance that told him to stay silent. I'd never been one to bow to the whim of another. Gods, even Emrys had struggled to make me see reason and obey. Now was no different - especially when there was a chance that I could be useful - truly useful - in saving the old man.

"Come with me, and I will show you."

CHAPTER TWENTY-SIX

I elbowed Thorn sharply as we wended our way through the tunnels once more. He threw me an irritated glare.

"What?" he hissed.

"If you don't like this, then turn back," I replied, keeping my eyes on Viane. The diviner walked with purpose - or in other words, much too fast. I was already panting behind her, trying to keep up with the quick pace she set.

"Not a chance. Someone has to be there to put a stop to all this when it gets out of hand."

"So much faith you put in me," I sniped in reply. We passed the lake and I shuddered, remembering yesterday and the near-death experience Viane now considered a favour.

Favour my arse.

"It's not a matter of faith," he said, "but rather of pragmatism. When you meddle in the affairs of demons, something is bound to go wrong."

I didn't reply. What could I have said? That I knew he made sense? That, yes, something would most likely go wrong? I was untrained and until yesterday, ignorant of the family history that had landed me square in this mess. I'd used the majority of the walk so far to tamp down my fear. Though if Viane was to be believed, then that fear was required.

The downward sloping of the tunnel grew gradually steeper until eventually, my footing was thready. Every step was a risk that I would end up eating dirt. I let Thorn take my hand. Every few steps he held me up, stopping me from landing on my rear and sliding the rest of the way.

"A toboggan might have come in handy," I said to hide my embarrassment on what had to be the dozenth misstep.

"I've never tobogganed before."

"I have," I replied. "Quite a fair bit, too. Naiva would snow half the year and honestly, it was the only real fun to be had. The toboggan Emrys made for me was crude at best but it lasted till I was old enough."

Thorn was silent for a moment. And then - "Emrys?"

I paused, not realising that along with my feet, my tongue had also slipped.

"Who is he to you?"

I shook my head. "No one. Forget I said anything."

But still, Thorn pushed. "Was he a brother?"

"I'm an only child."

"A friend?"

"Sometimes." Gods, what was wrong with me? The replies were falling from my lips before I could stop them. But would they have really hurt? The answers were bland enough, generic to the point of being of no real value at all.

"He was a friend sometimes," I said, remembering that one period when Emrys and I were constantly at odds, forever fighting and bickering. That had been a tense few years before eventually, I learned to master my temper.

Somewhat.

Thorn gripped me under my arms, hauling me to my feet before I could fall yet again. This tunnel had to end soon, surely. I thought of the walk back and how tedious it would be. After months in captivity, athleticism wasn't something I possessed. I got tired just watching the fire burn in the evenings. Make it back up to the surface? That would be a death march.

Just when I thought he had dropped the subject, Thorn asked one final question.

One that made me choke mid-swallow.

"A lover?"

I coughed for several moments before peals of laughter rang out, filling the tunnel. Not from me, but from Viane, far up ahead. It was the tinkling of bells, that sound, full of mirth and hidden knowledge.

"Mother spare me," I gasped. "No. *Not* a lover."

Relief relaxed Thorn's posture. I hadn't noticed till now how rigid and tight he had been. A smile slowly crept across my face and I playfully narrowed my gaze at him.

"You're not…jealous…are you, *my king*?"

He cleared his throat, looking away as we navigated through the tunnel. Stairs with worn down, rounded edges came into view, carved into the rock floor. Why couldn't there have been stairs the entire way? That would have made things infinitely easier, much less of a near-death experience.

"What you did before is history," he replied with a huff. "I've no right to be jealous of anything you may or may not have done."

I laughed at his obvious discomfort at having been caught.

"I am *not* jealous," he insisted.

I nodded, lips pressed firmly together to trap in the laughter that threatened to burst forth.

"I'm *not*," he said again.

"You protest too much," Viane called from up ahead, her voice echoing around us.

Thorn opened his mouth to speak again, whether to insist once more that there was no hint of jealousy, I didn't know. Instead, I decided to put him out of his misery.

"Emrys was like a father to me," I explained. A heavy weight settled in my chest at the last memory I had of him, huddled into a corner of a damp cell, face gaunt and pale and scared. Not for himself, but for me. That man would have protected me to the bitter end. I just hoped that I would reach him before that came about. "He raised me after my mother died."

That seemed to satisfy Thorn as he loosed a breath.

I smirked a moment later as I said, "If you want to talk about lovers, however, I can tell you all about *her*."

His head snapped up at that. "Her?"

"*Her*," I agreed. "Fret not. She turned out to be a lying, back-stabbing cunt. My fidelity to you is once more assured."

"I wasn't worried about that," he replied, wiping a hand over his face. The memory of Emrys declaring I was aging him terribly came to mind and I wondered how much Thorn would agree with him. "But now, I'm not so certain."

The tunnel - thankfully, blissfully, finally - evened out. Down so far, it was so dark I had to squint up at Thorn and even then, it was hard to see him. The torch Viane held up ahead was a faint glow. It was as though the dark were swallowing the light itself, thirstily consuming any radiance it contained.

I squeezed Thorn's hand. "Who else am I going to meet here?"

"Methinks he thinks me," Viane called out in a sing-song voice. She hadn't lost any traces of humour, obviously enjoying eavesdropping on our conversation. "And I would not object, nephew, let me say as much. So best you keep your wife satisfied or I'll not shy from the task."

Thorn's face paled in the darkness, turning ghostly white. "There's a reason she was exiled to the isle."

"I wasn't *exiled*," Viane said, her voice instantly closer. We ground to a halt, narrowly avoiding a collision. "I *chose* to leave. Nimue has been many things but progressive it was not. At least, not when I left. We can thank your father's rule for moving things along, albeit slowly."

There wasn't a chance for me to reply, not when a low growling filled the air. The sound was laced with scratching and clawing against rock, the vibrating through to my very bones. I went entirely still as I listened to what was most *definitely* the thing that went bump in the night.

*

My eyes roamed overhead. Honeycomb. That's what I immediately thought of.

Hexagonal gaps fanned out around the walls and ceiling, each one as wide as a man was tall and just as deep. They weren't part of the rock, hadn't been formed with the birthing of the isle as so many other features had been. I eyed a part of the honeycomb as we moved past. Veins spider-webbing through glossy raw, membranous meat. Organic matter, a kind not entirely unfamiliar to me after all I'd done with Emrys.

Thorn held onto me tighter still. "It almost looks like-"

"Placenta," I finished, unable to hide the disgust in my voice. When Viane raised a brow in my direction, I shrugged. "I've seen enough afterbirth to recognise one when I see it."

She led us to the centre of a space the size of her cavern. If it weren't for the honeycomb all around, the space would have been twice the size. Feelings of claustrophobia danced in the middle of my chest.

"Truthfully, you're not far off," Viane said. She placed the torch on the ground. Compared to the tunnel, the light was better here, reflecting off the hard edges of the honeycomb. It was almost pretty, the luminescence that flittered around us.

"Viane, what is this?" Thorn looked physically uncomfortable. I found myself wishing he'd opted to stay behind.

"A nest," the diviner replied. Hands on her hips, she surveyed the cavern. "A mighty fine one, at that."

"A…nest…" Thorn repeated slowly. "A nest for what?"

Her eyes glowed with wicked mischief. I knew the kind far too well - and instantly dreaded what she had in store.

"Hellions."

Thorn was pulling me back to the entrance before she could finish the word, grip so tight around my hand, it was almost painful. I was caught somewhere between running right along with him and staying out of a morbid sense of curiosity. Because if I was being truly honest with myself, I wanted to know what Viane had planned. How she intended to pull magic from my veins like the air from my lungs.

Just as we reached the doorway, I dug my heel in.

"Sparrow," Thorn warned, his voice deep and impatient.

"Just…" I inhaled deeply. The scent of sulphur and rot was overpowering here. The same scent I'd smelled in Viane's room. I swallowed against the bile rising in my throat. "Let's hear her out, just see what Viane has to say."

"Family or not," he replied, "she's mad. I'm not putting you in harm's way. This is insanity, Artura."

"I agree. But I still think we should hear her out."

He wasn't relenting, still firmly with one foot out the door. I reached up to cup the side of his face, feeling the clipped beard beneath my fingers, the warm, smooth skin that stretched across his cheekbones. Emerald eyes full of nothing but concern looked into mine and I almost relented.

Almost.

I turned, dropping Thorn's hand, and moved to stand across from Viane. The diviner had the good sense not to look too triumphant, though there was a suspicious gleam in her eye. With a heavy sigh, Thorn left the entrance and retreated to the torchlight.

"Now you see sense," Viane said. "Glad you decided to stay."

"When this goes south," Thorn bit out, barely concealing his fury, "and it will, just know that I told you so."

Dramatically, Viane rolled her eyes and threw her head back with a groan. "Have a little faith."

The scratching started up again, echoing around the room.

"They know we're here."

I gulped. "Sure. But why are we here?"

Viane drew a blade from her belt. The handle was inlaid with blood-red rubies that sparkled in the light of the torch. The craftsmanship was flawless and the weapon itself was completely unmarred by use. The edges gleamed with the promise of being razor sharp. I'd only seen this kind of blade once before and then, it had sold for a godsdamned fucking fortune.

"You best hold this," Viane said. I took the blade from her as she pulled its twin from the other side of her belt. "When I say so, fight."

I glanced up, panic dousing me like a cold bucket of water. "What?"

Viane didn't look back as she moved to a nearby honeycomb, raised her dagger and pierced the flesh.

*

The scream was ear-shattering and guttural all at once. It tore through me as fast as Viane's blade sliced through the fleshy placenta. Foul-smelling liquid poured out, pooling at our feet. Had I thought the sulphur and rot were bad? I was wrong. So wrong. Thorn was already dropping into the stance of a warrior, a finely trained soldier. I had seen it only once before. The night where he killed Malik, slitting the man's throat from ear to ear. And now, that same steely determination fell over him as he studied the scene before us.

Viane stood beside the placenta. Cocoon? Nest? What was it? Now wide enough to glimpse the internal structure, I saw it was unlike anything I'd ever seen before. The spider-webbing veins were more like actual webs, weaving back and forth in a secondary layer behind the placenta wall. Any other day, I'd have wanted a closer look. But there was no time to question and wonder. Not when a bony, clawed hand weaved its way through the webbing and tore it apart.

The torchlight flickered dangerously at my feet, the placenta's liquid oozing around it. I bent down and blindly reached for the wooden handle, not once taking my eyes off the creature that slowly emerged.

It was identical to the one Thorn had killed in Viane's room, right down to the parchment-esque skin and dual faces. One face, the larger, had its eyes still closed as though sleeping. If anything, it looked peaceful. The second face, however, was the distinct opposite. It stared right through me, furious and maddened and murderous. It's eyes glowed in the darkness, swirling orange and crimson and gold.

Like fire.

A fire hellion.

"Fight," Viane said, her tone cool and calm despite how closely she stood to the demon.

"Are you insane?" I hissed, holding the blade the same way Thorn held his own, pulled from somewhere on his person. I hadn't seen him withdraw a weapon but now he held two - a dagger that in my hands would have been more like the sword held in his other hand.

"Do you want your magic to manifest?"

I hesitated.

Emrys.

His name was a whisper in my mind. A reminder of what I stood to lose if I didn't act and give his rescue my all. I swallowed past the lump in my throat, the memory of him and nodded.

"Good." Viane smiled, genuinely pleased. Definitely insane. "Kill the demon."

Across the space, the hellion was still righting itself, stretching and testing joints that a moment ago had been bent at odd angles. The same sticky liquid that I decided had to be a kind of amniotic fluid dripped from his skeletal frame.

I held up the dagger. "With this? You must be joking."

Viane looked down at her hand, studying her nails as if this were just any other morning. As if we weren't square in a nest of hellions.

"You can use the dagger if you want," she replied. "Use your fists or gods, even your teeth. Are you afraid, Artura? Fear is what will bring out your magic. Be afraid, fall into that fear and find yourself."

This was lunacy. All of it. Fear to bring out my magic? If you had asked me even a day ago what I thought would be the best way to learn, I would never have said this. Would have likely assumed there would be countless days bent over volumes and tomes, tinkering with vials and cauldrons.

But fighting a demon?

No. That wasn't even my hundredth guess.

Thorn crept incrementally in front of me, prepared to strike at a moment's notice. He could kill the hellion easily enough. He had already, the body was still cooling in Viane's room. But if Thorn fought this battle, would I truly know fear? Would I accomplish what I needed to? He could fight and I would hide, and yes, I might be afraid.

But not enough.

I placed a hand on Thorn's shoulder. He knew what I was about to say before the words left my mouth.

"Forget it, sparrow."

"Please," I whispered, daring a quick glance at him. "I need to do this."

"I beg to differ," he ground out, a muscle in his jaw ticking.

"Thorn."

He softened - just enough that I knew he was about to relent.

"You can stay by my side," I amended. "Just let me take the lead?"

In the split second he took his eyes off the hellion to look back at me, the demon lunged forward. The cry that tore from its two mouths working in unison was shrill as it rang through my ears. I felt dizzy at the sound echoing through the cavern, bouncing off each one of the honeycomb cocoons. I shook my head to clear it, that one sound disorienting me in a way I could barely comprehend.

"Artura," Thorn shouted.

I looked up just in time. The hellion bounded off its hind legs, arcing into the air. Its clawed hands dug into my shoulders as it used its full weight to push me to the sticky ground. For something that looked so lean, emaciated even, the demon was heavy. I struggled against it, trying to pry myself out from under its grasp as the smaller of the two heads snapped its jaws at me. Saliva dripped from behind blackened, pointed teeth, and when it hit the exposed skin of my neck, it seared, hotter than fire.

I screamed in surprise and pain, unsettling the creature long enough to twist out of its grasp. I rolled to the side, slipping in the fluid and scrambled back on hands and knees. With enough distance put between us, I pushed myself to my feet and wiped my hands on my dress. The ooze covering the ground was hot and clinging to me, stickier than honey.

Once my hands were clean enough to be usable, I looked around. In the struggle, I'd dropped the dagger. It glinted faintly from under the demon where it poised on its haunches.

Are you afraid, Artura?

Yes. Very much afraid.

The hellion circled me, biding its time. After the initial attack, the creature realised that this battle would be easy. I was an opponent of no consequence. Easy prey. My death would be swift and painless.

For the demon, anyway.

I warily eyed its claws, feeling their phantom touch against my shoulder. I reached a hand up to prod the wound left behind. Not deep. It hadn't been an attack designed to kill, just to unsettle.

A job well done.

As the hellion circled and moved away from the dagger, I moved in turn. Every step put me closer and closer, the tightness in my chest easing. I reached the blade easily enough, crouching to retrieve it without taking my eyes off the hellion. It tipped the two heads to the side, studying me. I stared back, a thousand thoughts racing through my mind as I debated the best way to kill such a creature. Yes, Thorn had done it. But he was a soldier. He was lethal, the blades he held superfluous to what was already innate.

I was no soldier. I was a healer and a mediocre one at that. The only life I had ever taken was by accident. Emrys had raised me with the belief that taking life was abhorrent. True, the past months had challenged that belief and I now realised there were exceptions to every rule. But committing what amounted to cold-blooded murder? I didn't know where to begin.

Those glowing eyes, all four of them, narrowed.

Icy dread gnawed at my gut.

Before I could register what happened, Thorn was on the ground, pinned by the hellion. It hadn't intended to kill *me* moments ago. I knew that now. Because the way it fought with Thorn, tooth and nail and all fiery anger...this was what it looked like when a demon sought death.

I didn't think as my boots pounded against the floor, headed directly for Thorn. He was strong but the hellion was stronger. Just when Thorn managed to push himself up an inch or two, the hellion shoved him back, a sickening crack bouncing off the honeycomb all around. Fear chased away every last thought, every ounce of self-preservation as I launched myself atop the demon.

I realised my mistake almost instantly.

The larger of the two heads turned around to look at me, a self-satisfied smirk growing across its face. A hunter that had tricked and trapped its prey. One clawed hand wrapped around to press against my back, holding me to its body. I swung with the blade, trying to make purchase. Twice I scraped the blade against the leathery skin of its back but it wasn't deep enough. Barely a drop of blood oozed from the wound. The hellion seemed almost amused as I fought against it.

I was a fly in a spider's web. Helpless.

Afraid.

Thorn didn't move, didn't pull away as the hellion's full attention turned on me. I hazarded a glance at his lifeless form on the ground. Blood flowed from a wound on his throat. I opened my mouth to scream but no sound came out, just a whooshing of breath as the clawed hand held me tighter. I couldn't breathe, couldn't pull in enough air. Just as I had nearly drowned yesterday, I was now slowly suffocating. If I made it through this, I would never again take fresh air for granted.

I felt my body grow heavy and limp as I fought for air.

But then the heaviness shifted, turned into something else.

Heat.

It pulsated through me like a heartbeat, starting deep in my core. I felt it grow, spread, turning into a blaze as it reached my chest. It moved through to my arms, my legs, my hands and my feet. With one final pulsation, it filled my head. An all-consuming inferno, wrapping around me like a second skin.

I felt the heat, knew it was hotter than any flame I'd been near before, but it didn't burn me. Beneath my hands, already pushing against the hellion's skin in my efforts to free myself, I felt a slow bubbling, melting. Seared flesh filled my nostrils as the hellion screeched in agony. I pulled my hands back, tendrils of melted skin and muscle pulling away with them.

I wasted no time, latching onto the head facing me with both hands. Again, the creature screeched, the sound morphing into a wail, almost like it was crying, begging. I didn't stop, didn't let go. Digging my fingers in, I found ridged sockets that held the haunting, glowing eyes that had stared at me with that predatory gaze. A moment later, I felt more than heard the skull cracking as it collapsed in on itself. Beneath my hands, there was nothing but charred bone, fragmenting and falling into the stump that once bore the hellion's head. I reached for the second head, going through the same motions, only this time with more certainty of what I was doing.

Thorn still hadn't moved so much as an inch. The blood oozing from him had quickly become a competing stench with the melted flesh of the hellion. It spurred me on, fuelling the rage that had once been fear. Again, cracking vibrated up my arms before the second skull caved in.

The creature froze and the hellion's hand fell from my back. I slipped to the floor, scuttling around the headless form still standing on two gnarled hind legs. I reached Thorn within a heartbeat, sheltering his body with my own as the hellion teetered forward and collapsed atop us.

CHAPTER TWENTY-SEVEN

I pushed inky, matted hair away from Thorn's brow, studying the smooth features splattered with blood - both his own and the hellion's. He didn't stir, barely breathed and then-

A groan. It was low, almost too quiet to hear. But I could have sworn it was there. Ear against his chest, I stroked his face with my only free hand, the other still trapped beneath the hellion, willing Thorn to wake up. My heart pounded relentlessly, an ice-cold sweat coating me from head to toe. Or was that the cooling demon blood, soaking through the back of my dress? I half shoved, half wiggled out from the hellion, trying to shift it even a fraction off Thorn. With both the demon and I atop him, breathing would be difficult, near impossible. The hellion weighed a godsdamned tonne despite its frail appearance. What was it made up of? Solid rock? It didn't make sense how something so lean could be so damned heavy.

The hellion's torso slipped to the side, just enough that with one more shove, it fell to the ground beside me. I followed a second later, our positions now reversed. With one hand I pushed up, ignoring the fact that what I used for leverage was the gaping chasm that had once been a neck. There was only silence surrounding us, not a hint of life within the other cocoons. Safe for now, at least.

My hands fussed over Thorn, lifting fabric and searching for injuries. At his throat was a nasty gouge, bleeding much too fast. His chest bore a long cut. The outermost edges of the wound were blackened and, I realised, singed. As though the hellion's claws had been so hot they cauterised the wound as it was made. It was the same for the other three injuries on Thorn. I turned back to the bite mark at the base of his neck - from teeth that were not only pointed but also serrated. I glanced at the smaller of the two heads. Serrations along both sides of each tooth and half an inch apart, designed to inflict as much damage as possible. I shuddered, turning away.

The hem of my dress was torn from the fray and I ripped an arm-length piece that I promptly folded to create a pad. I placed it against Thorn's neck, silently praying the hellion's bite contained no traces of poison or venom.

Thorn's chest lifted on a deep inhale. His eyes flickered, the normally rich emerald muddied by exhaustion and pain. He winced as I pushed against the bite hard, willing it to stop bleeding and clot. It was far too close to the jugular. Any closer and it would have been torn clean in two, instantly becoming a life-threatening injury. Not that this was much better. His golden skin was sallow, his face covered in a fine sheen of sweat.

"Sparrow," he murmured. "Are you well?"

I couldn't help the laugh that bubbled. "Am I well? *Am I well?* Look at you! You…"

He smiled weakly, the familiar mischief returning. "It's nothing I've not dealt with before."

"I highly doubt you've been wounded by a fire hellion before now." I pulled the corner of the pad back. Still bleeding. I suspected it would need to be stitched back together. Emrys had taken care of sewing wounds. I had only ever watched, too nervous to keep a steady hand. I loosed a breath. "I'm sorry."

He frowned. "Sorry for what?"

"I should've realised the demon would go for you."

"How could you have? No one knows the mind of a creature of The Pit."

"I need to get you out of here," I said, wondering how - or even if - Thorn might cope with the return journey. Downhill had been taxing enough. Uphill would be murder. "Can you stand?"

"Parts of me can." He winked. The idiot actually *winked*.

My free hand gently swatted at his head in a mock uppercut. "Stop thinking with your cock and start thinking with your brain."

"But my cock has a brain of its own, too."

I ignored him. "We've a long way to go and I need you lucid at the very least."

Groaning and failing to hide the way his face paled even further, Thorn pushed himself up. I didn't remove the pad. The best option to stem the blood flow would be to secure it somehow and ensure there was enough pressure. Wrapping it would prove near impossible, though, with the position of the bite. I was fairly certain the vein itself wasn't pierced. There was a lot of blood but not nearly as much as there had been with Malik.

I glanced around the room, searching for a solution. My eyes landed on Viane.

She stood silently, hands clasped in front of her. There was no hint of panic or worry for her nephew. Just a soothing peace. I scowled at her, wondering how angry Thorn would be if I slipped a tincture of oleander, nightshade and hemlock into her tea. She would be dead within minutes, payback a bitch. Of course, the fact that I couldn't get my hands on a single one of those ingredients did put a dent in my plan.

"I actually have all three," she said, a hint of amusement in her tone. When I glanced up, her violet eyes were twinkling. "If you do decide to kill me."

"The day is young yet," I murmured. "I dare you to give me another reason."

Damned telepatia. No inner thoughts were safe.

Thorn stood to his feet, swaying. I pressed one hand against the pad, the other against his back to steady him. He grunted as he lifted an arm to wrap around my shoulders to balance himself. No. Not to balance. His thumb stroked at the exposed skin of my shoulder, soothing my racing heartbeat. It thumped so hard against my chest that I was certain he could hear it. Did he have any idea how terrified I was - both then and now? His returning to consciousness eased that terror somewhat but I had come too close to losing him.

And again, I wondered how I could be so concerned for someone I barely knew. Nearly a month had passed since we were wed and yet, I felt drawn to him, like one magnet to another. Already I knew that if I lost Thorn now, it would hurt.

Really fucking hurt.

*

Viane was testing my patience.

It felt like some cosmic joke. No sooner had we hobbled back into her cavern than she had pulled from a wooden crate three pouches, each one containing the ingredients that would kill her in no time at all. I ignored them, knowing she was just trying to bait me, and focused instead on Thorn.

The bite mercifully clotted on the return journey. I washed and dressed the wound with provisions from Viane, taking them silently and without meeting her gaze. The hellion's bite was benign with no signs of contamination and I breathed a sigh of relief. One less problem.

Thorn's gaze didn't slip from my face as I worked. I felt the heat of his stare, felt my core turn molten. The reaction was instantaneous. I breathed heavily, unable to focus. I licked at my dry lips, noticing the way his eyes flickered to the small movement, how they darkened to a shade of forest green that reminded me of home.

Viane left, muttering something about 'attending to duties' and the cavern fell silent.

"I want you," he breathed.

My eyes narrowed, hands going to my hips. "The only thing you should want is sleep."

He shook his head and reached up to twirl a lock of my obsidian hair that fell along the side of my breast. His fingertips dusted across the curve, trailing fire in their wake, and I couldn't stop the way I shifted into that touch, silently begging for more.

"No," he said, voice smoother than velvet. "I want my wife."

I forced myself to concentrate, to not get swept away in the moment. I wanted him, too, more than anything. But if I let myself be caught up in the heat of the moment, would I regret it?

Perhaps.

That was enough to give me pause.

"Do you want me simply because I am your wife? Or because I am Artura?"

He leaned forward, pressing his forehead to mine. "I want you because you are *mine*. In every sense of the word. My wife, my heart, my soul and every desire. I could have died down there. You could have..." He worked to swallow past a lump in his throat, face turning grave. "I've never been so distracted in a battle in my life but the moment I saw you facing down that hellion, every thought ground to a halt. All I could think was that if you died, I would have died right there with you. It would have devastated me, *eviscerated* me. Sparrow, we haven't had enough time."

"Why?" I found myself asking. The gnawing need in my core was driving me insane but I had to know. "Neither of us asked for this." I waved a hand between his chest and mine. "I certainly didn't. The last person I gave my heart to destroyed it. How do I know you won't do the same?"

"Sparrow, I could no sooner hurt you than I could extinguish the stars," he murmured, placing a warm, tender kiss on my brow.

I shivered in delight under the gentle press of his lips, closing my eyes to savour the moment. Never had I ever wanted anyone as much as I wanted Thorn. The aching need I felt was so acute that if I didn't have him, it would cleave me clean in two. I lifted my lips to return the gesture, kissing him, and when I pulled away, I sighed against his warm skin.

"And I could no sooner let you go than I could bring the heavens to ruin." My hands cupped his face, thumbs stroking against his cheeks. "I want you, too. Painfully, desperately, completely. But you terrify me, Thorn. I'm no stranger to love but what I feel for you? It feels more like obsession. From the moment I met you, I couldn't put you out of my head. You drove yourself under my skin and became an indelible mark upon my very soul. I don't understand how this can be what it is so soon. I don't even think there's a name for what we are."

Married sounded too formal. Partner, too clinical. Lovers felt almost cheap with the way I burned for him - like the very air in my lungs depended upon his presence.

He smiled in my hands, turning slightly to kiss one palm and then another. "Then do not name it. Just live for it."

I lowered my mouth to his, hovering an inch apart for an agonising moment. So close. We'd kissed before. Neither of us was unfamiliar with the touch and feel of our lips melting together, but somehow this was different. We stood on a precipice, one more step and we would fall, never to be saved.

I don't want to be saved.

Thorn's hand wrapped in my hair, yanking my mouth against his own in a fevered kiss. His tongue tangled with mine, tasting like honey and cinnamon, warm summer days and long winter nights with a book by the hearth. I drove forward, pushing him back against our makeshift bed. He landed with a grunt.

"I'm sorry," I said, a hand flying to my mouth, suddenly remembering how mauled he was. I inwardly chastised myself, *Stupid, stupid, stupid*. "Are you okay?"

He huffed a laugh past the pained look on his face. "With you? Always."

*

The sound of heavy boots echoed around me.

King Helmar. He was here.

Nowhere to run. Nowhere to hide. Back to Purgatory. I wouldn't leave this time. He wouldn't be so reckless as to let me wander the tunnels, searching for an escape.

This was it.

Thump, thump, thump.

Closer, closer closer.

A hand pressed around my mouth. I couldn't breathe. I was drowning. A moment from now I would be face down in The Tub, struggling not to inhale vomit and feces, blood and urine. I gagged against the hand.

"Sshh," a low voice commanded.

Feminine. Had King Helmar sent another to torture me? I fought against the hand once more only to feel a stinging slap against my cheek.

My eyes flew open and instantly I jerked back. Viane hovered over me, her gaze going to Thorn who slept on soundly, not moving a muscle. He'd been exhausted, utterly wrecked after the day. I hadn't intended to sleep beside him - not when someone needed to tend to injuries and ensure he didn't develop an infection. I searched Thorn quickly, only to find his bare, wounded torso dressed with fresh cloth and sweet-smelling herbs. All traces of blood had been washed away. Had he been wearing a shirt, he might have simply been resting rather than sleeping off a near-death experience.

Viane turned back to me, tendrils of snow-white hair brushing against my face. She held out a hand, one which I looked at warily for a moment before taking. I still hadn't fully decided not to hurt her - just whether or not it ought to be lethal. There was no denying she had been reckless today, putting Thorn and I in danger...again. True, the king had managed just fine with a hellion on his own but he said he'd been distracted. I was a liability when it came down to it, one that nearly cost him his life.

She motioned for me to follow and I trailed a step behind her, leaving the cavern behind. Once in the tunnel, she folded her arms and turned back to me.

"What do you want?" I asked, stifling a jaw-cracking yawn. I'd slept, yes, but quality of sleep? That was a foreign concept to me after the past few months.

"Firstly," she said, voice low. "I would like to thank you for my stay of execution."

"Early days yet," I interjected.

"Secondly, we need to talk about what happened."

I leaned back against the tunnel wall, feeling the cool rock leeching through the back of my dress. Before falling asleep, I'd hastily changed into one of the few dresses Denard delivered in a trunk the previous day. It was a velvet blue so deep, it neared on black. Sewn along the wrists, neckline and hem were tiny six-pointed stars, the thread a bright silver that sparkled in the torchlight. I chose it over a burnt orange high-necked gown, the colour too close to blood for my liking. In the past months, I had seen more blood than I cared for.

"I suppose we do," I replied. "So I'd like to begin with, what the fuck?"

Viane, for the first time, looked ashamed. It was only there for a fraction of a second but enough to satisfy me.

"I've been somewhat remiss in my efforts thus far." She gave me a tight-lipped smile, her full lips thinning slightly. "I've been rather hell-bent on helping you develop your magic."

"Which I'm still not convinced I have."

"Aren't you?" she countered, head cocking to the side. Viane eyed me with intense curiosity, trying to see something that wasn't there. At least, something I didn't *think* was there. "Did you not feel it today? The heat? The burn? I saw the marks your touch left upon the demon. You branded the creature with the fire in your veins, melted the very skin from its bones. Gods above, you even turned bone to ash."

I said nothing, my gut stirring with unease. Memories of fighting the hellion resurfaced, already buried deep despite the short time between then and now. The memory of searing flesh and skin that stretched apart like too wet dough, of the unearthly screams that erupted from the hellion as it fought to loose itself from me... I shuddered at it. Every single moment flashed through my mind.

"Artura, you can pretend all you want that you are average, ordinary even."

I put up a hand to stop her. "You know as well as I do that what I've been through these past months was anything but ordinary."

No need to explain, not when Viane had seen it all. She pulled me into her mind, behind a curtain for me to see all she knew. It was as if I stood outside my body, watching everything beneath Dearmond unfurl. All the horrors of Purgatory, Emrys wasting away in his cell as he lived off naught but scraps, the loneliness in my eyes, my body turning into little more than a ghost of what it was as the images sped past, faster and faster in a dizzying whirlwind.

"Get out of my head," I ground out, trying to block every single image that infiltrated my mind. I pressed shaking, clammy palms against my temples, as though I could somehow shield myself from Viane. I hadn't noticed the tightness, like one giant fist around my brain until it relented. My mind went blissfully blank once more and I panted, more tired than if I had run from one end of the tunnel to another.

"Compared to what awaits you, Artura," Viane said, tone gentle as if in apology, "all that has passed is very much *ordinary*. Let me teach you, help you unlock the magic you possess. You could be great, incredible, utterly *untouchable*."

I shook my head, about to object when the last four words to leave her mouth made me instantly pause.

"You could save Emrys."

"I know," I whispered after several seconds had passed in silence, save for the whistling of wind down the tunnel. It stirred the hem of my star-speckled dress, winding its way underneath and up my legs. I shivered and banded my arms around my chest in a feeble attempt to ward off the chill. "Don't you think I haven't thought about that? I know I could save Emrys. But there's a chance I could also damn him. You know what it's like in Cimran. You've seen it. People are killed for simply breathing the word 'witch' - it's madness there. Emrys could hardly give an elixir to cure a cold without fearing for his life."

Of course, he had done it anyway. Because some things were worth risking it all for. To help another, show kindness and mercy in the face of unquenchable wrath. That had been important to Emrys, valued above all.

Except me. My life was the one thing he valued the most. It was why he had been hesitant at first to teach me to heal. Still, I had insisted. And proven myself to be the worst student known to man. Ruining remedies, wrapping wounds too tightly…

Killing Soraya before killing her in a whole other manner with her resurrection. That one act had hurt her the most and it had all been my fault. Every moment, everything that happened after. Without me, Emrys would still be safe in Naiva.

"He wouldn't be, Artura," Viane whispered.

"Stay. Out. Of. My. Head." I bit out every word with enough venom to kill but she remained unaffected. If anything, her gaze softened even further.

"It is hard," she replied. "Especially when your thoughts are so loud that you might as well shout them."

I slid down the wall, pulling my knees against my chest and wrapping my arms around them. "I don't want to make things worse."

"I know."

"Or jeopardise what little safety Emrys has right now."

Viane sat beside me, placing a delicately boned hand on my elbow. "Is it better to try and fail? Or never try at all?"

"It is better to succeed."

"Then let me teach you," the diviner said, her words earnest, almost pleading. "I see strength in you, Artura. You're capable of far more than you know."

I let her words fall to the ground, to become one with the dust.

"What you did today…will I have to do more like it?" She was silent for so long that I turned to look at her. "Viane?"

"Yes," she finally said. "There is no other way. Fear is what will unlock your magic and jolt it out of where it lurks far below the surface of your subconsciousness. If there were another way, believe you me, I would give it to you in a heartbeat."

I sighed, letting my head fall back against the wall. No other way. I toyed with a wavy strand of my hair, dried at strange angles after I'd fallen asleep with it still damp. Its previous lustre was slowly returning, bringing back a shred of the woman I had once been. I would never truly be the same but perhaps, scars aside, I could look similar.

Not shy away from my reflection. For once.

Glancing sideways at Viane, I pushed myself to my feet.

"Fine. But Thorn cannot come this time."

CHAPTER TWENTY-EIGHT

"What have you two been up to?"

Viane and I froze in the entryway to her room, both looking towards the glowering figure standing in the centre. Speckled daylight trickled in from cracks between the amethyst geode ceiling, illuminating only part of his face. Thorn was the very picture of fury, jaw clenched, a small muscle jumping as he exhaled roughly.

I half shrugged. "Better you not know?"

Viane dropped her head beside me, placing a thumb and forefinger against the bridge of her nose.

"Nephew, ever heard that it is better to beg forgiveness than ask permission?"

Thorn lifted his chin, folding his arms against his bare chest. Gods, he looked good. Whatever Viane had applied worked fast, the wounds this morning now little more than angry red marks. Tomorrow, they'd look even better. Perhaps by week's end, they'd be faint scars. I'd seen Emrys treat injuries like that before, but only twice - and on both occasions, the injuries had been life-threatening. He'd used treatments I had never seen before, practices that he swore me to secrecy over. I was young then, and didn't object. But now I recognised it for what it was - witchcraft, magic.

Thorn grunted. "So you're asking me for forgiveness?"

"I'll gladly take it if you offer it freely." Viane strode forward, positively regal despite the thick band of blood that soaked the hem of her dress. "But as for asking? I intend on asking neither forgiveness nor permission, nephew. I've no real need of either. And before you turn on her, neither does your wife. You should be proud of her."

His eyes widened, perfect emerald surrounded by a rim of stark white. "Proud? If you did what I think you did then I'm furious. She could have been killed."

"I wasn't," I mumbled, though I felt every bit as close to death as he had been just yesterday - physically and mentally.

"Irrelevant," Thorn spat.

The journey back down the tunnel to the hellion nest had proved useful, giving Viane a chance to explain her plan. It was simple:

Scare me so much, so horribly that my magic had no choice but to manifest, to pull itself from deep within to protect me from harm. It was a tactic once utilised by those who received no training as children. Viane had said as much the day before but it had been hard to focus, what with the demon about to emerge and all that.

The following two hours were nothing short of horrifying as she released three fire hellions, each one more grotesque than the previous. I fought with each one, knowing at least a little of what to expect but still shocked when each hellion launched itself like the feral beast it was, set on destroying me.

Towards the end, my magic had finally bubbled, just enough to prove it really was there, lurking around behind a door I couldn't unlock. It was wedged tight and no matter how afraid I was as I fought for my life, growing more and more tired by the minute, that magic refused to budge.

"I don't understand," I'd grumbled on all fours as I sucked in steadying breaths of sulphur-tainted air. "I felt something when Thorn was here. I burned the fire hellion. All I'm doing now is stabbing blindly. Why can't I do it again?"

"Keep trying," was all Viane had said. "Keep trying. It's there. The first time we saw your magic it was merely raising its head in curiosity. Now we need to drag it out - kicking and screaming if necessary."

I had a strong feeling she'd meant that I would be the one kicking and screaming. By the end of our time below, I was ready to do as much.

"I told you, Viane, not to take her back there," Thorn continued, pointing an accusatory finger. "You swore to me you wouldn't."

The diviner sat back against her work table, placing her hands on the edge of either side of her. She smiled widely at her nephew. "And I held to that. If anything, it was your wife who took *me*."

Thorn's eyes whipped to mine, shocked and outraged. "Why would you go back, Artura?" No sparrow this time, not when he was shaking with rage. "Why would you put yourself in danger again?"

I walked towards him slowly, a mouse approaching a lion. I saw him soften, saw the anger abate in his eyes only to be replaced with fear of his own. He was scared for me, for my safety. His words from before echoed in my mind.

If you died, I would have died right there with you. It would have devastated me, eviscerated me.

Taking his hand in mine, I placed it against my chest. His fingers splayed as he felt the steady thrumming of my heart, how it picked up fractionally as I held his gaze.

"I'm still here," I whispered, low enough that only he could hear. "I'm still whole, still alive."

"But *why?*" he asked again, voice breaking. "Sparrow…"

I pushed myself up on my toes, wrapping my arms around his neck. My lips found his in a gentle kiss that lingered for what felt like an eternity.

"I have no intention of going anywhere," I whispered. "None. I meant what I said, I cannot give you up. But neither can I give up…"

My sentence trailed off as he nodded in understanding. "Emrys. He was with you, wasn't he?"

I nodded once. "Beneath Dearmond. There were things that happened…" I sucked in cold air, suddenly shaking at the memory. "I can't leave him there, Thorn. Not after all he's done for me. I love him like a father. He's only in this mess *because* of me. If I have to go to the ends of the earth to save him, I will. But this, I need it. To be able to stand on my own two feet. I've felt powerless long enough. No more."

"About that," Viane piped up. "I may have a solution to our problem of manifesting your magic."

Thorn and I both turned at the same time, eyeing the diviner sceptically.

"Naturally, you won't like it."

*

"You're mad." I laughed. Surely Viane was joking.

"On the contrary," she replied. "I am quite sane."

I sipped at a cup of tea again, letting the rich peppermint thaw me from the inside out. The hellion nest carried a chill with it so unlike that of winter - this one felt more permanent, suffocating. It was a film coating my skin that I couldn't easily shrug off with a blanket or coat.

"Dragons aren't real," I went on. "They're a myth."

Viane ladled out soup as Thorn cut thick slices of perfectly cooked bread that bore a rich, golden crust and light, airy centre. My stomach growled and my mouth watered in appreciation. It had been too long since I last ate and after dealing with four fire hellions in less than twenty-four hours? I was ready to eat my left arm.

"Have you ever seen one?" I asked.

Viane looked up, an eyebrow raised. "Have you?"

"No," I replied, rolling my eyes like a petulant child. Emrys hated that. It was why I'd kept doing it. "Because they do not exist."

"Who says they do not?" she countered, passing me a bowl and a spoon. I took only the bowl, raising it to my lips to sip at the scalding broth. I was too famished to manage a utensil.

"Everyone. Ever."

"I should think you smarter than to listen to the opinions of others, Artura."

"It's not an opinion. It's a fact. Dragons are stories and nothing more."

She settled back onto a cushion with perfect posture. Definitely of royal blood, however humble her surroundings might be. There was something innate with nobility that couldn't be removed no matter how hard you tried. I let myself really look at her, at the set of her jaw and gaze, the unrelenting look in her eye.

A stubborn royal, too, then.

"Where do you think stories come from?" She took a sip from her soup, unhurried. She hadn't eaten in as long as I had but it didn't seem to bother her at all. Then again, only one of us had been routinely starved for the better part of four months and had significant catching up to do.

I fished a chunk of fish out of the broth with my fingers, stifling a yelp at the burn. The moment I popped the meat in my mouth, flavour burst across my tongue and I moaned in delight. Thorn threw me a glance at that moan, his eyes heating.

"Behave yourself, nephew," Viane smirked.

"Good to know she doesn't just get into my head, too," I muttered grimly.

Viane gave me a disapproving look. "I told you last night, Artura. Strong emotions produce strong thoughts, ones that are akin to shouting a mere handspan away from another. And from what I'm hearing, my nephew has...*very* strong emotions."

Thorn flushed a little at that, throwing an abashed glance my way. I tried not to react, conscious of the telepatia sitting across from us. She'd heard enough these past few days. I wasn't about to let her hear any more.

Especially when the man that was now my husband and I were on the same page.

"The stories," I said, trying to distract myself, "are nothing more than that - stories. People have wild imaginations. No doubt someone saw a bird once and thought, 'Hey, what would make this a thousand times worse? Perhaps scales and fire.'"

"Might I remind you, that until three days ago you'd not seen a hellion in the flesh. That was also just a story."

"Viane," I said, placing my bowl down on the floor where I sat. "Show me one shred of proof that dragons are real and I'll believe you."

The diviner sat silent and still.

"See?" I said after a moment. "You can't prove it because *they are not real*."

Viane sighed, turning to Thorn. "Nephew?"

Thorn didn't look up from his soup. "No."

"Yes," she replied.

"*No*," Thorn said again, slowly, emphasising the word.

She rocked back on her rear, eyes on the amethyst above. "Help me out here."

My eyes narrowed on Thorn. "What aren't you telling me? And why?"

The king, looking much more like a commoner in a simple linen shirt and pants, normally smooth hair now ruffled around his forehead, growled low in his throat. "I'll not tell you the *what* but I will tell you the *why*."

"And that is?"

"You'll go along with Viane's deranged plan."

I popped a cube of potato into my mouth, letting it fall apart on my tongue before I answered. "That would imply dragons are real, if you think I would go along with Viane's plan."

Thorn said nothing, just turned his gaze back to his empty bowl.

"Thorn," I pushed. "That would imply that they're real."

"As I said," he replied. "If I tell you the *what*…"

I gasped. "You lie."

It couldn't be. Could it?

"To you?" he said, looking almost regretful. "I never do."

*

"Let me get this straight." I stopped the chatter between Thorn and Viane with a hand over the former's mouth. The latter fell silent all on her own with an entertained smile. I was beginning to learn that not many had willingly put Thorn in his place. Not that he often needed it. But when he did, I was more than willing to oblige. Always would be. For him or anyone else. "You want to track down a dragon, which is apparently entirely possible because they're apparently entirely real...and you want me to *kill it*?"

Neither spoke. I waited for confirmation or denial - *please, gods, let it be a denial* - but neither response came. They waited, not quite patiently, but expectantly. Almost as though the truth weren't so hard to grasp, that I was taking far too long to come to terms with what had been revealed.

How many stories were true? How many times had Emrys tucked me into bed with tales of mermaids, ogres, fairies and...*gods, dragons?* I knew nothing. Nothing at all. In just a few short days, everything I believed had been called into question without mercy. I would never walk this world the same again. I would forever second-guess everything I heard.

"'Kill' is such a harsh word," Viane crooned, a mocking pout puckering her full lips.

Thorn pulled my hand away from his mouth, quickly pecking the back of it. "Sparrow, you're not killing anyone or anything."

I bobbed my head from side to side, debating. "Let's not be too hasty on the 'anyone' - you know if I get the chance, there's a certain king who could do without a head."

"Semantics." He waved a hand before placing it against my knee. In the light and warmth of the fire, I'd pulled my dress - the hated orange one - past my knees. His thumb drifted across my bare skin. "My point is, you barely survived killing a hellion. A dragon? That's ridiculous."

My lips pressed firmly together as I levelled a deadpan stare his way.

"She survived just fine," Viane interrupted. "You, nephew, are the one who struggled."

Thorn threw her a wounded look, pulling back slightly. "I killed one. And I also survived the other."

"But so very nearly didn't after you got gooey eyes looking at your wife," Viane replied. "You didn't fare so well and you'll not convince me otherwise."

"Why would I need to kill the dragon?" I asked, cutting off Thorn before he could speak again. The bickering between the two of them was starting to get on my nerves. Every hour that passed had me more and more grateful that Viane resided in the isle and that once this madness was done, and if we survived, Thorn and I would depart for Hafan. Some distance between nephew and aunt would do us all some good - me, most of all.

"I'll admit, it's a hunch," Viane began.

"Risking my wife's life on a hunch is not acceptable."

Viane looked past Thorn to where I sat, continuing with the conversation as though he weren't there. "But my hunches generally pay off. Your ancestors practised fire magic on two levels: one, simple manipulation. That is what we've been trying to draw out during our time with the hellions. I'm still hopeful that will work. House Igneous, when wanting to develop their magic further, would kill a dragon, and consume its fire. By drawing in the magic the dragon possessed, it pushed their own magic far beyond its limits until it became something more. Your ancestors - a select few - could summon fire at will and birth it anew with naught but a breath."

"She can't even manipulate fire as it is," Thorn said. He gestured to the fire with the remnants of the soup still cooking over it. "Go ahead, sparrow. Try and…do something."

"First of all," I replied tartly. "'She' has a name. Do not speak of me as if I wasn't here. Secondly, I've got the same question. How will this help me if I can't even master simple manipulation?"

"Perhaps it'll give you the push you need," Viane replied. "There's no doubt in my mind that your magic can manifest, it's just finding the right combination of fear to pull it out."

"Good luck with that," I chimed with a fake smile. "I've lived my life in fear, Viane. As a healer, a gender traitor and also as a citizen of Cimran. You'll be hard-pressed to find something that will truly terrify me."

"I'm sure I'll think of something." Her answering smile was positively predatory. "We'll continue to try things here for the time being. Failing that, we should travel east, to Galdua. There's an island your ancestors kept watch over. Dragons roamed free there, awaiting the moment a member of Igneous would require their heart."

"Heart?" I gulped, suddenly not liking - even more than before - where this was going.

Viane absentmindedly played with her snow-white hair, as though she wasn't about to once again upend my world.

"Heart. You'll need to eat it."

CHAPTER TWENTY-NINE

"Where are you going now?"

I breezed past Thorn and Viane. "The nest."

Silence rang out, only to be broken a second later by three solid thumps as Thorn caught up to me, grabbing hold of my elbow. The look of confusion on his face was matched only by the one of determination on mine.

"You were just down there."

I shrugged. "I'd rather go down there a hundred times than go and kill a fucking *dragon*. Do you honestly believe that's a better plan?"

"I don't think either option is a good plan," he hissed back. "You are my wife, I'll not stop you from doing what you wish but I will make it damn clear that I think it's a fucking terrible idea."

"All of this is a terrible idea! But it's the only one we've got." I felt wetness spread across my cheeks and angrily swiped at it. I could not be crying right now, not when I needed to appear strong. Not 'kill a dragon' strong, but 'kill a hellion' strong at the very least. "Emrys is waiting for me. I'm not a warrior like you. I can't lift a sword worth a damn. Can barely pick up a dagger. If there's a chance I can use what little magic I possess, then you're damned right I'll do it, even if it kills me in the long run. So either get on board or fuck off."

His grip didn't loosen but his expression softened, the emerald in his eyes brightening. "I can't say I fully understand, sparrow, not when you've not told me about what happened." I opened my mouth to object, only to be silenced with a finger on my lips. "I'm not saying you have to tell me everything now. If you want vengeance, I'm right there with you. Your enemies are my enemies. The burdens you carry, I carry, too. If you wanted to walk into hell tomorrow, I would walk at your side. I know I can't stop you from facing what's to come, no matter how much I want to keep you close, keep you safe. Just be careful. I've only just gotten you. We haven't had enough time."

"Be at my side, be with me," I concluded, echoing some of the first words he said to me on our wedding night. I'd asked then what he wanted from me, what he wanted in a queen. He hadn't demanded the world but rather just asked for my place beside him. That was all I needed now. I didn't want him to fight my battles, didn't want to be the wife that cowered behind her husband. But to have him by my side?

That would be worth everything.

He nodded, thumb brushing away another tear as it fell. "Come sleep. If this is truly what you want, at least do it rested."

*

There's a mirror.

There's not been a mirror here before and I've not seen one since Naiva, some eight weeks ago. I try to look into it but Helmar pushes me towards the bed of nails. He likes to do this once a week, force me to lie upon it, my slight weight enough to bear me down so each pointed nail pushes into my back. It's worst along my spine, now bonier than ever thanks to limited food. I'm always careful not to show my back to Emrys after days like today. He can't do anything to stop this, can't help me. Seeing the signs of my torture would be torture in kind for the old man. I won't give Helmar the satisfaction of breaking both of us.

Helmar doesn't say a word. He knows I know the routine and what is required of me. There's no easy way to place yourself upon a bed of nails, some part of you needs to bear the brunt of the pain, bracing yourself until you've evened out and gone completely horizontal. The first time, I fought. Helmar pushed me down, one nail driving so far into my side that I'd struggled to bend for days. It was a miracle I'd survived to this point and escaped infection.

I learned long ago not to use my hands to ease myself onto the nails. I needed my hands most. Hands and feet, really. I can sleep on my stomach or rest on my side to avoid sitting square on my rear. So it is that I place upon the nails first, struggling not to cry out at the pain as I sit.

Helmar likes it when I scream.

So I stay silent where possible.

It takes some careful manoeuvring but eventually, I'm flat against the bed. I begin to sweat, shaking as my body teeters on the edge of shock.

No. Don't start that now, I beg. You've got a long way to go.

Helmar takes his time, every time. I'll be here all day. Or is it night? I can't tell. Not in this room nor below this mountain, both utterly devoid of windows and life. I watch as the king saunters back and forth as if to study every inch of my body. He likes it most when I bleed and when he bends to turn my thigh inwards, he pushes down slightly, just enough to pierce that most tender piece of flesh. I can't stop the scream then, can't stop it rolling into a howl of agony. His impassive face turns into a wicked grin of delight and he pulls back.

"Good," he says. "You've done well."

Done well. As if this is something to be graded, a test I might fail or pass. Perhaps this is a test, one sent by gods I don't believe in. Maybe that's why they sent this test, this trial. Because of my disbelief. I'd have rather they turn rain into diamonds to show their might. Anything but this fate they've heaped upon my throbbing, aching head. The weight of their punishment is far too great for one person.

"I have a gift for you, witch. You'll quite like it, I think."

I never like his gifts. I never have. His rewards and favours are the same as his punishments. Once, I'd been deluded enough to believe that a gift would be exactly that - a gift. Perhaps an extra scrap of food or more time to search the tunnels for the promised exit that would grant freedom for Emrys and I.

Helmar turns, picks something up from the table where he keeps a myriad of tools he uses on me. He's particularly fond of a barbed rolling pin. He's used it four times now, each time increasing the pressure. There are scars on my abdomen that will never go away, even if I survive this godsforsaken place. I glance out of the corner of my eye, not daring to turn my head, carefully placed in the least painful position. Helmar holds something soft-looking. It falls over the side of his hands as he cradles it.

"You've been such a good witch," he says, though I know the last word he would ever ascribe to me is 'good.' "Every

punishment you've taken so well these past weeks. I thought perhaps, for the face that has become so damaged, that this gift would be fitting."

Helmar leans over and places something cold over my face. There are two holes for my eyes and one for my mouth. A mask. It smells foul and I can't quite place the scent over the one wafting towards me from The Tub. I can't move to touch it without putting unwanted pressure elsewhere on my body. I wouldn't dare move anyway, not when he's standing so close. Any attempt at weaselling out of a punishment is met with an even greater one.

Footsteps recede, only to grow louder a moment later as Helmar returns. I hear him chuckle softly to himself. He pauses, silent, unmoving. I try to swallow the lump of panic in my throat. I can't. My mouth is too dry, too in need of water. For two days now, Emrys and I have been given only a cup a day. I've lied every time, telling the old man that I had water while he slept. He's drunk all that's been on hand. Anything I can do to keep him alive a little longer. Any chance to survive this hell. But it is taking its toll on me and I feel dusty, dry, as though I might crack at any moment.

Helmar's fingers stroke over the mask and all I feel is the pressure of his touch, setting my insides roiling in revulsion.

"Beautiful," he murmurs. And now I really panic, really get scared. Because what is beautiful to him can be nothing short of horrifying.

And when he lifts the mirror above me to show me my reflection, I discover just how true that is.

No. Not a mask. I gaze up at my reflection in utter horror as I no longer recognise myself save for the pale blue eyes ringed by redness from lack of sleep. What I thought was a mask is in fact someone else's face. It covers all but my eyes and mouth, distorting and changing the face I've always known would stare back at me. I'm no longer there, I'm covered in death.

A scream tears from my throat, shrill in my ears, sending a wave of blinding pain through a head already set aching by the nails pressing into it. I turn, ignoring the sharpened points, as I try to shuck off the face of another prisoner who'd spent less than a week under Dearmond. I can taste copper on my lips and my tongue. Instinctively I know it is not my blood. It belongs to the flesh covering my own. I gag, bile rising in my throat, and begin to choke.

"No," Helmar croons. He places a hand atop my head, digs in his fingers until a bundle of dirt-encrusted hair is wrapped around them. He turns my face back up, keeping the mask in place. His nails dig into my scalp harder, breaking the skin, so that I have no choice but to stare up at the mask with its edges cut so they are smooth and un-torn. He doesn't care how much pressure he needs to exert, only that I watch the horror before me, memorise the face, so carefully sliced off the woman who cried till she was hoarse in the cell beside mine..

"Look at how beautiful you are," he whispers in my ear. "Look at the new face I've given you. It belonged to a whore, one who made the mistake of stealing from me. And now it is yours. Better to be a whore than a witch, wouldn't you agree?"

I whimper, too terrified to cry anymore. It won't do me any good. Not while he's like this. Not while he's having his fun.

The chill of the skin mask was replaced by the cooling sensation of water cascading over my face, drenching my hair and the bed beneath me. I coughed and spluttered, trying to suck in air as nothing but water filled my nose. In the background, there was the sound of crackling, like dozens of tiny twigs snapping in half. I let that sound lead me out of the depths of a nightmare - a repressed, forgotten memory. So much from Purgatory had been locked away, thrown to my subconsciousness where not even my nightmares dared venture. But this one had, had pulled the banished memory from its exile and made me relive it while I was helpless to stop it, caught in a world between awake and truly asleep.

More water lapped at my skin and my eyes flew open. Red and orange light filled my vision, blocking the view of anything else. There should have been a pillow beside me. I'd fallen asleep with it next to my head, surplus when I needed only one to lay my head upon. It was gone and in its place, flames.

They danced all around me, a wreath and blanket and tomb all at once. I was engulfed by fire. I screamed again, realising that the scream in my nightmare had been real, too. My throat was raw. But perhaps that was also from the all-consuming heat enveloping me as the fire raged. I lifted a hand to swat away flames that slowly ate away at my clothes. It burned. But there was no pain only…

Peace.

Why was there peace? I was alight, burning with the intensity of fires that ravaged my home a week before I was torn away. But no, that was peace that filled me now. Calming, reassuring, blissful peace. It had been too long since I'd last felt it, the feeling almost alien. It had been hard to place but now, the familiarity of it came rushing back like an old friend, wrapping me in its welcoming arms.

"Artura!"

I zeroed in on the voice. Thorn. He called to me, from how far away I didn't know. His voice was faint above the roaring and crackling of the flames.

Another wave of water cascaded only this time, it barely touched my skin before it vaporised, vanishing into steam that billowed out and away like a cloud. I watched it twist and turn until it met with the geode ceiling, now blackened like coal.

Again, Thorn shouted. His voice was drowned out by the constant buzzing in my ears.

I pushed myself to my feet, mouth gaping as I examined my body. My clothes fell apart, reduced to ashes, and I stood naked. Burning. A living flame, one with a will and power and an unquenchable thirst for retribution.

As I looked up, it wasn't Thorn's gaze I met, but Viane's. Approving, satisfied and every bit triumphant.

CHAPTER THIRTY

In and out, in and out.

Breathe, one, two, three. Rinse and repeat.

My heart raced painfully in my chest. Not because of the fire. No, something about that had felt all too right. Like donning a well-worn cardigan, or perhaps more akin to a warm hug from an old friend. The only shock related to the fire that had coated me like a second skin was that I hadn't been afraid for even a second. I wasn't hurt. Not a single hair on my head singed so much as an inch.

My bed, however, was a different matter. Pillows and blankets were unrecognisable as they disintegrated into watery ashes. I'd lost count of how many buckets of water Thorn had poured over me in vain, as he attempted to extinguish the fire.

A fire that still raged even now as I sat atop the rock floor, naked.

Thorn and Viane kept their distance. The diviner eyed me with intense curiosity. Her beautiful face glowed nearly as bright as my own. She was waiting for something. Expectation hung thick in the air. Thorn sat across from me, giving me a wide enough berth that he wasn't in any danger. Though he had been before. The left side of his body was blackened from the fire and the skin peeking through holes in the linen was bright red and blistered. He ignored it, focusing solely on me.

"What happened?" His voice was low but still, I heard it over the crackling of the flames that licked at my neck and my face. They felt as soft as my hair when blown about by the wind. The sensation was almost pleasant, if not a little ticklish.

I shook my head slowly, trying to remember. Memories were faint, distant, veiled as if behind a sheer curtain. I could glimpse only snippets but it told me enough. I knew there were things from Purgatory I'd blocked from my memory and tucked away, the lid on the box they resided forced shut so hard to the point of breaking. But one memory had snaked its way out, slipped to the forefront of my mind and terrified me so much, it achieved what no hellion in all its horror and grotesqueness could do.

It had unleashed the dormant magic deep within. And at a moment where there was no awareness, no hope to control it before it could get out of hand. Hurt someone.

Someone like Thorn who had slept soundly beside me. Too close, too at risk. I shuddered at the possibilities, what might have happened had he not awoken. Our marriage, or whatever the bond was between us, could have been over almost before it began.

"I was dreaming," I murmured. A flash of skin, the scent of rusty blood, these were the first things to trickle back to my mind. "Something that happened."

"With King Helmar?" Thorn asked.

I nodded, chewing on my thumbnail. I forced myself to remember. I had to, even if it was the last thing I wanted. If I didn't remember, how could I be prepared to control my reaction to the memory when it inevitably returned as another nightmare? I was far from short on material to fuel my every unconscious moment but some memories came to mind more than others. With how I'd combusted so spectacularly, this had to be one of them.

The curtain in my mind pulled back inch by inch and there it was. I was staring up at a mirror, screaming. My face wasn't my own, it belonged to another. Had belonged to another, someone now long since dead. Helmar was beside me, offering up his approval and praise.

The fire around me grew hotter, wilder. It seemed to grow tentacles, ones that tried to snake outwards to Thorn and Viane. The former pushed himself back and out of harm's way. I shook where I sat, locked on the memory of that day in Purgatory. It had been one of the worst. Not in terms of physical punishment. I was used to the bed of nails, painful as it was. No. This had been psychological, the kind of trauma that couldn't be healed by a tincture or poultice. While the memories that plagued me daily were mental scars, this was a deep gouge, taking something intrinsic away from me. A sliver of innocence I had possessed until that day.

I was vaguely aware of Viane still staring and when I looked up at her finally, she unfolded her arms.

"Breathe through it," she instructed. "Quiet your mind."

I bit back my retort. Quieting my mind had never been my strong suit. I was fiery, Emrys had said. If only he knew just how right he was. Fiery, indeed. I was the very essence of a flame.

I forced myself to refocus on my breathing. In and out, in and out, until it was a rhythm my body danced to. One by one the tentacle-like fires pulled back, disappearing deep within me where it formed a ball of warmth and light. I let it fill me, let the peace and tranquillity that came with it drive out my fear of the detached face and the screams that even now echoed in my ears.

I simmered down to little more than a smoulder and then finally extinguished.

Viane clapped. "Marvellous. I knew you could do it."

Thorn hurried forward, a blanket from Viane's bed in his hands. He tentatively touched my skin, as though worried I might have still been piping hot, and when satisfied, draped the blanket around my shoulders. He sat down, tucked me into his lap and I rested my head against his shoulder. I was suddenly bone weary, more than I had ever been before. Sleep would be bliss but for the first time, it worried me. What if the nightmare came again and I reignited?

As if he could read my thoughts, Thorn said, "I'm not afraid to be beside you, sparrow."

I bit my lip, not trusting myself to say anything. I didn't even know what to say.

"That memory seemed to be effective enough." Viane handed me a cup of peppermint tea as she mused. "Quite a decent reaction. I would have thought it would be minor at first. Maybe a spark or two. But Artura, you are the most spectacular thing I have ever witnessed."

Something in her wording caught my attention. "Were you listening?"

"To your thoughts?" she clarified, one eyebrow in a perfect arch. Her lips pulled into a sly smile. "Something along those lines, yes."

It wasn't a denial. "The other day, you changed my nightmare and took it away. Did you cause this? I had no recollection of that day. But now, I remember everything in perfect detail. The nightmare was too real. And yes, I was foggy when I awoke but now I see it all."

Viane simply shrugged her bony shoulders. "It worked, didn't it?"

"You had no right," I spat. "No right to get in my head like that."

"Time is a precious commodity, Artura, and we are poorer than most. I simply did what was necessary."

I pulled the blanket tighter around myself, willing the tears that threatened to fall to stay at bay. "What you did wasn't right, Viane. I locked that memory away for a reason."

"Yes," she interrupted, the word sharp. "For a time such as this, to be used to make you *great*. Powerful. Do you have any idea how many of House Igneous remain?" When I didn't answer, she continued. "You, Artura. You. Are. *It*. You have a precious gift that was being squandered."

"I didn't know about it!"

"But *now you do*."

It was the first time I'd seen Viane angry. Well and truly angry. I shied away from it, from the coldness in her eyes as she threw the mug in her hand at the wall. It shattered into a dozen pieces, the clay flying in several different directions. One fell to beside Thorn and he eyed it with disdain.

Viane's chest heaved with every rough breath. "I've tried to be patient-"

"It's been four days," I interjected.

She continued as if I'd not said a word. "But patience is a luxury we do not have time for. You know what I am, Artura. You know that there is little hidden from me. How much longer do you think Emrys has? Because we are running out of time. Helmar is not a man of his word, no matter what he may have you believe."

I was eternally grateful for Thorn holding me, for his silence. Part of me still wanted to fight my own battles - likely always would.

"Not for one second have I believed Helmar to be honourable," I replied. Heat simmered beneath my skin, comforting. "And I know Emrys doesn't have long. Why do you think I've gone back to the hellions? What other reason would I have to do something so reckless as manifest magic that is as good as a noose around my neck?"

"It wasn't enough," she snapped.

"So you took matters into your own hands?" I asked. Thorn slid a hand beneath the blanket and pressed his palm flat against my stomach. I melted into his touch, letting my body mould to his. I was suddenly bone-weary, the outburst of my magic draining what little energy I'd accumulated as I slept.

"Yes," Viane replied. "I did. I'm sorry if it was a hard thing for you to relive, and believe me, I listened, I watched. I saw it all. Never could I comprehend what you endured beneath Dearmond but I have to believe it means more than what it was. That you can use all that pain and punishment, turn it back on Helmar, and have your vengeance."

"I want to," I admitted. And it was true. It had always been true. I would have my revenge on Helmar, no matter the means. "But I don't like how you went about it. You are to never do it again, Viane, you understand me? That is an order from your queen."

It felt strange, alien to demand something as queen, yet I was desperate enough to try. I didn't even know if I technically could where Viane was concerned, given that she resided on the isle and not within Nimue's borders. However, the fear I felt over the nightmare was rivalled only by the fear that Viane might recall more repressed memories. Just when I thought she would object, the diviner dipped her head once in a curt nod.

"Now that you've awoken it," I continued, feeling a little relieved, "you best teach me how to control my magic."

*

The water was clearer than I remembered, the scent of salt cleansing in more ways than one.

I sat on the edge of the rocks, toes dipped into the lapping ocean, now at high tide. Somewhere behind me, Edric snored and Leo sharpened his knife, blunted, apparently, from some foolish bet made between him and his brother. Edric had wagered that Leo couldn't cut through solid rock. Not one to concede to his big brother, Leo had tried and failed - but not until he had stubbornly tried for an hour and nearly ruined his knife altogether.

Thorn's legs bracketed my own and I leaned back against his chest, soaking in his spiced scent. His arms wound around my middle and his chin rested in the crook of my neck. We were silent, simply enjoying the distance between Viane and ourselves. Things were tense, to say the least, and when it looked like Thorn would combust right along with me, I'd suggested a trip above for some fresh air.

"Is this really what you want?" he murmured, his lips moving softly against my skin. He placed a lingering kiss below my jaw. "For Viane to teach you?"

"Yes."

"I don't trust her."

I half turned to meet his gaze. "She's your aunt."

He huffed a breath, tightening his hold. "Just because she's family doesn't mean she's trustworthy. This isn't what we came here for."

"But it's the hand we've been dealt," I replied. A bright blue, iridescent fish swept around my right foot before darting into salmon and lilac coral with tubular protrusions. Each one was large enough to house a small fish and I glimpsed the tips of fins as several wiggled their way in further. "I need to tell you, Thorn. About what Helmar did."

He tensed behind me, his whole body going rigid. The air surrounding us instantly cooled, as though his burgeoning anger was summoning a storm.

"You don't have to." He spoke through gritted teeth. I almost regretted bringing it up, shifting the lighter mood of a moment ago into one that was darker, heavier.

I swivelled between his legs to straddle him and wrapped an arm around his shoulders to stop myself from falling into the water. His face was dangerously blank, the only thing betraying that were his emerald eyes, now full of quiet wrath and fury.

"Thorn," I whispered, placing a hand on his cheek. His jaw relaxed a fraction under my touch. "I trust you. You need to know so you can understand why I'm willing to do anything to get Emrys out of there."

He still looked unsure. "Sparrow, I need *you* to understand that what you tell me will have repercussions."

I nodded. Of course, there would be. I hadn't anticipated anything else. As to what those repercussions were, well, that was what worried me most. Would he be able to look at me the same way again after hearing what I endured at Helmar's hands? There were times when I couldn't even look at or think of myself the same way as before. Times when I caught sight of my reflection and felt only revulsion for what I'd been made to do. Not a day went by where I couldn't still smell The Tub or feel my skin being sliced open by one of Helmar's many tools.

"I'll understand if you don't want me after I tell you," I whispered, eyes falling away from his to the bobbing of his throat. I couldn't look at him. It hurt too much, the feeling that these were our last moments of relative normalcy. If such a thing had ever existed for us.

"Not this shit again, sparrow." Thorn tipped my chin up. "Have I not proven my loyalty to you? Don't get me wrong, if need be, I'll remind you daily that I want you. Not just with my words but with my actions, my body and my choices as first a husband and then king. I've no idea what you're about to tell me but I can say with absolute certainty that it won't change a thing about how I see you. Strong, courageous. And now both literally and metaphorically, hot."

I smiled at that and rolled my eyes mockingly. "Is that all you can think about? My body?"

"No." He winked. "I also think about all the delicious things I can do *to* your body."

Shoving a hand against his chest, I laughed, feeling light despite the impending storm my story would bring.

*

"I was beginning to think you had both boarded the *Scylla*," Viane said.

"It's not entirely out of the question yet," I replied, plastering a fake smile across my face. "You're still public enemy number one. Maybe we'll take you with us and drop you in the middle of the ocean."

Viane carried on with her sewing, mending Thorn's singed shirt. "I'm favoured by the old gods, child, remember that when you try to kill me."

"If you're so favoured, they can have you."

Night had fallen long before Thorn and I hurried back down the tunnel to Viane's cavern. Growls and scratching echoed in time with our every footstep and I was grateful to be back by the fire, watching the reflected flames dance amidst the thousands of faceted amethyst faces.

Despite his easy stance, Thorn was anything but calm. He was a brewing tempest and had been since the first words describing my time in King Helmar's hands had been uttered. Once I'd begun talking, it was as though a damn had broken. Everything came out, one thing after another. I left out nothing - despite Thorn reminding me that I didn't have to share everything if I wasn't comfortable - describing every moment in as much detail as I could remember. It struck me just how much I'd buried, though, like the nightmare that had finally manifested my magic. But as I relived all that took place in Purgatory, I couldn't bring myself to be even the faintest bit regretful at the loss of chunks of time.

It had taken the better part of the afternoon and evening to lay it all out, every dark and twisted memory, every building block that had created the woman I now was. But when it was done I felt lighter. Freer. As though with telling my story I'd loosed the final shackles still binding me to Purgatory. Emrys was still there, however, so I couldn't be truly free.

Nevertheless, it was a relief to have someone else know.

Someone I'd decided could know, anyway. Viane knew everything that had happened. It was her job to know, her 'gift' from the gods. It felt much more like an invasion of privacy but it was nice to know I didn't need to retell everything to another. Because after telling Thorn, I was tired. In sharing my story, I had lived a thousand emotions all over again in a short space of time.

Thorn paced across from his aunt, throwing a furtive glance every so often. The last thing we had discussed was something equally contentious - the repercussions that what we needed to do next might fail. It was all too overwhelming.

"Out with it," Viane said, almost bored. Another stitch through the singed linen. Her needle moved gracefully, arcing before sliding back in to loop another stitch. Thorn had said it wasn't necessary, that he had more clothes aboard the *Scylla*. But Viane kept sewing anyhow, simply for something to do, I suspected.

I chewed on my bottom lip, considering my words carefully. "I need to train."

"Yes." Again, she didn't look up. Just continued to sew.

"And we've not a lot of time."

"Not if you want to save Emrys before it is too late," she agreed.

"So we need to begin tomorrow," I continued, now twisting my fingers in my clammy palms. Eels writhed in my stomach, threatening to bring up what little food I'd eaten. For so long I'd been taught that magic was evil, a one-way ticket to a Burning. Now, I was actively running towards it. The switch was jarring.

Viane bit off the thread. "Tomorrow is too late."

My eyes narrowed. "So we start today."

"Today is too late." She tied the thread, completing the repair on Thorn's sleeve.

Thorn stalked forward. "What do you know?" he asked his aunt. "What have you seen?"

Viane carefully examined the sleeve, turning it every which way before giving herself a satisfied nod. "Merely that Helmar grows restless with every passing day. His anger with Artura continues to increase and he's none too pleased with what happened with your father."

Thorn wiped a hand over his mouth before speaking. "I doubt he knows what he speaks of."

Viane levelled a glare at the king, mouth thinning. She looked positively radiant with the light of the fire around her, turning her snow-white hair luminescent and making her violet eyes stand out. "Do not doubt, nephew. Helmar has spies everywhere."

"He couldn't possibly know," Thorn snapped. "I trust every man at my side. There's not a traitor among them."

"Know what?" I asked. I hated feeling like I was being left in the dark, that things were intentionally being hidden from me. True, our marriage was very much still in its infancy and I had no real right to demand answers to things that didn't concern me, but after all I'd told Thorn this afternoon, a little reciprocation wouldn't have gone amiss.

Viane didn't let her gaze leave Thorn's. Unconsciously, she smoothed out her skirts, as black as the sky above the isle. "Would you care to tell your wife? Or should I?"

She didn't give Thorn a chance to reply before she said five little words that changed everything.

"Your husband killed his father."

CHAPTER THIRTY-ONE

"I don't understand." I looked between Viane and Thorn, numbness slowing every thought. "Why? How?... *Why?*"

Thorn's look was nothing short of murderous as he stood over Viane. To her credit, the diviner smiled, entertained more than anything. She turned that smile up towards her nephew, patted him on the arm and stood to her feet. Viane held the shirt out to him and when he didn't take it from her hands, she draped it over his head like a veil.

"Because, child," she said as she side-stepped Thorn who had already tossed the newly mended shirt on the floor, "my brother was both a fool and an ingrate. He never treasured the gifts given to him and wore through possessions faster than a rich man in a brothel can go through whores. If you wound up married to him, you'd have begged to return to Helmar."

I lifted a sceptical eyebrow. "I very much doubt that."

Viane came to a stop in front of me and took my hand. "Perhaps life would have been decent, for a year. Maybe a little more. But then his true colours would have shown, the king he truly was. As his wife, you would have been given everything you asked for, no doubt, but he'd have ruled you with an iron fist as surely as he did his people."

"The real reason," Thorn interjected from where he stood simmering, "was that he was also dying. He had been for some time. My father was many things, a man of vice being the first. He indulged throughout his life to the point of no return and when I finally reunited with him in Nimue, a month before we arrived in Lanceris, he was very much at death's door."

"What did you do?" I asked, my voice barely above a whisper.

"Gave him milk of the poppy," Thorn replied.

"And promptly smothered him in his sleep," Viane concluded.

I jerked back, horrified. "You really *did* murder him? It wasn't just a turn of phrase?"

"All in accordance with his wishes, sparrow."

I shook my head. "Do not 'sparrow' me. You're a murderer." I threw my hands up in the air. "I honestly cannot believe this."

Was Helmar right? Had I been given to a ruthless king? He'd implied as much just before I was wed. Perhaps like called to like. Perhaps in Thorn, Helmar saw himself reflected.

"It was all detailed in his final will," Thorn explained. "I didn't do anything he didn't wish for."

I barked a harsh laugh. "Doubtful. You *killed* the man."

"Out of mercy." Thorn's tone was pleading. He took a step towards me and I promptly took another back. "He was incredibly sick, Artura."

At least he'd dropped the 'sparrow.'

"I've misrepresented things," Viane said. She put both hands up in surrender. "I am guilty of causing drama on any given day and today is no different. What can I say? I *thrive* on the chaos. Usually, I am alone here on this isle and I've no one to share that chaos with. Forgive me for indulging myself a little."

This time, Thorn wasn't the only one shooting daggers at the diviner.

"My brother truly was sick," she continued. "And Thorn did kill him, though perhaps a better term is 'put him out of his misery.' If you had been married to Juriel, you'd have been made a widow within the turn of the moon and in accordance with our customs, returned to King Helmar."

"Whatever happened to living miserably with Juriel?" I asked. "Not a moment ago you made it sound as though I would have been bound to him for decades to come."

Viane shrugged her delicate shoulders. "It's still the truth, though one that will never come to pass. I've told you before, Artura, that I've had my eye on you for quite some time - on futures that will and won't eventuate, a marriage to Juriel being one of them."

I folded my arms, leaning into the cool rock wall. Since igniting the night before, the blood in my veins felt white hot, like molten metal coursing throughout my body, filling every nook and cranny, even those I didn't know existed. I wiped a trickle of sweat from my brow.

"Are you saying this was all planned? Juriel's death? Thorn's crowning? My marriage to the son instead of the father?"

Viane nodded. "You have no idea just how important you are, Artura. I'd have no sooner risked a complication weaving itself into your world than I would have cut off my own arm."

"Fantastic job you've done of it, then," I bit back. "Because I would call Purgatory a fucking massive complication."

I glanced past Viane to where Thorn stood, noting that he was far too silent. Etched across his face I saw pain echoing that of this afternoon as I'd recalled the details of my imprisonment. I wanted so badly to take back the truths whispered, to take away the aching sadness I knew was plaguing him. But this was better, surely, to have everything out in the light of day. No more secrets.

At least I hoped there would be.

"There are things we must go through, Artura. Things that seem without reason until the time is right." Viane smiled, the look almost angelic despite how positively wretched she had been in the past few days. "Trust that all you've been through thus far is just that - something seemingly without reason though valuable for a later time."

The fire crackled across the cavern, the scent of smoke intermingling with the richly spiced incense that hung heavy in the warm air. Sandalwood and something headier that tickled my nose and made me want to sneeze. Violently.

"And speaking of things one must go through," she continued, "tell me of your plans."

The tension in the cavern eased a fraction. I let loose the breath I didn't know I'd been holding, my lungs aching as I drew in a new breath.

"What did you mean when you said I could 'consume the fire' of a dragon?"

Viane circled the room to her table where she withdrew a tome from beneath several others, a plume of dust fanning out around their crinkled edges. As she walked back to her stool beside the fire, she quickly flicked through to the last quarter of the book. She was silent as she read and I didn't dare move. If I was going to do this, go through with what was most definitely an insane plan, then it needed to be done right. There had been far too many complications lately.

Thorn moved to my side and took my hand in his, bringing it to his lips where he pressed a kiss to my palm. His lips were velvety soft and I felt a new surge of heat travel down my arm, stronger than any fire that fuelled my veins.

"I'm sorry I didn't tell you," he murmured.

I sighed, weariness enveloping me like the waves we watched earlier. "You tell me to trust you and yet you do not trust me. Where is the fairness in that?"

"I do trust you, Artura," he murmured, thumb rubbing across my knuckles. "I trust you with my body, my heart, my very soul. There is nothing I wouldn't give to you. I just didn't want to burden you with yet another thing."

"I am already burdened," I said with a smile that didn't reach my eyes. "What's one more to the pile?"

He shook his head, hair rustling around his face. His beard was looking a little more unruly than it had been when we married and I stroked it, letting my fingers explore and wander until they grazed his collarbone.

"Trust works two ways," I whispered. "It is both given and earned. But I only give to those who earn which is what I did today in telling you all that has happened. I thought things might be the same for you but perhaps I was wrong."

Thorn pressed his forehead to mine, our breath intermingling as he searched for the words. "From the moment I knew of you, I knew you would be someone to protect, someone to keep safe above all else. What I did carries the potential for the treaty with Cimran to become null and void. Regicide, even when it's done out of mercy, is a seed for civil unrest - even war - especially when committed on foreign soil. I couldn't jeopardise the treaty my father worked so hard for but neither could I jeopardise you by letting you be bound to him in marriage."

"But why?" I couldn't pull back from Thorn with my head trapped between the wall and his own. Not that I wanted to. His presence was soothing, a balm for the soul. "What need does Nimue have for a treaty that benefits only Cimran? It doesn't make sense. Tell me you see that."

"Sparrow, it does make sense." he said as he pulled back to show the determined look in his eyes, "All will be clear when Nimue invades Cimran."

*

"Regicide to genocide," I gasped. "This is your answer?"

I paced fast enough that I might have worn a path clear through the cavern floor. Thorn leaned back against the wall I'd only a moment ago stood against, cradled there by his massive form. He looked perfectly at ease with folded arms across his muscled chest and one leg bent, the sole of his boot flat against the smooth rock behind him. The moment the words left his mouth, he'd released me as though he knew I needed the space to think.

And did I ever. The thought of my homeland being invaded, more unrest and pain wrought across already desolated lands, made me murderous, sickened to my very core. I thought of the past decades, the hell caused by Helmar and The Cleanse. Of Burnings that filled the skies with cloying black smoke and ash that fell in a poisonous layer across fields that would never again bear produce. I thought of the families torn apart, men sent to fight in a war they didn't believe in. How birth rates had drastically fallen since with towns and bloodlines now slowly dying out entirely.

I turned to look at the man who promised more of everything I hated most and spat at his feet.

"You're no better than Helmar."

Thorn exhaled sharply through his nose. "I'm a good deal better than Helmar and you know it."

I laughed, the sound hysterical. "Why? Because you haven't raised a hand to me? Well, it's early days, husband. Plenty of opportunity for you to strike while you lay waste to foreign lands. All hail the mighty conqueror."

"I'll never raise a hand to you," Thorn replied before adding with a small smirk, "unless you're into that. In which case, I might oblige, my preferences notwithstanding."

The look I threw at him was lethal. "Do *not* turn this sexual."

"At some level, sparrow, things between the two of us always will be."

I reached for the thing closest to me, an embroidered pillow placed as a seat beside the roaring fire, and pegged it directly at him. Thorn didn't move, letting it rebound off his shoulder to the floor.

"You're planning to destroy everything I love."

"Do you?"

I paused. "Do I what?"

"Love it? Cimran?"

I loosed a breath, more and more exasperated as time went on. "Yes, I love it. Parts of it anyway."

Thorn pushed off the wall, letting his arms fall to his side. He approached slowly, gaze unflinching. "If you're worried about Emrys, I will protect him to the best of my ability. Of course, his proximity to Helmar is a concern. Naturally, there will be a window once the invasion begins where things will be...dicey. Just know that Emrys will be the first retrieved. After you, he is my top priority."

Part of me eased at that and I hated it. Yes, more than anything I wanted Emrys safe. He was my family, the only family I had. But the fact that my one thought had been for his safety and not that of the innocents living in Cimran? It felt selfish, almost like a betrayal to all those who suffered under that sick bastard.

"Just answer why," I said, pleading. "What purpose would an invasion serve? Nimue is strong enough in its own right. Does it really need more land? More people to conquer? You don't have to be the king your father was and vie for what is not yours. Be content and leave Cimran well enough alone."

I glared at the hand Thorn extended towards me and a moment later he let it drop.

"Nimue has stood by for more than twenty years and watched the hell wrought across your home," he explained, a hand scrubbing through week-old stubble across his jaw. "My father was cowardly enough that he did not seek to intervene. He was content, so long as The Cleanse left us well enough alone, to let Cimran lie solely in Helmar's murderous hands." His eyes fell to his feet and I got the impression he was no longer seeing what was beneath him, his words taking on a distant tone. "I was seven when I first visited Cimran with my father. There was a celebration for the birth of Princess Cerana, royalty near and far were invited for a week-long feast. Do you know what your king did to celebrate?"

I shook my head but the unsettled feeling gnawing at my gut told me it wasn't good.

Thorn swallowed hard and when he looked up, his eyes glistened. "Many think there was a build-up to Helmar's wickedness, that he wasn't always the man he is now. I know for a fact that is not the case and as I said already, my father was too cowardly to put a stop to it."

"To what?" I almost didn't want to ask.

A lone tear fell from Thorn's eye. "Did you know I had a sister? Ten years my senior. She was something of a little mother to me, always fussing and ensuring I was well-cared for. My mother frequently fell into a depression and through no fault of her own became absent. Elinor was all I needed, more often than not. So while we were partaking of your king's hospitality, Elinor took it upon herself to put me to bed each night before the real debauchery began. No one ever put a dozen kings in one room and expected it to be a wholesome affair. Elinor knew that well enough. She tucked me in one night, recited prayers and kissed my brow. The next thing I knew, I woke before dawn to her bloodied body in the bed across the room. There were things done to her…things I'd struggled to comprehend."

An ice-cold shudder raced down my spine. "She was taken to Purgatory."

I thought back to what Helmar had said. One-hundred-thirty-nine souls, including my own, were taken to Purgatory. And now to find out that the sister-in-law I never met was one of them. Had I touched her dried blood? Been wounded by the same implements? Nausea swept over me at the thought.

He nodded solemnly. "There wasn't a name for that place then. It was simply referred to as King Helmar's playroom. It took my father's men years to piece together what happened to Elinor but I'm sure you can draw your own conclusions. Helmar used, abused and discarded my sister as though she were no more than trash. I hated my father for the fact that he let it go. He hated Helmar, of course, but retribution? Revenge? These were concepts unfamiliar to my father. Not because he was a benevolent man but because he was afraid of what might befall his kingdom should he stir the pot."

"What happened to Elinor?" I ached for Thorn and what he'd lived through, the ache rivalling my memories of what Helmar was capable of.

Thorn loosed a harsh breath, refusing to look up at me. "We left the celebrations two days early when Elinor grew feverish and it was clear that Cimran had little to offer her in the way of care. We never made it back. Elinor succumbed to her injuries on the journey home."

I felt sick all over again, thinking of the woman who would have been my sister-in-law enduring the same pain and torture as I did.

"You knew already of what I endured."

"The finer details? No," he replied. This time when he reached out, I didn't flinch. He caught a lock of my inky, silken hair and twirled it around his fingers, a mesmerised air taking over. "But I suspected. You weren't ready to divulge and I wasn't about to pry. I knew whatever had happened to you would have had to be vile for all the shadows that linger in your eyes. I see the way it haunts you, all those months spent in his hands. Tell me, sparrow, is that not enough to wage war? Is your suffering worth so little that you'd spare a kingdom woven with evil at its very core?"

"There are good people in Cimran," I whispered, leaning into the rhythmic movements of his fingers. "To kill them would be an affront to everything I believe in."

"Who said anything about harming innocents?" Thorn asked. I opened my mouth to reply before he placed a finger over my lips. "Artura, you assumed far too quickly that my approach to invasion would be that of a bull in a china shop. Trust that I'm a little more careful than to run roughshod when the disease that must be eradicated is only a small fraction of Cimran."

"You're only after Helmar and The Cleanse?" I didn't dare fall into the relief I was holding at bay, not until I knew for a fact that the people I'd lived amongst would be safe. People who were good and even in their moments of weakness were still so. People who wanted nothing of the decades-long war wrought upon the kingdom by Helmar. People I had lived alongside all my life and even though kept at an arm's length to protect me, were people I still cared for. Even Soraya, in light of her betrayal, didn't deserve to die. There was good in most - not everyone, I knew that to be true. "Why the weapons, then? Why provide Cimran with the means to wreak more havoc?"

I let Thorn lead me to the fire and when he sat down, pulling me into his lap, I didn't resist. The closeness was soothing, his warmth far more needed than anything else. One calloused hand stroked up and down my back, the thin linen of my dress barely masking the roughness of his fingers, while his other hand stroked from my knee to my ankle and back again, raising goosebumps across flesh that slowly grew more and more fevered under his touch with every pass.

"Helmar is a man of greed," Thorn said, placing a kiss on my shoulder. "And men of greed are not men concerned with the finer details. Every weapon we've provided to Cimran is about as effective as a feather is to a sword. When the time comes, The Cleanse will struggle to protect themselves. Denard expects a swift victory with little to no casualties."

I frowned. "That seems a little too good to be true. There are other ways for Helmar to hurt Cimran. And who is to say you'll apprehend him so swiftly? The kingdom is not a small place. All Helmar needs is an hour before he can put enough distance between the two of you to be problematic."

"He'll not know we're coming, sparrow."

"You can't be certain of that."

"I can," he breathed, his words barely audible. "Denard knows how to get into Dearmond. There's a pathway-"

"That son of a bitch," I gasped. "I asked him to find a way and he said it could not be done."

Thorn had the hide to smirk, making no move to hide his amusement. "Is that so?"

"I can't believe him."

"No doubt he thought he was protecting his queen from a foolhardy rescue mission."

I slapped Thorn's shoulder. "I blame you."

"Me?"

"Yes, *you*. Your men follow your example. Keep things from your wife and they'll presume they can keep them from their queen."

He raised a hand in defeat. "Have I not said now that I'll not keep secrets from you?"

I grabbed his hand, pulling it into my lap. "Truthfully? I'm too relieved to be truly mad with you and Denard. Can it really be so simple to save Emrys?"

"Simple? No," he said, face turning grave. "Nothing about war is ever simple."

"But we can save him?"

Thorn nodded.

We sat in silence and I let my head fall against his shoulder, the first bright sparks of hope dancing in my chest. The nightmare might soon be over. It felt all too surreal, the thought that I might once again hold Emrys in my arms, the only person who had truly loved me unconditionally. My heart ached for him, for the last memories I had of the old man huddled in a corner of a cold, damp cell.

"Where do I fit into all of this?" I asked, breaking the silence after some time.

Viane cleared her throat, making the both of us jump.

"You possess fire magic, Artura, and while it is yet in its infancy, it is strong," she said, her finger firmly stuck at a place on the page before her. "While victory might be attainable enough for Nimue, having a summoner on their side? That would guarantee it."

CHAPTER THIRTY-TWO

We rowed back to the *Scylla* with an extra passenger. Viane turned her face up towards the sun, basking in the warmth it showered each one of us with. The way she sighed made me wonder how long it had been since she ventured from within the isle, a place so dark that night seemed everlasting.

"Four years, three months and six days," she murmured.

"Why?"

She merely shrugged, giving no more of an answer than that.

Thorn entwined his fingers with my own, rough callouses scraping against my skin. I shivered at the sensation, not finding it entirely unpleasant. He was a king completely at ease, not a single concern marring his young face. His eyes scanned the gently lapping waves, looking for what, I didn't know. But then a moment later I caught sight of a fin, and then a tail, and then before I could take a breath, the boat was doused in a wave of chill water. No, not a wave, a splash. Thorn jutted his chin to the side and I followed his gaze to see a dolphin retreating into the clear waters of the isle. As we rowed back to the *Scylla*, the dolphin followed, acting as though it were his duty to guide us homeward.

Home. It was strange that the grand ship, anchored offshore for a week, felt like home. But that was what it was. The first home I'd had in quite some months. My own in Naiva was likely long gone. Either scavenged by those desperate enough to venture near the home of an accused witch or burned as a sign of good faith to the crown. All I had remaining in this world was that one ship.

"I've missed it," I admitted, eyes on the perfectly white sails being readied to once more catch the wind. Sailors milled about on deck, preparing for departure.

Thorn leaned closer, his lips brushing the shell of my ear as he whispered. "When this is all over, you may do with the *Scylla* as you wish. You are my wife and my queen, what is mine is yours."

I threw him a sideways glance. "You mean what belonged to your father?"

"If you wish, we will retire the *Scylla* and take up a new ship for our own. There are others in Nimue. Simply ask and it shall be done."

"I've no need to waste resources."

Thorn frowned. "It's hardly a waste if it pleases you."

"I was taught all my life to not waste that which is in good enough condition to still be of use. We had little growing up, and what we did have we looked after well. Dresses were worn till they bore holes and then redesigned into a blouse or undergarments or simply turned into other useful items such as cloths and wrappings. Food scraps were eaten instead of discarded, vegetable peelings could easily plump up a stew. Even herbs that were no longer of use were dried out and made into bags of potpourri to sell at the markets. Anything to cover the stench of Burnings sold for a pretty coin."

"So no new boat?" Thorn chuckled.

"No."

Denard caught the end of a rope ladder once we reached the *Scylla*, holding it steady as Viane gracefully climbed aboard, not missing a single step. Unlike myself. Thorn rushed to catch me, his hand slipping up my dress to my rear where he cupped it and squeezed it.

I threw an exasperated look back down at him. "How am I supposed to concentrate now?"

He shrugged and when he spoke, there was gravel in his voice. "Think of it as an enticement to board quickly."

Last night had been quiet with not an ounce of intimacy as nerves stole the air from my lungs and peace from my mind. I barely slept, tossing and turning until eventually, Viane awoke, declaring the day had begun. A day that I still couldn't believe I'd ever agreed to. What we were about to embark upon was madness. To describe it as anything else would have been laughable.

After all, it's not every day you agree to fight a dragon.

*

The cabin was silent, save for the echoes of Denard instructing men above deck.

Oh, that and the storm beating against *Scylla*.

High winds and furious seas whipped at the sides of the boat, sails now long since pulled down and secured. Within a matter of moments, the few unsecured possessions in the cabin had been tucked away. I'd not been quick enough to take hold of a clay mug full of piping hot tea, now shattered upon the floorboards. Jagged pieces slid back and forth as I sat on the bed, keeping my bare feet safe.

Unlike other inexperienced travellers, I wasn't squeamish. I enjoyed the chaos the storm brought. A hurricane, Denard warned. A product of the seas we traversed as we neared a collection of islands known for the downfall of many a ship. I'd been warned to expect rough seas and merely smiled. After Purgatory, there was little that could be thrown at me that would, in turn, throw me.

A knock barely sounded above the roar of the wind before the door to the cabin opened. Thorn swept inside, face serious.

"What is it?"

"The storm isn't letting up."

I shrugged. "You trust Denard, as do I. So what is the problem?"

Thorn's stern face turned to me and then I saw it. Something dark burned in his eyes, something that ignited my core and made my heart flutter. I tried to slow my breathing, sucking in a sharp intake of humid air. It did nothing to settle me, instead giving power to the flame that now licked slowly throughout my core, sending tingles of awareness through every inch of my being.

"The problem is that I've wasted time trying to manage this storm," he replied, "when I could have been down here making you scream with no one to hear."

Heat pooled between my thighs. I tilted up my chin, determined not to crumble. At least not right away. "Is that so?"

Like a predator closing in on its prey, Thorn stalked ever closer, his eyes not once leaving my own. The intensity in them was brutal and all-consuming, threatening to pull me apart as easily as the seas had pulled apart many a ship over years past.

"I want you to scream for me, sparrow. I want your moans and cries of pleasure to rival the roar of the storm. If I don't have you quivering and soaking beneath me in the next minute, I'll die. But first, I want to see how you pleasure yourself. Show me that pretty cunt, darling."

I opened my mouth once, twice, struggling to find the words. "I...you...what?"

The sexual tension between us had dimmed somewhat over the few days on the isle but it had lingered nevertheless. Small touches or looks throughout the day reminded us both that we were yet to consummate our marriage, that so far all we'd shared were stolen kisses, gentle touches and that one moment on our journey from Cimran where Thorn had devoured me so desperately that even now, the memory sent a ripple of pleasure coursing through me.

Thorn exhaled sharply through his nose, placing one hand against the bedpost that led to the willowy canopy overhead. "Spread those beautiful legs for me, sparrow. Show me that perfect cunt."

My jaw dropped a fraction at the roughness of his voice, the pressing need his words held. In a haze, I obeyed, drawing up my skirts around my waist and slipping off my undergarments.

"Is this what you want?" I whispered.

"More," was all he said.

I slipped my hand down my thigh, the skin clammy. The islands were humid, forever caught amid an oppressive summer, and it only heightened the sensations barrelling through me. My fingers brushed across the curls of my sex, seeking out that little nub that would make me fall apart. Parting my folds, I let a finger slip across my clit. A low whimper fell from my lips.

"That's it, darling," Thorn crooned. "Just like that. Show me how you touch yourself when you think of me."

"Bold of you to assume," I gasped, circling my finger, "that I think of *you*."

The smile Thorn gave me as his eyes slid from my pussy to my face was pure predator - confident and assured. "You think of me, sparrow, because I think of *you* and only *you* while I stroke my cock. Do you really think I don't? You're in my head forever and always."

I circled my clit with my finger, teasing the careful balance between sanity and insanity. Already I felt myself growing wetter, almost more than I'd ever been before. This, being so exposed before my husband, only made me wilder, more determined to please him. I'd never been one to seek the approval of another and even though on many levels we were still relative strangers, I craved it almost as much as I craved release.

"Tell me what you feel."

My tongue darted out to lick my dry lips, the movement slow and pronounced as I slipped my finger back and forth across my clit. "Desperate."

Thorn chuckled, the sound low and throaty. "Oh sparrow, you know nothing of desperation…not yet."

My hand slid further down until my middle finger found my entrance, tracing around the opening, not yet moving in. My back arched, pushing my breasts out. My clothing felt too tight, too constricting, but I didn't want to move my hand away. I needed that friction more than breath itself. But when I slipped a finger inside, feeling that delicious warmth, I realised I was wrong. I needed this. So, so, so very much.

Moans - either my own or Thorn's, I couldn't tell - rivalled the crashing of the sea and I fell back against the bed. My free hand slid up my stomach to my breasts, trying to tease my nipple through the stiff fabric. I whimpered in frustration.

Footsteps echoed in the room and then a second later, Thorn's firm hand curled around the neckline of my bodice. A sharp ripping sound made me jump and looking down I saw he held a dagger in one hand and the shredded fabric of my dress in his other. My breasts, now exposed, felt heavy under his gaze, the nipples peaking and hardening.

Touch me, I silently begged. *Lick me. Something. Anything. Please.*

Instead, Thorn withdrew to his previous position where he watched. His eyelids were heavy, mouth parted slightly.

I slipped a second finger into my core as I pulled and twisted at my nipples with my free hand. At first, the tempo was slow, deliberately slow, as my fingers rhythmically plunged in and withdrew. They were slippery, coated in the slickness of my cunt. I was practically dripping, melting right before him.

Thorn groaned. "Mmm, you look good enough to eat."

"Then have at it," I replied, breathless.

"Not until you come for me, sparrow. I want to see you shatter."

His words spurred me on and I picked up the pace. I fucked myself with my fingers, letting my palm push against my clit to create that so-needed friction. I was lost to the sensations building in my core, driving me higher and higher. The hand teasing my nipples slipped up my chest to my throat where my hand wrapped around it, acting purely on instinct, on what felt right.

"Oh, darling," Thorn crooned, "An admirable effort but you can do better."

I redoubled my efforts, the hand around my throat tightening. I could feel my cunt clenching helplessly around my fingers, searching for something better, thicker. I needed to be filled, consumed, and despite there being two fingers, it wasn't enough. The frustration I felt almost equalled that of my need to come.

"If you're wanting to be choked, sparrow, you need only ask."

I nodded at his words, pleading with my eyes.

Thorn's smirk grew. "Words, Artura, use them."

"Choke me," I gasped, not daring to let go.

He tisked. "Manners."

"Please." My voice was barely audible.

Thorn surged forward in an instant. I had barely let my hand drop before his rougher, larger one took hold of my throat. It was the touch I needed, the lightheadedness only adding to the pleasure roaring throughout my body.

"Fuck yourself," he growled.

I obeyed, unashamed in the way I thrust my hips up into my hand. I came apart a second later, the world spinning around me. My cunt clenched down but I didn't pull out my fingers, revelling in the tightness. Thorn pulled his hand away, smug.

"On your knees," he commanded.

I scrambled from the bed, neatly dodging the broken mug sliding around the floor. My legs felt like jelly as I fell to my knees, helped by the sharp twist of the boat as a wave crested over the side. Salty water splashed across the window of our cabin.

Thorn undid his buckle and let his pants fall. His cock sprang free, thick and heavy, the head already glistening with a bead of precum. I'd yet to taste him and my mouth watered at the sight of him, swollen and ready. I took hold of his cock in my hand but his fingers clamped around my wrist, pulling it away.

"Just your mouth, sparrow."

I swallowed hard, doubting that I'd fit him in. He looked thicker than any other cock I'd seen before and my core clenched down, feeling deliriously empty. I traced my tongue along the underside of his cock, following the thick vein that wound its way to the swollen head where I lapped up the salty cum. I moaned in delight at his taste and Thorn's breath hissed through his teeth. I repeated the process over again and again.

Thorn fisted his hand in my hair, jerking my head up to look at him. I felt myself shudder under the heat of his gaze. Slowly that smirk, spelling nothing but wicked mischief, widened.

"Don't be shy."

Those three little words preceded his hand roughly shoving my head towards his cock. It slipped past my lips, further and further until it hit the back of my throat. But instead of pulling back, he held steady, letting me adjust to his girth and length. I breathed through my nose, trying to relax but instead gagged. Thorn withdrew to the tip and then repeated the process all over again. And again, I gagged. On the fourth time, my eyes began to water. On the seventh, tears spilled down my cheeks.

"Fuck, sparrow, that's such a pretty picture. You've never been more beautiful."

I hollowed my cheeks and drew him in again. Each time he grew faster and faster until finally, Thorn was fucking my throat with abandon. I gave myself over to him, letting him use me for his pleasure. My hands, not allowed to touch, moved back to the apex of my thighs. I was soaked. Never had I been so turned on, so aroused.

You know nothing of desperation.

I knew now. As well as I knew the back of my hand.

"So eager," he murmured. "So needy."

I moaned around his length until suddenly, he withdrew completely. I tried to lunge towards him but his hand, still fisted in my hair, stopped me.

"I want you sparrow," Thorn said, pulling my head back. "Tell me you do not want me and I will leave right now. This is your decision."

I panted, still catching my breath but managed to nod. More than anything, I wanted him, too. Needed him. I was aching so acutely that it was almost painful. The need to be filled by Thorn was overwhelming.

"Take off your dress. Get on the bed. On your hands and knees."

With the bodice of my dress torn down to my waist, it was easy to push past my hips until it pillowed on the floor. I kicked it away, climbed onto the bed as instructed and waited.

Thorn's hand whipped sharply across my rear. I gasped, lurching forward for a moment before pushing back in a silent plea for him to spank me again. Instead of hitting me again, though, I felt the head of his cock slide easily through my folds. I moaned at the feeling, heated steel against supple flesh. In one swift movement, Thorn sheathed himself inside me, giving no time to adjust before he pummelled relentlessly.

I cried out, the sound echoing in the cabin.

"Try harder, sparrow. Sing for me."

Sharply and without warning, my head was pushed down into the bed, my rear still high. Thorn didn't miss a beat, moving continuously. There was no mercy with each thrust, no reprieve and certainly no gentleness. I didn't want it. After everything, I wanted to be fucked, consumed, taken by the man fate had delivered me to.

"More," I gasped, my voice muffled by the blanket. "I need more."

"Be careful what you wish for," he growled.

On the next thrust, Thorn's thumb pressed against the pucker of my rear, massaging it, adding pressure every time he bottomed out. Each thrust was met by my cries of pleasure, my voice growing louder and louder until eventually, my throat felt hoarse. His thumb pushed in and I'd never felt so full.

"I can't," I gasped.

"You can," he countered. "Take it, Artura. Take it all."

"It's too much, Thorn." My eyes rolled back in my head, feeling another orgasm fast building. My cunt clenched around Thorn's cock and the groan I heard from him was the most delicious sound I'd ever heard.

"Take all of me," he ground out, punctuating each word with a thrust.

My release barrelled through me and I screamed out, the pleasure far too much to cope with. Tears streamed down my face from the brutal fucking Thorn dealt out. Heat washed through me as he followed me over the edge of bliss, his thrusts slowing as he held himself still, pouring every last drop into me.

He sighed, stroking his hand down my back soothingly, approvingly. "Yes, sparrow. Just like that."

*

Something cold and hard was pressed against my lips and a second later, cool liquid spilt down my throat. Half in a daze, I swallowed, letting the water soothe the dull ache that lingered there. Once I'd drained the cup, I opened my eyes, blinking in the sudden darkness that was broken only by a lone candle flickering across the room.

"What time is it?" I groaned, pushing myself up on the bed.

"Past midnight," Thorn replied, his voice smooth in the dark. Beside me, the bed shifted, the mattress dipped and then his arms banded around me, spooning me to his chest. "You've dozed most of the day."

"Really?"

He chuckled. "You needed it."

"No need to sound so smug," I mumbled, stifling a yawn.

"Should I not? When even now I can feel my seed dripping from you?"

I shifted uncomfortably against his lap and immediately felt the truth of his words. We were both naked and very much in need of a clean-up. A cloth. Anything. My cheeks flushed.

"Don't be ashamed, sparrow."

"Should I not?" I replied, echoing his earlier question.

"Not even a little," he murmured, pressing his lips to the dip below my ear. When he spoke again, I felt his warm breath mist across my damp skin. The lateness of the hour had done nothing to dispel the humidity, made all the worse by the now-dissipated storm. "I want there to be no shame between us. Just trust and pleasure."

"Yours?" I asked. "Or mine?"

"Have I not made it clear that I very much intend that we be equal *in all things*?"

I was silent for a moment as his hand slid up and down my arm, leaving a trail of goosebumps in its wake. I shivered and he mistook it instantly for me being cold because he groped in the darkness, pulling a blanket to drape across us.

"Sparrow? Do you honestly still believe I would put a higher importance on my pleasure as opposed to your own?"

I shrugged. "Men everywhere consider their own needs and then little else. Women, too, from my experience." I couldn't stop the image of Soraya flashing across my mind, a pang of anger and sadness mingling in my chest. She and I had both been guilty of taking without giving. The last time we'd been together, I'd done as much, refusing her touch when she was sated. "How can I be certain that you will be different? That you will break the mould, so to speak. I've barely had any time with you. We still know little about each other beyond simple facts. How do I know this isn't some carefully curated facade that you put on for all the women?"

"Firstly," Thorn replied, his voice soft, "other men are obtuse. There's no greater pleasure than watching you unravel beneath my fingertips. No amount of stroking my cock will rival that."

"Don't be crass," I muttered.

"It's not crass, it's the truth. I could pleasure myself every day for a year straight but would give it up in an instant to watch your pleasure take hold just once. There's a light in your eyes, sparrow, when you tip over the edge. That light is brighter than any rising sun I've seen on the horizon. It's like seeing god, something so incredibly holy. I would worship at your altar, more devout than the most ardent monk or priest, just to glimpse that light even once in a lifetime."

I blushed. Sweet nothings had been whispered in my ear more than once in my lifetime but there was a surety in the way he spoke, a conviction so deep-seated I doubted it could ever be shaken. For a moment, my flight instinct kicked in. It was such a rare thing that it took me by surprise. I couldn't bear to be wounded again by someone I cared for, even loved.

Was that what this was? Love?

I shook my head to clear it. A few weeks was nowhere near long enough to get to that point.

"Secondly," Thorn continued. "I'll not lie to you. There have been others. I was away in the southern kingdoms for quite a number of years and whilst I might claim to worship as a monk, I am far from one."

I rolled away, turning to face Thorn. His jade green eyes were luminous in the dark, two shining orbs full of serenity and contentment.

"So are you saying this because you'll take others into our bed? That no matter how much it pleases you to 'watch my pleasure take hold' I'll still somehow not be enough for you? Because hear me now, King Thorn of Nimue, I'll not share my marital bed with another beyond you. I'm not the generous kind of wife."

Thorn growled low in his throat, irritated. "Do you truly think that my eyes, although having been locked on you since the moment I saw you beside Helmar, layered up in all that so-called finery to hide the evil you endured, would suddenly find another and be pleased with them?" There was something beneath his words, something that sounded almost…hurt. Like my assumption had wounded him in some unseen way.

"I trust you," I said, only to be cut off before I could finish my sentence.

"Clearly not."

"Let me finish," I snapped. "I trust you with my *life*. My *heart* is another thing entirely. Some days I think it might be yours but others… The last time I gave myself completely to another, I was betrayed."

"I know this."

"Then understand where I'm coming from," I begged, taking his hands in my own. I lifted each one, pressing a kiss to each fingertip. "I told you before that there are broken parts of me slowly healing. It will take time for me to be that vulnerable again."

"I'm prepared to wait," he said and then repeated the gesture, pressing a lingering kiss to each one of my fingers. "You are something incredible, Artura."

I scoffed. "Incredibly infuriating, sure."

I felt more than heard his answering chuckle as Thorn pulled me forward, the two of us nestling down in the bed. He folded me into his arms, my head resting against his firm chest. I placed an arm atop him, my fingertips playing with his cheek, his beard and neck, idly exploring the man who was unexpectedly stealing my whole heart.

Just as I was falling asleep, Thorn pressed a kiss to my brow and whispered, "You are eternal torture and I am a masochist. Destroy me and I will worship at your altar for all my days, sparrow. I am utterly, wholly and irrevocably yours."

CHAPTER THIRTY-THREE

A subtle crest of greenery on the horizon broke the monotony of the endless ocean two weeks later. At first, it was faint and I thought I'd imagined it, my eyes still bleary from sleep. But as the morning wore on, it grew, became more solidified and...*real*.

Galdua.

For the first time, I saw the homeland of my mother, someone I'd known so little of till recently. I waited for some feeling of connection, a sense of rightness. This was my homeland, also, by blood.

But nothing came. The winds were warm as they whispered around me yet nothing stirred in my heart or mind.

Denard hadn't lied when he said the *Scylla* was the fastest ship in the northern kingdoms. We'd sailed the northern border of Cimran in no time at all. And thankfully so, as I'd all but held my breath those four days. It was like I could feel Helmar's eyes upon me, watching my every move, studying and criticising. And worst of all, planning what more he could do to me in Purgatory.

I had stayed in our cabin below deck until the all-clear was given.

And now we were here, having travelled so far into the east that I'd thought land might not be seen again. Galdua wasn't what I thought. From the brief history Viane had given of a small kingdom where House Igneous spent the remainder of their days, I'd assumed something grand - even a little. Instead what greeted us was lush forest and nary a hint that civilisation had ever existed within its borders.

We arrived at the reefs surrounding Galdua late that night and decided to wait till sunrise before disembarking. Denard and Viane were wary of what the island held, and rightfully so if the low growls carried towards us on the offshore winds were anything to go by. At Viane's insistence, I drank an herbal remedy she prepared and slept like the dead until Thorn roused me from sleep, the first rays of light tickling my face through the window.

"I've sent a boat ahead to set up camp," Denard informed us as we emerged on deck. "I know you're against being so close to the shore but until we're certain of what is in the forest, I'll not prepare for my king and queen to reside in it."

Thorn clapped Denard on the shoulder, the captain swaying a little at the force. "Kind of you, though perhaps unnecessary."

"My king?" Denard cocked an eyebrow.

Thorn placed his hand at the small of my back, the simple gesture barely steeling my already fraught nerves. Because before he said it, I knew what Thorn would tell his most trusted soldier.

We were going alone, my husband and I, and wouldn't emerge until what was done was done.

If it could be done at all, that was.

"Forgive me for speaking out of turn," Denard began, brow furrowed. He stood with his hands clasped behind his back as he did so often while watching the horizon as we sailed. Only now his stance was tense, wary. His normally tan skin was pale with unease.

"Never," Thorn smirked.

"But I know we have a relationship where I can speak my mind when necessary. This is lunacy," Denard grumbled. "I've not stepped foot on Galdua but even I know the legends."

"Legends cannot harm us," Thorn replied, all confidence and bustling, eager energy. When Denard relaxed a fraction, Thorn's smirk grew. "But these can. There is a dragon out there somewhere that Artura and I must find. And we will. Once it is done, we'll return. Recall your men and await further instruction. I do not need the beast to detect more than one scent. It'll drive it to insanity and be harder to kill."

My stomach flipped. No amount of preparation from Viane was enough for me to come to terms with the fact that I would have to stare down a dragon and slay it. Beneath my cloak that trapped the stifling humidity to my skin, I was armed to the teeth. Thorn had spent more time dressing me than he had himself. Knives were sheathed at my thighs and ankles, hidden in my boots and strapped to my wrists. Those at the wrists contained a mechanism, designed to quickly produce the blades with a mere flick. No such 'flicking' had happened from the moment Thorn bound them to me. With my luck, I'd stab myself and this whole trip would be null and void.

"I have to insist," Denard pleaded. "It's not safe."

"You're a good man, Denard. And that is why I place my trust solely in you to protect this ship." Thorn looked out over Galdua, carefully searching through the towering greenery. "But I am also your king and my word must be obeyed. If there was another way around this, it would be done. There are things Artura needs before we can sail back to Cimran. This is the fastest way to it."

I couldn't shake the niggling guilt in the back of my mind. Because I'd asked for this. It was my decision to drag us all here and into unknown danger. To Galdua and dragons and slaying such a beast when the largest creature I'd killed my entire life was a rabbit - and even then I'd mourned it for months.

As though sensing my inner turmoil, Thorn lowered his face to mine and whispered in my ear.

"No matter what, sparrow, let it be done. I would cross oceans a thousand times over and follow you into the heart of hell if it meant you could be the woman you were born to be."

I gulped but said nothing.

A tender boat was lowered into the turquoise waters lapping around the reef and once Thorn and I were seated, he began to row us towards the shores of Galdua. I sat, fiddling with my fingers, picking at the worn skin around my nails, and tried not to think about what was about to happen. Would we even make it off the island? I was under no grand illusions. I wasn't a fighter. Far from a warrior. I couldn't hold my own in battle. The closest I'd come to a fight was striking at the odd reprobate in Naiva and even then I'd been selective about it so as not to stir unnecessary trouble. I had a sharp tongue but I doubted the dragon would fall to a few choice words. All I truly had as we rowed ever closer was hope.

And that hope had been born already waning.

*

"I have to question the logic of House Igneous setting up their home in such a flammable location."

Thorn snorted beside me, squeezing my hand once. "It's likely why they died out. Much of Galdua has regrown over the past years. If you're still long enough, you can sense it in the earth, the feeling of rebirth and new life. It sings of past heartbreak and torment but also the hope of starting anew."

"Keep talking like that. You sound just like Viane," I grumbled.

Thorn lifted a heavy palm frond, moisture dripping from it onto my head as I crouched low and slid under. The forest was thicker than I realised and I was glad of the cloak, no matter how much I dripped with sweat beneath. Without it, I'd have already been cut to high heaven. I'd never before laid eyes on palms and vines bristling with inch-long thorns. It was unnerving, almost like Galdua was trying to make us retreat to its shores and the tender boat we'd left moored there.

"There is a familial connection to my aunt that is inescapable," he replied. "Her likeness is bound to come out in me every so often."

"Perhaps I ought to have just married her then," I retorted. I'd partly been grateful to leave the *Scylla* because it meant putting distance between the diviner and myself. Except now, she still found small ways to plague me.

Thorn winked back at me as he effortlessly swatted away a bug that was far too big for my liking.

"You'd miss my cock too much."

"And your charming wit, clearly."

He grinned, all mischief and playfulness.

I couldn't find it in myself to return his cheerful mood. Not when I knew what awaited us. And I had the distinct feeling that it was all an act on Thorn's part, a way to distract me from the terror bubbling in my veins, chilling the fire I'd felt coursing through over the past weeks. For what was about to come, that terror would disarm me. I tried to push it down, deny its existence altogether. But that terror was potent and only redoubled its efforts. I shivered.

"How are we even going to find a dragon in all this?" I asked, my voice just above a whisper in case my simple question summoned the creature. I could barely see several feet ahead, so dense was the foliage.

"We're not," Thorn replied, shaking out his hand as he released another frond. I noticed for the first time the dozens of hairline cuts along his palm and the back of his hand from where he'd grasped stems littered with thorns and pinprick spikes. "The dragon will find us."

"How do you intend to make that happen? Are you going to cover me in spices and marinades to attract it? Turn me into a meal?"

"Don't forget the garnish on your head."

I swatted at his arm, my hand grazing a nearby spike in the process. Instant karma.

"Dragons operate firstly by scent," Thorn explained. "It's partly why I sent our men back to the ship, so as not to confuse the creature. We will find an opening in the forest and wait. The breeze on shore felt strong enough and if we can make it to higher ground then that very same breeze ought to attract him."

"And then what?" I asked, trying to swallow past the lump in my throat. I already knew the answer but I asked anyway, hoping somehow that it had changed.

"You fight like hell, Artura." He stopped, turning to face me. The hand that gripped mine squeezed almost painfully but brought only comfort. "I will be nearby, ready to step in at a moment's notice. If it looks like the dragon is about to get the better of you, I'll pull you out."

I shifted restlessly from one foot to another. "I can't do this, Thorn."

"You can."

"I can't."

"Yes, you can."

I groaned and tilted my head up towards the sky, only to realise it was completely hidden from view by the thick canopy overhead. All around was the insistent humming and buzzing of insects, both crawling and flying. In Naiva, such things didn't exist. Save for the odd cockroach, lured in by the filth and stench of poverty, the weather was usually too cold and inhospitable. I decided that, despite the conditions of my home, I would trade it any day over Galdua. How had my mother managed to grow up here amongst this? We were hardly two hours into marching through the forest and already I was on the brink of madness.

"Artura, I wouldn't have let you come here if I didn't think you capable," Thorn said, tilting my face to his with a lone finger under my chin.

"So much for letting me be independent and my own person," I grumbled.

It earned a small smile from him. "You can independently kill a dragon, how about that?"

"You're a bastard."

We continued for several hours more and when I felt what had to be the dozenth blister pop in my boot, we began to climb. The ground sloped sharply upwards and as I took each step, I found myself placing a hand on the ground, my body nearly horizontal to it. Bracken and dirt caked under my nails and turned my palm into a disgusting brownish-green but I relaxed as the forest began to thin out.

Until I realised that we were here. And now it was time to summon a dragon.

*

I felt like a fool, standing in the middle of a meadow. In another world, it might have looked sweet, perhaps even innocent, if seen from a distance. Flowers the colour of sunset surrounded my feet and a warm breeze tangled in my hair, undone from the braid I'd carefully wound it into this morning. All the better for the dragon to latch onto my scent, Thorn had said. My cloak was gone, too, left beside Thorn who stood just inside the tree line, a fraction down the slope of the hill.

It was, in reality, far from a pretty picture. I jerked as something nipped at my ankle again and when I glanced down I yelped.

"It has teeth," I hissed at Thorn. "Why the ever-loving fuck does a flower have teeth?"

He shrugged, his reply low and carried on the breeze. "Most plants on Galdua have some sort of defence mechanism."

"Defence mechanism?" I scoffed. "I'm not doing a godsdamned thing and it's trying to eat my ankle."

I felt blood trickle into my boot.

"Well, it is carnivorous. Probably hungry, too, given how few people venture here."

"Outstanding," I sarcastically muttered, kicking the flower aside. It reared back, reminding me of an asp prepared to strike. I kept my eyes on it. "Try it. I dare you. I'll flatten you in a split second."

Perhaps House Igneous had simply been devoured by the flora on Galdua and died out that way.

Just as another flower began nipping at the exposed flesh of my other ankle, I felt the ground quake. Just enough that the flower paused mid-bite. Another quake rumbled through the earth and the flower closed in an instant. On the third rumble, this one bigger than the rest, it nearly threw me off balance.

The flower slid into the ground, disappearing into the grass almost too fast to catch.

My breathing turned shallow.

Roaring filled the humid air surrounding us. It was long and drawn out and full of unmatched ferocity. Even the hellions I'd encountered in the Isle of the Old Gods were no match for the acute terror that lanced through me like a hot knife. My knees threatened to buckle.

"Breathe, sparrow," I heard Thorn say. "Everything will be fine."

I wanted to snap back that no, everything wouldn't be alright. Perhaps it would be for him, safely ensconced within the forest. But my mouth hung slack as the first glimpse of the dragon slid over the meadow.

It prowled towards me with a preternatural grace, stalking its prey.

Me.

Stand your ground, I heard Viane say, the memory of her instructions from last night. *Show fear and you've already lost.*

But if a dragon could scent as well as I assumed it could, then surely it could smell the sweat pouring off me, the panic that coated every inch of me. Perhaps I'd already lost. Either way, I had no choice now. I was stuck. The only way out was through.

I drew a knife from my belt and awaited its attack.

CHAPTER THIRTY-FOUR

I waited.

And waited.

The dragon, all gleaming, iridescent onyx scales and piercing yellow eyes that reminded me of a cat, studied me. It didn't move a muscle and had I not seen it approach mere minutes ago, I might have assumed it to be a statue. It wasn't quite as large as I'd feared, perhaps thirty to forty feet. But that wasn't what worried me.

It was the fact that even from across the meadow, now devoid of the carnivorous flowers turned coward, I could see just how thick the plating was that covered every inch of the beast. He might as well have been made of stone, impenetrable and built to outlast any opponent. His head was as big as a carriage and protruding from the edge of his mouth, one end to the other, was a row of fangs, yellowed with age. One on the right side bore a crack, and another beside it was jagged, the tip broken off. Was I not the first to challenge the dragon, then? Or had he destroyed another of his kind in a bid for territory?

Because the way it looked at me now, shifting from one spiked hind leg to the next, could only be described as a challenge. I was competition, one that he needed to swiftly eviscerate to protect his home. I felt hostility rolling off him in waves and when his scaled lips pulled back in a feral snarl, also felt heat radiating from deep within him. The fires he held I could already tell were so much more than the average flame. From where I stood, the skin of my cheeks slowly blistered as if I'd fallen asleep in the sun all day.

The dragon's tail began to slowly flick. It was hypnotic in the way it moved and serpent-like. Bony spikes ran along the spine of the dragon and as I watched, rose like hackles. So when the creature finally lunged, I was somewhat prepared for the attack.

In three great leaps, the dragon closed the distance between us. I narrowly avoided it as I flung myself to the side, rolling along the grass. Stopping at the edge of the meadow, I quickly pushed myself to my feet. Already I'd dropped my knife. It made sense now why Thorn had armed me so heavily. I wasn't a trained warrior. I was bound to stuff up more than once.

Or more than a dozen times.

The dragon swung its muzzle around and this time I wasn't quick enough to dodge it. The hard head connected with my gut and flung me several feet into the air. When I landed it was with a painful thud. I gasped, clutching my ribs. If I lived through this, I would be covered with bruises again and the ones from Helmar had only just healed. The dragon turned its head to the side as it watched me clamber to my feet. I slid a knife from my ankle as my hand moved past it and held it in a white-knuckled grip, determined not to drop this one.

Again, the dragon charged across the meadow and instinctively, I rolled towards it, ducking under its muzzle. I flung my arm up, knife connecting with the underside of its jaw. It was like striking brick and the impact reverberated along my arm and into my shoulder. I hazarded a glance at where I'd made my mark only to realise that no such mark was left behind. The creature really was plated as thickly as I feared. I made a mental note not to strike the same place twice. I doubted I'd be lucky enough to have too many opportunities. I would have to be selective with where I chose to wound the dragon.

The dragon continued to step past me as I rolled, its hind legs narrowly missing my head and feet. I tucked into a ball at the last second and stayed like that until its tail was flicking overhead. Scrambling to the right on all fours, the knife still firmly clasped in my hand, I put as much distance between the dragon and I as the meadow would allow. I needed to regroup and reevaluate my plan.

Not that I had a plan beyond 'don't die.'

I assessed the dragon as it shook out its head, opening and closing its mouth as though to test for any wound I might have inflicted. I looked at the dragon's belly, noting that the further down it went, the smoother the scales became. No longer did they appear raised and stone-like, but rather softer and almost smooth like leather.

The belly, then.

But there was a far more pressing issue. It could see me. It turned its head from side to side, unable to look directly at me just like a bird. Perhaps there was an evolutionary connection somewhere. Its wings seemed similar to that of a bat's and Emrys had referred to bats on many occasions as 'rat birds.' If the dragon was anything like a bat and got airborne, I'd be in trouble. Would it attempt to carry me off to its nest or lair or wherever it was that a dragon resided? If it somehow took me away from Thorn, I doubted he would find me. Not on an island the size and density of Galdua. I would be lost, as good as dead.

I made a plan quickly in my head, gritted my teeth, and before I could give myself a moment to second guess myself, charged forward.

The look on the dragon's face could be described as nothing other than amused. I was a mouse to a cat as I slowly closed the distance between the two of us. But just as I hoped, the dragon took the bait and with little more than a bound towards me, I repeated my earlier move. This time when I ducked and rolled under the dragon, I didn't attempt to slice into its heavily plated jaw and bypassed the delicate flesh of its belly altogether. That would come later. Instead, the moment the hind legs passed by, I threw myself forward and latched onto its tail.

I felt surprise flicker through the dragon as it paused for a fraction of a second.

And then it began to wildly thrash from side to side.

I clung on for dear life. It wasn't enough.

I flew high into the air, arcing until I landed exactly where I began.

"Fine," I ground out, shaking out my arms as I tried to slow my breathing. I didn't dare look at Thorn. Not when it could cost me my concentration - or his life if the dragon discovered there was another delicious human nearby to sate its appetite.

The dragon and I danced around the edge of the meadow, neither one of us taking our eyes off the other.

It was the dragon that broke first and as I repeated the move I'd made twice now, I grinned. The beast hadn't expected me to try what had already failed and so when I made it to the tail and latched on, it didn't have time to thrash and fling me off. I shoved the knife between my teeth and took hold of each bone-like horn along its spine, using them as handholds as I climbed to between its shoulder blades. Once perched, my hands wrapped firmly around a thick, ash-coloured horn, I looked down at either wing. As I'd moved under the dragon, the wings had been neatly folded in and in my hurry to mount the beast, I hadn't felt it shifting in a whole new way. The thin, membranous wings were expansive, extending from one side of the meadow to the other, and a split second before the dragon took flight, I realised I'd made a very huge mistake.

CHAPTER THIRTY-FIVE

The ground disappeared from below. I swallowed the scream building in my throat, determined not to let the knife fall from between my teeth. My entire body instantly grew ice cold as we soared high into white clouds - clouds that had looked so peaceful while I'd stood on board the *Scylla* just this morning. Moisture coated my cheeks and I choked as a bug flew into my mouth. I spat it out and begged myself to think.

I had planned to disable the dragon's wings before it could take flight. Of course, in that plan, it hadn't occurred to me that the dragon might fly away before I could accomplish my task. I could try again now, dig my knife through the membrane and shred them as planned. But I would have to leave the safety of my perch, somehow make it along wings that rapidly beat and would surely shake me off like the inconsequential thing I was.

Higher and higher we flew and I felt desperation rising within. I could see nothing of Galdua below, only misting white stretching for endless miles, a blanket upon the world I knew. How far were we now from the island? I had no sense of direction, no way of knowing just how far we'd flown. The height made me dizzy and I narrowly fought and won against the nausea twisting in my gut.

Perhaps my earlier plan could still work somehow, I decided. Wrapping an arm around the horn I clung to, I reached up with my free hand and took the blade from my mouth. My hand shook with cold, each finger numb and stiff. But I gripped as hard as I could muster and in one swift motion, drove the blade downwards into the dragon's right shoulder, directly between a sliver of a gap between the scales.

Thunderous roaring tore through the sky, making my skin crawl. But it told me one thing - my aim was true. Hot liquid spurted as I withdrew the knife, the colour of the blood nearly as dark as the onyx scales. A second later, the dragon dipped to the side, favouring the undamaged shoulder and wing. The wounded wing continued to move, disjointed, ragged and far slower than it had been a moment ago. We began to spiral slowly, the dragon unable to maintain our position in the sky.

I carefully swivelled around in my seat and looked for a similar opening atop the left shoulder. Again, the dragon roared as my knife drove home in that fine gap in the scales - a gap that seemed to have been crafted for this very purpose.

We left my stomach somewhere high in the clouds. Both wings ceased beating, seeming to almost crumple in on themselves. The leathery sail of each wing creased as we fell faster and faster, passing through the cloud bank. I screamed, my throat tearing at the force, when Galdua came into view. It was coming up to meet us much too fast. We were going to crash and I knew for a fact that only one of us would potentially walk away.

But just as the finer details of palm fronds were seen and the buzzing of insects sounded dimly in my ears, the dragon forced its wings taut, the air catching under them. It roared, the sound no longer one of fury but of pain. For a moment I felt sickening guilt. I'd caused this. I'd wounded this beautifully terrifying creature beneath me. The dragon landed back in the meadow with an almighty crash, the ground cracking beneath its razor-sharp claws. Falling from its back, I was unable to catch myself. My elbow met the earth first, and I screamed in unison with the dragon.

Broken, definitely broken. At least it was the arm that bore the badly healed wrist. I still had one good hand at my disposal. Running across the meadow to buy some time, I one-handedly undid my belt, flung it over my shoulder and fumbled until I managed to secure my broken arm to my chest. The pain caused nausea to swell once more and I doubled over, heaving into the grass. Little came up after having no appetite this morning, dreading the oncoming mess I was now firmly in the grips of.

The dragon was still testing out its wings, gingerly extending one before bellowing in pain and withdrawing it. He wouldn't fly again and despite my earlier guilt, I couldn't bring myself to truly regret it. I never wanted to be so far from the blessed ground again. If the price of being on solid ground was that my ankles would be attacked by carnivorous flowers and insects would attempt to sting any exposed flesh they could find, I would gladly pay it.

I glanced behind me to the patch of trees where Thorn waited. There was a split second where I glimpsed panic and horror across his face before he schooled his features into a mask of confidence and calm. I recognised it as the face he showed his men, the trusted leader and king, unfazed by the impossible. But for a moment, he'd let his true feelings show, the terror he felt that I might not survive this. I shook my head and raised my uninjured arm in a silent sign for him to stay put. He nodded once before jerking his chin upward towards the dragon. It hadn't moved and I looked back at Thorn, both eyebrows lifted in a silent question.

All he did in reply was point to my wrist and then his eye. I understood enough.

While the dragon was distracted, fawning over now useless wings, I crept up slowly. Every step in the grass was carefully placed, avoiding any leaves that might crunch or twigs that could snap and give my position away. I danced from one spot to the next, on the balls of my feet. But then the wind changed, tangling my hair around my face, and my scent hit the dragon.

Instantly, the dragon's head swung towards me, slitted eyes narrowing, honing in on me where I stood rooted to the spot. It roared, showering me in scalding hot breath and droplets of saliva that burned on contact. The enormous scaled body turned on the spot and I leapt backwards, narrowly avoiding the tip of its muzzle. I pivoted and when the head swung back in an attempt to hit me, I flicked my uninjured wrist upwards, loosed the hidden blade there and made purchase with the dazzling yellow of the dragon's eye.

Had the creature been loud before? It was nothing compared to the ear-splitting cry that escaped from it now. My ears popped and I felt a trickle of water dripping from one ear. Touching it with trembling fingertips, I wasn't entirely surprised to find that it was blood. The cry of the dragon diminished slightly, just enough for me to focus. When I looked at the eye, blood teeming from the socket, I saw that it was milky, clouded over completely and bearing a jagged diagonal cut through the pupil. I moved a step to the side. The dragon didn't follow my movement. Another step and still, no awareness that I'd moved. Suddenly, my scent swam around the dragon's head as the wind blew hard and fast once more. I moved around the muzzle, careful not to draw any notice. The blade at my wrist dripped thick crimson blood and my hand was covered in it, growing stickier by the minute. The other eye came into view and before that pupil could flick in my direction, I drove the blade clean through, stopping only when my palm prevented it from sinking any further.

I raced backwards as the dragon roared again. Now completely blind, I was a ghost to it, able to move somewhat freely so long as the gusting wind remained constant, dizzying the dragon with my scent and preventing it from pinpointing my location. I flicked my wrist, attempting to withdraw the blade and when I couldn't, used my teeth to rip the buckle off. The metallic tang of dragon blood coated my tongue and I gagged silently as the weapon fell to the grass.

With one final gust, the wind came to a dead halt.

I cursed under my breath.

The dragon snapped its head in my general direction and blindly charged forward.

The greatest of all senses to a dragon was smell, Thorn had said on our journey to the meadow. Whilst removing sight had been advantageous, it hadn't quite levelled the playing field. So long as the dragon could smell *me*, it would find me.

I gasped, the answer suddenly hitting me.

It could smell *me*.

But if my scent suddenly disappeared…

I pushed my legs quickly, closing the distance between the dragon's previous spot, a thick puddle of blood oozing across the grass. I lunged at it, falling to the ground. My broken arm was the first thing to make contact and I bit down on the inside of my cheek. This time when I tasted blood, it was my own but I'd at least kept silent. I rolled back and forth in the blood, the rusty tang coating the inside of my nose. I covered every inch of my body with the dragon's blood and when satisfied that I reeked of it, stood to my feet and waited.

The wind picked up again, slowly at first before it hit the crescendo it had minutes ago. The dragon remained still, save for its head, turning in one direction and then the next, blindly searching. It growled, frustrated, as it stalked slowly across the meadow.

And away from me.

It couldn't smell me anymore.

I was *invisible*.

I slid down to a crouch and pulled the remaining dagger from my thigh.

Either this plan was genius…or the very last act I would ever do.

I whistled.

The dragon froze.

I whistled again, louder this time.

The growling grew, vibrating through the ground. The dragon followed the sound as I continued to whistle like one would for a dog. Slowly, it crept across the meadow, stopping and reassessing every few feet. What once had taken only a few bounds now took what felt like an eternity. I waited, too focused to acknowledge the fear clawing at my mind, as the dragon stepped closer and closer.

I was up too high. That was the first thing I realised when it was several feet from me. I rolled off my heels and onto my back, laying flat, and whistled again. The beast sidled up, first its head and then the long neck rising over me, dousing me in shadow. I waited, breathing slowly in through my nose and out through my mouth until the delicate flesh of its belly stopped directly above my face.

I shoved the dagger upwards and twisted.

The dragon lurched forward and I fought not to lower my blade, keeping it firmly pointed upwards. As the dragon thrashed in an attempt to dislodge the dagger, the incision in the belly grew from an inch wide, to a handspan, an arm length and finally right to where the scales grew thicker once more at the base of its tail. Overhead, the dragon shuddered and swayed. I abandoned the dagger and rolled out from under it just as the dragon collapsed to the ground.

Minutes felt like years as I waited with bated breath, silently willing the dragon not to move. Blood pooled around my feet, hot and cloying. One final exhalation of heated breath and the dragon fell impossibly still.

Dead.

I froze, numb and blank before slowly realising what I'd done.

Firm arms encircled me. I jumped with a yelp.

"Sshhh," Thorn soothed, one hand going to my matted hair. "It's me. You're safe."

Safe. I'd nearly died. But I'd survived. I shouldn't have but I did. I'd taken down a creature I'd believed to be a myth until a few weeks ago.

And survived.

A smile crept across my face. Hysterical giggles bubbled before I broke out into laughter, the sound echoing around the meadow. Thorn held me all the while as the adrenaline leeched itself from my body in the only way it could.

*

"Are you ready?"

I looked up at Thorn from where I stood beside the dragon's clawed foot. The body was quickly cooling and Thorn had acted fast. Another incision was made in the belly crosswise and the flaps of skin peeled back to reveal wide ribs encasing a multitude of organs. The space between each rib was wide enough that there was no need to pull them apart -

and thankfully so. The ribs of the dragon were stronger than iron, Thorn had grunted as he reached through, fumbling through the innards.

And now he held in his hands something round and smooth. At the recalled instructions from Viane, Thorn had carefully sliced through the dragon's heart, past veins and ventricles until he reached the centre where a low light pulsed from something no bigger than the palm of my hand. This. This was what Viane meant when she said I would have to consume the heart of the dragon. Not the literal, physical heart, but rather something *more*. Something *else*. It was the life force and soul of the dragon, the fire within and magic that gave it breath.

Thorn slipped the heart from his hands into my trembling ones. I gasped. For something that created such extreme heat, it was cool to the touch, pleasantly so.

"Is it…" I said, searching for the words. "Is it still…good?"

"Do you mean is it still viable and will it work?" Thorn clarified and when I nodded he continued. "Yes. Viane told me what to expect and so far as I can tell, this is exactly it."

I nodded mutely and brought the heart, the essence of the dragon to my lips. Hesitating, I drew a deep, steadying breath. For Emrys. This was all for Emrys.

The first wave of flavour across my tongue as my teeth drove into the smooth flesh was spicy. It tasted like chillies and I choked, thumping a hand against my chest as I forced myself to keep chewing. After a moment the taste melted into something sweeter, almost like cinnamon. It wasn't entirely unpleasant but with every single bite, the sweet taste of the spice grew. I felt my face grow hot and I began to sweat. And when I swallowed, heat permeated every part of my chest. My lungs felt like they were on fire and I fell to my knees. I couldn't cry, couldn't speak. The heart of the dragon had stolen the very breath from my lungs. I choked down the last few bites and felt the edges of my vision growing darker. Hands planted with splayed fingers, I fell forward on the grass and let it consume me, swallow me whole and drag me under.

I fell into a void. The flowering meadow, Thorn and gaping dragon carcass all melted away until there was nothing around me. A night so incredibly dark that I couldn't even see my hand before my face, swam all around, filling every part of my being. I called out into it but heard no sound. The darkness consumed everything and became all I knew.

I don't know how long I stayed down there, devoured by an endless, starless night. It could have been mere minutes or a decade. But that darkness began to shift. Hard to notice at first, I thought perhaps I was going mad. Was this it? Had I fallen into insanity when all I'd sought was to awaken the magic that lay dormant within?

The darkness shifted again and then a bolt of yellow suddenly appeared. Familiar dragon eyes no longer milky and clouded with blindness I'd inflicted. Pure onyx scales melted into the surrounding dark as it lowered its muzzle towards me where I lay. I couldn't move, no matter how much every instinct within begged, screamed, *pleaded* for me to. I braced for the sharp slicing of fangs but instead felt...something *much* different.

I felt peace, as alien to me as a winter without snow. The dragon nuzzled at my chest, right over my heart where the burning was greatest. It sniffed and blew out heavily through fist-sized nostrils, scenting within me what had once resided within it.

Dragon fire.

Dragon soul.

Dragon *spirit*.

The beast withdrew into darkness, closing its eyes until it became no more.

I could feel it then: a tremulous wave, slowly encroaching all around me. It seemed to pulsate as it swarmed ever closer, preparing to either strike me down for good or consume me, body and soul. I let it hit. Drawing out something hidden within, the wave uncovered a part of me buried so deep I might have never known it existed. I felt sparks, humble at first as they steadily grew from a pinprick within my soul. It was the faintest of faint lights that spoke directly into my mind.

Yes, life is here - yes, something more exists.

The full force of the wave hit me then, the heat of it so overpowering, it felt almost cold. A white-hot fire unlike any other. With that first caress of blinding pain across my skin, the sparks deep inside burst forth into an inferno. It moved fast, swifter than the wings of any dragon, and burned through everything I'd ever known. Every fear and insecurity, every nightmare and unfulfilled desire. It tore through, turned everything to ash. I watched as it then fell away from me like shackles. The sensation was one of release, freeing the old me, the woman I was. Someone who believed she was strong but was still all too vulnerable.

I shed it all, every last bit.

When the fire died down, the pitch black receded. Slowly, the meadow came back into view along with Thorn's face. Pride lit up his eyes and that all too familiar smirk stretched across his face. I felt my heart leap at the sight, wanting nothing more than to throw my arms around his neck and hold him close to me. He nodded towards the ground and I followed his gaze.

The once lush green grass was now charred, barren earth encircling me where I lay. I moved my fingers through it, ashes stirring and catching on the wind. There were no words and as I stood to my feet, I felt different. Exposed. Because along with the earth, every fibre of clothing had burned away, leaving me naked. Vulnerable was how I'd have once felt but instead I felt strong as I moved, testing out a body that felt unfamiliar.

My arm. I gasped, looking down at what had been broken only moments ago. No hint of an injury lingered, not one ounce of pain or discomfort. I rotated it gingerly, waiting for that familiar agony to return but instead felt only comforting heat. On closer inspection, I saw that the misshapen bones of my wrist from my time in Purgatory were no more. I bent my wrist back and forth, smiling as I realised I had full mobility again.

I continued searching my body excitedly, looking to where I knew ugly scars existed. In their place now was only clear, alabaster skin. I felt my face, for the long, puckered scar running down from my brow to cheek, and felt no trace of it.

Reborn.

The word flittered through my mind almost too quickly to catch but it was right. I felt new again, whole. For the first time in months, I felt like my old self but still so, so incredibly different. This girl would never have been captured by The Cleanse and subjected to months of torture. She would have been a victor, a champion, the furthest thing from a victim.

I turned to Thorn, speechless.

His eyes were full of unspoken words as he looked back at me and whispered, "You are majestic." Thorn outstretched his hand, in it a clean blade. "Look."

I took the blade from him, polished so perfectly that it reflected the sky above. I tilted it towards my face and saw that the creature staring back at me looked familiar enough but there was something else different, something I couldn't put a finger on. *Majestic*, Thorn had said. He was right. There was no other word for it. Glowing, swirling amber ringed the sea blue of my eyes, moving like molten fire even as I stood still. The was an otherworldly hypnotism and I felt myself steadily drawn in the longer I looked.

As I gazed at the stunning creature reflected in the blade, I felt something I hadn't felt in a very long time.

A sense of rightness.

That everything was *exactly* as it ought to be.

CHAPTER THIRTY-SIX

Sweat glistened across Thorn's back as he led me back through the forest of Galdua. In the absence of my clothes and with a firm, "No one gets to see such a delicious sight but me," Thorn had stripped and slipped his shirt over my head. I pulled the collar to my nose as I gingerly stepped around tree roots and sniffed. It smelled of Thorn's heady scent. I drank it in, letting it soothe the nerves that flitted about my gut like toxic butterflies, threatening to take over every part of me.

In the absence of all my fears, a new, even greater fear had birthed itself. I was an unknown quantity now, a wild card. There was little I knew about the magic contained within.

And just when I thought I was getting a handle on myself.

What could I do? What *would* I do? That scared me most of all.

As if sensing my unease, Thorn squeezed my hand once. With a backward glance as he held a branch for me to duck under, said, "I trust you."

Blind trust had never sat right with me.

The anxiety continued to gnaw at me over the next few hours and when we broke through the tree line and stepped onto the shore, doused in late afternoon light, I was shaking.

Not so long ago on the Isle of the Old Gods, I'd combusted, igniting a fire all around me. Hell, had I not done as much mere hours ago? It didn't take a genius to realise the idiocy of an uncontrollable, unpredictable open flame on a *wooden* ship. What if it happened again? What if I burned the damn thing to ashes?

"We can't." I yanked on Thorn's arm, jolting him to a stop.

"Unless you plan to swim back to Cimran, we have no other choice."

I looked at the *Scylla*, panicked. "I have no idea what I'm capable of, Thorn."

"Nor do I." He shrugged.

"Does that not concern you even a bit?" I snapped back. "What if I sink the ship? Kill everyone on board?"

"Good thing I'm an excellent swimmer and we've soldiers to spare."

"Be serious."

The wind ruffled the hem of my shirt, the linen tickling the tops of my thighs. I tugged it down, acutely aware of my lack of underwear.

"Where you are concerned, sparrow, I've never been more serious." Thorn tugged me close, tucking my head neatly under his chin as his arms banded around me in a crushing, though oddly comforting, embrace. "I don't know how many times I need to say it but hear me now: *I trust you*. I trust you with my life, with everything I have. Now I need you to trust me."

"How? You know as little about this as I do. I just consumed the heart of a dragon which, the more I think about it, sounds absolutely insane and hideously irresponsible. I might as well blow a hole through the *Scylla* to save us all some time."

"Viane is prepared for anything that might happen."

I pulled back to look up at Thorn. His eyes were full of nothing but a peace that I so desperately wished would turn infectious. "I'm beginning to hate that woman."

Thorn's laughter echoed across the beach. "She has that effect on people. Let's head back, sparrow."

The tender boat was tossed about the moment we passed the reef, the waves turning mercilessly. Overhead, storm clouds began to drift across Galdua, promising heavy rains. I was grateful that we were leaving. The humidity was already stifling without adding a torrential downpour.

I climbed the rope ladder alongside the *Scylla*. A warm breeze rushed past my rear, ballooning the borrowed shirt up around my waist. Thorn whistled teasingly and without looking back, I threw a vulgar gesture over my shoulder and continued to climb.

On deck, Viane stood patiently waiting. The moment her eyes fell on me, she pulled off the cloak she wore, madness amid the oppressive heat, and placed it over my shoulders. I was about to object but then caught the eye of an older sailor eagerly leering my way.

"I trust all is well?" Viane asked with a bright smile.

"Don't pretend you don't already know. And if by 'well' you mean 'volatile' and 'chaotic,' then yes," I replied. "*Well*, indeed."

The only confirmation I had that Thorn was now on deck was the firm touch he placed against my lower back. I ignored him, my mood having instantly turned sour at his teasing. When he slipped his fingers lower on my back, brushing against my backside, I elbowed him sharply. Thorn chuckled, the rumble of it reverberating through his splayed hand.

"Could you really expect me not to appreciate such a marvellous view, sparrow?" he whispered low into my ear.

I turned my head slightly in his direction. "I expect you to set an example for your men and not be such a womaniser."

His tongue darted out and dragged across the shell of my ear. "The only example I am prepared to set is one of matrimonial bliss. Very few have a wife so fine as you."

Viane cleared her throat. "There is a time for play and this is not it, nephew. For now, we must deal with the elephant on board. Your wife."

Denard appeared seemingly out of nowhere, coming to stand beside the diviner. Hands clasped behind his back, he fell into what might have been mistaken for an easy, calm stance. But I saw the slight rigidity of his shoulders, the firm press of his mouth when he thought I wasn't paying attention. My presence made him uneasy.

He wasn't the only one.

"We're to sail directly back to Cimran," Viane explained. "We've at least a fortnight's worth of travel ahead of us, weather permitting, and your powers have been fully awoken now, Artura. However, we've the added complication of you having not an ounce of training. My concern is that, with these things, high emotion could cause an *event*, shall we say. We've little idea of how high exactly that emotion must be to elicit a response from you. All we've witnessed so far was that it took Thorn being put in danger on the isle for your magic to manifest. However, now that your full abilities have been unleashed, something as simple as a tantrum could perhaps cause catastrophic damage. There would be no way to know until it is too late."

I barely stopped myself from pouting. "I do not throw tantrums. I'm no child."

There was nothing but deadly seriousness on Viane's face as she closed the few feet between us. "What you must understand, Artura, is that everything from here on in *will* be heightened. Sensitivity will be ten-fold to what it once was. The touch of a feather upon your skin will feel like the crushing blow of a fist. Sadness will be devastation. Happiness will make you delirious with joy." She threw a sideways glance at Thorn. "Intimacy will feel like utter ecstasy. Until you manage to control your emotions, you will be a danger to us all, make no mistake."

I stared back at her, dumbfounded. "But...you did this to me. You told me this was the only way."

"I know."

My chest tightened as I breathed in and out, each breath quicker than the last. "You said nothing of what this would be like. All you promised was that this would help me."

"And it will," she replied calmly.

I stepped back at the first prickles of sensation rolling down my spine. Something not too different from the feel of fingernails scraping across my skin. I shuddered at the subtle pain as it grew, flooding quickly past my spine and down my arms and legs. I scented smoke.

Thorn stepped between Viane and I, placing a hand on either side of my face. "Breathe, sparrow. Just breathe."

I couldn't breathe. My head swam, numbness tingled at my fingertips.

"In and out, sparrow. Focus on me. Look at me."

I forced my eyes upward, finding Thorn's face. Any trace of teasing was long gone now, replaced solely by concern. Smoke continued to fill my nostrils, reminding me of long, cold nights back in my cottage in Naiva. My home. The loss I felt only compounded the swirling emotions flooding my mind.

"Breathe," Thorn commanded. "Just breathe."

I drew in a shaking breath, mirroring Thorn, and held it for five seconds before releasing it. And again. And again. I kept forcing myself to breathe slowly until calm slowly leached back into my mind, the panic dying out.

"Good, sparrow," Thorn cooed, a thumb brushing across my cheek. "You're doing so well."

I shoved his hands away, noting that his palms were bright red and hot.

"Do not speak to me as though I am a child."

I heard something clunk against the deck. Craning my head around Thorn's shoulder, I saw a pail of water at Denard's feet. The captain looked up at me, brows pulled down and mouth now pressed so tightly, his lips had all but disappeared.

"Just in case," he murmured.

I couldn't fault him for being worried.

"If you're in control of yourself once more," Viane said, "then we've need to hurry. Before this happens again."

"What's the plan then?" I asked. The day was finally catching up with me and I struggled to stifle a jaw-cracking yawn. Had I really been airborne on dragon back only several hours ago? Already it seemed like a different life.

"You're going to sleep," the diviner replied. "I've prepared a brew that will put you into a deep slumber."

"For how long?" Thorn asked. I let him pull me against him protectively, knowing that he needed it more for his benefit. We were in unfamiliar territory, our world turned on its head just when it felt like things were becoming clearer, easier. "Will it harm her?"

The diviner motioned for us to follow her below deck. Instantly, the scent of lavender and jasmine hit me. I breathed it in, almost smiling as it brought memories of childhood and happiness to the forefront of my mind. We passed by the kitchens and mess hall before rounding a corner and moving through an open doorway. I hadn't stepped foot in Viane's quarters once on the crossing from the isle. She'd made it her own easily enough, the creature comforts of her home brought on board. Each one changed the space so drastically, that it felt as though we were back on the isle, seated around her fire pit. Thankfully, no such fire pit awaited us, but rather a simple stove, stolen from the kitchens. How she had moved it, I didn't know. Though with the way I caught Denard looking at her, I suspected she might have had help.

"Draught of the Dead," she said with a flourish of her hand.

"That doesn't at all sound ominous," I murmured.

I skirted the edge of her room. The name rang of forbidden magic that would have you burning upon a pyre before you even glimpsed a match. It didn't surprise me in the slightest that Viane knew of such things.

"No," Thorn said, that simple word unequivocal and final. "Not happening, Viane."

The diviner looked to her nephew and I saw a hint of sympathy in her delicate features. Her violet eyes softened. "We have no other choice. The surest way to avoid what nearly happened above, short of dragging Artura through the sea behind us, is to remove the liability."

I sighed. "Me."

"Yes," she nodded. "If you're asleep on this journey, the risk to the entire ship is instantly minimised."

"She has nightmares every single night," Thorn pointed out, tightening the arm around my shoulders. "High emotion is unavoidable even while unconscious. Who's to say she won't unknowingly turn the ship to ashes while we sleep?"

"Thanks for the vote of confidence," I muttered. But I had to agree with him. The nightmares of Purgatory that plagued me nightly were full of more fear than I could muster by daylight, were equal to that of ten thousand dragon back rides. Had I not violently lashed out in the past while in the grips of horrifying nightmares? Had I not already set myself ablaze, injuring Thorn in the process, just as he pointed out?

Viane loosed a heavy breath and folded her arms neatly. "I said the risk was minimised, not voided entirely."

Thorn looked down at me, his brows furrowed together. The light in his eyes dulled to a flat, dark green as the enormity of our situation weighed upon him. "I won't let anything happen to you," he swore. "I promised to protect you and I mean that, sparrow."

I stroked his cheek, my fingers lightly trailing across the prominent cheekbones. His eyes fluttered closed for a second and the tired creases lining his eyes smoothed. There was a vulnerability there, one I knew he never let his men see. But for me, his wife, he would show it all, everything he felt. There was nothing hidden between us anymore. And in that moment, I wanted to be the one to protect him more than anything else. Even if it cost me dearly.

"I know you will," I whispered. "I've not once doubted that. Not from the moment I met you on the altar. I've known all along that you would protect me to the very end. But this, it will be fine. *I* will be fine."

I prayed to any gods listening that Thorn wouldn't see the thinly veiled deception in my eyes, that he wouldn't recognise my promise for what it truly was: empty.

And then I prayed even more fervently that Viane would not say aloud what she now warned me of, speaking quietly into my mind.

That sometimes, the Draught of the Dead worked a little too well.

That sometimes…those who drank of it *never* woke up.

CHAPTER THIRTY-SEVEN

The darkness was cold. That was the least surprising aspect of the sleep I fell deep into. The Draught of the Dead was unlike anything I'd ever taken before, not that I'd taken much in the way of potions. Tonics and remedies provided by Emrys, naturally, but something more sinister? No.

It felt like a constricting rope, binding me so completely that I couldn't move an inch. There wasn't even the will to try. Rather, there was an all-encompassing passivity that I easily fell into. The draught provided both restful and restless sleep. There were moments when I felt my subconscious flicker, the magic I held within trying to break through and make itself known. But then the draught swallowed it like the beast it was and I sank further into listlessness, falling away from the world around me.

I don't know how long it was by the time I felt the weight of the draught easing. A fortnight of sailing between Cimran and Galdua, Viane had hoped, so perhaps no longer than that. I felt myself rising back to the surface of consciousness and was almost giddy with relief at the thought of seeing Thorn again. While time had been a non-existent concept thanks to the draught, it still felt like an age since I'd last taken in that stern face that melted into a smirk whenever he looked at me. The dazzling jade green eyes that turned molten when I stood bare before him and the silken obsidian strands of hair that fell around his face, framing it perfectly. I missed it all.

So when I awoke, it was with a smile.

Only to realise I was in the one place on earth that didn't deserve such a sweet emotion.

Shaking, I pushed myself backwards in an all too familiar cell, my bare back making contact with a stone-cold wall that still bore traces of my blood.

"No," I gasped, my voice barely audible as I scrunched my eyes shut. "This is still the draught, I'm having a nightmare."

Viane had prepared me for as much. Some experienced their worst fears while in the grips of the potion. I'd yet to experience the nightmares that wouldn't let me go but they'd finally arrived and in the most hideous form possible. This...it felt all too real. I shuddered, both a chill of fear and from arctic air lingering all around. I was completely naked, bared to the hell of Dearmond.

Footsteps echoed off the walls, growing steadily louder as someone passed cell after cell.

The other cells.

I scuttled forward on my hands and knees and peered around the corner.

Emrys' cell was empty, though evidence of its previous occupant remained in the form of a discarded crust of bread and a chamber pot full to overflowing. Beyond that, there was nothing of the man who raised me.

A nightmare. It's the draught, I told myself again, breathing deeply through my nose to calm my mind. Heat flickered in my chest. *That's all. Emrys isn't here. This isn't real. Breathe through it, Artura.*

The footsteps reached a deafening crescendo, each thump falling in time with the pounding of my heart. It was the boots I saw first. Finely polished black, bound with gleaming silver buckles. I knew those boots. I'd spent many days hunched over, being whipped and tortured, focused on the shoes of the man whom I swore one day I would seek vengeance upon.

He cleared his throat and when I gazed up, it was into the dead eyes of King Helmar.

He angled his head towards me, the look on his face one of utter victory. "Welcome back, witchling."

I shook my head, lowering it into my shaking hands. My eyes pressed closed, almost painfully as I tried to drown out the evil exuding from the King of Cimran, the man responsible for my existence.

"You're not here," I chanted. "I'm safe on the *Scylla*, I'm going to wake up with Thorn beside me. You're not here. You're not here."

Helmar barked a harsh laugh, the sound making me jump. "Oh, I assure you, I am very much *here*. As are you. I knew you'd be back eventually and not a moment too soon. I was just beginning to miss our time together."

"No." This time I looked up at the king, finding a surge of confidence. "This isn't real."

Helmar withdrew from his pocket a set of wrought iron keys that jangled and clanged deafeningly in the silence below Dearmond. "Shall I prove to you just how real this is?"

I stood to my feet, lifting my chin in a subtle show of defiance. "There's nothing you can do to me. *This isn't real.*"

He unlocked the door to my cell and swung it wide. In one long stride, Helmar entered, coming to stand before me. By no account was I short but the king moved swiftly enough that in a heartbeat he towered over me. A flicker of panic ran through my mind. I hoped it was too quick for him to notice but by the delighted light in his cold, uncaring eyes, I knew he'd seen it.

I felt the blow before I realised it had been delivered. Somewhere below my navel, sharp and winding me instantly. I doubled over, amazed by how real the pain was. I would wring Viane's thin neck for this, for giving me the Draught of the Dead and subjecting me to reliving this horror.

Viane, if you can hear me, you fucking bitch.

Another blow, this one to the side of my face. I fell, my knees making contact with the stone floor with a sickening crack. Pain lanced through my legs. And then a knee drove into the other side of my head and the cell began to spin. Nausea flooded my gut and bile rose in my throat.

Something cold touched my back. Fingers. Helmar tisked as he stroked across the exposed flesh.

"All my hard work erased. How did you do it, witch? A spell? A potion?" Helmar fisted his hand in my hair, half of it falling out of the braid I'd neatly wound it into before taking the draught. "This won't do. I'll have to redouble my efforts this time. Make sure you bear my marks for the rest of your life."

I couldn't catch my breath, couldn't hold the injured parts of me tight enough. My hands went to the one pulling at my hair and I held on, trying to counter the weight that threatened to pluck each and every hair from my scalp. Helmar dragged me along behind him, passing cells that were emptier than before.

Someone at least had cleared the skeleton from three doors down. That was new. Perhaps The Cleanse were readying the space for more victims. I couldn't muster the spare energy to feel sorry for them.

You don't have to, I chided myself. *This is not real. We're going to wake up, safe on the Scylla. Everything will be as it was.*

I knew where we were headed despite not being able to see a thing. Tears filled my eyes, brought on by the sharp pain lancing through my head.

Purgatory.

Helmar threw me into the room as if I were little more than a sack of grain, despite regaining the weight I'd lost during my previous venture beneath Dearmond. My naked body slid across the stone, rolling past the table with rusted chains and manacles still attached. I sucked in a deep breath.

Bad decision.

The overwhelming stench of The Tub filled my nostrils and I gagged.

"Remember, witch," Helmar warned. "Surely you haven't forgotten what happens if you're sick on my floors."

I remembered. How could I ever forget? The memory of scooping my vomit with shaking hands and dumping it into a tub that my head would be forced into until I could no longer breathe was indelible. As long as I lived, it would stay with me, a mark upon my psyche that could be triggered by little more than the barest of thoughts.

The door to Purgatory slammed shut and I heard the distinctive clicking of the padlock. When I looked up I saw the king tucking away the key - a lone key only he held - into the collar of his tunic. Helmar wore pale grey today, the colour similar to clouds that contemplated a storm but weren't yet ready to commit. It was always worse when he wore a lighter colour. All the better to see my blood splatted across him, a trophy he could hold onto for gods knew how long.

I didn't dare say out loud what I now silently chanted.

A nightmare. It's the draught. I'm safe.

Because even here, in the squeezing grip of my subconscious, it was all too possible for me to break. In my time back in Naiva, I'd witnessed just how easily one could fall apart at the memory of past trauma. Stronger men than I had been broken down to little more than a snivelling mess as they were held captive by the past. I refused to let that happen. Helmar couldn't win, not when I'd resisted him for so long before.

Not even in a nightmare would I give him that victory.

The king busied himself at his table of tools, everyday items that if used in a specific way, could torture in ways many could never dream of. He set several items aside, one of which I noted to be the flogger he'd used on me before. At some point, it had been adapted to his specific tastes, tweaked with sharpened scraps of metal that dug into your flesh with every lash. I shuddered and clenched my fists, digging my nails into the palms of my hands.

This was a nightmare, of that I was certain. But it felt so real. *How* could it feel so real?

"You know what to do," he called over his shoulder, his calm voice betraying a hint of underlying excitement. "Table. Now."

I didn't move. I was safe. I had to believe that. Nothing he could do to me here would truly hurt me.

"Did you not hear what I said?" Helmar turned, holding a simple, thin blade the length of his forearm.

"I heard you," I ground out. "That doesn't mean I'll make it easy for you."

He smiled and I forced myself not to recoil. "Good. After all, this wouldn't be nearly as fun if you were compliant. I've always enjoyed a fight from you, witch. Tell me, did you fight that husband of yours? Was your untried king as cruel as I prayed he would be?"

My head snapped up at the mention of Thorn, at the implication he was something far from what he was. Someone like Helmar. Instead of taking the bait, I replied, "The gods do not listen to the prayers of demons."

Helmar closed the distance between us. He knelt before me and used the tip of the blade to keep my face bent up towards his. He lowered his face, stopping an inch away from my own, and when he spoke I scented the familiar foul breath, tinged with ale.

"Who says I pray to the blameless, untainted gods my people pray to? Perhaps I beseech the help of the depraved and wicked."

Gritting my teeth together as I felt the tip of the blade prick my skin, I ground out, "Fitting considering how you are exactly so."

Helmar snickered. "Compliments won't save you here, witch."

With a swift flick of his wrist, Helmar drew the blade across my neck shallowly. It stung and I winced. Determined though I was not to show him fear, I felt it quaking through me already.

Words I'd clung to from months ago echoed through my mind.

Do not break.

Even here, in the grips of a horrid dream, I needed to heed that.

Helmar inhaled deeply, his eyes drifting closed. "Your blood is a homecoming, witch. I will delight in spilling yours the most."

At blade point, Helmar directed me to the table. I climbed atop it, a faint sense of bravado spurring me on. A nightmare. Nothing more. He couldn't hurt me.

Physically, anyway.

Helmar fastened the manacles around my wrists and ankles, the weight of them sickeningly familiar. For good measure, he yanked on each attached chain, forcing my wrists and ankles to bend at an unnatural angle. I was glad that my wrist had been made whole again by the dragon heart otherwise it might have snapped all too easily.

The king walked alongside the table, dragging the tip of the blade along my body. I felt my skin slice open as he went, the wound as shallow as the one on my neck. The light sting I could handle. As awful as it was, I'd grown used to this meagre torture, the entree before he moved onto the main meal - breaking me.

"It's been far too long, witch. No one else copes quite as well as you do. It makes pulling you apart all the more sweeter, watching you crumble before me."

I inhaled deeply through my nose, stilling my mind, but couldn't stop the sarcastic remark that slipped from my mouth.

"Do you talk purely for your benefit? Do you truly enjoy the sound of your voice that much? Get on with it - *silently* - and let's be done." Another deep breath and a heavy, slow exhale. "None of this is real. None of it. I'll wake and you'll be far away."

Not entirely true, I reminded myself. Not when we were sailing for Cimran right as I slept. But dream Helmar didn't need to know that. Even in this form, I wasn't prepared to give him more than he deserved. And all he deserved was a sharp tongue followed by arctic silence.

"How can I convince you, Artura, that this is *very* real?" I flinched at the way he said my name, making it sound like a threat. "I could carve into that pretty skin once more. Although, if you believe none of this to be real, then perhaps something new, something different. Something...*special*. Maybe that would suffice to convince you."

I refused to look at him as I waited, spread-eagled on the table.

That was a mistake.

Helmar seized my left hand, pulling it towards him as far as the chain would allow. He turned it this way and that, examining it as one would a ware in a market. I watched with a sickened feeling twisting my gut as he bent forward and inhaled.

"I see your king gifts you only the finest. Lavender. How sweet. Does he dote on you, witch? Is that it?" Another inhale. I tried to jerk my hand away but his grip only tightened. "Tell me, did you hear his screams as your ship sank?"

I froze.

Helmar sneered. "It was quite a spectacular sight, my men tell me, to see such grand craftsmanship ablaze. It was pure happenstance that a detachment of The Cleanse was travelling along the northern coast. You see, I've had quite some trouble with your kind trying to escape Cimran. It's become necessary in recent weeks to take my crusade to the seas. What a delight it was to stumble across a Nimuean ship, especially one slowly collapsing in on itself. Admittedly, Captain Brone was disappointed. He'd have taken great enjoyment in torching your sails. He tells me that soldiers and sailors were jumping into the sea to save themselves. Some were, of course, beyond saving, their flesh already peeling from their bones. I regret I did not see that for myself. But then Azazel saw you and recognised you instantly. That husband of yours held you as he jumped overboard in a bid to save you both. But while he was perhaps strong enough to save you, he wasn't strong enough to save himself."

A dream, I chanted, *it's all a dream. I'm safe.*

My chest rose and fell too quickly, each breath coming faster than the last.

"I'm glad your husband gave his life to save you. Not out of any paternal gratitude - you and I both know I possess none of that where you are concerned. No. Saving you, that was quite the gift to me. And to think, originally I had planned to kill you on your wedding night. I would have robbed myself of this luxury."

"He's not dead," I choked out. "Thorn's still alive. You're not real. None of this is."

Around my wrists and ankles, I felt the shackles heat as my panic ratcheted up a notch. The metal, heated by the fire within me, seared into my flesh. I knew it would leave no marks behind. Not when it was part of me.

Helmar barked a harsh laugh, squeezing my arm so tight I thought he might break it through brute strength alone.

"Still carrying on with that ridiculous notion? No matter. I will break you of it."

Once again bent towards my hand. Only this time, he didn't sniff the lavender that perfumed my skin. With a bolt of horror, I watched as Helmar quickly opened his mouth, drew in my pinky -

And bit down.

*

Rocking back and forth, back and forth, all the while clutching a filthy, stained rag around my left hand. A hand that now only bore four fingers.

It was real. All of it. I knew that now. There was no denying what Helmar had made so plainly obvious.

The nightmare was real.

Thorn was dead.

And I was alone.

CHAPTER THIRTY-EIGHT

My second time beneath Dearmond, I was a little more aware of time slipping by. But the only way I could have described it was with one simple word: eternal.

The days and nights were unending and alone I sat in my cell, mourning over what I'd lost.

This *was* real. All of it. I indeed had returned to hell, dragged back and forth from Purgatory each day by King Helmar. Each day he grew steadily more and more furious as I refused to show any emotion. After that first day back in Purgatory where he bit off my left pinky finger, now riddled with an infection I could feel leaching through my hand and arm, I'd shut down completely.

I needed to survive. Long enough to find out what happened to Emrys.

Helmar tortured me both physically and psychologically. The physical was never as bad as the psychological. He refused to tell me where Emrys was, what had happened to the only father I'd ever known. That was my one lifeline here, the hope that Emrys' absence meant he had somehow gotten free, and so I endured. However, the not knowing hurt the most.

Or so I thought.

Because when the king was done teasing me with the mystery of Emrys' disappearance, he would begin on Thorn, weaving one lie after another until they all blurred together and became indiscernible. How he looked as he drowned, how he screamed. How the moment he was aware he would die, he'd sacrificed me in an attempt to save his own skin. That was the least believable of all he said. But then…

I was here. *Thorn* was not.

I was pulled from the water. *Thorn* had drowned.

No. The fact that he didn't survive and I did? Thorn had protected me till his very last breath, just as he always swore he would do. I never doubted that promise, never thought him incapable of keeping it. Now was no different.

Dead, though? That I did believe. Because the alternative was too painful to bear.

That he was still alive and had as of yet not come for me.

*

Days were crudely marked on the stone walls of my cell, one strike after another indicating that a full month had passed from the day I awoke and lost a finger. Whether or not those days were correct to the hour was irrelevant, the only real way to track time being the one meal I received each day. The bottom line was that I was definitely alone now. No one was coming to save me.

Vengeance was the only thing fuelling my will to live now. That and the hope that Emrys was still alive. Many nights I'd dreamed of releasing every last ounce of tenuous control I held over my newly awoken magic. Dreams of bursting into flames, igniting and setting Lanceris ablaze just as I had reportedly done to the *Scylla*. Images of the charred husk of Helmar soothed me, grounded me enough with the promise that one day, one day it would come to pass. It was enough that I was able to pull back within myself, bypassing the fury and grief until I found a numbness that enveloped me and buried me far beneath the ability to feel a single potent emotion.

Without feeling, Helmar was still none the wiser that I was exactly what he claimed me to be. He couldn't know. The moment he had his proof, I was as good as dead. Here, with ambiguity hanging over my head, I was worth more alive, kept as a plaything.

I never thought I'd be grateful to be tortured and yet here I was.

In the past weeks, I'd grown familiar enough with Helmar's footsteps that I could pick his out from those of The Cleanse who kept guard of the cells. Far too many men for one woman. At all times there were at least three of them below - one stationed at either end of the hallway and one in the middle, able to keep a direct eye on me where I sat huddled and freezing in the corner. After the first week, one of the men threw a sack-like shift through the cell bars, the intention clear for me to cover up. With naught but a backward glance, he'd moved to the side of another soldier, muttering how he couldn't stand to look at me.

There was little chance I would ever blame him.

Cuts and bruises covered my body in a patchwork that boasted the cruelty of the king. Dried blood, cracked from each movement I made, covered my left arm. Turning my head was difficult with the thin cut on my neck. It had reopened more than once until I learned to just stay still and chew slowly on the meagre portions delivered once a day.

Bread, water and, if I was 'lucky' a piece of mouldy meat. I did my best to scrape off the fuzzy layer of green and white but it was never enough. I brought up my dinner more than once. Perhaps food poisoning was merely another form of the king's torture.

The bars creaked open and Helmar entered.

"Shall we have some fun today?"

I didn't look up. My knees were tucked up tightly against my chest, my arms folded atop them with my wounded hand neatly hidden against my chest. Silence was safety. Silence was key to my survival.

He didn't like it. But I learned he also didn't hate it. For all Helmar's talk of how it was fun to torture me while I fought back, he just as much enjoyed working uninterrupted. Screams were no longer loosed from my lungs and tears fell silently. I was precariously close to having nothing left to live for with no news still of Emrys. Any moment now I would become a ghost, haunting Dearmond for all eternity.

"I've something special planned for us."

Us. As though this was a group activity, a game children played together willingly.

Helmar reached for my hair, his new favourite way of dragging me from my cell. Patches had begun to fall out in clumps from the strain. I didn't have the energy to mourn the beauty I had long ago. Beauty that was brought back to me for half a day before I entered that fateful sleep and wound up back here.

A place devoid of any semblance of beauty.

I pushed myself to my feet before he could take hold. With a small shrug as if to say 'Suit yourself,' Helmar turned and I followed. At this point, I could find my way to Purgatory blindfolded. I walked slowly, almost in a zombie-like state.

Do not break.

I tripped, caught off guard by the words that ran through my mind. So clear that they might have been spoken by someone right beside me. My hands scraped against the stone floor as I clumsily caught myself before my face could break my fall. I glanced around wildly, searching for the speaker, yet the only one nearby was the king, looking at me with a quizzical look on his face.

"This will be a long day if you're already giving up, witch."

I swallowed a 'sorry' and stood, ignoring the droplets of blood blooming on the tender skin of my palms and knees. There would be more blood before the day was out. So much had been spilled so far that I was constantly light-headed, struggling to focus on the most basic of tasks, like toileting or holding a cup of water steady.

The Tub loomed in the corner of Purgatory. Small mercies and all that, but not once since my return had Helmar forced me into it. I wasn't about to look a gift horse in the mouth, no matter what else he might do.

"Quite a special day, if I do say so myself," Helmar said conversationally. When I stayed silent he again spoke. "Ask me why."

I sighed. "Why?"

He inclined his head to the table and like an obedient dog, I went to it, taking off my shift before laying down. I hated what I'd become, even though I knew that it was necessary for the moment.

Thorn. Emrys. Survival. Revenge.

Four words. The simplest plan there ever was. Enacting it? Not so simple. At least not yet.

"A convoy from the southern kingdoms has come to Lanceris, seeking an alliance," he said. Helmar picked up a thick chain, snaking it around his hand and forming a fist. "It would seem that Cimran is not the only kingdom that desires war on your kind. Princess Xayla of House Mortae has come with quite the proposal. It's put me in a rather good mood."

"Then go celebrate and let me rest," I muttered, unable to stop myself. Parts of me still snuck through the numbness, determined not to go quietly.

Helmar chuckled to himself before drawing back his chain letting it fly to whip against my thigh. I forced myself not to cry out, biting down on my tongue until I tasted copper.

"Why celebrate with those above when what I really want is right here?"

Another blow. And another. The chain had become a favourite in the past week, used almost daily. Bruises in the shape of thick links patterned my body. If I squinted, they almost looked like scales. But then I'd inevitably think of the dragon, of Thorn's proud gaze as I took the beast down on my own and consumed its heart.

Do not break.

Again, that voice. I recognised it this time and hissed.

Viane. Of course, it would be her voice I would hear while fighting the ever encroaching madness. What better way to ensure insanity than to hear the diviner's voice in my head, louder than my own?

Do. Not. Break, the voice insisted, growing louder with each word.

Fuck you, I mentally replied.

A chuckle ran through my mind.

I gasped.

Stay there, Artura.

Viane! All traces of anger eddied as I realised what this was. The diviner was in my head, which meant she had to be nearby.

Where are you? Where's Thorn? Is he-?

I groaned around the sixth blow, this one directly into my gut. With my body bound to the table, there was nowhere for me to go and the impact of Helmar's fist was tenfold. Tears leaked from the corners of my eyes.

You must listen to me, Artura, Viane said. *We are coming to get you but you must hold on a little longer.*

We? Who's 'we?' Thorn's dead.

Silence.

Viane? I prompted. *He's dead, isn't he?*

The thought of Thorn's death, one I'd ignored for weeks, threatened to undo me. I tucked it neatly away and focused on my breathing. In and out, in and out, ignoring the sharp stab that followed each breath. I'd suspected a broken rib yesterday and now felt it acutely. Definitely broken. At least it wasn't my wrist again.

He's alive.

I froze.

Artura, Viane said, the hint of a question in her voice as though she were unsure I was still listening. *Thorn's alive. He survived.*

A sob wracked through me, shaking my entire body. Helmar smiled.

"Finally," he crooned. "I always get you in the end."

I ignored him. Thorn was alive. *Alive.* I didn't kill him.

Where is he? Tell me, Viane, is he safe?

He's coming for you. Just be patient a little longer.

How much longer?

Helmar discarded the chain on his table of tools, picking through them until he found the thin blade I'd come to hate most. To my surprise, he unchained me, letting the manacles drop and clang against the table legs. I sat up slowly, every nerve in my body going on full alert.

"Do you know what I love most, witch?" Helmar asked.

He held the handle of the blade in one hand, the tip poking the pad of the forefinger of his other hand. He turned the blade back and forth until a droplet of blood oozed out and slipped down his finger. The king lifted his hand to my face and with the bloodied finger, drew a line down each cheek from just below my eye socket to my jaw. Blood tears staining my face.

"Ask me what I love most, witch."

"What do you love most?" I mumbled, feeling weak as I warily stared at his finger. The king had shed plenty of my blood in the past but never his own, not even such a minuscule amount. It was off-putting, to say the least, and I eyed that finger as though it might have been the most dangerous weapon in Purgatory.

"Symmetry. There's something exquisitely beautiful about two halves of a whole in perfect alignment, indiscernible from the other." He reached for my four-fingered hand, still wrapped in its pitiful bandage. Helmar pulled the crusted fabric away with what I presumed he thought to be tenderness but looked more akin to pleasure. When my hand was finally exposed, he pulled it to his lips and placed a kiss against the palm. I jerked back, hating how he tainted my skin in a way this room never could. "Take your hand for example. It's no longer in perfect symmetry with your other. How would we rectify that, witch?"

Cold dread washed over me. No. He couldn't...

"You turn back time and give me back my finger," I breathed, stalling.

"Hmm." He bounced his head back and forth as he thought my proposal over. I knew he was mocking me. There was no way to return what had been taken. It was all for show, to appear as the benevolent king The Cleanse claimed him to be.

"You don't have to do this," I whispered. I was dangerously close to breaking. My mantra was now the furthest thing from my mind. To survive, I would grovel if necessary, beg at his feet. Whatever it took.

Helmar sat down the blade on the table and placed a thumb against the stub that was all that remained of my finger. And then, with a cruel grin, he pressed - hard. I cried out, unable to deny the pain. But still, he pressed again, and again. The wound opened and blood and foul-smelling pus oozed out around his thumb. I kept crying all the while, tears falling in earnest now.

"Shut up," he barked. "Remember what happens when you cry."

I couldn't stop it. Of all that I'd endured in Purgatory, this felt the worst. Because I knew help was close by, so close I could almost taste it. But it wasn't here *yet*. I was still trapped in this hell and unable to free myself.

Helmar growled and released my hand, only to place both his hands around my throat. His fingers were strong as they clamped down on my airway, choking me with more force than I'd thought possible. By no means was the king a weak man, no matter how much he relied heavily on his torture implements. But his hands, they were vice-like, growing steadily tighter by the second. I couldn't breathe.

Panic drenched me in a cold sweat. Images of my life flashed through my mind in quick succession.

Emrys. Soraya. Apothecary. Burnings. Pain. Humiliation. Thorn. Love. Pleasure. Desire. *Salvation*.

I scented smoke.

Helmar swore but refused to let go and doubled down. I heard his knuckles crack with the force exerted. My head grew light. I couldn't suck in that sweet, much-needed oxygen. I was suffocating. Not long now and I would pass out. Die. Leave Thorn behind. Leave Emrys with no chance of salvation, wherever he was.

Sizzling filled the air.

Helmar shouted and threw himself back, instantly releasing me. I choked down lung-fulls of stale, putrid-smelling air. My chest ached and I couldn't tell where the bruising pain of each blow or the agony of oxygen-deprived lungs began.

Helmar didn't stop shouting.

When my head finally stopped spinning enough for me to focus, I looked towards what had now twisted into screams.

The king sat slumped against the wall. His face was chalk white and his eyes wild as tears brimmed. Beneath those tears was an anger like I'd never seen. It threatened to strike me down where I sat.

But it wasn't his face that caught my attention. No, it was his hands, palms up in his lap. They were blistered, raw in parts where the skin had melted away. Undeniably burned. All the emotion I'd kept a tight hold on over the past month had come undone in one moment, the magic within fighting back when my body could fight no more.

"*You*," he gritted out, breathless. "You *are* a witch."

I shook my head even though I knew there was no use denying it. I was as good as dead now that he had his proof. The final puzzle piece completed a hideous picture in the king's eyes.

He had everything he needed to finally destroy me.

Well, if I was going to go down, I might as well go down fighting.

I snatched up the blade Helmar had foolishly left on the table and threw myself across the room. He didn't have time to react, couldn't even hold me off if he wanted to with his hands being so destroyed. I drew the dagger back and with one swift movement, sank it into his shoulder, missing his heart entirely. The king howled as I withdrew the blade and plunged it in again - and again missed his heart. Rage clouded every thought, made it impossible to think and in a last-ditch attempt at a fatal wound, I lashed out.

The blade sliced across his forehead, down to his eye and plunged through the pupil.

There was no sound from Helmar now. All that could be heard was my rapid breathing in the quiet of the room. Nausea hit like a wave crashing in a storm and I doubled over, vomiting on the stone floor beside the king. I scrambled backwards, my hand finding my shift, and clutched it to my chest, eyes still firmly on the motionless form of the king.

I killed him.

The realisation swept over me, bringing with it a mixture of relief and horror.

I was *definitely* dead now.

I glanced around the room, my gaze pausing on the door.

A lone word slipped through my mind.

Run.

CHAPTER THIRTY-NINE

I didn't stop running.

In one hand I clutched the blade and in the other, the key to Purgatory. In seconds I'd dressed, ripped the key on its leather thong from Helmar's neck, pulled the dagger from his eye and fled. I couldn't escape by going up through the castle. If it was as the king said and there was a delegation from the southern kingdoms, then the castle would be swarming with people. I wouldn't go undetected for nearly long enough and I wasn't stealthy enough to chance it.

So I took off for the tunnels beneath Dearmond, not caring to avoid the jagged rock walls. It was darker than moonless midnight. Cuts opened up on my hands as I felt my way through, determined to find the path I'd found long ago, the one that I was certain guaranteed freedom.

Distantly, I heard the sounds of dozens of hurried footsteps followed by a gruff shout.

"The king! Send for help!"

The Cleanse, no doubt, had discovered my handiwork.

I didn't dare stop as I continued to frantically search.

Corner after corner. Doubling back and rechecking paths I was unsure I'd ventured down already. It was a maze and far worse than I remembered. Pure adrenaline was all that spurred me onward as I tried my best to ignore the sharp stinging of a broken rib in my side.

I gasped when I saw it up ahead. Light. Freedom. I didn't stop, not with the sounds echoing through the tunnels behind me, promising a swift death to whoever murdered the king. This was my last chance and I wouldn't squander it.

So when I rounded the corner and found myself face to face not with the sun, but rather glowing torchlight, I couldn't stop in time. I crashed into the solid form of a man dressed in white and fell back on my rear.

Azazel Brone, Captain of The Cleanse, glared down at me. Before I could move back half an inch, his calloused hand reached down and took hold of the front of my shift, pulling me to my feet.

"I knew it was you," he growled. "Trouble from the moment I saw you."

Footsteps echoed. His men knew these tunnels better than anyone, barring the king. It would be minutes if that before I was surrounded and carted off to a death that would be far from merciful.

"Do not for a second think that just because we know now of your lineage we won't give you a death befitting that of a murderer," he said, his voice gravelly in the dim. "Too bad, witchling. Had things been different, they might have called you King Slayer, given you a parade and a banquet. Instead, we're going to make your last days a living hell."

Fight back.

Viane's voice whispered all around.

Now, Artura.

I swung up a hand and slapped Azazel straight across the face. It barely turned his head and for a moment, he laughed.

"A cub cannot stand against a lion," he sneered.

"No," said a voice behind me. "But a dragon can."

I whipped my head around.

Thorn stood several feet away, sword held in one hand, dagger in the other. He was covered in blood, his clothes sun-bleached and torn in places but he was *here*. He was alive and whole and still...*mine*. The thought settled within me, feeling so right and pure and good. It was the relief and rebirth of a promise all in one. I felt my chest swell with love and pain and determination.

So I let go.

One moment the tunnel was lit only by the light of Azazel's torch. The next, I was a beacon, blinding and chasing away every inch of darkness. Azazel didn't have time to scream, to even whimper. One moment he was there, holding onto me. The next, he was charred at my feet, one hand still frozen in the fist that had grabbed my shift. Coating his body was molten metal, the armour he wore beneath his white cloak melted by the flames that whipped around me. The blade I'd held and the key to Purgatory were now indistinguishable from one another, both forming a neat molten puddle at my feet.

I spun on the spot, searching for Thorn.

I couldn't see him. My chest rose and fell as I peered in the darkness, returned now that I no longer blazed brightly. No movement. He'd been too close. He was burned. One scenario after another ran through my mind.

"Thorn!" I screamed.

Silence. All I heard was my panicked breathing.

Again, I screamed his name. And then-

"I'm here, sparrow."

I saw a subtle shift in the darkness before Thorn rounded the corner, patting out embers clinging to his sleeve as they threatened to turn into flame. I rushed towards him, stepping over Azazel without a second glance, and threw my arms around his neck.

"Sparrow," he murmured. "At least let me put myself out first."

I laughed, the sound more of a strangled sob as I pulled back. Thorn beat out the flame on his sleeve, extinguishing it with little trouble at all.

"This is the third time you've burned me, sparrow." But he yanked me against him, my chest crashing into his. One hand went to the back of my neck, still tender even in his eagerness, as he tucked me against him. For the first time in weeks, I felt safe.

But not safe enough.

"We need to go," I said as I pulled away, catching one of his hands in my own. I didn't realise that it was my left hand and in the dark, Thorn's fingers gently drifted across the absence of a pinky finger.

"I'm going to kill him," Thorn bit out with lethal fury.

"No!" I grabbed onto him with both hands, rooting him to the spot. "It's done, Thorn. He's dead. Stay with me."

"You're sure he's dead?"

I nodded. "I killed him myself."

Thorn sighed and then I felt his lips pressing against my sweaty brow. Not so much a kiss as it was desperately needed contact. He murmured against my skin, "That's my girl."

Thorn tugged off his singed shirt and pulled it over my head. Despite the sheer number of holes and tears in it, I wasn't about to argue. It was another way I could be close to Thorn, to relish in the knowledge that he really *was* here, alive and safe and in my arms.

"How will we get out? How did you get in here?"

"I had help," Thorn explained. "Come, he's back here."

I let Thorn lead me back the way I'd initially come, only this time we turned down a passage I could have sworn I'd already checked before deeming it a dead end. We moved through, turning so many corners that I began to fear I'd never find my way out if we got separated. I tightened my grip on Thorn's hand and he matched it.

I glimpsed something in the darkness. Light.

I pulled on Thorn's arm. "There's someone up there."

"I hope so."

I couldn't see it in the darkness but somehow I knew he was wearing that smirk I'd come to love most.

When we rounded the corner, all my fears eased.

Denard stood alone and what I'd thought to be torchlight was sunlight. My knees wobbled as I sagged in relief. Thorn didn't pause as he bent down and scooped me up against his chest, silently following Denard out of one of the precious few tunnels to freedom.

*

Two chestnut horses awaited and we rode till nightfall, Denard on one, Thorn and I on the other. None of us spoke until Dearmond was little more than a hill on the horizon, a safe enough distance put between us and Lanceris. Still, we were careful, setting up camp in a copse of trees and securing the horses out of sight. Denard produced a pack with bread and fruit, a simple meal compared to what was provided on the *Scylla* but a veritable feast in light of all I'd been given to eat in the cells. As I ate, I moaned in delight, relishing the sweetness.

"What happened?" I asked, turning towards Thorn.

Denard had retired a while ago and now Thorn and I huddled on a blanket spread over the grass. I let him hold me, knowing that he needed it as much as I did. There was something about being wrapped up in Thorn that soothed me, despite the emotions bubbling within. He was a much-needed anchor, keeping me grounded in my new, very welcome, reality.

"What we thought would happen," he murmured. "You went just over a week and we were rounding the north coast of Cimran when you changed. It was a dream, I think. Something. There was a small spark at first, at your fingertips. Viane was with you at the time. I'd not taken a break all week so I stole a few hours of sleep and a meal when I thought it was safe. But the ship caught fire. That one spark was all it took. All the draught did was buy us time before you inevitably combusted. The men fought to extinguish the flames but it was no use. A wooden ship does not so easily survive something like that - the *Scylla* was no different. I got you out, jumped into the sea." His chest shuddered on a deep exhale. "Next thing, I woke on the shores of Cimran. I had no clue where I was and as I looked around at the few who'd made it to safety, I realised you were gone."

"And then you came for me."

He snorted a laugh. "It wasn't that simple. We were without supplies. Aside from Viane, Denard and myself, two other sailors survived. They both deserted us the moment they could. I cannot fault them but Denard is livid."

"And I will be for some time," the captain groggily mumbled from where he lay.

I stifled a giggle into Thorn's chest.

"It took nearly two full weeks of walking before we reached a village. Viane was able to barter the gold ring she wore for two horses and supplies. But by the time we finally reached you, a full month had passed. We were slow going after nearly drowning. I worried you were dead, no matter what Viane said. I couldn't shake the feeling that she was feeding me what I wanted to hear to serve some greater purpose. A diviner is a dangerous thing."

"You don't say," I dryly replied.

"It wouldn't have been the first time Viane led me astray 'for the greater good.' But I knew that even if you were… gone…I would rip Helmar limb from limb. I wouldn't stop until he was destroyed."

I stroked a hand up and down Thorn's chest. Denard had given him a spare shirt the moment we reached the horses and I had to wonder at just how expensive Viane's ring had been to buy enough supplies to support three people. People in Cimran had little need for gold - not when grain, medicine and linen were worth far more in these times. Whoever they traded with wasn't Cimranean, I was willing to bet.

Silently, I toyed with Thorn's hand in mine. His other hand held my newly bandaged left hand. It had been a tense half-hour as Denard sewed closed what skin he could, disinfected with a little of the alcohol they had with them - a necessity, he'd explained. I couldn't bring myself to be shocked at how prepared the captain was. I'd come to learn that he was just that sort of man, the kind who planned for the worst but hoped for the best - sometimes, anyway.

"I heard her," I said. "Viane."

"I know."

"How could she communicate from so far away?"

He bent his head to mine, kissing my temple softly before speaking. "Why are you assuming she wasn't nearby?"

I sat up, leaning on my elbow, and looked down at my husband. "Where exactly was she?"

The corner of Thorn's mouth twitched upward. "Ever heard of Princess Xayla?"

I gasped. "You've got to be joking."

Thorn reached out a hand, his fingers playing with the neckline of his old shirt I still wore. His fingertips brushed across my collarbone and it was a battle not to melt under his touch. The heat in his eyes told me he knew exactly how I felt. The way I craved him was acute, punishing. My body had gone far too long without his.

"We needed a distraction," he explained, clearing his throat. The spell dissipated and I could focus once more. "So I could sneak into Dearmond and get you out. It was Viane's idea to impersonate a southern royal who wanted to share in Helmar's vision. It was sickening to hear her plan and how she would swear up and down to want to destroy the very thing she is. But it worked. Helmar welcomed her with open arms."

"Where is she now?"

Thorn's face turned grave. "Still in Lanceris."

I tried to push myself up more but winced at the pain in my ribs. "We have to go back for her."

Thorn shrugged. "We can't."

I swatted my right hand at his chest. "We can and we will."

"Sparrow, we won't. I'll not risk you again." His eyes softened and for a second I glimpsed overwhelming pain. His voice turned hoarse. "Never again."

"If she's discovered, she'll be executed," I pushed. "You know she will."

"My aunt is a grown woman. She can handle herself. Besides, I didn't think you cared for her all that much."

Laying back down, I rolled my eyes. "Not exactly. I just know how awful that place is."

Through a gap in the trees above, I watched the stars shine brightly, feeling that same sense of relief from months ago when I'd seen the night sky after months in the cells. Even that small sliver of sky was full of so much wonder and magnificence that I felt the hot prick of tears behind my eyes.

"Emrys is dead," I whispered. Thorn said nothing, just continued stroking my arm. "He wasn't there. I couldn't find him. I think Helmar held out on telling me for so long because not knowing hurt more than knowing. But he's gone. Of that, I'm certain now."

A silent, heavy moment passed, broken only by the soft shooting of a silvery star far, far above us. I wondered if the gods truly did watch us from above, if they bore witness to our every plight as so many down here attested. With all that had happened, I was certain now that they turned a blind eye. The gods didn't know - didn't want to know - what it was to suffer, to be one of us. I envied them that ignorance. I knew too much now. I had seen and felt things I would *never* erase.

"Did you see a body?" Thorn tilted my head towards his face.

"No. I..." My words trailed off as I swallowed against the mental image of what Emrys might have looked like. Would The Cleanse have left him to turn into a dusty skeleton just as the other they'd left in the cells for so long? Would they have left the man who raised me to be a warning for all those to come? I refused to believe that was all Emrys' life had been worth in the end - a mere warning.

"No body, no proof, no reason to mourn yet, sparrow." Thorn pressed his lips to my brow before tucking me tight against his chest. I burrowed closer, inhaling the woodsy, spicy scent that was so uniquely him, and let the tears fall.

"I have to know."

"I know you do," he replied. "We'll find him, Artura. I promise."

EPILOGUE

Rouge could cover a multitude of sins, including the pale skin that made others wary of me.

I finished blotting the pink along my cheekbones before pinching them for good measure. The sooner I left this godsforsaken city, the better. But ever since Artura had taken things into her own hands, Lanceris had been on lockdown. No one in. No one out.

Including me.

Once I was satisfied with my skin, I pulled out the veil I'd worn every day since my arrival to conceal the violet of my eyes, the dead giveaway that I wasn't like the others. The veil was black, suitably so for one in mourning. Gods, the whole city was. The dress I wore was equally as dark. My lips twisted in disgust. I thrived on colour and light. Lanceris was nothing but emptiness and pain now.

A few more days. That was all I needed before I could don brighter, more cheerful colours. Not that I was exactly the happiest of people but to wear black was an affront to the Old

Gods. They considered it a betrayal of sorts, a silent worship of death where they favoured life.

I left my room, heading down the gilded halls of the castle. Such finery and wealth when the people of Cimran struggled to rub two oats together. It sickened me to see such a blatant disregard for the people. Wealth should never be hoarded. It should be shared equally, with everyone given a fighting chance at survival. Instead, for decades the royal family had lived in grotesque luxury while beating down a kingdom that couldn't fight back, no matter how much they wanted to.

People milled about, all headed for the throne room. There was to be an announcement and many surmised whether Princess Cerana would finally be crowned today. It had been a week since the king was fatally wounded. The kingdom could not survive much longer without a leader, if not a simple figurehead. A shepherd for the sheep that followed blindly.

I sighed as I filed into the throne room behind a noblewoman bearing a sweeping veil that dusted the floor. She didn't seem the least bit devastated by the events of the past week and instead spoke excitedly with the woman beside her.

"I heard he bled out completely."

The other woman shook her head. "I heard he was missing an eye. That his attacker *ate* it."

"That's gross, Arna," said the first. "Cannibalism? Really? That's where your mind went?"

"What other explanation could there be for it missing altogether?"

The heavily veiled woman fumbled through her purse, pulling a handkerchief. She pretended to dab at her eyes beneath the veil. All an act.

The second woman inelegantly snorted. "Just how do you suppose an eye, pierced by a sword, could be saved? Why wouldn't the victor eat it?"

"Because it's disgusting? The sword likely obliterated any traces of the eye. They're not small weapons."

For a moment I wanted to interject that it wasn't a sword. Their king had been brought down by a blade much smaller than that, something legends would no doubt be remiss in telling. Kings weren't allowed to fall victim to simple injuries. It was always grand battles and weapons with ludicrous, vicious names that were their undoing.

Beside the throne stood a woman with masses of deep red hair wound high atop her head in an intricate bun. She wore a glittering black gown that plunged low between her breasts, stopping just above her navel. As she surveyed the court, she held her chin high.

"Cerana's become quite the looker." Under my veil, my eyes darted to the man beside me. He spoke to a woman wrapped around his arm, covering his mouth as he did. "I'd fuck her six ways to Sunday if given the chance."

The woman smacked his arm and I noted a wedding ring on her finger. Classy, a husband detailing would be conquests to his wife. Then again, after a week of living amongst the members of the court, I'd come to learn it was normal behaviour.

A throat cleared and the room fell silent.

"Thank you for all coming," Princess Cerana began, her voice low but clear as it echoed across the room. "As many of you may well know by now, my father was attacked last week. Rumours at court are that he succumbed to his injuries and passed away. That you now await my crowning as your queen. I'm here to tell you that I've no intention of taking the throne." She paused, her eyes moving across the room. "Not when my father has happily survived his gruesome attack."

A collective gasp of shock rose up from the members of the court.

All save for one.

I'd been waiting on this announcement for three days now, growing increasingly frustrated as it was delayed again and again. No doubt the king wanted to present a strong front when he once more greeted his people.

The heavy groaning of the wide, gilded doors sounded and then the room fell impossibly silent. Heavy footsteps thundered. I waited, not turning as the others did to watch a far too ostentatious crown bobbing through the crowd, headed for the throne and Princess Cerana. It seemed to take an age before King Helmar came into sight, taking the three steps of the dais with the ease of one who'd not suffered what would have most certainly been fatal to any other man. When he turned, a wave of unease spread out from the throne like ripples on the pond. Someone screamed.

The kings normally handsome face was now hideously distorted. A thick scar ran from his hairline diagonally across his eye - an eye that was indeed no longer there - pulling half of his face taut. The socket was puckered and badly stitched closed. Many averted their gazes, whether out of fear or respect, I didn't care to know, though I strongly suspected the former.

King Helmar took a seat upon his golden throne, holding the arms with a white knuckled grip.

"Let it be known that from today, Cimran is at war with Nimue."

No one gasped this time, the war a foregone conclusion after the foreign queen attacked, driven mad by this, that and whatever other rumour had surfaced. It was anyone's guess why Queen Artura of Nimue had done what she did.

Helmar looked around the room, eyes roaming over every face until he landed on mine. From so far back, I wondered if he could actually tell who I was. That I wasn't Princess Xayla of House Mortae but rather Viane, High Priestess, Keeper of the Old Gods, diviner, telepatia...witch.

I was dangerously close to no longer caring whether the king knew or not.

After all, if he did know, then all bets were off. His death - certain death this time - would be fair game.

"As of now," Helmar said, voice echoing across the room, "The Cleanse march on Nimue with my armies. I want that murderous witch Artura and her husband, King Thorn of House Sorega. I want their heads mounted on spikes at my front gates and their innards left for the crows. If I have to burn entire kingdoms, I *will* find them. For the crimes they have committed, I will relish in bringing about their deaths."

I sighed heavily.

I hope you both know what you've gotten yourselves into, I silently sent up. *I hope you're both safe*.

Then again, hope had never been so kind to me.

KING OF BLOOD & TIDES

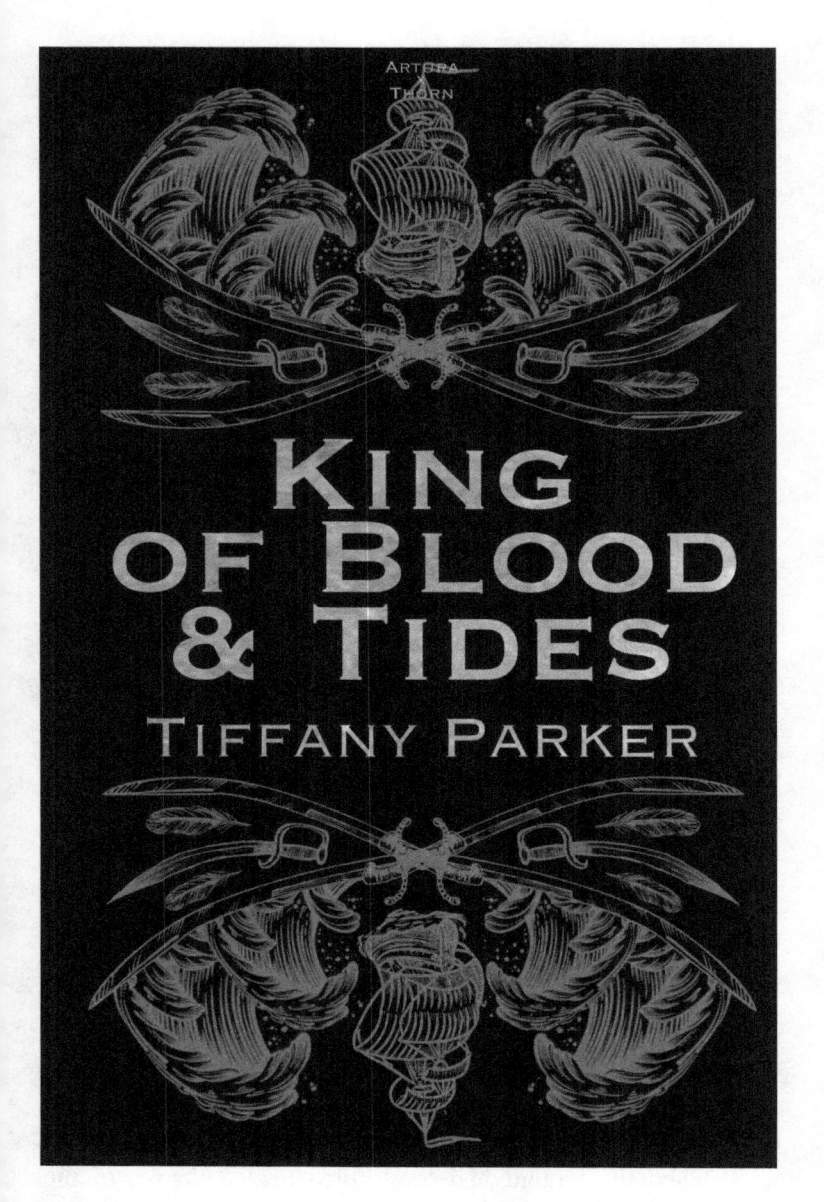

TIFFANY PARKER

CHAPTER ONE PREVIEW
COMING 2024

CHAPTER ONE

Blood.

I had never shied away from the sickly sweet scent of it. Oftentimes it carried a sense of comfort. It told me I was doing right, helping the sick and injured. A healer knows that when blood smells sour, there is yet more work to be done. The task not complete, you pushed onward, applying carefully crafted tinctures and salves, dressing the wound in sterilised gauze to aid in warding off infection.

I'd never shied away from blood.

Until the scent of my own was all I knew.

It was overwhelming in its intensity. A heady stench that reeked of failure and desolation. Fear and hopelessness. Even now, when the wound had long since healed thanks to the careful ministrations of Viane, the loss still haunted me.

I gazed down at where my pinky finger had once existed on my left hand. It was nothing more than a shrivelled stump now, oddly shaped at the tip where Viane had done her best to give it a clean, straight scar. Nothing, no amount of hard work or steady hand with a needle was going to make my hand look normal again.

Not when my finger had been bitten and torn off by human teeth.

The *Endurance* surged on through cresting waves. *Endurance*. A silly name for a silly ship. I had to wonder if the name was chosen specifically for my benefit, if Thorn perhaps intended it to be something to upend the foul, miserable mood I was trapped in nowadays. As if by throwing the word 'endurance' in my face multiple times a day would manifest the very concept within me. I might somehow toughen up, shake off the past... *endure* the hardships of life.

'Hardship' was putting the past months lightly. I narrowly surpassed the urge to spit on the salt-stained deck.

I was drenched thanks to the wild seas we rode but I made no move to return below deck. After once more escaping Purgatory, that hellish prison beneath Dearmond Mountains surrounding Lanceris, I had no inclination to be away from the sky. Even if it was a miserable grey.

At least it and I had something in common.

Another wave misted across my face and I could taste the tang of salt on my tongue. If I closed my eyes, I could almost pretend it was the sweat that coated my upper lip while King Helmar 'played' with me. I shuddered at the memory of his face, at the knowledge that we shared the one thing that made my stomach - nay, my very being - revolt.

Blood.

It had been five weeks since I escaped, since I stabbed Helmar clear through the eye and made a run for it through tunnels bearing walls as sharp as the edge of a blade. I'd been quiet, much to my husband's dismay. I needed the solitude, at least mentally, to process what had transpired.

And now, I'd come to a conclusion that satisfied me. Somewhat.

I felt him over my shoulder before a warm hand grabbed it. Thorn, the King of Nimue, a man I was effectively sold off to in marriage to garner Helmar's much-needed treaty. We'd formed a bond that defied all logic and reason. It still puzzled me how, in such a short space of time, I could come to feel his heart as keenly as my own. It didn't make one iota of sense and I'd given up trying to make the puzzle pieces fit together.

"Do not name it," Thorn had once told me. "Just live for it."

How could I possibly live for anything now? When the very act of living itself was agony, splinter-like knives slicing through every ventricle and vein in my heart? Leaving me to slowly bleed out until I withered away into nothing…into no one.

"Can I sit?"

I nodded, not looking at him. In the distance, I glimpsed a sliver of land. By the brownish tinge, I knew it was still Cimran, my home no longer. To step foot back on its soil would be certain death. And besides, I was a queen now by marriage.

Queen Artura of Nimue, First of Her Name.

The title still didn't sit right with me. Nor did the need for one. I had always simply been 'Artura' and until recently, didn't even know my true heritage as the daughter of King Helmar and the late Queen Iseult. None of that had ever bothered me, the lack of known history. Yet now, as royalty, heritage and breeding were paramount. If not for my lineage then at least for the legacy I would one day leave behind in the form of offspring. Gods, the word was like bile on my tongue. I'd always wanted children but now? Now I knew the horrors this world held - and not just the simple ones such as cheating, theft and murder, we learned long ago to put up with. But the truly gruesome ones, instead. The horrors that no one knew of simply because no average human could summon such possibilities even in their darkest nightmares.

Thorn was silent for a moment, his gaze following mine. I appreciated the quiet solidarity, the calm wafting off him in waves as powerful as the Ocaran Sea. This time of year, it was necessary to sail around the north of Cimran to reach Nimue. Crazy when you considered how close Lanceris was to my new homeland. But if Denard, captain of the king's guard, was to be believed, the journey would have been a treacherous one. The western seas were plagued with monsters great and small during the warmer months.

No one wanted to risk the life of their new queen to save a few weeks of travel.

And, Viane had argued, the extra time aboard the *Endurance* would ensure a full recovery for me.

Thorn took my hands in one of his own, careful not to touch my left where it sat atop my right. I glanced down and saw how irritated the stump of my finger looked, red and near raw still in parts. The pain was welcome, something to ground me amidst all the uncertainty. I couldn't stop playing with the stitched seam of skin in the moments when memories flooded my mind.

"I have a gift for you," Thorn murmured.

I turned to look at him, noting the purpling under his eyes. He'd been listless since pulling me from the cells. Sleep had been hard to come by for Thorn but he refused the very same tea I was forced to drink once. While dozing off one afternoon, I heard him whisper the reason to his aunt.

"I worry that the moment I close my eyes, she'll be gone again. She'll be so far out of my reach and hurt in a way she

can never come back from. I'll not risk it. I love her too much, Viane."

I couldn't fault him for that.

Beyond the sleeplessness etched deep on his face, he was as handsome as ever. Eyes such a pure jade green, no artist could ever hope to replicate it. His skin was a warm caramel that I'd too often licked across, savouring him as if he tasted just as sweet. The beard was a little longer these days, no longer immaculately cropped with its fine edges along his cheeks and jaw. He was dressed warmly in a black fur coat so dark, it matched the inkiness of his hair. There was an unmistakable gentility about him as he looked back at me. Hoping to see…what? What was it that he looked for in my eyes? Pain? Suffering? A desire for death?

All would have been expected given the hell I'd endured.

There was that word again…endure.

Thorn dug a hand into his coat pocket and withdrew a carefully wrapped bundle. The material was bright blood red and for a moment, the overwhelming urge to shy away threatened to consume me. But instead, I gritted my teeth, tilted up my chin and took the parcel from him.

Once unwrapped and the cloth tucked out of sight behind me, I tried to make sense of the thing I held. It was brown leather with neat hand-stitching. One long, protrusion that fanned out at the base to a wide band of the same material. On either end of the band, several inches wide, were leather thongs like those I used to tie up my hair. The protrusion was the length of a finger and solid but yet soft, almost pillow-like inside the leather.

"I don't understand what this is," I finally admitted with a frown.

Thorn took the leather and my left hand. Making quick work of it, he slipped the finger-length material onto my nub of a pinky finger and tied the band around my wrist. Leather covered the back of my hand and a slim strap wound over my palm to steady the whole contraption.

A prosthetic finger.

I was no stranger to the concept of prosthetics. I had grown up ensconced by a senseless war and Emrys had, on many occasions, treated men missing limbs of every variety. While the prosthetics were at best aesthetic, they provided some degree of confidence to the wearer. Perhaps that was what Thorn intended for me now.

I turned my hand back and forth, examining the false appendage from every angle with thinly veiled disgust.

"I can't undo what has been done," Thorn murmured, voice thick with unshed tears, just as it had been for the past several weeks. "But I can perhaps ease the embarrassment and shame of what occurred."

He reached out to touch my hand. I snapped it back.

Fury, sudden and volatile, choked me. When I managed to squeeze out the words bubbling in the back of my throat, they were sharp, pained.

"I am not embarrassed, nor am I ashamed. I survived something horrible, truly evil. That makes me a victor, not a victim. I beat the odds twice over now. Very few escape Helmar's clutches but *I* did. *I* escaped. *I* defied the odds that were stacked against me so high, they were an impassable wall I could not see the sun beyond. Do not presume I am embarrassed when I am nothing but proud."

Thorn grimaced, lines indenting the smooth crease of his forehead. "I didn't mean it that way."

My eyes narrowed on my husband. "Then how, pray tell, did you mean it?"

"Sparrow, our people will expect to see a queen whole and untouched. They'll expect to see a woman who exudes strength."

I stood to my feet, fingers deftly untying the knotted leather holding the prosthetic in place. I let it fall to the glistening floor of the ship where it landed in a puddle.

"That's exactly what they will see," I replied, tilting my chin even higher. I knew I must have looked ridiculous, looking down my nose at the man who had been nothing but supportive and attentive during my recovery. But it steeled my nerves, the ones plaguing the dark recesses of my mind. They threatened to undo me daily. Even more so now.

"When our people see me as I am, they will see a strong queen. They will see someone who didn't back down and let reality consume her body and soul. I am stronger than I've ever been. And I will be an even stronger queen. That I can guarantee."

My words hung on the salt thick air for a split second before I turned away and marched to the opposite end of the ship.

Because if I stayed before Thorn, he would see confirmation of a truth he suspected all along.

I wasn't strong. I was teetering on a precipice.

One that promised a long descent into a place as horrid as Purgatory, a place I'd not escape from this time.

*

"I worked hard on that."

I glanced back over my shoulder. Pure white hair flitted about the wind, the spider silk webbing seeking out prey. Of the search for prey, I was not uncertain. Viane had spent much of our journey thus far toying with the sailors, much to Thorn's chagrin. As I fully turned to watch her approach, I noticed a young man, no older than nineteen, practically swooning over the healer.

"On what?" I replied. "On having every man on this ship fall over their feet to get to you?"

Viane's lips quirked up in a sly smile. "No. That was effortless."

"Humble."

"Life is far too short to waste it away on humility, Artura." Viane bundled her arms tighter around her body. She was wrapped in an olive-coloured shawl that had most definitely seen better days. The faint scent of horse danced around her. We'd not exactly fled Cimran with much in the way of supplies. "And no, I was not referring to the fine specimens on board but rather to the glove I heard you discarded."

"Discarded is a strong word."

"Is it not fitting?"

I turned away from Viane, looking out over the ocean. The stern of the ship wasn't much quieter than the rest of it but those who worked nearby paid me little to no mind. It was about as much as I could have hoped for given the circumstances. The *Scylla*, the ship Thorn and I had travelled on from Cimran to the Isle of the Old Gods some time ago, now lay at the bottom of the northern sea, slowly rotting away or becoming the foundation of a new reef. The ship Denard had sought out as its temporary replacement was about half the size, idiotically named, and of far inferior quality. I'd woken to a leak under my bed the previous night and was certain we were about to sink.

"I didn't discard the glove, as you call it," I replied. "I simply refused the gift."

The witch quirked an eyebrow at me. "By letting it be sullied by the slush on board?"

"For a diviner, your part in this little 'gift' was awfully misguided. Surely you would've seen that I wouldn't want the glove? Why waste your time making it?"

Viane shook out her snow-white hair. "My nephew is headstrong at best. When he desires something, it's best that I abide by his wishes and leave him to suffer the revelations of his actions alone. As he is currently doing. You had quite the wicked tongue, Artura."

"You're testy today, aren't you?"

Viane snorted. "I'm testy every day. Some days I just do a better job of concealing it."

I said nothing to that, half hoping she'd take the hint and finally leave me to my thoughts. I'd taken to wallowing, sinking into dark moods or altogether zoning out from life. It was the safest way to go. If I let myself think, to dwell on what happened, I would feel. And if I felt things too keenly?

Fire.

By now, I was all too familiar with why fire on a ship made of wood was a very, very bad idea.

Viane didn't leave. Instead, she took hold of my elbow, twisting me around to face her.

"Look at me, Artura."

Reluctantly, I let my gaze meet her violet one. Her eyes were mesmerising. It was easy to see why the sailors on board were practically at each other's throats to get into her bed. Siren eyes, Thorn had said. And he was right. There was nothing ordinary about the woman lingering within. I loosed an unsteady breath when I realised there was no pity in her eyes, no sympathy. Just curiosity. Safe, manageable curiosity.

"Why not take the gift?"

I shrugged her hand off. "I don't need it."

"Your husband would believe otherwise."

I'd deliberately not been thinking about Thorn since leaving his side and the mention of his name made me wince.

"My husband thinks there is something to hide."

"Is there not?"

I bounced my head from one side to another, contemplating. "No. I don't think so. I'll not cover up what Hel...*he* did. I feel that if I cover up for him, I'm just making excuses, permitting his behaviour. I'm not going to hide and play the victim."

Viane thought quietly for a moment, tucking a stray hair behind her ear. "Even if you feel like one?"

My gaze narrowed on her. "Stay out of my head."

The diviner shrugged her slender shoulders. "You broadcast, love. Practically shout. It's hard to ignore."

"Then go elsewhere," I suggested. "Plenty of space on the ship for us both."

Neither one of us said anything, letting my words sink in. In a rush, we both broke out in laughter. There was little to no sense in it. Peals rang out across the sea. There wasn't exactly joy behind the emotion. If anything, it was nothing more than a vessel, setting sail to a myriad of complex emotions I couldn't have hoped to ever sift through. I laughed until my sides ached, until the wind whipping at my face dried out my throat and made it hard to swallow. And even then, when my laughter turned silent, it continued to shake my body.

I didn't notice a change until Viane, already sober, reached out and brushed away something from my cheek. A tear. At some point, laughter had given way to grief, to heaving sobs that echoed the mania of laughter. I couldn't stop. Now that the first tear had been shed, they fell in earnest. One after another, my face chilling in the cold wind. Viane said nothing.

Didn't move. Didn't leave. Just waited patiently while my body purged what had plagued it for the past weeks.

Slowly, the tears receded until all that was left was bleary vision and a streaming nose. I wiped the back of my hand under it, not caring how disgusting it might have looked to anyone else. In that moment, nothing beyond the twisting emotions and gentle rocking of the boat existed.

"There is nothing wrong with being a victim," Viane finally whispered.

I shook my head, hiccuping. "That's where you're wrong. No one wants a victim for a leader. How can I be a queen like this? I put on a brave face for Thorn but for thousands of people? I don't have the energy to keep a facade up that long."

"Then don't," she replied, all too matter-of-fact. "The greatest leaders aren't the ones that present an impenetrable facade. They are the ones that allow themselves to feel, and allow their people to see them feel. Yes, it might be disconcerting to step into a role feeling less than whole. But you're stepping into a role where you will govern people who feel just the same. Use this tragedy to grow. Use it to become great."

"And if I fail?" My words were small, nearly completely silent. One of my deepest fears I'd yet to acknowledge. Failure wasn't an option. This was no hobby I was to undertake - one where I could simply change my mind about tomorrow and move on to the next thing. 'Queen' wasn't a position I could easily reject.

Well, I *could*. But that would mean rejecting Thorn, also, and despite how I felt at the moment, he was the one thing in this world I couldn't bear to let go of.

Viane smiled, revealing straight white teeth. Her canines were a little too sharp, something I hadn't ever really noticed before. I wondered if she could tear a man's throat out with them.

"So what?" The diviner countered. "So what if you fail? You try again, Artura. No one expects you to get this right the first time. Show me a ruler alive or dead who was flawless from the start and I'll show you a thousand more who weren't."

"I doubt this is the kind of thing I can make repeated attempts at," I replied. Absentmindedly, my fingers started poking at the nub on my left hand. "Coups have taken place over less."

Viane linked her arm through mine, breaking the grasp I had on my hand before I could open the wound and draw blood.

"If you fail and the people revolt, you are more than welcome to come and stay with me on the isle."

Laughing hollowly, I replied, "You mean with the hellions?"

The diviner winked. "Them? They're harmless. And besides, I'll keep you safe."

PLAYLIST

King - Florence & The Machine
Bow (Slowed) - Reyn Hartley
Water Witch - The Secret Sisters, Brandi Carlile
Which Witch - Florence & The Machine
Everything Matters - AURORA, Pomme
I'm Coming For It - UNSECRET, Sam Tinnesz, GREYLEE
Savage Daughter - Sarah Hester Ross
Dream Girl Evil - Florence & The Machine
Pray - Ryan Vasquez
How Villains Are Made - Madalen Duke
Throne - Saint Mesa
The Calling - The Amazing Devil
Villains Aren't Born (They're Made) - PEGGY
Play With Fire (Alternate Version) - Sam Tinnesz, Ruelle, Violents
Mother's Daughter - Miley Cyrus
<u>Artura & Thorn's Theme:</u>
Atom 6 - Sleeping At Last

ACKNOWLEDGEMENTS

I genuinely don't know where to begin with this one. Simply because QPF was the book that snuck up on me. Mid 2022, while struggling to write *Rule of Shadow & Stars*, I started a little side project. Within a week, I'd belted out over fifty thousand words. It's insane to even think about now but somehow I managed to do that while sick with Covid and dealing with three terror children.

Sadly, I had to shelve QPF not long after so I could make my deadline for ROSAS but I knew it was the one I had to come back to next. I couldn't escape Cimran and Artura was constantly in my head (and let's be real, Thorn, too *swoon*).

Firstly, I have to thank my ever supportive husband. Toby is my cheerleader, my sounding board, editor, talk-down-off-a-ledge-erer and everything in between. He kept me hydrated and sane while banging this book out. I could not be half the author I am without his support and love. Thank you, darling.

I'd like to thank the amazing author & reader communities formed across social media. Being an indie author can be absolutely terrifying. There's so much conflicting information out there on what you should or shouldn't do, what publishing platforms to go to, how to advertise, etc, etc. I admit I'm still trying to get this right and I am so far from it. So if you've fielded one of my many panicked questions/meltdowns, thank you. I owe you one.

Now to some incredibly random thank you notes:

- Coffee. My lover, my life. I couldn't function without a triple shot caramel iced coffee. I shook most of the first draft because I was so hopped up.

- Ruby Dixon's books for giving me an escape when the worlds I wrote were too intense to stay in. Needless to say by now, you've likely worked out what I'm referring to. Reading about dragons and their penchant for panties or 7ft tall blue guys was a great way to unwind each evening.

- My kids who are banned from ever reading my books but also supported me insane amounts every step of the way. My four-year-old is particularly fond of sitting on my lap to 'help' me write...whereby she asks about every single key on the keyboard and giggles like a loon when I hit one.

- My besties Alida and Zoe for having a ready ear when I needed to vent. Also for providing top notch distractions in the form of babies and TikToks.

I could go on. For now, thank you for reading. Catch you on the flip side in book two: *King of Blood & Tides*!

Tiffany xx

Tiffany grew up in Sydney, Australia. She likes wine, nuggets, good books, tattoos and zombie movies. She strongly dislikes laundry - something there is always an endless supply of while writing.

In her free time you can find her with her husband and three insane(ly cute) kids or, alternatively, napping…again.

This marks her third book but hopefully not her last, sanity permitting. Because let's be real - this shit *tough*.

IG + TikTok
@tiffanyparker.author
WEBSITE
www.tiffanyparkerbooks.com

Printed in the USA
CPSIA information can be obtained
at www.ICGtesting.com
LVHW040607071123
763198LV00005B/46